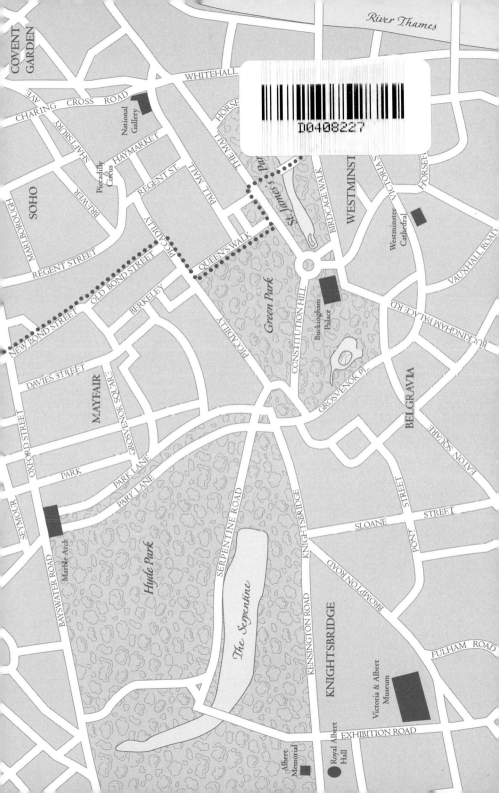

THE
MRS.
DALLOWAY
READER

THE
MRS. DALLOWAY READER

VIRGINIA WOOLF ET AL.

EDITED BY  FRANCINE PROSE

HARCOURT, INC.

Orlando   Austin   New York   San Diego   Toronto   London

www.HarcourtBooks.com

Library of Congress Cataloging-in-Publication Data
Woolf, Virginia, 1882–1941.
The Mrs. Dalloway reader/edited by Francine Prose.—1st ed.
p.   cm.
ISBN 0-15-101044-7
1. Parties—Fiction. 2. Married women—Fiction. 3. London
(England)—Fiction. 4. Woolf, Virginia, 1882–1941. Mrs. Dalloway.
I. Prose, Francine, 1947–   II. Title.
PR6045.O72M7 2003
823'.912—dc22   2003015608

Text set in Garamond MT
Designed by Cathy Riggs

Printed in the United States of America

First edition
A C E G I K J H F D B

Contents

Introduction

*W*HAT WE KNOW, OR HALF KNOW, OR THINK WE KNOW ABOUT Virginia Woolf—that sad litany of childhood trauma, illness, madness, suicide, death, dark decades brightened by flashes of acid Bloomsbury wit—has come to seem like a cautionary tale about the pitfalls of a brilliant, blighted life and about the particular perils of being a writer and a woman. Yet every sentence Virginia Woolf wrote, every word she wrote about writing, tells a parallel but altogether different and contradictory story—a narrative at once courageous, inspirational, and far more valuable to us, her grateful heirs, than the pitiable image of the fragile, haunted, still-beautiful woman who, at fifty-nine, methodically filled her pockets with stones and walked into the river.

To begin with, she was one of her century's most dazzlingly productive and consistently first-rate authors. She completed dozens of novels and stories, hundreds of book reviews and long essays and volumes of letters, plus biographies, a comedy, and the diaries that so seamlessly combine ruthless self-examination, social observation, provocative literary opinion, and delightful turns of phrase such as her description of a gathering populated by "a bunch of young men no bigger than asparagus." "More than anything," she noted in her diary, "I want beautiful prose," and that is what she wrote; her style is eloquent, graceful, precise, and never inadequate to the original, playful, and incisive operations of her mind. She translated from the Greek, learned Russian in order to co-translate Chekov, read widely and voraciously. During the years of work on *Mrs. Dalloway,* from the summer of 1922 until the late autumn of 1924, she read—to select just a few names from a very long list—Sophocles, Homer, Shakespeare, Proust, Joyce, Chaucer. Despite recurrent bouts of illness and madness, she helped Leonard Woolf run the Hogarth Press and maintained a social schedule so demanding that the healthiest, youngest, and most popular guests might have had trouble attending that many dinners and parties—and, the morning after, going to their desks and picking up their pens.

Here is a part of her "work list" for January 1923. "I shall write at *Mrs. Dalloway* till, next Monday, perhaps, bringing her into full talk, I hope. Shall I dash off an article for *Squire* upon memoirs . . . then do the Greek chapter, for which I shall have to read *Odyssey* (6 books) *Agamemnon: Oedipus Tyrranus* . . . & some dialogue of Plato's? This puts off writing rather till late in the day; but I want to make myself a certain amount of money regularly, if only for pocket money. Now, therefore, I must finish Greek regularly: & tackle, perhaps, another volume of Proust."

She was periodically insane. She endured horrifying hallucinations. But on her healthy, lucid days—which is to say, most days—she was seemingly indefatigable, a phenomenon of sheer productivity. And if Virginia Woolf's career represents a series of prodigious accomplishments and costly but extraordinary victories, the writing of *Mrs. Dalloway* was one of the first and most remarkable of these triumphs.

In the summer of 1922, Virginia and Leonard were, for reasons mostly having to do with Virginia's health, living in the suburbs, where she was beginning to feel increasingly exiled and deprived by her distance from the city. As she began *Mrs. Dalloway*, or more correctly, the story, "Mrs. Dalloway in Bond Street," which would later turn into the novel, she imagined her way back into the hustle and thrum of Westminster; and by the time she finished the book, she and Leonard had moved back to London, to a house in Tavistock Square.

That September, just after starting the novel, she noted that "this has been the most sociable summer we've ever had," but the same could be said of most seasons in the Woolfs' eventful lives. During the time she worked on the book, she was surrounded by friends and acquaintances; she weathered periods of illness and depression, and all manner of major and minor crises. Katherine Mansfield—with whom she had had a very complex and, as Woolf herself admitted, fiercely competitive friendship—died in January 1923. Several passages in Woolf's diary record her conviction that, with Katherine gone, there was no longer any reason to write, no one to prove herself against. And when she found that she had written "the last words of the last page of *Mrs. Dalloway*," her mind tracked almost instantly to Katherine's death and to the idea that, had her friend lived, readers would now realize that Virginia was the more gifted of the two.

Happily, other friendships flourished. Six months or so into the writing of the novel, Virginia met Vita Sackville-West, with whom she was to form an intensely romantic relationship. And here is how that January 1923 "work list," quoted earlier, actually ends: "I must master the *Agamemnon* . . . & before doing that I must write to the new apparition, Vita, who gives me a book every other day."

Clearly, the diaries and the letters can be read as a history of distraction. "It is fatal to have visitors in the middle of a story." So many events were transpiring in the household and the press, Virginia was reading and writing so much in addition to her novel that, in all the pages of journal entries that span the years spent composing *Mrs. Dalloway,* there are less than thirty direct references to the book, and most of them are quite brief.

Yet somehow we have the sense that she is thinking about it all the time. And ultimately she tells us so. "Here I am, peering across Vita at my blessed *Mrs. Dalloway*; & can't stop, of a night, thinking of the next scene, and how I'm going to wind up."

Reading and rereading *Mrs. Dalloway,* along with the relevant diary entries and letters, the sketches and short stories collected in "Mrs. Dalloway's Party," and the other selections gathered here in *The Mrs. Dalloway Reader,* you can watch a magical process taking place on the page. That is, you can observe a great writer realizing what she wants to do in her work, figuring out how to do it, and discovering that she can do it—and, in the end, knowing that she has done it.

Along the way, there are the usual complaints, the inevitable worries, which—if you are a writer, or are fortunate or unfortunate enough to know a writer well—you will be relieved to hear coming from one of Virginia Woolf's caliber. She fears that her work is going alarmingly quickly, or disturbingly slowly. She wonders how much she needs to protect herself from society in general and "unsympathetic" society in particular. Is she trying to force too many ideas into the novel? Is she writing from deep emotion? The book seems like such "sheer weak dribble" that she can only assume that she has no gift for fiction, and consequently a sort of breezy resignation has to suffice for confidence. "There is no principle, except to follow the whimsical brain implicitly, parc away the ill fitting, till I have the shape exact." "Parts of it are so bad," she writes, "parts so good . . . Only I must note this odd symptom; a conviction that I shall go on, see it through, because it interests me to write it."

And, of course, we can see why. The diaries, letters, and the Dalloway stories shed light on what she imagined and planned and hoped for, what she was trying to achieve. She longed to fill the book with "speed and life," to "give life & death, sanity &

insanity; I want to criticize the social system & to show it at work, at its most intense." Indeed, among the most striking and admirable things about *Mrs. Dalloway* is how far it reaches, how many characters, how much personal history and sheer experience it crams into a book that is—I suppose you could say—nominally about a woman getting ready for a party during a single day in London. But, in fact, it's all here: life, death, sex, love, marriage, parenthood, youth, age, the present and the past, memory, London, war, reason and unreason, loyalty, medicine, social snobbery, friendship, compassion, cruelty; the occasionally apt but more often unfounded snap judgements we make about ourselves, each other, loved ones, strangers, and the world in which chance and fortune have thrown us all together.

One of Virginia Woolf's earliest notes on the book—an entry about the importance of the character of the shell-shocked war veteran Septimus Warren Smith—reveals how much she knew in advance about the novel's thematic shape. "I adumbrate here a study of insanity & suicide: the world seen by the sane & the insane side by side." Clearly, writing about Septimus was painful for her, chillingly close to her own agonies. In one letter, she referred to the mad scenes: "It was a subject that I have kept cooling in my mind until I felt I could touch it without bursting into flame all over." And you can sense that hesitation lurking just beneath the surface of her flinty resolve to "use up everything I've ever thought" and "pour everything in." And so Septimus and his hapless Italian wife are made to endure versions of the Woolfs' appalling and damaging consultations with pompous, uncomprehending medical specialists about Virginia's health, while the young man's frightening, alienating, exhilirating—and fatal—delusions echo her own.

At the same time, we feel the decision to write about Septimus provided her with the key to what she truly wanted to do in the book: a revelation partly responsible for the contrast between "Mrs. Dalloway in Bond Street" (in which there is no Septimus) and the first chapter of the novel. The dissimilarities are so striking and so instructive that the two sections, studied side by side, should be required reading for every beginning writer or serious lover of literature. The significant changes in image and detail—substituting the buying of flowers for the purchase of gloves—pale beside the huge difference in perspective and tone. And what can be learned by comparing them is nothing less than the secret of using language to penetrate a character's consciousness, to probe beneath the surface, to go deeper.

Look, for example, at one small moment: Hugh Whitbread's explanation of his presence in London. In the story, we have a brief exchange.

> 'We've just come up,' said Hugh Whitbread. 'Unfortunately to see doctors.'
> 'Milly?' said Mrs. Dalloway, instantly compassionate.
> 'Out of sorts,' said Hugh Whitbread.

All perfectly sufficient, competent, and correct. But in the novel, the same conversation takes place in indirect dialogue, filtered through Clarissa's awareness. And every sentence and sentence fragment takes us deeper into her psyche. So, instead of "instant compassion," we get something rather more complex: Clarissa feels "very sisterly and oddly conscious at the same time of her hat."

When, in the diaries, Woolf contrasts conveying "true reality" with "writing essays about myself," or when she remarks that "I think it most important in this book to go for the central things, even though they don't submit, as they should however, to beautification in language," what else is she referring to but the way in which word choice, cadence, tone, and diction transform the essayistic and the objectively removed into the psychological and the interior? Consider two more paragraphs, the first from the story, the second from the novel.

Big Ben was striking as she stepped out into the street. It was eleven o'clock and the unused hour was fresh as if issued to children on a beach. But there was something solemn in the deliberate swing of the repeated strokes; something stirring in the murmur of wheels and the shuffle of footsteps. No doubt they were not all bound on errands of happiness . . . Big Ben struck the tenth, struck the eleventh stroke. The leaden circles dissolved in the air. Pride held her erect, inheriting, handing on, acquainted with discipline and with suffering.

And then, thought Clarissa Dalloway, what a morning . . . fresh as if issued to children on a beach . . . For having lived in Westminster—how many years now? over twenty,—one feels even in the midst of traffic, or waking at night, Clarissa was positive, a particular hush, or solemnity; an indescribable pause; a suspense (but that might be her heart, affected, they said, by influenza) before Big Ben strikes. There! Out it boomed. First a warning, musical; then the hour, irrevocable. The leaden circles dissolved in the air. Such fools we are, she thought, crossing Victoria Street. For Heaven only knows why one loves it so, how one sees it so, making it up, building it round one, tumbling it, creating it every moment afresh.

What we instinctively respond to here is the way in which Woolf is exchanging the measured, reflective, faintly magisterial tone of the essayist for the psychological novelist's ability to portray the swift, sensory, associative workings of perception and of consciousness. Because that is her true subject here: consciousness, awareness, action, and reaction, what we remember and say and keep hidden, the distance between the interior and the exterior, how very differently we appear to ourselves and to others. What she wants is something like what E. M. Forster said to her in praise of *Jacob's Room:* to get "further into the soul."

In a moment of optimism, she records that the novel is becoming "more analytical & human... less lyrical; but I feel as if I had loosed the bonds pretty completely and could pour everything in." And it's in the service of this—of this loosing the bonds and pouring everything in—that she deploys what she calls her "prime discovery... my tunneling process... tell(ing) the past in installments, as I have need of it." Thus she sets out to "dig out beautiful caves behind my characters; I think that gives exactly what I want; humanity, humour, depth. The idea is that the caves shall connect, & each comes to daylight at the present moment."

And now we come to the very heart of things, to the secret behind all the other secrets. Let me suggest that readers try the following experiment. Ask any writer of serious fiction why they write, what continues to engage them. And nearly all of them will tell you that what interests them—the reason why one becomes that sort of a writer in the first place—is consciousness, human awareness, the mind and soul of one's characters. It's why most writers cringe when even the most favorable reviews doggedly recount the plot or focus on some abstract theme that had nothing to do with whatever sparked the author's initial interest. And this is also part of what makes *Mrs. Dalloway* so successful and so impressive—the fact that Virginia Woolf somehow managed to write a novel about consciousness in such a way that it is virtually impossible to mistake her intention. What else could we say the book is about? Shell shock? Hosting a party?

Woolf did what she set out to do and used language to do it. And though it's an analogy that she herself probably would have despised, it's tempting to suggest that reading *Mrs. Dalloway* feels a bit like looking at Jackson Pollock's greatest paintings and reflecting that, for one brief moment, an artist was able, employing the most seemingly unlikely methods, to make paint do exactly what he wanted.

A writer's doubts can never, or hardly ever, be put to rest. But even so, Virginia Woolf intuited that she had accomplished something real and important. On completing the book, she noted that she felt "more fully relieved of my meaning than usual." And two months later, after an interval during which a blow-up at the Hogarth Press and a series of negotiations about journalistic pieces kept her from working, she returned, with deep happiness, to the retyping and the revision of *Mrs. Dalloway.*

"I can write & write & write now: the happiest feeling in the world." That is how she describes the pleasure of returning to her desk, with an uncharacteristic burst of such exuberance and bliss that she almost sounds more like Clarissa Dalloway than like whatever we know, or half know, or imagine we know about Virginia Woolf—but which we can easily discover by reading her marvelous novel and the evidence, collected here, of her early attempts, her thoughts, her struggles, and her astonishing success.

JUNE 2003

VIRGINIA WOOLF

An Introduction to
Mrs. Dalloway

$\mathcal{I}$T IS DIFFICULT—PERHAPS IMPOSSIBLE—FOR A WRITER TO SAY anything about his own work. All he has to say has been said as fully and as well as he can in the body of the book itself. If he has failed to make his meaning clear there it is scarcely likely that he will succeed in some pages of preface or postscript. And the author's mind has another peculiarity which is also hostile to introductions. It is as inhospitable to its offspring as the hen sparrow is to hers. Once the young birds can fly, fly they must; and by the time they have fluttered out of the nest the mother bird has begun to think perhaps of another brood. In the same way once a book is printed and published it ceases to be the property of the author; he commits it to the care of other people; all his attention is claimed by some new book which not only thrusts its predecessor from the next but has a way of subtly blackening its character in comparison with its own.

It is true that the author can if he wishes tell us something about himself and his life which is not in the novel; and to this effort we should do all that we can to encourage him. For nothing is more fascinating than to be shown the truth which lies behind those immense façades of fiction—if life is indeed true, and if fiction is indeed fictitious. And probably the connection between the two is highly complicated. Books are the flowers or fruit stuck here and there on a tree which has its roots deep down in the earth of our earliest life, of our first experiences. But here again to tell the reader anything that his own imagination and insight have not already discovered would need not a page or two of preface but a volume or two of autobiography. Slowly and cautiously one would have to go to work, uncovering, laying bare, and even so when everything had been brought to the surface, it would still be for the reader to decide what was relevant and what not. Of *Mrs. Dalloway* then one can only bring to light at the moment a few scraps, of little importance or none perhaps; as that in the first version Septimus, who later is intended to be her double, had no existence; and that Mrs. Dalloway was originally to kill herself, or perhaps merely to die at the end of the party. Such scraps are offered humbly to the reader in the hope that like other odds and ends they may come in useful.

But if one has too much respect for the reader pure and simple to point out to him what he has missed, or to suggest to him what he should seek, one may speak more explicitly to the reader who has put off his innocence and become a critic. For though criticism, whether praise or blame, should be accepted in silence as the legitimate comment which the act of publication invites, now and again a statement is made without bearing on the book's merits or demerits which the writer happens to know to be mistaken. One such statement has been made sufficiently often about *Mrs. Dalloway* to be worth perhaps a word of contradiction. The book, it was said, was the deliberate offspring of a method. The author, it was said, dissatisfied with the form of fiction then in vogue, was determined to beg, borrow, steal or even create another of her own. But, as far as it is possible to be honest about the mysterious process of the mind, the facts are otherwise. Dissatisfied the writer may have been; but her dissatisfaction was primarily with nature for giving an idea, without providing a house for it to live in. The novelists of preceding generation had done little — after all why should they?— to help. The novel was the obvious lodging, but the novel it seemed was built on the wrong plan. Thus rebuked the idea started as the oyster starts or the snail to secrete a house for itself. And this it did without any conscious direction. The little note-book in which an attempt was made to forecast a plan was soon abandoned, and the book grew day by day, week by week, without any plan at all, except that which was dictated each morning in the act of writing. The other way, to make a house and then inhabit it, to develop a theory and then apply it, as Wordsworth did and Coleridge, is, it need not be said, equally good and much more philosophic. But in the present case it was necessary to write the book first and to invent a theory afterwards.

If, however, one singles out the particular point of the book's methods for discussion it is for the reason given — that it has been made the subject of comment by critics, not that in itself it deserves notice. On the contrary, the more successful the method, the less it attracts attention. The reader it is to be hoped will not give a thought to the book's method or to the book's lack of method. He is concerned only with the effect of the book as a whole on his mind. Of that most important question he is a far better judge than the writer. Indeed, given time and liberty to frame his own opinion he is eventually an infallible judge. To him then the writer commends *Mrs. Dalloway* and leaves the court confident that the verdict whether for instant death or for some years more of life and liberty will in either case be just.

JUNE 1928

VIRGINIA WOOLF

Mrs. Dalloway's Party

A SHORT STORY SEQUENCE

Long before Mrs. Dalloway *became a classic, Virginia Woolf was exploring in a series of sketches and stories her fascination with the mental and physical excitement that surrounds parties. The seven stories in* Mrs. Dalloway's Party *create a portrait of what Woolf called "party consciousness." Whether considered as parallel expressions of the themes of* Mrs. Dalloway *or as stand-alone stories, this collection provides a valuable window into Woolf's writing mind.*

1

Mrs. Dalloway in Bond Street

$\mathcal{M}$RS. DALLOWAY SAID SHE WOULD BUY THE GLOVES HERSELF. Big Ben was striking as she stepped out into the street. It was eleven o'clock and the unused hour was fresh as if issued to children on a beach. But there was something solemn in the deliberate swing of the repeated strokes; something stirring in the murmur of wheels and the shuffle of footsteps.

No doubt they were not all bound on errands of happiness. There is much more to be said about us than that we walk the streets of Westminster. Big Ben too is nothing but steel rods consumed by rust were it not for the care of H.M's Office of Works. Only for Mrs. Dalloway the moment was complete; for Mrs. Dalloway June was fresh. A happy childhood—and it was not to his daughters only that Justin Parry had seemed a fine fellow (weak of course on the Beach); flowers at evening, smoke rising; the caw of rooks falling from ever so high, down down through the October air—there is nothing to take the place of childhood. A leaf of mint brings it back: or a cup with a blue ring.

Poor little wretches, she sighed, and pressed forward. Oh, right under the horses' noses, you little demon! and there she was left on the kerb stretching her hand out, while Jimmy Dawes grinned on the further side.

A charming woman, posed, eager, strangely white-haired for her pink cheeks, so Scope Purvis, C.B., saw her as he hurried to his office. She stiffened a little, waiting for Durtnall's van to pass. Big Ben struck the tenth; struck the eleventh stroke. The leaden circles dissolved in the air. Pride held her erect, inheriting, handing on, acquainted with discipline and with suffering. How people suffered, how they suffered, she thought, thinking of Mrs. Foxcroft at the Embassy last night decked with jewels, eating her heart out, because that nice boy was dead, and now the old Manor House (Durtnall's van passed) must go to a cousin.

'Good morning to you,' said Hugh Whitbread raising his hat rather extravagantly by the china shop, for they had known each other as children. 'Where are you off to?'

'I love walking in London,' said Mrs. Dalloway. 'Really it's better than walking in the country!'

'We've just come up,' said Hugh Whitbread. 'Unfortunately to see doctors.'

'Milly?' said Mrs. Dalloway, instantly compassionate.

'Out of sorts,' said Hugh Whitbread. 'That sort of thing. Dick all right?'

'First rate!' said Clarissa.

Of course, she thought, walking on, Milly is about my age— fifty—fifty-two. So it is probably *that*. Hugh's manner had said so, said it perfectly— dear old Hugh, thought Mrs. Dalloway, remembering with amusement, with gratitude, with emotion, how shy, like a brother—one would rather die than speak to one's brother—Hugh had always been, when he was at Oxford, and came over, and perhaps one of them (drat the thing!) couldn't ride. How then could women sit in Parliament? How could they do things with men? For there is this extraordinarily deep instinct, something inside one; you can't get over it; it's no use trying; and men like Hugh respect it without our saying it, which is what one loves, thought Clarissa, in dear old Hugh.

She had passed through the Admiralty Arch and saw at the end of the empty road with its thin trees Victoria's white mound, Victoria's billowing motherliness, amplitude and homeliness, always ridiculous, yet how sublime thought Mrs. Dalloway, remembering Kensington Gardens and the old lady in horn spectacles and being told by Nanny to stop dead still and bow to the Queen. The flag flew above the Palace. The King and Queen were back then. Dick had met her at lunch the other day—a thoroughly nice woman. It matters so much to the poor, thought Clarissa, and to the soldiers. A man in bronze stood heroically on a pedestal with a gun on her left hand side—the South African war. It matters, thought Mrs. Dalloway walking towards Buckingham Palace. There it stood foursquare, in the broad sunshine, uncompromising, plain. But it was character she thought; something inborn in the race; what Indians respected. The Queen went to hospitals, opened bazaars—the Queen of England, thought Clarissa, looking at the Palace. Already at this hour a motor car passed out at the gates; soldiers saluted; the gates were shut. And Clarissa, crossing the road, entered the Park, holding herself upright.

June had drawn out every leaf on the trees. The mothers of Westminster with mottled breasts gave suck to their young. Quite respectable girls lay stretched on the grass. An elderly man, stooping very stiffly, picked up a crumpled paper, spread it out flat and flung it away. How horrible! Last night at the Embassy Sir Dighton had said, 'If I want a fellow to hold my horse, I have only to put up my hand.' But the religious question is far more serious than the economic, Sir Dighton had said, which she thought extraordinarily interesting, from a man like Sir Dighton. 'Oh, the country will never know what it has lost,' he had said, talking, of his own accord, about dear Jack Stewart.

She mounted the little hill lightly. The air stirred with energy. Messages were passing from the Fleet to the Admiralty.

Piccadilly and Arlington Street and the Mall seemed to chafe the very air in the Park and lift its leaves hotly, brilliantly, upon waves of that divine vitality which Clarissa loved. To ride; to dance; she had adored all that. Or going long walks in the country, talking, about books, what to do with one's life, for young people were amazingly priggish—oh, the things one had said! But one had conviction. Middle age is the devil. People like Jack'll never know that, she thought; for he never once thought of death, never, they said, knew he was dying. And now can never mourn—how did it go?—a head grown grey.... From the contagion of the world's slow stain.... Have drunk their cup a round or two before.... From the contagion of the world's slow stain! She held herself upright.

But how Jack would have shouted! Quoting Shelley, in Piccadilly! 'You want a pin,' he would have said. He hated frumps. 'My God Clarissa! My God Clarissa!'—she could hear him now at the Devonshire House party, about poor Sylvia Hunt in her amber necklace and that dowdy old silk. Clarissa held herself upright for she had spoken aloud and now she was in Piccadilly, passing the house with the slender green columns, and the balconies; passing club windows full of newspapers; passing old Lady Burdett Coutt's house where the glazed white parrot used to hang; and Devonshire House, without its gilt leopards; and Claridge's, where she must remember Dick wanted her to leave a card on Mrs. Jepson or she would be gone. Rich Americans can be very charming. There was St. James's Palace; like a child's game with bricks; and now—she had passed Bond Street—she was by Hatchard's book shop. The stream was endless—endless—endless. Lords, Ascot, Hurlingham—what was it? What a duck, she thought, looking at the frontispiece of some book of memoirs spread wide in the bow window, Sir Joshua perhaps or Romney; arch, bright, demure; the sort of girl—like her own Elizabeth—the only *real* sort of girl. And there was that absurd book, *Soapy Sponge,* which Jum used to quote by the yard; and Shakespeare's Sonnets. She knew them by heart. Phil and she had argued all day about the Dark Lady, and Dick had said straight out at dinner that night that he had never heard of her. Really, she had married him for that! He had never read Shakespeare! There must be some little cheap book she could buy for Milly—*Cranford* of course! Was there ever anything so enchanting as the cow in petticoats? If only people had that sort of humour, that sort of self-respect now, thought Clarissa, for she remembered the broad pages; the sentences ending; the characters—how one talked about them as if they were real. For all the great things one must go to the past, she thought. From the contagion of the world's slow stain. . . . Fear no more the heat o' the sun. . . . And now can never mourn, can never mourn, she repeated, her eyes straying over the window; for it ran in her head; the test of great poetry; the moderns had never written anything one wanted to read about death, she thought; and turned.

Omnibuses joined motor cars; motor cars vans; vans taxicabs; taxicabs motor cars—here was an open motor car with a girl, alone. Up till four, her feet tingling, I know, thought Clarissa, for the girl looked washed out, half asleep, in the corner of the car after the dance. And another car came; and another. No! No! No! Clarissa smiled good-naturedly. The fat lady had taken every sort of trouble, but diamonds! orchids! at this hour of the morning! No! No! No! The excellent policeman would, when the time came, hold up his hand. Another motor car passed. How utterly unattractive! Why should a girl of that age paint black round her eyes? And a young man with a girl, at this hour, when the country—The admirable policeman raised his hand and Clarissa acknowledging his sway, taking her time, crossed, walked towards Bond Street; saw the narrow crooked street, the yellow banners; the thick notched telegraph wires stretched across the sky.

A hundred years ago her great-great-grandfather, Seymour Parry, who ran away with Conway's daughter, had walked down Bond Street. Down Bond Street the Parrys had walked for a hundred years, and might have met the Dalloways (Leighs on the mother's side) going up. Her father got his clothes from Hill's.

There was a roll of cloth in the window, and here just one jar on a black table, incredibly expensive; like the thick pink salmon on the ice block at the fishmonger's. The jewels were exquisite — pink and orange stars, paste, Spanish, she thought, and chains of old gold; starry buckles, little brooches which had been worn on sea-green satin by ladies with high head-dresses. But no looking! One must economise. She must go on past the picture dealer's where one of the odd French pictures hung, as if people had thrown confetti—pink and blue—for a joke. If you had lived with pictures (and it's the same with books and music) thought Clarissa, passing the Aeolian Hall, you can't be taken in by a joke.

The river of Bond Street was clogged. There, like a queen at a tournament, raised, regal, was Lady Bexborough. She sat in her carriage, upright, alone, looking through her glasses. The white glove was loose at her wrist. She was in black, quite shabby, yet, thought Clarissa, how extraordinarily it tells, breeding, self-respect, never saying a word too much or letting people gossip; an astonishing friend; no one can pick a hole in her after all these years, and now, there she is, thought Clarissa, passing the Countess who waited powdered, perfectly still, and Clarissa would have given anything to be like that, the mistress of Clarefield, talking politics, like a man. But she never goes anywhere, thought Clarissa, and it's quite useless to ask her, and the carriage went on and Lady Bexborough was borne past like a queen at a tournament, though she had nothing to live for and the old man is failing and they say she is sick of it all, thought Clarissa and the tears actually rose to her eyes as she entered the shop.

'Good morning,' said Clarissa in her charming voice. 'Gloves,' she said with her exquisite friendliness and putting her bag on the counter began, very slowly, to undo the buttons. 'White gloves', she said. 'Above the elbow,' and she looked straight into the shopwoman's face—but this was not the girl she remembered? She looked quite old. 'These really don't fit,' said Clarissa. The shop-girl looked at them. 'Madame wears bracelets?'

Clarissa spread out her fingers. 'Perhaps it's my rings,' And the girl took the grey gloves with her to the end of the counter.

Yes, thought Clarissa, it's the girl I remember, she's twenty years older.... There was only one other customer, sitting sideways at the counter, her elbow poised, her bare hand drooping vacant; like a figure on a Japanese fan, thought Clarissa, too vacant perhaps, yet some men would adore her. The lady shook her head sadly. Again the gloves were too large. She turned round the glass. 'Above the wrist,' she reproached the grey-headed woman, who looked and agreed.

They waited; a clock ticked; Bond Street hummed, dulled, distant; the woman went away holding gloves. 'Above the wrist,' said the lady, mournfully, raising her voice. And she would have to order chairs, ices, flowers, and cloak-room tickets, thought Clarissa. The people she didn't want would come; the others wouldn't. She would stand by the door. They sold stockings — silk stockings. A lady is known by her gloves and her shoes, old Uncle William used to say. And through the hanging silk stockings, quivering silver she looked at the lady, sloping shouldered, her hand drooping, her bag slipping, her eyes vacantly on the floor. It would be intolerable if dowdy women came to her party! Would one have liked Keats if he had worn red socks? Oh, at last — she drew into the counter and it flashed into her mind:

'Do you remember before the war you had gloves with pearl buttons?'

'French gloves, Madame?'

'Yes, they were French,' said Clarissa. The other lady rose very sadly and took her bag, and looked at the gloves on the counter. But they were all too large — always too large at the wrist.

'With pearl buttons,' said the shop-girl, who looked ever so much older. She split the lengths of tissue paper apart on the counter. With pearl buttons, thought Clarissa, perfectly simple — how French!

'Madame's hands are so slender,' said the shop-girl, drawing the glove firmly, smoothly, down over her rings. And Clarissa looked at her arm in the looking-glass. The glove hardly came to the elbow. Were there others half an inch longer? Still it seemed tiresome to bother her—perhaps the one day in the month, thought Clarissa, when it's an agony to stand. 'Oh, don't bother,' she said. But the gloves were brought.

'Don't you get fearfully tired,' she said in her charming voice, 'standing? When d'you get your holiday?'

'In September, Madame, when we're not so busy.'

When we're in the country thought Clarissa. Or shooting. She has a fortnight at Brighton. In some stuffy lodging. The landlady takes the sugar. Nothing would be easier than to send her to Mrs. Lumley's right in the country (and it was on the tip of her tongue). But then she remembered how on their honeymoon Dick had shown her the folly of giving impulsively. It was much more important, he said, to get trade with China. Of course he was right. And she could feel the girl wouldn't like to be given things. There she was in her place. So was Dick. Selling gloves was her job. She had her own sorrows quite separate, 'and now can never mourn, can never mourn', the words ran in her head, 'From the contagion of the world's slow stain,' thought Clarissa holding her arm stiff, for there are moments when it seems utterly futile (the glove was drawn off leaving her arm flecked with powder)—simply one doesn't believe, thought Clarissa, any more in God.

The traffic suddenly roared; the silk stockings brightened. A customer came in.

'White gloves,' she said, with some ring in her voice that Clarissa remembered.

It used, thought Clarissa, to be so simple. Down, down through the air came the caw of the rooks. When Sylvia died, hundreds of years ago, the yew hedges looked so lovely with the diamond webs in the mist before early church. But if Dick were to die to-morrow? As for believing in God—no, she would let the children choose, but for herself, like Lady Bexborough, who opened the bazaar, they say, with the telegram in her hand— Roden, her favourite, killed—she would go on. But why, if one doesn't believe? For the sake of others, she thought taking the glove in her hand. The girl would be much more unhappy if she didn't believe.

'Thirty shillings,' said the shop-woman. 'No, pardon me Madame, thirty-five. The French gloves are more.'

For one doesn't live for oneself, thought Clarissa.

And then the other customer took a glove, tugged it, and it split.

'There!' she exclaimed.

'A fault of the skin,' said the grey-headed woman hurriedly. 'Sometimes a drop of acid in tanning. Try this pair, Madame.'

'But it's an awful swindle to ask two pound ten!'

Clarissa looked at the lady; the lady looked at Clarissa.

'Gloves have never been quite so reliable since the war,' said the shop-girl, apologising, to Clarissa.

But where had she seen the other lady?—elderly, with a frill under her chin; wearing a black ribbon for gold eyeglasses; sensual, clever, like a Sargent drawing. How one can tell from a voice when people are in the habit, thought Clarissa, of making other people—'It's a shade too tight,' she said—obey. The shop-woman went off again. Clarissa was left waiting. Fear no more she repeated, playing her finger on the counter. Fear no more the heat o' the sun. Fear no more she repeated. There were little brown spots on her arm. And the girl crawled like a snail. Thou thy worldly task hast done. Thousands of young men had died that things might go on. At last! Half an inch above the elbow; pearl buttons; five and a quarter. My dear slowcoach, thought Clarissa, do you think I can sit here the whole morning? Now you'll take twenty-five minutes to bring me my change!

There was a violent explosion in the street outside. The shop-women cowered behind the counters. But Clarissa, sitting very upright, smiled at the other lady. 'Miss Anstruther!' she exclaimed.

2

The Man Who Loved His Kind

TROTTING THROUGH DEANS YARD THAT AFTERNOON, PRICK-ett Ellis ran straight into Richard Dalloway, or rather, just as they were passing, the covert side glance which each was casting on the other, under his hat, over his shoulder, broadened and burst into recognition; they had not met for twenty years. They had been at school together. And what was Ellis doing? The Bar? Of course, of course—he had followed the case in the papers. But it was impossible to talk here. Wouldn't he drop in that evening. (They lived in the same old place—just round the corner.) One or two people were coming. Joynson perhaps. 'An awful swell now,' said Richard.

'Good—till this evening then,' said Richard, and went his way, 'jolly glad' (that was quite true) to have met that queer chap, who hadn't changed one bit since he had been at school—just the same knobbly, chubby little boy then, with prejudices sticking out all over him, but uncommonly brilliant—won the Newcastle. Well—off he went.

Prickett Ellis, however, as he turned and looked at Dalloway disappearing, wished how he had not met him or, at least, for he had always liked him personally, hadn't promised to come to this party. Dalloway was married, gave parties; wasn't his sort at all. He would have to dress. However, as the evening drew on, he supposed, as he had said that, and didn't want to be rude, he must go there.

But what an appalling entertainment! There was Joynson; they had nothing to say to each other. He had been a pompous little boy; he had grown rather more self-important—that was all; there wasn't a single other soul in the room that Prickett Ellis knew. Not one. So, as he could not go at once, without saying a word to Dalloway, who seemed altogether taken up with his duties, bustling about in a white waistcoat, there he had to stand. It was the sort of thing that made his gorge rise. Think of a grown up, responsible men and women doing this every night of their lives! The lines deepened on his blue and red shaven cheeks as he leant against the wall in complete silence, for though he worked like a horse, he kept himself fit by exercise; and he looked hard and fierce, as if his moustaches were dipped in frost. He bristled; he grated. His meagre dress clothes made him look unkempt, insignificant, angular.

Idle, chattering, overdressed, without an idea in their heads, these fine ladies and gentlemen went on talking and laughing; and Prickett Ellis watched them and compared them with the Brunners who, when they won their case against Fenners' Brewery and got two hundred pounds compensation (it was not half what they should have got) went and spent five of it on a clock for him. That was a decent sort of thing to do; that was the sort of thing that moved one, and he glared more severely than ever at these people, overdressed, cynical, prosperous, and compared what he felt now with what he felt at eleven o'clock that morning when old Brunner and Mrs. Brunner, in their best clothes, awfully respectable and clean looking old people, had called in to give him that small token, as the old man put it, standing perfectly upright to make his speech of gratitude and respect for the very able way in which you conducted our case, and Mrs. Brunner piped up, how it was all due to him they felt. And they deeply appreciated his generosity—because, of course, he hadn't taken a fee.

And as he took the clock and put it on the middle of his mantelpiece, he had felt that he wished nobody to see his face. That was what he worked for—that was his reward; and he looked at the people who were actually before his eyes as if they danced over the scene in his chambers and were exposed by it, and as it faded—the Brunners faded—there remained as if left of that scene, himself, confronting this hostile population, a perfectly plain unsophisticated man, a man of the people (he straightened himself), very badly dressed, glaring, with not an air or a grace about him, a man who was an ill hand at concealing his feelings, a plain man, an ordinary human being, pitted against the evil, the corruption, the heartlessness of society. But he would not go on staring. Now he put on his spectacles and examined the pictures. He read the titles on a line of books; for the most part poetry. He would have liked well enough to read some of his old favourites again—Shakespeare, Dickens—he wished he ever had time to turn into the National Gallery, but he couldn't—no, one could not. Really one could not—with the world in the state it was in. Not when people all day long wanted your help, fairly clamoured for help. This wasn't an age for luxuries. And he looked at the armchairs and the paper-knives and the well-bound books, and shook his head, knowing that he would never have the time, never, he was glad to think, have the heart, to afford himself such luxuries. The people here would be shocked if they knew what he paid for his tobacco; how he had borrowed his clothes. His one and only extravagance was his little yacht on the Norfolk Broads. And that he did allow himself. He did like once a year to get right away from everybody and lie once a year on his back in a field. He thought how shocked they would be—these fine folk—if they realised the amount of pleasure he got from what he was old-fashioned enough to call the love of nature; trees and fields he had known ever since he was a boy.

These fine people would be shocked. Indeed, standing there, putting his spectacles away in his pocket, he felt himself grow more and more shocking every instant. And it was a very disagreeable feeling. He did not feel this—that he loved humanity, that he paid only five-pence an ounce for tobacco and loved nature—naturally and quietly. Each of these pleasures had been turned into a protest. He felt that these people whom he despised made him stand and deliver and justify himself. 'I am an ordinary man,' he kept saying. And what he said next he was really ashamed of saying, but he said it. 'I have done more for my kind in one day than the rest of you in all your lives.' Indeed, he could not help himself; he kept recalling scene after scene, like that when the Brunners gave him the clock—he kept reminding himself of the nice things people had said of his humanity, of his generosity, how he had helped them. He kept seeing himself as the wise and tolerant servant of humanity. And he wished he could repeat his praises aloud. It was unpleasant that the sense of his goodness should boil within him. It was still more unpleasant that he could tell no one what people had said about him. Thank the Lord, he kept saying, I shall be back at work to-morrow; and yet he was no longer satisfied simply to slip through the door and go home. He must stay, he must stay until he had justified himself. But how could he? In all that room full of people, he did not know a soul to speak to.

At last Richard Dalloway came up.

'I want to introduce Miss O'Keefe,' he said. Miss O'Keefe looked him full in the eyes. She was a rather arrogant, abrupt-mannered woman in the thirties.

Miss O'Keefe wanted an ice or something to drink. And the reason why she asked Prickett Ellis to give it her in what he felt a haughty, unjustifiable manner, was that she had seen a woman

and two children, very poor, very tired, pressing against the railings of a square, peering in, that hot afternoon. Can't they be let
in? she had thought, her pity rising like a wave; her indignation
boiling. No; she rebuked herself the next moment, roughly, as if
she boxed her own ears. The whole force of the world can't do
it. So she picked up the tennis ball and hurled it back. The whole
force of the world can't do it, she said in a fury, and that was
why she said so commandingly, to the unknown man:

'Give me an ice.'

Long before she had eaten it, Prickett Ellis, standing beside
her without taking anything, told her that he had not been to a
party for fifteen years; told her that his dress suit was lent him
by his brother-in-law; told her that he did not like this sort of
thing, and it would have eased him greatly to go on to say that
he was a plain man, who happened to have a liking for ordinary
people, and then would have told her (and been ashamed of it
afterwards) about the Brunners and the clock, but she said:

'Have you seen the *Tempest*?' then (for he had not seen the
Tempest), had he read some book? Again no, and then, putting
her ice down, did he ever read poetry?

And Prickett Ellis feeling something rise within him which
would decapitate this young woman, make a victim of her, mas-
sacre her, made her sit down there, where they would not be interrupted, on two chairs, in the empty garden, for everyone was
upstairs, only you could hear a buzz and a hum and a chatter
and a jingle, like the mad accompaniment of some phantom or-
chestra to a cat or two slinking across the grass, and the wavering of leaves, and the yellow and red fruit like Chinese lanterns
wobbling this way and that—the talk seemed like a frantic
skeleton dance music set to something very real, and full of
suffering.

'How beautiful!' said Miss O'Keefe.

Oh, it was beautiful, this little patch of grass, with the towers of Westminster massed round it black, high in the air, after

the drawing-room; it was silent, after that noise. After all, they had that—the tired woman, the children.

Prickett Ellis lit a pipe. That would shock her; he filled it with shag tobacco—fivepence-halfpenny an ounce. He thought how he would lie in his boat smoking, he could see himself, alone, at night, smoking under the stars. For always to-night he kept thinking how he would look if these people here were to see him. He said to Miss O'Keefe, striking a match on the sole of his boot, that he couldn't see anything particularly beautiful out here.

'Perhaps,' said Miss O'Keefe, 'you don't care for beauty.' (He had told her that he had not seen the *Tempest*; that he had not read a book; he looked ill-kempt, all moustached, chin, and silver watch chain.) She thought nobody need pay a penny for this; the Museums are free and the National Gallery; and the country. Of course she knew the objections—the washing, cooking, children; but the root of things, what they were all afraid of saying, was that happiness is dirt cheap. You can have it for nothing. Beauty.

Then Prickett Ellis let her have it—this pale, abrupt, arrogant woman. He told her, puffing his shag tobacco, what he had done that day. Up at six; interviews; smelling a drain in a filthy slum; then to court.

Here he hesitated, wishing to tell her something of his own doings. Suppressing that, he was all the more caustic. He said it made him sick to hear well-fed, well-dressed women (she twitched her lips, for she was thin, and her dress not up to standard) talk of beauty.

'Beauty!' he said. He was afraid he did not understand beauty apart from human beings.

So they glared into the empty garden where the lights were swaying, and one cat hesitating in the middle, its paw lifted.

Beauty apart from human beings? What did he mean by that? she demanded suddenly.

Well this; getting more and more wrought up, he told her the story of the Brunners and the clock, not concealing his pride in it. That was beautiful, he said.

She had no words to specify the horror his story roused in her. First his conceit; then his indecency in talking about human feelings; it was a blasphemy; no one in the whole world ought to tell a story to prove that they had loved their kind. Yet as he told it—how the old man had stood up and made his speech—tears came into her eyes; ah, if any one had ever said that to her! but then again, she felt how it was just this that condemned humanity for ever; never would they reach beyond affecting scenes with clocks; Brunners making speeches to Prickett Ellises, and the Prickett Ellises would always say how they had loved their kind; they would always be lazy, compromising, and afraid of beauty. Hence sprang revolutions; from laziness and fear and this love of affecting scenes. Still this man got pleasure from his Brunners; and she was condemned to suffer for ever and ever from her poor, poor women shut out from squares. So they sat silent. Both were very unhappy. For Prickett Ellis was not in the least solaced by what he had said; instead of picking her thorn out he had rubbed it in; his happiness of the morning had been ruined. Miss O'Keefe was muddled and annoyed; she was muddy instead of clear.

'I am afraid I am one of those very ordinary people,' he said, getting up, 'who love their kind.'

Upon which Miss O'Keefe almost shouted: 'So do I.'

Hating each other, hating the whole houseful of people who had given them this painful, this disillusioning evening, these two lovers of their kind got up, and without a word, parted for ever.

3

The Introduction

LILY EVERIT SAW MRS. DALLOWAY BEARING DOWN ON HER from the other side of the room, and could have prayed her not to come and disturb her; and yet, as Mrs. Dalloway approached with her right hand raised and a smile which Lily knew (though this was her first party) meant: 'But you've got to come out of your corner and talk,' a smile at once benevolent and drastic, she felt the strangest mixture of excitement and fear, of desire to be left alone and of longing to be taken out and thrown into the boiling depths. But Mrs. Dalloway was intercepted, caught by an old gentleman with white moustaches. So Lily Everit had two minutes respite there in which to hug to herself, as a drowning man might hug a spar in the sea, her essay on the character of Dean Swift. It had been given back to her that morning by Professor Miller marked with three red stars: First rate. First rate; she repeated that to herself, she took a sip of that cordial that was ever so much weaker now than it had been when she stood before the long glass being finished off (a pat here, a dab there) by her sister and Mildred, the housemaid. For as their hands moved about her she felt that they were fidgeting agreeably on the surface but beneath lay untouched like a lump of glowing metal—her essay on the character of Dean Swift, and all their praises when she came downstairs and stood in the hall waiting for the cab—Rupert had come out of his room and said what a swell she looked—ruffled the surface like a breeze among ribbons; but no more. Essays were the facts of life.

One divided life (she felt sure of it) into fact and into fiction, into rock and into wave, she thought, driving along and seeing things with such intensity that for ever and ever she would see the driver's back through the glass, and her own white phantom reflected in his dark coat. Then as she came into the house, at the very first sight of people moving upstairs and downstairs, this hard lump (her essay on the character of Swift) wobbled began wilting, she could not keep hold of it, and all her being (no longer sharp as a diamond cleaving the heart of life asunder) turned to a mist of alarm, apprehension, and defence, as she stood at bay in her corner. This was the famous place: the world.

Looking out, Lily Everit instinctively hid that essay of hers, so ashamed was she now, so bewildered too. And on tiptoe, nevertheless, to adjust her focus and get into right proportions (the old had been shamefully wrong) these diminishing and increasing things (what could one call them? people—impressions of people's lives?) which seemed to menace and mount over her, to turn everything to water, leaving her only the power to stand at bay.

Now Mrs. Dalloway, who had never quite dropped her arm, had shown by the way she moved it that she was coming, left the old soldier with the white moustaches, and came straight down on her, and said to the shy charming girl, with the clear eyes, the dark hair which clustered poetically round her head and the thin body in a dress which seemed to be slipping off, 'Come and let me introduce you,' and there Mrs. Dalloway hesitated, and then remembering that Lily was the clever one who read poetry, looked about for some young man, some young man just down from Oxford, who would have read everything and would talk about himself. And holding Lily Everit's hand she led her towards a group where there were young people talking.

Lily Everit hung back a little, might have been in the wake of a steamer; felt as Mrs. Dalloway led her on, that it was now going to happen; that nothing could prevent it, or save her (and she only wanted it to be over now) from being flung into a whirlpool where either she would perish or be saved. But what was the whirlpool?

Oh it was made of a million things and each so distinct to her; Westminster Abbey; the sense of enormously high solemn buildings surrounding them; grown up; being a woman. Perhaps that was the thing that came out, that remained, it was part of the dress, and all the little chivalries and respects of the drawing-room; all made her feel that she had come out of her chrysalis and was being proclaimed what in the long comfortable dark-ness of childhood she had never been—this frail and beautiful creature, this limited and circumscribed creature who could not do what she liked, this butterfly with a thousand facets to its eyes, and delicate fine plumage, and difficulties and sensibilities and sadnesses innumerable: a woman.

As she walked with Mrs. Dalloway across the room she ac-cepted the part which was now laid on her, and, naturally, over-did it a little, as a soldier proud of the traditions of an old and famous uniform might overdo it, feeling conscious as she walked of her finery; of her tight shoes; of her coiled and twisted hair; and how if she dropped a handkerchief (this had happened with strangers) a man would stoop precipitately and give it to her; thus accentuating the delicacy, the artificiality of her bearing unnaturally, for they were not hers after all.

Hers it was, rather, to run and hurry and ponder on long solitary walks, climbing gates, stepping through the mud, and through the blur, the dream, the ecstasy of loneliness, to see in the plover's wheel and surprise the rabbits, and come in the hearts of woods or wide lonely moors upon little ceremonies which had no audience, private rites, pure beauty offered by beetles and lilies of the valley and dead leaves and still pools, without any care whatever what human beings thought of them, which filled her mind with rapture and wonder—all this was, until tonight, her ordinary being, by which she knew and liked herself and crept into the heart of mother and father and brothers and sisters; and this other was a flower which had opened in ten minutes. And with the flower opened there came too, incontrovertibly, its world, so different, so strange; the towers of Westminster; the high and formal buildings; the talk; this civilisation, she felt, hanging back, as Mrs. Dalloway led her on.

This regulated way of life which fell like a yoke about her neck, softly, indomitably, from the skies, a statement which there was no gainsaying. Glancing at her essay; the three red stars dulled to obscurity, but peacefully, pensively, as if yielding to the pressure of unquestionable might, that is the conviction that it was not hers to dominate, or to assert; rather to air and embellish this orderly life where all was done already; high towers, solemn bells, flats built every brick of them by men's toil, parliaments too; and even the criss-cross of telegraph wires she thought looking at the window as she walked. What had she to oppose to this massive masculine achievement? An essay on the character of Dean Swift! And as she came to the group, which Bob Brinsley dominated (with his heel on the fender, and his head back), with his great honest forehead, and his look of self-assurance, and his delicacy, and honour and robust physical well-being, and sunburn, and airiness and direct descent from Shakespeare, what could she do but lay her essay, oh and the whole of her being, on the floor as a cloak for him to trample on, as a rose for him to rifle. Which she did, emphatically, when Mrs. Dalloway said, still holding her hand as if she would run away from this supreme trial, this introduction. 'Mr. Brinsley—

Miss Everit'. Both of you love Shelley. But hers was not love compared with his.

Saying this, Mrs. Dalloway felt, as she always felt remembering her youth, absurdly moved; youth meeting youth at her party, and there flashing, as at the concussion of steel upon flint (both stiffened to her feeling perceptibly) the loveliest and most ancient of all fires as she saw in Bob Brinsley's change of expression from carelessness to conformity, to formality, as he shook hands, which foreboded Clarissa thought, the tenderness, the goodness, the carelessness of women latent in all men, to her a sight to bring tears to the eyes, as it moved her even more intimately, to see in Lily herself the shy look, the startled look, surely the loveliest of all looks on a girl's face; and man feeling this for woman, and woman that for man, and there flowing from that contact all those homes, trials, sorrows, profound joy and intimate staunchness in the face of catastrophe, humanity was sweet at its heart, thought Clarissa, and her own life (to introduce a couple made her think of meeting Richard for the first time!) infinitely blessed. And on she went.

But, thought Lily Everit. But—But—But what?

Oh nothing, she thought hastily smothering down softly her sharp instinct. In the direct line from Shakespeare she thought and parliaments and churches she thought, oh and the telegraph wires too she thought, and ostentatiously of set purpose begged Mr. Brinsley to believe her implicitly when she offered him her essay upon the character of Dean Swift to do what he liked with, trample upon and destroy, for how could a mere child understand even for an instant the character of Dean Swift. Yes, she said. She did like reading.

'And I suppose you write?' he said, 'poems presumably?'

'Essays,' she said. And she would not let this horror get possession of her. She wanted to have her handkerchief picked up on the staircase and be a butterfly. Churches and parliaments, flats, even the telegraph wires—all, she told herself, made by men of toil, and this young man, she told herself, in direct descent from Shakespeare, so she would not let this terror, this suspicion of something different, get hold of her and shrivel up her wings and drive her out into loneliness. But as she said this, she saw him—how else could she describe it—kill a fly. That was it. He tore the wings off a fly, standing with his foot on the fender his head thrown back, talking insolently about himself, arrogantly. But she didn't mind how insolent and arrogant he was to her, if only he had not been brutal to flies.

But she said, fidgeting as she smothered down that idea, why not, since he is the greatest of all worldly objects? And to worship, to adorn, to embellish was her task, her wings were for that. But he talked; but he looked; but he laughed; he tore the wings off a fly. He pulled the wings off its back with his clever strong hands, and she saw him do it and she could not hide the knowledge from herself. But it is necessary that it should be so, she argued, thinking of the churches, of the parliaments and the blocks of flats, and so tried to crouch and cower and fold the wings down flat on her back.

But—but, what was it, why was it? In spite of all she could do her essay upon the character of Swift became more and more obtrusive and the three stars burnt quite bright again, only with a terrible lustre, no longer clear and brilliant, but troubled and bloodstained, as if this man, this great Mr. Brinsley, had just by pulling the wings off a fly as he talked (about his essays, about himself and once laughing, about a girl there) charged her light being with cloud, and confused her for ever and ever and shrivelled her wings on her back, and, as he turned away from her, she went nearer to the window and thought of the towers and civilisation with horror, and the yoke that had fallen from the skies onto her neck crushed her, and she felt like a naked wretch who having sought shelter in some shady garden is turned out and made to understand (ah, but there was a kind of passion in it too) that there are no sanctuaries, or butterflies, and this civilisation, said Lily Everit to herself, as she accepted the kind compliments of old Mrs. Bromley on her appearance, depends upon me. Mrs. Bromley said later that like all the Everits, Lily looked 'as if she had the weight of the world upon her shoulders'.

4

Ancestors

*M*RS. VALLANCE, AS SHE REPLIED TO JACK RENSHAW WHO HAD
made that rather silly remark of his about not liking to watch
cricket matches, wished that she could make him understand
somehow what became every moment more obvious at a party
like this, that if her father had been alive people would have realised how foolish, how wicked—no, not so much wicked as
silly and ugly—how, compared to really dignified simple men
and women like her father, like her dear mother, all this seemed
to her so trivial. How very different his mind was, and his life;
and her mother, and how differently, entirely differently she herself had been brought up.

'Here we all are,' she said suddenly, 'cooped up here in one
room the size of an oven, when up in Scotland where I was
born we should all be—': she owed it to these foolish young
men who were after all quite nice, though a little under-sized, to
make them understand what her father, what her mother and
she herself too, for she was like them at heart, felt. And then it
came over her in a rush, how she owed it to the world to make

men understand how her father and her mother, how she too, were quite different.

He had stopped in Edinburgh for a night once, Mr. Renshaw said.

'Was she Scotch?' he asked.

He did not know then who her father was, that she was John Ellis Rattray's daughter and her mother was Catherine Macdonald; and one night in Edinburgh! And she had spent all those wonderful years there, there and at Elliotshaw on the Northumbrian border. There she had run wild among the currant bushes; there her father's friends had come and only a girl as she was, she had heard the most wonderful talk of her time. She could see them still; her father, Sir Duncan Clements, Mr. Rogers (old Mr. Rogers was her ideal of a Greek sage) sitting under the cedar tree; after dinner in the starlight.

They talked about everything in the world, it seemed to her now; they were too large-minded ever to laugh at other people; they had taught her, though she was only a girl, how to revere beauty. What was there beautiful in this stuffy London room?

'Oh, those poor flowers,' she exclaimed. For a carnation or two were actually trodden under foot, for petals of flowers were all crumpled and crushed. For she felt almost too much for flowers. Her mother had loved flowers; ever since she was a child she had been brought up to feel that to hurt a flower was to hurt the most exquisite thing in nature. Nature had always been a passion with her; the mountains, the sea. And here in London, one looked out of the window and saw more houses. One had a dreadful sense of human beings packed on top of each other in little boxes. It was an atmosphere in which she could not possibly live; herself; now she could not bear to walk in London and see the children in the streets. She was perhaps too sensitive; life would be impossible if everyone was like her, but when she remembered her own childhood, and her father and mother, and the beauty and care that were lavished on them—

'What a lovely frock!' said Jack Renshaw. And that seemed to her altogether wrong—for a young man to be noticing women's clothes at all. Her father was full of reverence for women, but he never thought of noticing what they wore. And of all these girls—the girls might be pretty—there was not a single one of them one could call beautiful as she remembered her mother, her dear stately mother who never seemed to dress differently summer or winter, whether they had people or not, but always looked herself in some lace and a black dress or, as she grew older, a little cap. When she was a widow she would sit among her flowers by the hour, and she seemed to be more with ghosts than with them all, dreaming of the past which is, Mrs. Vallance thought, somehow so much more real than the present. But why!

It is in the past with those wonderful men and women, she thought, that I really live; it is they who knew me; it is those people only (and she thought of the starlit garden and the trees and old Mr. Rogers, and her father, in his white linen coat, smoking) who understood me. She felt her eyes soften and deepen as at the approach of tears, standing there in Mrs. Dalloway's drawing-room, looking at these people, these flowers, this noisy bright chattering crowd; at herself, that little girl who was to travel so far, running picking Sweet Alice, then sitting up in bed in the attic which smelt of pine-wood reading stories, poetry. She had read all Shelley between the age of twelve and fifteen, and used to say it to her father, holding her hands behind her back, while he stared. The tears began, down in the back of her head, to rise, as she looked at this picture of herself, and added the suffering of a lifetime (she had suffered abominably, life had passed over her like a wheel, like was not what it had seemed then—it was like this party) to the child standing there, reciting Shelley, with her dark wild eyes. But what had they not seen later.

And it was only those people, dead now, laid away in quiet Scotland, who had ever seen all that she had it in her to be; who had known her, who knew what she had it in her to be. And now the tears came closer, as she thought of the little girl in the cotton frock; how large and dark her eyes were; how beautiful she looked repeating the "Ode to the West Wind'; how proud her father was of her, and how great he was, and how great her mother even, and how when she was with them she was entirely so pure, so good, so gifted that she had it in her to be anything; that if they had lived, and she had always been with them in the garden (which now appeared the only place where she had spent her whole childhood, and it was always starlit, and always summer, and they were always sitting out under the cedar tree smoking, and except that somehow her mother was dreaming alone, in her widow's cap, among her flowers; and how good and kind and respectful the old servants were, Andrews the gardener, Jersy the cook; and old Sultan the Newfoundland dog; and the vine, and the pond, and the pump; and)—Mrs. Vallance looking very fierce and proud and satirical, compared her life with other people's lives—and if that life could have gone on for ever, then Mrs. Vallance felt none of this—and she looked at Jack Renshaw and the girl whose clothes he admired—could have had any existence, and she would have been oh perfectly happy, perfectly good, instead of which here she was forced to listen to a young man saying—and she laughed almost scornfully and yet tears were in her eyes—that he could not bear to watch cricket matches!

5

Together and Apart

MRS. DALLOWAY INTRODUCED THEM, SAYING YOU WILL LIKE him. The conversation began some minutes before anything was said, for both Mr. Serle and Miss Anning looked at the sky and in both of their minds the sky went on pouring its meaning, though very differently, until the presence of Mr. Serle by her side became so distinct to Miss Anning that she could not see the sky, simply, itself, any more, but the sky shored up by the tall body, dark eyes, grey hair, clasped hands, the stern melancholy (but she had been told 'falsely melancholy') face of Roderick Serle, and, knowing how foolish it was, she yet felt impelled to say:

'What a beautiful night!'

Foolish! Idiotically foolish! But if one mayn't be foolish at the age of forty in the presence of the sky, which makes the wisest imbecile—mere wisps of straw—she and Mr. Serle atoms, motes, standing there at Mrs. Dalloway's window, and their lives, seen by moonlight, as long as an insect's and no more important.

'Well!' said Miss Anning, patting the sofa cushion emphatically. And down he sat beside her. Was he 'falsely melancholy' as they said? Prompted by the sky, which seemed to make it all a little futile—what they said, what they did—she said something perfectly commonplace again:

'There was a Miss Serle who lived at Canterbury when I was a girl there.'

With the sky in his mind, all the tombs of his ancestors immediately appeared to Mr. Serle in a blue romantic light, and his eyes expanding and darkening, he said: 'Yes.'

'We are originally a Norman family, who came over with the Conqueror. That is a Richard Serle buried in the cathedral. He was a Knight of the Garter.'

Miss Anning felt that she had struck accidentally the true man, upon whom the false man was built. Under the influence of the moon (the moon which symbolised man to her, she could see it through a chink of the curtain, and she took dips of the moon) she was capable of saying almost anything and she settled in to disinter the true man who was buried under the false, saying to herself: 'On, Stanley, on'—which was a watchword of hers, a secret spur, or scourge such as middle-aged people often make to flagellate some inveterate vice, hers being a deplorable timidity, or rather indolence, for it was not so much that she lacked courage, but lacked energy, especially in talking to men, who frightened her rather, and so often her talks petered out into dull commonplaces, and she had very few men friends— very few intimate friends at all, she thought, but after all, did she want them? No. She had Sarah, Arthur, the cottage, the chow and, of course *that,* she thought, dipping herself, sousing herself, even as she sat on the sofa beside Mr. Serle, in *that,* in the sense she had coming home of something collected there, a cluster of miracles, which she could not believe other people had (since it was she only who had Arthur, Sarah, the cottage, and the chow), but she soused herself again in the deep satisfactory possession, feeling that what with this and the moon (music that was, the moon), she could afford to leave this man and that pride of his in the Serles buried. No! That was the danger—she must not sink into torpidity—not at her age. 'On, Stanley, on,' she said to herself, and asked him:

'Do you know Canterbury yourself?'

Did he know Canterbury! Mr. Serle smiled, thinking how absurd a question it was—how little she knew, this nice quiet woman who played some instrument and seemed intelligent and had good eyes, and was wearing a very nice old necklace—knew what it meant. To be asked if he knew Canterbury. When the best years of his life, all his memories, things he had never been able to tell anybody, but had tried to write—ah, had tried to write (and he sighed) all had centred in Canterbury; it made him laugh.

His sigh and then his laugh, his melancholy, and his humour, made people like him, and he knew it, and yet being liked had not made up for the disappointment, and if he sponged on the liking people had for him (paying long calls on sympathetic ladies, long, long calls), it was half-bitterly, for he had never done a tenth part of what he could have done, and had dreamed of doing, as a boy in Canterbury. With a stranger he felt a renewal of hope because they could not say that he had not done what he had promised, and yielding to his charm would give him a fresh start—at fifty! She had touched the spring. Fields and flowers and grey buildings dripped down into his mind, formed silver drops on the gaunt, dark walls of his mind and dripped down. With such an image his poems often began. He felt the desire to make images now, sitting by this quiet woman.

'Yes, I know Canterbury,' he said reminiscently, sentimentally, inviting, Miss Anning felt, discreet questions, and that was what made him interesting to so many people, and it was this extraordinary facility and responsiveness to talk on his part that he had been his undoing, so he thought often, taking his studs out and putting his keys and small change on the dressing-table after one of these parties (and he went out sometimes almost every night in the season), and, going down to breakfast, becoming quite different, grumpy, unpleasant at breakfast to his wife, who was an invalid, and never went out, but had old friends to see her sometimes, women friends for the most part, interested in Indian philosophy and different cures and different doctors, which Roderick Serle snubbed off by some caustic remark too clever for her to meet, except by gentle expostulations and a tear or two—he had failed, he often thought, because he could not cut himself off utterly from society and the company of women, which was so necessary to him, and write. He had involved himself too deep in life—and here he would cross his knees (all his movements were a little unconventional and distinguished) and not blame himself, but put the blame off upon the richness of his nature, which he compared favourably with Wordsworth's, for example, and, since he had given so much to people, he felt, resting his head on his hands, they in their turn should help him, and this was the prelude, tremulous, fascinating, exciting, to talk; and images bubbled up in his mind.

'She's like a fruit tree—like a flowering cherry tree,' he said, looking at a youngish woman with fine white hair. It was a nice sort of image, Ruth Anning thought rather nice, yet she did not feel sure that she liked this distinguished, melancholy man with his gestures; and it's odd, she thought, how one's feelings are influenced. She did not like *him*, though she rather liked that comparison of his of a woman to a cherry tree. Fibres of her were floated capriciously this way and that, like the tentacles of a sea anemone, how thrilled, now snubbed, and her brain, miles away, cool and distant, up in the air, received messages which it would sum up in time so that, when people talked about Roderick Serle (and he was a bit of a figure) she would say unhesitatingly: 'I like him,' or 'I don't like him,' and her opinion would be made up for ever. An odd thought; a solemn thought; throwing a green light on what human fellowship consisted of.

'It's odd that you should know Canterbury,' said Mr. Serle. 'It's always a shock,' he went on (the white-haired lady having

passed), 'when one meets someone' (they had never met before), 'by chance, as it were, who touches the fringe of what has
meant a great deal to oneself, touches accidentally, for I suppose
Canterbury was nothing but a nice old town to you. So you
stayed there one summer with an aunt?' (That was all Ruth Anning was going to tell him about her visit to Canterbury.) 'And
you saw the sights and went away and never thought of it again.'

Let him think so; not liking him, she wanted him to run away
with an absurd idea of her. For really, her three months in Canterbury had been amazing. She remembered to the last detail,
though it was merely a chance visit, going to see Miss Charlotte
Serle, an acquaintance of her aunt's. Even now she could respect
Miss Serle's very words about the thunder. 'Whenever I wake, or
hear thunder in the night, I think "Someone has been killed".'
And she could see the hard, hairy, diamond-patterned carpet,
and the twinkling, suffused, brown eyes of the elderly lady, holding the teacup out unfilled, while she said that about the thunder.
And always she saw Canterbury, all thundercloud and livid apple
blossom, and the long grey backs of the buildings.

The thunder roused her from her plethoric middle-aged
swoon of indifference; 'On, Stanley, on,' she said to herself; that
is, this man shall not glide away from me, like everyone else, on
this false assumption; I will tell him the truth.

'I loved Canterbury,' she said.

He kindled instantly. It was his gift, his fault, his destiny.

'Loved it,' he repeated. 'I can see that you did.'

Her tentacles sent back the message that Roderick Serle was
nice.

Their eyes met; collided rather, for each felt that behind the
eyes the secluded being, who sits in darkness while his shallow
agile companion does all the tumbling and beckoning, and
keeps the show going, suddenly stood erect; flung off his cloak;
confronted the other. It was alarming; it was terrific. They were
elderly and burnished into a glowing smoothness, so that Roderick Serle would go, perhaps to a dozen parties in a season, and

feel nothing out of the common, or only sentimental regrets, and the desire for pretty images—like this of the flowering cherry tree—and all the time there stagnated in him unstirred a sort of superiority to his company, a sense of untapped resources, which sent him back home dissatisfied with his life, with himself, yawning, empty, capricious. But now, quite suddenly, like a white bolt in a mist (but this image forged itself with the inevitability of lightning and loomed up), there it had happened; the old ecstasy of life; its invincible assault; for it was unpleasant, at the same time that it rejoiced and rejunvenated and filled the veins and nerves with threads of ice and fire; it was terrifying. 'Canterbury twenty years ago,' said Miss Anning, as one lays a shade over an intense light, or covers some burning peach with a green leaf, for it is too strong, too ripe, too full.

Sometimes she wished she had married. Sometimes the cool peace of middle life, with its automatic devices for shielding mind and body from bruises, seemed to her, compared with the thunder and the livid apple-blossom of Canterbury, base. She could imagine something different, more like lightning, more intense. She could imagine some physical sensation. She could imagine—

And, strangely enough, for she had never seen him before, her senses, those tentacles which were thrilled and snubbed, now sent no more messages, now lay quiescent, as if she and Mr. Serle knew each other so perfectly, were, in fact, so closely united that they had only to float side by side down this stream.

Of all things, nothing is so strange as human intercourse, she thought, because of its changes, its extraordinary irrationality, her dislike being now nothing short of the most intense and rapturous love, but directly the word 'love' occurred to her, she rejected it, thinking again how obscure the mind was, with its very few words for all these astonishing perceptions, these alternations of pain and pleasure. For how did one name this. That is what she felt now, the withdrawal of human affection, Serle's disappearance, and the instant need they were both under to cover up what was so desolating and degrading to human nature that everyone tried to bury it decently from sight—this withdrawal, this violation of trust, and seeking some decent and acknowledged and accepted burial form, she said:

'Of course, whatever they may do, they can't spoil Canterbury.'

He smiled; he accepted it; he crossed his knees the other way about. She did her part; he his. So things came to an end. And over them both came instantly that paralysing blankness of feeling, when nothing bursts from the mind, when its walls appear like slate; when vacancy almost hurts, and the eyes petrified and fixed see the same spot—a pattern, a coal scuttle—with an exactness which is terrifying, since no emotion, no idea, no impression of any kind comes to change it, to modify it, to embellish it, since the fountains of feeling seem sealed and as the mind turns rigid, so does the body; stark, statuesque, so that neither Mr. Serle nor Miss Anning could move or speak, and they felt as if an enchanter had freed them, and spring flushed every vein with streams of life, when Mira Cartwright, tapping Mr. Serle archly on the shoulder, said:

'I saw you at the *Meistersinger,* and you cut me. Villain,' said Miss Cartwright, 'you don't deserve that I should ever speak to you again.'

And they could separate.

6

The New Dress

MABEL HAD HER FIRST SERIOUS SUSPICION THAT SOMETHING was wrong as she took her cloak off and Mrs. Barnet, while handing her the mirror and touching the brushes and thus drawing her attention, perhaps rather markedly, to all the appliances for tidying and improving hair, complexion, clothes, which existed on the dressing-table, confirmed the suspicion— that it was not right, not quiet right, which growing stronger as she went upstairs and springing at her, with conviction as she greeted Clarissa Dalloway, she went straight to the far end of the room, to a shaded corner where a looking-glass hung and looked. No! It was not *right*. And at once the misery which she always tried to hide, the profound dissatisfaction—the sense she had had, ever since she was a child, of being inferior to other people—set upon her, relentlessly, remorselessly, with an intensity which she could not beat off, as she would when she woke at night at home, by reading Borrow or Scott; for oh these men, oh these women, all were thinking—'What's Mabel wearing?

What a fright she looks! What a hideous new dress!'—their eyelids flickering as they came up and then their lids shutting rather
tight. It was her own appalling inadequacy; her cowardice; her
mean, water-sprinkled blood that depressed her. And at once
the whole of the room where, for ever so many hours, she had
planned with the little dressmaker how it was to go, seemed sordid, repulsive; and her own drawing-room so shabby, and herself, going out, puffed up with vanity as she touched the letters
on the hall table and said: 'How dull!' to show off—all this now
seemed unutterably silly, paltry, and provincial. All this had been
absolutely destroyed, shown up, exploded, the moment she
came into Mrs. Dalloway's drawing-room.

What she had thought that evening when, sitting over the
teacups, Mrs. Dalloway's invitation came, was that, of course,
she could not be fashionable. It was absurd to pretend it even—
fashion meant cut, meant style, meant thirty guineas at least—
but why not be original? Why not be herself, anyhow? And,
getting up, she had taken that old fashion book of her mother's,
a Paris fashion book of the time of the Empire, and had thought
how much prettier, more dignified, and more womanly they
were then, and so set herself—oh, it was foolish—trying to be
like them, pluming herself in fact, upon being modest and old-
fashioned, and very charming, giving herself up, no doubt about
it, to an orgy of self-love, which deserved to be chastised, and so
rigged herself out like this.

But she dared not look in the glass. She could not face the
whole horror—the pale yellow, idiotically old-fashioned silk dress
with its long skirt and its high sleeves and its waist and all the
things that looked so charming in the fashion book, but not on
her, not among all these ordinary people. She felt like a dressmaker's dummy standing there, for young people to stick pins into.

'But, my dear, it's perfectly charming!' Rose Shaw said, looking her up and down with that little satirical pucker of the lips
which she expected—Rose herself being dressed in the height
of fashion, precisely like everybody else, always.

We are all like flies trying to crawl over the edge of the saucer, Mabel thought, and repeated the phrase as if she were crossing herself, as if she were trying to find some spell to annul this pain, to make this agony endurable. Tags of Shakespeare, lines from books she had read ages ago, suddenly came to her when she was in agony, and she repeated them over and over again. 'Flies trying to crawl,' she repeated. If she could say that over often enough and make herself see the flies, she would become numb, chill, frozen, dumb. Now she could see flies crawling slowly out of a saucer of milk with their wings stuck together; and she strained and strained (standing in front of the looking-glass, listening to Rose Shaw) to make herself see Rose Shaw and all the other people there as flies, trying to hoist themselves out of something, or into something, meagre, insignificant, toiling flies. But she could not see them like that, not other people. She saw herself like that—she was a fly, but the others were dragonflies, butterflies, beautiful insects, dancing, fluttering, skimming, while she alone dragged herself up out of the saucer. (Envy and spite, the most detestable of the vices, were her chief faults.)

'I feel like some dowdy, decrepit, horribly dingy old fly,' she said, making Robert Haydon stop just to hear her say that, just to reassure herself by furbishing up a poor weak-kneed phrase and so showing how detached she was, how witty, that she did not feel in the least out of anything. And, of course, Robert Haydon answered something, quite polite, quite insincere, which she saw through instantly, and said to herself, directly he went (again from some book), 'Lies, lies, lies!' For a party makes things either much more real, or much less real, she thought; she saw in a flash to the bottom of Robert Haydon's heart; she saw through everything. She saw the truth. *This* was true, this drawing-room, this self, the other false. Miss Milan's little workroom was really terribly hot, stuffy, sordid. It smelt of clothes and cabbage cooking; and yet, when Miss Milan put the glass in her hand, and she looked at herself with the dress on, finished, an extraordinary bliss shot through her heart. Suffused with light, she sprang into existence. Rid of cares and wrinkles, what she had dreamed of herself was there — a beautiful woman. Just for a second (she had not dared look longer, Miss Milan wanted to know about the length of the skirt), there looked at her, framed in the scrolloping mahogany, a grey-white, mysteriously smiling, charming girl, the core of herself, the soul of herself; and it was not vanity only, not only self-love that made her think it good, tender, and true. Miss Milan said the skirt could not well be longer; if anything the skirt, said Miss Milan, puckering her forehead, considering with all her wits about her, must be shorter; and she felt, suddenly, honestly, full of love for Miss Milan, much, much fonder of Miss Milan than of anyone in the whole world, and could have cried for pity that she should be crawling on the floor with her mouth full of pins, and her face red and her eyes bulging — that one human being should be doing this for another, and she saw them all as human beings merely, and herself going off to her party, and Miss Milan pulling the cover over the canary's cage, or letting him pick a hemp-seed from between her lips, and the thought of it, of this side of human nature and its patience and its endurance and its being content with such miserable, scanty, sordid, little pleasures filled her eyes with tears.

And now the whole thing had vanished. The dress, the room, the love, the pity, the scrolloping looking-glass, and the canary's cage — all had vanished, and here she was in a corner of Mrs. Dalloway's drawing-room, suffering tortures, woken wide awake to reality.

But it was all so paltry, weak-blooded, and petty-minded to care so much at her age with two children, to be still so utterly dependent on people's opinions and not have principles or convictions, not to be able to say as other people did, 'There's Shakespeare! There's death! We're all weevils in a captain's biscuit'— or whatever it was that people did say.

She faced herself straight in the glass; she pecked at her left shoulder; she issued out into the room, as if spears were thrown at her yellow dress from all sides. But instead of looking fierce or tragic, as Rose Shaw would have done—Rose would have looked like Boadicea—she looked foolish and self-conscious, and simpered like a schoolgirl and slouched across the room, positively slinking, as if she were a beaten mongrel, and looked at a picture, an engraving. As if one went to a party to look at a picture! Everybody knew why she did it—it was from shame, from humiliation.

'Now the fly's in the saucer,' she said to herself, 'right in the middle, and can't get out, and the milk,' she thought, rigidly staring at the picture, 'is sticking its wings together.'

'It's so old-fashioned,' she said to Charles Burt, making him stop (which by itself he hated) on his way to talk to someone else.

She meant, or she tried to make herself think that she meant, that it was the picture and not her dress, that was old-fashioned. And one word of praise, one word of affection from Charles would have made all the difference to her at the moment. If he had only said, 'Mabel, you're looking charming tonight!' it would have changed her life. Charles said nothing of the kind, of course. He was malice itself. He always saw through one, especially if one were feeling particularly mean, paltry, or feeble-minded.

'Mabel's got a new dress!' he said, and the poor fly was absolutely shoved into the middle of the saucer. Really, he would like her to drown, she believed. He had no heart, no fundamental kindness, only a veneer of friendliness. Miss Milan was much more real, much kinder. If only one could feel that and stick to it, always. 'Why,' she asked herself—replying to Charles much too pertly, letting him see that she was out of temper, or 'ruffled' as he called it ('Rather ruffled?' he said and went on to laugh at her with some woman over there)—'Why,' she asked herself, 'can't I feel one thing always, feel quite sure that Miss Milan is right, and Charles wrong and stick to it, feel sure about the canary and pity and love and not be whipped all round in a second by coming into a room full of people?' It was her odious, weak, vacillating character again, always giving at the critical moment and not being seriously interested in conchology, etymology, botany, archaeology, cutting up potatoes and watching them fructify like Mary Dennis, like Violet Searle.

Then Mrs. Holman, seeing her standing there, bore down upon her. Of course a thing like a dress was beneath Mrs. Holman's notice, with her family always tumbling downstairs or having the scarlet fever. Could Mabel tell her if Elmthorpe was ever let for August and September? Oh, it was a conversation that bored her unutterably!—it made her furious to be treated like a house agent or a messenger boy, to be made use of. Not to have value, that was it, she thought, trying to grasp something hard, something real, while she tried to answer sensibly about the bathroom and the south aspect and the hot water to the top of the house; and all the time she could see little bits of her yellow dress in the round looking-glass which made them all the size of boot-buttons or tadpoles; and it was amazing to think how much humiliation and agony and self-loathing and effort and passionate ups and downs of feeling were contained in a thing the size of a threepenny bit. And what was still odder, this thing, this Mabel Waring, was separate, quite disconnected; and though Mrs. Holman (the black button) was leaning forward and telling her how her eldest boy had strained his heart running, she could see her too, quite detached in the looking-glass, and it was impossible that the black dot, leaning forward, gesticulating, should make the yellow dot, sitting solitary, self-centred, feel what the black dot was feeling, yet they pretended.

'So impossible to keep boys quiet'—that was the kind of thing one said.

And Mrs. Holman, who could never get enough sympathy and snatched what little there was greedily, as if it were her right (but she deserved much more for there was her little girl who had come down this morning with a swollen knee-joint), took this miserable offering and looked at it suspiciously, grudgingly, as if it were a halfpenny when it ought to have been a pound and put it away in her purse, must put up with it, mean and miserly though it was, times being hard, so very hard; and on she went, creaking, injured Mrs. Holman, about the girl with the swollen joints. Ah, it was tragic, this greed, this clamour of human be-ings, like a row of cormorants, barking and flapping their wings for sympathy—it was tragic, could one have felt it and not merely pretended to feel it!

But in her yellow dress to-night she could not wring out one drop more; she wanted it all, all for herself. She knew (she kept on looking into the glass, dipping into that dreadfully showing-up blue pool) that she was condemned, despised, left like this in a backwater, because of her being like this, a feeble, vacillating creature; and it seemed to her that the yellow dress was a penance which she had deserved, and if she had been dressed like Rose Shaw, in lovely, clinging green with a ruffle of swans-down, she would have deserved that; and she thought that there was no escape for her—none whatever. But it was not her fault altogether, after all. It was being one of a family of ten; never having money enough, always skimping and paring; and her mother carrying great cans, and the linoleum worn on the stair edges, and one sordid little domestic tragedy after another— nothing catastrophic, the sheep farm failing, but not utterly; her eldest brother marrying beneath him but not very much—there was no romance, nothing extreme about them all. They petered out respectably in seaside resorts; every watering-place had one of her aunts even now asleep in some lodging with the front win-dows not quite facing the sea. That was like them—they had to squint at things always. And she had done the same—she was just like her aunts. For all her dreams of living in India, married to some hero like Sir Henry Lawrence, some empire builder (still the sight of a native in a turban filled her with romance), she had failed utterly. She had married Hubert, with his safe, permanent underling's job in the Law Courts, and they managed tolerably in a smallish house, without proper maids, and hash when she was alone or just bread and butter, but now and then—Mrs. Holman was off, thinking her the most dried-up, unsympathetic twig she had ever met, absurdly dressed, too, and would tell everyone about Mabel's fantastic appearance—now and then, thought Mabel Waring, left alone on the blue sofa, punching the cushion in order to look occupied, for she would not join Charles Burt and Rose Shaw, chattering like magpies and perhaps laughing at her by the fireplace—now and then, there did come to her delicious moments, reading the other night in bed, for instance, or down by the sea on the sand in the sun, at Easter—let her recall it—a great tuft of pale sand-grass standing all twisted like a shock of spears against the sky, which was blue like a smooth china egg, so firm, so hard, and then the melody of the waves—'Hush, hush,' they said, and the children's shouts paddling—yes, it was a divine moment, and there she lay, she felt, in the hand of the Goddess who was the world; rather a hard-hearted, but very beautiful Goddess, a little lamb laid on the altar (one did think these silly things, and it didn't matter so long as one never said them). And also with Hubert sometimes she had quite unexpectedly—carving the mutton for Sunday lunch, for no reason, opening a letter, coming into a room—divine moments, when she said to herself (for she would never say this to anybody else), 'This is it. This has happened. This is it!' And the other way about it was equally surprising—that is, when everything was arranged—music, weather, holidays, every reason for happiness was there—then nothing happened at all. One wasn't happy. It was flat, just flat, that was all.

Her wretched self again, no doubt! She had always been a fretful, weak, unsatisfactory mother, a wobbly wife, lolling about in a kind of twilight existence with nothing very clear or very bold, or more one thing than another, like all her brothers and sisters, except perhaps Herbert—they were all the same poor water-veined creatures who did nothing. Then in the midst of this creeping, crawling life, suddenly she was on the crest of a wave. That wretched fly—where had she read the story that kept coming into her mind about the fly and the saucer?—struggled out. Yes, she had those moments. But now that she was forty, they might come more and more seldom. By degrees she would cease to struggle any more. But that was deplorable! That was not to be endured! That made her feel ashamed of herself!

She would go to the London Library to-morrow. She would find some wonderful, helpful, astonishing book, quite by chance, a book by a clergyman, by an American no one had ever heard of; or she would walk down the Strand and drop, accidentally, into a hall where a miner was telling about the life in the pit, and suddenly she would become a new person. She would wear a uniform; she would be called Sister Somebody; she would never give a thought to clothes again. And for ever after she would be perfectly clear about Charles Burt and Miss Milan and this room and that room; and it would be always, day after day, as if she were lying in the sun or carving the mutton. It would be it!

So she got up from the blue sofa, and the yellow button in the looking-glass got up too, and she waved her hand to Charles and Rose to show them she did not depend on them one scrap, and the yellow button moved out of the looking-glass, and all the spears were gathered into her breast as she walked towards Mrs. Dalloway and said 'Good night.'

'But it's too early to go,' said Mrs. Dalloway, who was always so charming.

'I'm afraid I must,' said Mabel Waring. 'But,' she added in her weak, wobbly voice which only sounded ridiculous when she tried to strengthen it, 'I have enjoyed myself enormously.'

'I have enjoyed myself,' she said to Mr. Dalloway, whom she met on the stairs.

'Lies, lies, lies!' she said to herself, going downstairs, and 'Right in the saucer!' she said to herself as she thanked Mrs. Barnet for helping her and wrapped herself, round and round, in the Chinese cloak she had worn these twenty years.

7

A Summing Up

SINCE IT HAD GROWN HOT AND CROWDED INDOORS, SINCE there could be no danger on a night like this of damp, since the Chinese lanterns seemed hung red and green fruit in the depths of an enchanted forest, Mr. Bertram Pritchard led Mrs. Latham into the garden.

The open air and the sense of being out of doors bewildered Sasha Latham, the tall, handsome, rather indolent looking lady, whose majesty of presence was so great that people never credited her with feeling perfectly inadequate and gauche when she had to say something at a party. But so it was; and she was glad that she was with Bertram, who could be trusted, even out of doors, to talk without stopping. Written down what he said was in itself insignificant, but there was no connection between the different remarks. Indeed, if one had taken a pencil and written down his very words—and one night of his talk would have filled a whole book—no one could doubt, reading them, that the poor man was intellectually deficient. This was far from the case, for Mr. Pritchard was an esteemed civil servant and a Companion of the Bath; but what was even stranger was that he was almost invariably liked. There was a sound in his voice, some accent of emphasis, some lustre in the incongruity of his ideas, some emanation from his round, chubby brown face and robin redbreast's figure, something immaterial, and unseizable, which existed and flourished and made itself felt independently of his words, indeed, often in opposition to them. This Sasha Latham would be thinking, while he chattered on about his tour in Devonshire, about inns and landladies, about Eddie and Freddie, about cows and night travelling, about cream and stars, about continental railways and Bradshaw, catching cod, catching cold, influenza, rheumatism and Keats—she was thinking of him in the abstract as a person whose existence was good, creating him as he spoke in a guise that was different from what he said, and was certainly the true Bertram Pritchard, even though one could not prove it. How could one prove that he was a loyal friend and very sympathetic and—but here, as so often happened, talking to Bertram Pritchard, she forgot his existence, and began to think of something else.

It was the night she thought of, hitching herself together in some way, taking a look up into the sky. It was the country she smelt suddenly, the sombre stillness of fields under the stars, but here, in Mrs. Dalloway's back garden, in Westminster, the beauty, country born and bred as she was, thrilled her because of the contrast presumably; there the smell of hay in the air and behind her the room full of people. She walked with Bertram; she walked rather like a stag, with a little give of the ankles, fanning herself, majestic, silent, with all her senses roused, her ears pricked, snuffing the air, as if she had been some wild, but perfectly controlled creature taking its pleasure by night.

This, she thought, is the greatest of marvels; the supreme achievement of the human race. Where there were osier beds and coracles paddling through a swamp, there is this; and she thought of the dry, thick, well-built house, stored with valuables, humming with people coming close to each other, going away from each other, exchanging their views, stimulating each other. And Clarissa Dalloway had made it open in the wastes of the night, had laid paving stones over the bog, and, when they came to the end of the garden (it was in fact extremely small), and she and Bertram sat down on deck chairs, she looked at the house veneratingly, enthusiastically, as if a golden shaft ran through her and tears formed on it and fell in profound thanksgiving. Shy though she was and almost incapable when suddenly presented to someone of saying anything, fundamentally humble, she cherished a profound admiration for other people. To be them would be marvellous, but she was condemned to be herself and could only in this silent enthusiastic way, sitting outside in a garden, applaud the society of humanity from which she was excluded. Tags of poetry in praise of them rose to her lips; they were adorable and good, above all courageous, triumphers over night and fens, the survivors, the company of adventurers who, set about with dangers, sail on.

By some malice of fate she was unable to join, but she could sit and praise while Bertram chattered on, he being among the voyagers, as cabin boy or common seaman—someone who ran up masts, gaily whistling. Thinking thus, the branch of some tree in front of her became soaked and steeped in her admiration for the people of the house; dripped gold; or stood sentinel erect. It was part of the gallant and carousing company, a mast from the mast from which the flag streamed. There was a barrel of some kind against the wall, and this, too, she endowed.

Suddenly Bertram, who was restless physically, wanted to explore the grounds, and, jumping on to a heap of bricks, he peered over the garden wall. Sasha peered over too. She saw a bucket or perhaps a boot. In a second the illusion vanished. There was London again; the vast inattentive impersonal world; motor omnibuses; affairs; lights before public-houses; and yawning policemen.

Having satisfied his curiosity, and replenished, by a moment's silence, his bubbling fountains of talk, Bertram invited Mr. and Mrs. Somebody to sit with them, pulling up two more chairs. There they sat again, looking at the same house, the same tree, the same barrel; only having looked over the wall and had a glimpse of the bucket, or rather of London going its ways unconcernedly, Sasha could no longer spray over the world that cloud of gold. Bertram talked and the Somebodies—for the life of her she could not remember if they were called Wallace or Freeman—answered, and all their words passed through a thin haze of gold and fell into prosaic daylight. She looked at the dry, thick Queen Anne House; she did her best to remember what she had read at school about the Isle of Thorney and men in coracles, oysters, and wild duck and mists, but it seemed to her a logical affair of drains and carpenters, and this party—nothing but people in evening dress.

Then she asked herself, which view is the true one? She could see the bucket and the house half lit up, half unlit.

She asked this question of that somebody whom, in her humble way, she had composed out of the wisdom and power of other people. The answer came often by accident—she had known her old spaniel answer by wagging his tail.

Now the tree, denuded of its gilt and majesty, seemed to supply her with an answer; became a field tree—the only one in a marsh. She had often seen it; seen the red-flushed clouds between its branches, or the moon split up, darting irregular flashes of silver. But what answer? Well that the soul—for she was conscious of a movement in her of some creature beating its way about her and trying to escape which momentarily she called the soul—is by nature unmated, a widow bird; a bird perched aloof on that tree.

But then Bertram, putting his arm through hers in his familiar way, for he had known her all her life, remarked that they were not doing their duty and must go in.

At that moment, in some back street or public-house, the

usual terrible sexless, inarticulate voice rang out; a shriek, a cry. And the widow bird, startled, flew away, describing wider and wider circles until it became (what she called her soul) remote as a crow which has been startled up into the air by a stone thrown at it.

VIRGINIA WOOLF

Selected Entries from the Diary of Virginia Woolf

Virginia Woolf's famed diary is cherished by her readers for its insight, scope, and depth. The five volumes that make up the diary she kept all her life are nothing less than the map of the thoughts behind Woolf's writing, as well as the daily preoccupations, encounters, and curiosities of this literary master.

MONDAY 20 SEPTEMBER, 1920

To go on with Eliot, as if one were making out a scientific observation—he left last night directly after dinner. He improved as the day went on; laughed more openly; became nicer. L. whose opinion on this matter I respect, found him disappointing in brain—less powerful than he expected, & with little play of mind. I kept myself successfully from being submerged, though feeling the waters rise once or twice. I mean by this that he completely neglected my claims to be a writer, & had I been meek, I suppose I should have gone under—felt him & his views dominant & subversive. He is a consistent specimen of his type, which is opposed to ours. Unfortunately the living writers he admires are Wyndham Lewis & Pound. —Joyce too, but there's more to be said on this head. We had some talk after tea (I put off the Mayors) about his writing. I suspect him of a good deal of concealed vanity & even anxiety about this.) I taxed him with wilfully concealing his transitions. He said that explanation is unnecessary. If you put it in, you dilute the facts.

You should feel these without explanation. My other charge was that a rich & original mind is needed to make such psychological writing of value. He told me he was more interested in people than in anything. He cant read Wordsworth when Wordsworth deals with nature. His turn is for caricature. In trying to define his meaning ('I dont mean satire') we foundered. He wants to write a verse play in which the 4 characters of Sweeny act the parts. A personal upheaval of some kind came after Prufrock, & turned him aside from his inclination—to develop in the manner of Henry James. Now he wants to describe externals. Joyce gives internals. His novel *Ulysses,* presents the life of man in 16 incidents, all taking place (I think) in one day. This, so far as he has seen it, is extremely brilliant, he says. Perhaps we shall try to publish it. *Ulysses,* according to Joyce, is the greatest character in history[.] Joyce himself is an insignificant man, wearing very thick eyeglasses, a little like Shaw to look at, dull, self-centred, & perfectly self assured. There is much to be said about Eliot from different aspects—for instance, the difficulty of getting into touch with clever people.—& so forth—anaemia, self-consciousness; but also, his mind is not yet blunted or blurred. He wishes to write precise English; but catches himself out in slips; & if anyone asked him whether he meant what he said, he would have to say no, very often. Now in all this L. showed up much better than I did; but I didn't much mind.

WEDNESDAY 8 APRIL, 1925

Just back from Cassis. Often while I was there I thought how I would write here frequently & so get down some of the myriad impressions which I net every day. But directly we get back, what is it that happens? We strip & dive into the stream, & I am obsessed with a foolish idea that I have no time to stop & write, or that I ought to be doing something serious. Even now, I pelt along feverishly, thinking half the time, but I must stop & take Grizzle [*dog*] out; I must get my American books in order; the truth is, I must try to set aside half an hour in some part of my day, & consecrate it to diary writing. Give it a name & a place, & then perhaps, such is the human mind, I shall come to think it a duty, & disregard other duties for it.

I am under the impression of the moment, which is the complex one of coming back home from the South of France to this wide dim peaceful privacy—London (so it seemed last night) which is shot with the accident I saw this morning & a woman crying Oh oh oh faintly, pinned against the railings with a motor car on top of her. All day I have heard that voice. I did not go to her help; but then every baker & flower seller did that. A great sense of the brutality & wildness of the world re-mains with me—there was this woman in brown walking along the pavement—suddenly a red film car turns a somer-sault, lands on top of her, & one hears this oh, oh, oh. I was on my way to see Nessa's new house, & met Duncan in the square, but as he had seen nothing, he could not in the least feel what I felt, or Nessa either, though she made some effort to connect it with Angelica's accident last spring. But I assured her it was only a passing brown woman; & so we went over the house composedly enough.

Since I wrote, which is these last months, Jacques Raverat has died; after longing to die; & he sent me a letter about *Mrs. Dalloway* which gave me one of the happiest days of my life. I wonder if this time I have achieved something? Well, nothing anyhow compared with Proust, in whom I am embedded now. The thing about Proust is his combination of the utmost sensi-bility with the utmost tenacity. He searches out these butterfly shades to the last grain. He is as tough as catgut & as evanescent as a butterfly's bloom. And he will I suppose both influence me & make me out of temper with every sentence of my own. Jacques died, as I say; & at once the siege of emotions began. I got the news with a party here—Clive, Bee How, Julia Strachey, Dadie. Nevertheless, I do not any longer feel inclined to doff the cap to death. I like to go out of the room talking, with an unfinished casual sentence on my lips. That is the effect it had

on me—no leavetakings, no submission—but someone stepping out into the darkness. For her though the nightmare was
terrific. All I can do now is to keep natural with her, which is I
believe a matter of considerable importance. More & more do I
repeat my own version of Montaigne "Its life that matters".

WEDNESDAY 16 AUGUST, 1922

I should be reading Ulysses, & fabricating my case for &
against. I have read 200 pages so far—not a third; & have been
amused, stimulated, charmed interested by the first 2 or 3 chapters—to the end of the Cemetery scene; & then puzzled, bored,
irritated, & disillusioned as by a queasy undergraduate scratching his pimples. And Tom, great Tom, thinks this on a par with
War & Peace! An illiterate, underbred book it seems to me: the
book of a self taught working man, & we all know how distressing they are, how egotistic, insistent, raw, striking, & ultimately
nauseating. When one can have the cooked flesh, why have the
raw? But I think if you are anaemic, as Tom is, there is a glory in
blood. Being fairly normal myself I am soon ready for the classics again. I may revise this later. I do not compromise my critical sagacity. I plant a stick in the ground to mark page 200.

For my own part I am laboriously dredging my mind for
Mrs. Dalloway & bringing up light buckets. I don't like the feeling I'm writing too quickly. I must press it together. I wrote 4
thousand words of reading in record time, 10 days; but then it
was merely a quick sketch of Pastons, supplied by books. Now I
break off, according to my quick change theory, to write Mrs. D.
(who ushers in a host of others, I begin to perceive) then I do
Chaucer; & finish the first chapter early in September. By that
time, I have my Greek beginning perhaps, in my head; & so the
future is all pegged out; & when Jacob is rejected in America &
ignored in England, I shall be philosophically driving my plough
fields away. They are cutting the corn all over the country, which
supplies that metaphor, & perhaps excuses it. But I need no ex-

cuses, since I am not writing for the Lit Sup. Shall I ever write for them again?

I see I have said nothing about our day in London [on *9 August*]—Dr. Sainsbury, Dr. Fergusson, & the semi-legal discussion over my body, which ended in a bottle of quinine pills, & a box of lozenges, & a brush to varnish my throat with. Influenza & pneumonia germs, perhaps, says Sainsbury, very softly, wisely & with extreme deliberation. "Equanimity—practise equanimity Mrs. Woolf" he said, as I left; an unnecessary interview from my point of view; but we were forced into it by one step after another on the part of the bacteriologists. I take my temperature no more till Oct. 1st.

THURSDAY 14 MAY, 1925

The first day of summer, leaves visibly drawing out of the bud, & the Square almost green. Oh what a country day—& some of my friends are now reading Mrs. D. in the country.

I meant to register more of my books temperatures. C.R. does not sell; but is praised. I was really pleased to open the Manchester Guardian this morning & read Mr. Fausset on The Art of V. W. Brilliance combined with integrity; profound as well as eccentric. Now if only the Times would speak out thus, but the Times mumbles & murmurs like a man sucking pebbles—did I say that I had nearly 2 mumbling columns on me there? But the odd thing is this: honestly I am scarcely a shade nervous about Mrs. D. Why is this? Really I am a little bored, for the first time, at thinking how much I shall have to talk about it this summer. The truth is that writing is the profound pleasure & being read the superficial. I'm now all on the strain with desire to stop journalism & get on to *To the Lighthouse*. This is going to be fairly short: to have father's character done complete in it; & mothers; & St. Ives; & childhood; & all the usual things I try to put in—life, death &c. But the centre is father's character, sitting in a boat, reciting We perished, each alone, while he crushes a dying mackerel—However, I must refrain. I must write a few little stories first, & let the Lighthouse simmer, adding to it between tea & dinner till it is complete for writing out.

FRIDAY 15 MAY, 1925

Two unfavourable reviews of Mrs. D (Western Mail & Scotsman): unintelligible, not art &c: & a letter from a young man in Earls Court "This time you have done it—you have caught life & put it in a book..." Please forgive this outburst, but further quotation is unnecessary; & I dont think I should bother to write this, if I weren't jangled what by? The sudden heat, I think, & the racket of life. It is bad for me to see my own photograph. And I have been lunching with Desmond, & reading that dear old Owl's journalism. The thing is, he cant thrust through an article. Now, Lytton or I, though we mayn't think better or write better, have a drive in us, which makes an article whole. And yet there are things worth keeping, & he becomes moved, & irrational when he thinks of it, & I want him to be pleased— So we lunched in the grill of the Connaught Rooms where other men were talking business, had a bottle of wine & delved into the filth packets as he calls them. Home to find Vogue sending photographs—more photographs: T.P. wants one, the Morning Post another. & the C.R. sells 2 or 3 copies a day.

We are going to the play out into this tawny coloured London—but journalism is the devil. I cannot write after reading it. No time—& I must change, & write about clothes some day soon.

THURSDAY 18 JUNE, 1925

No, Lytton does not like Mrs. Dalloway, &, what is odd, I like him all the better for saying so, & don't much mind. What he says is that there is a discordancy between the ornament (extremely beautiful) & what happens (rather ordinary—or unimportant). This is caused he thinks by some discrepancy in

Clarissa herself; he thinks she is disagreeable & limited, but that I alternately laugh at her, & cover her, very remarkably, with myself. So that I think as a whole, the book does not ring solid; yet, he says, it is a whole; & he says sometimes the writing is of extreme beauty. What can one call it but genius? he said! Coming when, one never can tell. Fuller of genius, he said than anything I had done. Perhaps, he said, you have not yet mastered your method. You should take something wilder & more fantastic, a frame work that admits of anything, like Tristram Shandy. But then I should lose touch with emotions, I said. Yes, he agreed, there must be reality for you to start from. Heaven knows how you're to do it. But he thought me at the beginning, not at the end. And he said the C.R. was divine, a classic; Mrs. D. being, I fear, a flawed stone. This is very personal, he said & old fashioned perhaps; yet I think there is some truth in it. For I remember the night at Rodmell when I decided to give it up, because I found Clarissa in some way tinselly. Then I invented her memories. But I think some distaste for her persisted. Yet, again, that was true to my feeling for Kitty, & one must dislike people in art without its mattering, unless indeed it is true that certain characters detract from the importance of what happens to them. None of this hurts me, or depresses me. Its odd that when Clive & others (several of them) say it is a masterpiece, I am not much exalted; when Lytton picks holes, I get back into my working fighting mood, which is natural to me. I don't see myself a success. I like the sense of effort better. The sales collapsed completely for 3 days; now a little dribble begins again. I shall be more than pleased if we sell 1500. Its now 1250.

A Letter from Virginia Woolf

Virginia Woolf's earliest surviving letter was written when she was six years old, to her godfather, the American poet James Russell Lowell. The last was addressed to her husband, Leonard Woolf, on the day she ended her life. Throughout her lifetime she corresponded with many great thinkers and writers, reveling with them in the world of the written word.

To Vanessa Bell   *Asheham [Rodmell, Sussex]*

SATURDAY [28 DECEMBER 1918]

Dearest,

Owing to this beastly weather I have had to yield to Leonard and not come this morning, much against my will. I'm fearfully cross and disappointed, especially as the wind seems to be going down now—but I shall try to come tomorrow anyhow, about 12.30. and stay to luncheon. You cant imagine how excited I was to hear of my niece—in fact I think even you would have been touched to know how completely my pleasure here was spoilt until I heard it was over. I see I'm going to become a perfectly sentimental old Aunt (I'm dropping into Aunt Marys language already) about her. She must be the most adorable little creature.

But I want most to know how you are—whether sensible, ruminative, tender, peaceful and sublime.

Perhaps Leonard will bring me some news. I should only bore you if I went on saying be careful.

Ka and Will are not coming, so its easier than ever to have the children, and the servants are enraptured. It is just possible that Nelly is in touch with two friends who might come to you—but I'll tell you all about it tomorrow.

> Clarissa.
> Miriam.
> Rachel.
> Venetia.
> Sabina.
> Clara.
> Sarah.
> Sara.
> Euphrosyne.

I think on the whole I prefer Clarissa but I know there's a better one on the verge of my brain which I cant remember.

O damn! how I wish I were with you and had disregarded my husband flatly. It's not going to rain after all, and I said it wasn't.

A thousand embraces in all the tenderest parts from your Apes. Has Clarissa got a lovely little down at the back of her neck. Shall we all be allowed to kiss her?

Yr.

B.

Berg

KATHERINE MANSFIELD

The Garden-Party

The author of dozens of short stories, poetry collections, critical essays, letters, and journals, Katherine Mansfield enjoyed a creatively competitive relationship with Virginia Woolf. Years later, Woolf confided to her journal that "Mansfield's was the only writing [she] had ever been jealous of."

*A*ND AFTER ALL THE WEATHER WAS IDEAL. THEY COULD NOT have had a more perfect day for a garden-party if they had ordered it. Windless, warm, the sky without a cloud. Only the blue was veiled with a haze of light gold, as it is sometimes in early summer. The gardener had been up since dawn, mowing the lawns and sweeping them, until the grass and the dark flat rosettes where the daisy plants had been seemed to shine. As for the roses, you could not help feeling they understood that roses are the only flowers that impress people at garden-parties; the only flowers that everybody is certain of knowing. Hundreds, yes, literally hundreds, had come out in a single night; the green bushes bowed down as though they had been visited by archangels.

Breakfast was not yet over before the men came to put up the marquee.

"Where do you want the marquee put, mother?"

"My dear child, it's no use asking me. I'm determined to

leave everything to you children this year. Forget I am your mother. Treat me as an honoured guest."

But Meg could not possibly go and supervise the men. She had washed her hair before breakfast, and she sat drinking her coffee in a green turban, with a dark wet curl stamped on each cheek. Jose, the butterfly, always came down in a silk petticoat and a kimono jacket.

"You'll have to go, Laura; you're the artistic one."

Away Laura flew, still holding her piece of bread-and-butter. It's so delicious to have an excuse for eating out of doors, and besides, she loved having to arrange things; she always felt she could do it so much better than anybody else.

Four men in their shirt-sleeves stood grouped together on the garden path. They carried staves covered with rolls of canvas, and they had big tool-bags slung on their backs. They looked impressive. Laura wished now that she had not got the bread-and-butter, but there was nowhere to put it, and she couldn't possibly throw it away. She blushed and tried to look severe and even a little bit short-sighted as she came up to them.

"Good morning," she said, copying her mother's voice. But that sounded so fearfully affected that she was ashamed, and stammered like a little girl, "Oh—er—have you come—is it about the marquee?"

"That's right, miss," said the tallest of the men, a lanky, freckled fellow, and he shifted his tool-bag, knocked back his straw hat and smiled down at her. "That's about it."

His smile was so easy, so friendly that Laura recovered. What nice eyes he had, small, but such a dark blue! And now she looked at the others, they were smiling too. "Cheer up, we won't bite," their smile seemed to say. How very nice workmen were! And what a beautiful morning! She mustn't mention the morning; she must be businesslike. The marquee.

"Well, what about the lily-lawn? Would that do?"

And she pointed to the lily-lawn with the hand that didn't hold the bread-and-butter. They turned, they stared in the direction. A little fat chap thrust out his under-lip, and the tall fellow frowned.

"I don't fancy it," said he. "Not conspicuous enough. You see, with a thing like a marquee," and he turned to Laura in his easy way, "you want to put it somewhere where it'll give you a bang slap in the eye, if you follow me."

Laura's upbringing made her wonder for a moment whether it was quite respectful of a workman to talk to her of bangs slap in the eye. But she did quite follow him.

"A corner of the tennis-court," she suggested. "But the band's going to be in the corner."

"H'm, going to have a band, are you?" said another of the workmen. He was pale. He had a haggard look as his dark eyes scanned the tennis-court. What was he thinking?

"Only a very small band," said Laura gently. Perhaps he wouldn't mind so much if the band was quite small. But the tall fellow interrupted.

"Look here, miss, that's the place. Against those trees. Over there. That'll do fine."

Against the karakas. Then the karaka trees would be hidden. And they were so lovely, with their broad, gleaming leaves, and their clusters of yellow fruit. They were like trees you imagined growing on a desert island, proud, solitary, lifting their leaves and fruits to the sun in a kind of silent splendour. Must they be hidden by a marquee?

They must. Already the men had shouldered their staves and were making for the place. Only the tall fellow was left. He bent down, pinched a sprig of lavender, put his thumb and forefinger to his nose and snuffed up the smell. When Laura saw that gesture she forgot all about the karakas in her wonder at him caring for things like that—caring for the smell of lavender. How many men that she knew would have done such a thing? Oh, how extraordinarily nice workmen were, she thought. Why couldn't she have workmen for friends rather than the silly boys she danced with and who came to Sunday night supper? She would get on much better with men like these.

It's all the fault, she decided, as the tall fellow drew something on the back of an envelope, something that was to be looped up or left to hang, of these absurd class distinctions. Well, for her part, she didn't feel them. Not a bit, not an atom. . . . And now there came the chock-chock of wooden hammers. Some one whistled, some one sang out, "Are you right there, matey?" "Matey!" The friendliness of it, the — the — Just to prove how happy she was, just to show the tall fellow how at home she felt, and how she despised stupid conventions, Laura took a big bite of her bread-and-butter as she stared at the little drawing. She felt just like a work-girl.

"Laura, Laura, where are you? Telephone, Laura!" a voice cried from the house.

"Coming!" Away she skimmed, over the lawn, up the path, up the steps, across the verandah, and into the porch. In the hall her father and Laurie were brushing their hats ready to go to the office.

"I say, Laura," said Laurie very fast, "you might just give a squiz at my coat before this afternoon. See if it wants pressing."

"I will," said she. Suddenly she couldn't stop herself. She ran at Laurie and gave him a small, quick squeeze. "Oh, I do love parties, don't you?" gasped Laura.

"Ra-ther," said Laurie's warm, boyish voice, and he squeezed his sister too, and gave her a gentle push. "Dash off to the telephone, old girl."

The telephone. "Yes, yes; oh yes. Kitty? Good morning, dear. Come to lunch? Do, dear. Delighted of course. It will only be a very scratch meal—just the sandwich crusts and broken meringue-shells and what's left over. Yes, isn't it a perfect morning? Your white? Oh, I certainly should. One moment—hold the line. Mother's calling." And Laura sat back. "What, mother? Can't hear."

Mrs. Sheridan's voice floated down the stairs. "Tell her to wear that sweet hat she had on last Sunday."

"Mother says you're to wear that *sweet* hat you had on last Sunday. Good. One o'clock. Bye-bye."

Laura put back the receiver, flung her arms over her head, took a deep breath, stretched and let them fall. "Huh," she sighed, and the moment after the sigh she sat up quickly. She was still, listening. All the doors in the house seemed to be open. The house was alive with soft, quick steps and running voices. The green baize door that led to the kitchen regions swung open and shut with a muffled thud. And now there came a long, chuckling absurd sound. It was the heavy piano being moved on its stiff castors. But the air! If you stopped to notice, was the air always like this? Little faint winds were playing chase, in at the tops of the windows, out at the doors. And there were two tiny spots of sun, one on the inkpot, one on a silver photograph frame, playing too. Darling little spots. Especially the one on the inkpot lid. It was quite warm. A warm little silver star. She could have kissed it.

The front door bell pealed, and there sounded the rustle of Sadie's print skirt on the stairs. A man's voice murmured; Sadie answered, careless, "I'm sure I don't know. Wait. I'll ask Mrs. Sheridan."

"What is it, Sadie?" Laura came into the hall.

"It's the florist, Miss Laura."

It was, indeed. There, just inside the door, stood a wide, shallow tray full of pots of pink lilies. No other kind. Nothing but lilies — canna lilies, big pink flowers, wide open, radiant, almost frighteningly alive on bright crimson stems.

"O-oh, Sadie!" said Laura, and the sound was like a little moan. She crouched down as if to warm herself at that blaze of lilies; she felt they were in her fingers, on her lips, growing in her breast.

"It's some mistake," she said faintly. "Nobody ever ordered so many. Sadie, go and find mother."

But at that moment Mrs. Sheridan joined them.

"It's quite right," she said calmly. "Yes, I ordered them. Aren't they lovely?" She pressed Laura's arm. "I was passing the shop yesterday, and I saw them in the window. And I suddenly thought for once in my life I shall have enough canna lilies. The garden-party will be a good excuse."

"But I thought you said you didn't mean to interfere," said Laura. Sadie had gone. The florist's man was still outside at his van. She put her arm round her mother's neck and gently, very gently, she bit her mother's ear.

"My darling child, you wouldn't like a logical mother, would you? Don't do that. Here's the man."

He carried more lilies still, another whole tray.

"Bank them up, just inside the door, on both sides of the porch, please," said Mrs. Sheridan. "Don't you agree, Laura?"

"Oh, I *do* mother."

In the drawing-room Meg, Jose and good little Hans had at last succeeded in moving the piano.

"Now, if we put this chesterfield against the wall and move everything out of the room except the chairs, don't you think?"

"Quite."

"Hans, move these tables into the smoking-room, and bring a sweeper to take these marks off the carpet and— one moment, Hans—" Jose loved giving orders to the servants, and they loved obeying her. She always made them feel they were taking part in some drama. "Tell mother and Miss Laura to come here at once."

"Very good, Miss Jose."

She turned to Meg. "I want to hear what the piano sounds like, just in case I'm asked to sing this afternoon. Let's try over 'This life is Weary.'"

Pom! Ta-ta-ta *Tee*-ta! The piano burst out so passionately that Jose's face changed. She clasped her hands. She looked mournfully and enigmatically at her mother and Laura as they came in.

> *This Life is* Wee-*ary,*
> *A Tear—a Sigh.*
> *A Love that* Chan-*ges,*
>   *This Life is* Wee-*ary,*
> *A Tear—a Sigh.*
> *A Love that* Chan-*ges,*
> *And then . . . Good-bye!*

But at the word "Good-bye," and although the piano sounded more desperate than ever, her face broke into a brilliant, dreadfully unsympathetic smile.

"Aren't I in good voice, mummy?" she beamed.

> *This Life is* Wee-*ary,*
> *Hope comes to Die.*
> *A Dream—a* Wa-*kening.*

But now Sadie interrupted them. "What is it, Sadie?"

"If you please, m'm, cook says have you got the flags for the sandwiches?"

"The flags for the sandwiches, Sadie?" echoed Mrs. Sheridan dreamily. And the children knew by her face that she hadn't got them. "Let me see." And she said to Sadie firmly, "Tell cook I'll let her have them in ten minutes."

Sadie went.

"Now, Laura," said her mother quickly. "Come with me into the smoking-room. I've got the names somewhere on the back of an envelope. You'll have to write them out for me. Meg, go upstairs this minute and take that wet thing off your head. Jose, run and finish dressing this instant. Do you hear me, children, or shall I have to tell your father when he comes home to-night? And—and, Jose, pacify cook if you do go into the kitchen, will you? I'm terrified of her this morning."

The envelope was found at last behind the dining-room clock, though how it had got there Mrs. Sheridan could not imagine.

"One of you children must have stolen it out of my bag, because I remember vividly—cream cheese and lemon-curd. Have you done that?"

"Yes."

"Egg and—" Mrs. Sheridan held the envelope away from her. "It looks like mice. It can't be mice, can it?"

"Olive, pet," said Laura, looking over her shoulder.

"Yes, of course, olive. What a horrible combination it sounds. Egg and olive."

They were finished at last, and Laura took them off to the kitchen. She found Jose there pacifying the cook, who did not look at all terrifying.

"I have never seen such exquisite sandwiches," said Jose's rapturous voice. "How many kinds did you say there were, cook? Fifteen?"

"Fifteen, Miss Jose."

"Well, cook, I congratulate you."

Cook swept up crusts with the long sandwich knife, and smiled broadly.

"Godber's has come," announced Sadie, issuing out of the pantry. She had seen the man pass the window.

That meant the cream puffs had come. Godber's were famous for their cream puffs. Nobody ever thought of making them at home.

"Bring them in and put them on the table, my girl," ordered cook.

Sadie brought them in and went back to the door. Of course Laura and Jose were far too grown-up to really care about such things. All the same, they couldn't help agreeing that the puffs looked very attractive. Very. Cook began arranging them, shaking off the extra icing sugar.

"Don't they carry one back to all one's parties?" said Laura.

"I suppose they do," said practical Jose, who never liked to be carried back. "They look beautifully light and feathery, I must say."

"Have one each, my dears," said cook in her comfortable voice. "Yer ma won't know."

Oh, impossible. Fancy cream puffs so soon after breakfast. The very idea made one shudder. All the same, two minutes later Jose and Laura were licking their fingers with that absorbed inward look that only comes from whipped cream.

"Let's go into the garden, out by the back way," suggested Laura. "I want to see how the men are getting on with the marquee. They're such awfully nice men."

But the back door was blocked by cook, Sadie, Godber's man and Hans.

Something had happened.

"Tuk-tuk-tuk," clucked cook like an agitated hen. Sadie had her hand clapped to her cheek as though she had toothache. Hans's face was screwed up in the effort to understand. Only Godber's man seemed to be enjoying himself; it was his story.

"What's the matter? What's happened?"

"There's been a horrible accident," said cook. "A man killed."

"A man killed! Where? How? When?"

But Godber's man wasn't going to have his story snatched from under his very nose.

"Know those little cottages just below here, miss?" Know them? Of course, she knew them. "Well, there's a young chap living there, name of Scott, a carter. His horse shied at a traction-engine, corner of Hawke Street this morning, and he was thrown out on the back of his head. Killed."

"Dead!" Laura stared at Godber's man.

"Dead when they picked him up," said Godber's man with relish. "They were taking the body home as I come up here." And he said to the cook, "He's left a wife and five little ones."

"Jose, come here." Laura caught hold of her sister's sleeve and dragged her through the kitchen to the other side of the green baize door. There she paused and leaned against it.

"Jose!" she said, horrified, "however are we going to stop everything?"

"Stop everything, Laura!" cried Jose in astonishment. "What do you mean?"

"Stop the garden-party, of course." Why did Jose pretend?

But Jose was still more amazed. "Stop the garden-party? My dear Laura, don't be so absurd. Of course we can't do anything of the kind. Nobody expects us to. Don't be so extravagant."

"But we can't possibly have a garden-party with a man dead just outside the front gate."

That really was extravagant, for the little cottages were in a lane to themselves at the very bottom of a steep rise that led up to the house. A broad road ran between. True, they were far too near. They were the greatest possible eyesore, and they had no right to be in that neighbourhood at all. They were little mean dwellings painted a chocolate brown. In the garden patches there was nothing but cabbage stalks, sick hens and tomato cans. The very smoke coming out of their chimneys was poverty-stricken. Little rags and shreds of smoke, so unlike the great silvery plumes that uncurled from the Sheridans' chimneys. Washerwomen lived in the lane and sweeps and a cobbler, and a man whose housefront was studded all over with minute bird-cages. Children swarmed. When the Sheridans were little they were forbidden to set foot there because of the revolting language and of what they might catch. But since they were grown up, Laura and Laurie on their prowls sometimes walked through. It was disgusting and sordid. They came out with a shudder. But still one must go everywhere; one must see everything. So through they went.

"And just think of what the band would sound like to that poor woman," said Laura.

"Oh, Laura!" Jose began to be seriously annoyed. "If you're going to stop a band playing every time some one has an accident, you'll lead a very strenuous life. I'm every bit as sorry about it as you. I feel just as sympathetic." Her eyes hardened. She looked at her sister just as she used to when they were little and fighting together. "You won't bring a drunken workman back to life by being sentimental," she said softly.

"Drunk! Who said he was drunk?" Laura turned furiously on Jose. She said, just as they had used to say on those occasions, "I'm going straight up to tell mother."

"Do, dear," cooed Jose.

"Mother, can I come into your room?" Laura turned the big glass door-knob.

"Of course, child. Why, what's the matter? What's given you such a colour?" And Mrs. Sheridan turned round from her dressing table. She was trying on a new hat.

"Mother, a man's been killed," began Laura.

"*Not* in the garden?" interrupted her mother.

"No, no!"

"Oh, what a fright you gave me!" Mrs. Sheridan sighed with relief, and took off the big hat and held it on her knees.

"But listen, mother," said Laura. Breathless, half-choking, she told the dreadful story. "Of course, we can't have our party, can we?" she pleaded. "The band and everybody arriving. They'd hear us, mother; they're nearly neighbours!"

To Laura's astonishment her mother behaved just like Jose, it was harder to bear because she seemed amused. She refused to take Laura seriously.

"But, my dear child, use your common sense. It's only by accident we've heard of it. If some one had died there normally— and I can't understand how they keep alive in those poky little holes—we should still be having our party, shouldn't we?"

Laura had to say "yes" to that, but she felt it was all wrong. She sat down on her mother's sofa and pinched the cushion frill.

"Mother, isn't it really terribly heartless of us?" she asked.

"Darling!" Mrs. Sheridan got up and came over to her, carrying the hat. Before Laura could stop her she had popped it on. "My child!" said her mother, "the hat is yours. It's made for you.

,It's much too young for me. I have never seen you look such a picture. Look at yourself!" And she held up her hand-mirror.

"But, mother," Laura began again. She couldn't look at herself; she turned aside.

This time Mrs. Sheridan lost patience just as Jose had done.

"You are being very absurd, Laura," she said coldly. "People like that don't expect sacrifices from us. And it's not very sympathetic to spoil everybody's enjoyment as you're doing now."

"I don't understand," said Laura, and she walked quickly out of the room into her own bedroom. There, quite by chance, the first thing she saw was this charming girl in the mirror, in her black hat trimmed with gold daisies, and a long black velvet ribbon. Never had she imagined she could look like that. Is mother right? she thought. And now she hoped her mother was right. Am I being extravagant? Perhaps it was extravagant. Just for a moment she had another glimpse of that poor woman and those little children, and the body being carried into the house. But it all seemed blurred, unreal, like a picture in the newspaper. I'll remember it again after the party's over, she decided. And somehow that seemed quite the best plan....

Lunch was over by half past one. By half past two they were all ready for the fray. The green-coated band had arrived and was established in a corner of the tennis-court.

"My dear!" trilled Kitty Maitland, "aren't they too like frogs for words? You ought to have arranged them round the pond with the conductor in the middle on a leaf."

Laurie arrived and hailed them on his way to dress. At the sight of him Laura remembered the accident again. She wanted to tell him. If Laurie agreed with the others, then it was bound to be all right. And she followed him into the hall.

"Laurie!"

"Hallo!" He was half-way upstairs, but when he turned round and saw Laura he suddenly puffed out his cheeks and goggled his eyes at her. "My word, Laura; you do look stunning," said Laurie. "What an absolutely topping hat!"

Laura said faintly "Is it?" and smiled up at Laurie, and didn't tell him after all.

Soon after that people began coming in streams. The band struck up; the hired waiters ran from the house to the marquee. Wherever you looked there were couples strolling, bending to the flowers, greeting, moving on over the lawn. They were like bright birds that had alighted in the Sheridans' garden for this one afternoon, on their way to—where? Ah, what happiness it is to be with people who all are happy, to press hands, press cheeks, smile into eyes.

"Darling Laura, how well you look!"

"What a becoming hat, child!"

"Laura, you look quite Spanish. I've never seen you look so striking."

And Laura, glowing, answered softly, "Have you had tea? Won't you have an ice? The passion-fruit ices really are rather special." She ran to her father and begged him. "Daddy darling, can't the band have something to drink?"

And the perfect afternoon slowly ripened, slowly faded, slowly its petals closed.

"Never a more delightful garden-party . . ." "The greatest success . . ." "Quite the most . . ."

Laura helped her mother with the good-byes. They stood side by side in the porch till it was all over.

"All over, all over, thank heaven," said Mrs. Sheridan. "Round up the others, Laura. Let's go and have some fresh coffee. I'm exhausted. Yes, it's been very successful. But oh, these parties, these parties! Why will you children insist on giving parties!" And they all of them sat down in the deserted marquee.

"Have a sandwich, daddy dear. I wrote the flag."

"Thanks." Mr. Sheridan took a bite and the sandwich was gone. He took another. "I supposed you didn't hear of a beastly accident that happened to-day?" he said.

"My dear," said Mrs. Sheridan, holding up her hand, "we

did. It nearly ruined the party. Laura insisted we should put
it off."

"Oh, mother!" Laura didn't want to be teased about it.

"It was a horrible affair all the same," said Mr. Sheridan.
"The chap was married too. Lived just below in the lane, and
leaves a wife and half a dozen kiddies, so they say."

An awkward little silence fell. Mrs. Sheriden fidgeted with
her cup. Really, it was very tactless of father...

Suddenly she looked up. There on the table were all those
sandwiches, cakes, puffs, all uneaten, all going to be wasted. She
had one of her brilliant ideas.

"I know," she said. "Let's make up a basket. Let's send that
poor creature some of this perfectly good food. At any rate, it
will be the greatest treat for the children. Don't you agree? And
she's sure to have neighbours calling in and so on. What a point
to have it all ready prepared. Laura!" She jumped up. "Get me
the big basket out of the stairs cupboard."

"But, mother, do you really think it's a good idea?" said
Laura.

Again, how curious, she seemed to be different from them
all. To take scraps from their party. Would the poor woman
really like that?

"Of course! What's the matter with you to-day? An hour or
two ago you were insisting on us being sympathetic, and now—"

Oh, well! Laura ran for the basket. It was filled, it was
heaped by her mother.

"Take it yourself, darling," said she. "Run down just as you
are. No, wait, take the arum lilies too. People of that class are so
impressed by arum lilies."

"The stems will ruin her lace frock," said practical Jose.

So they would. Just in time. "Only the basket, then. And,
Laura!"—her mother followed her out of the marquee—"don't
on any account—"

"What, mother?"

No, better not put such ideas into the child's head! "Nothing! Run along."

It was just growing dusky as Laura shut their garden gates. A big dog ran by like a shadow. The road gleamed white, and down below in the hollow the little cottages were in deep shade. How quiet it seemed after the afternoon. Here she was going down the hill to somewhere where a man lay dead, and she couldn't realize it. Why couldn't she? She stopped a minute. And it seemed to her that kisses, voices, tinkling spoons, laughter, the smell of crushed grass were somehow inside her. She had no room for anything else. How strange! She looked up at the pale sky, and all she thought was, "Yes, it was the most successful party."

Now the broad road was crossed. The lane began, smoky and dark. Women in shawls and men's tweed caps hurried by. Men hung over the palings; the children played in the doorways. A low hum came from the mean little cottages. In some of them there was a flicker of light, and a shadow, crab-like, moved across the window. Laura bent her head and hurried on. She wished now she had put on a coat. How her frock shone! And the big hat with the velvet streamer—if only it was another hat! Were the people looking at her? They must be. It was a mistake to have come; she knew all along it was a mistake. Should she go back even now?

No, too late. This was the house. It must be. A dark knot of people stood outside. Beside the gate an old, old woman with a crutch sat in a chair, watching. She had her feet on a newspaper. The voices stopped as Laura drew near. The group parted. It was as though she was expected, as though they had known she was coming here.

Laura was terribly nervous. Tossing the velvet ribbon over her shoulder, she said to a woman standing by, "Is this Mrs. Scott's house?" and the woman, smiling queerly, said, "It is, my lass."

Oh, to be away from this! She actually said, "Help me, God," as she walked up the tiny path and knocked. To be away from those staring eyes, or to be covered up in anything, one of those women's shawls even. I'll just leave the basket and go, she decided. I shan't even wait for it to be emptied.

Then the door opened. A little woman in black showed in the gloom.

Laura said, "Are you Mrs. Scott?" But to her horror the woman answered, "Walk in please, miss," and she was shut in the passage.

"No," said Laura, "I don't want to come in. I only want to leave this basket. Mother sent—"

The little woman in the gloomy passage seemed not to have heard her. "Step this way, please, miss," she said in an oily voice, and Laura followed her.

She found herself in a wretched little low kitchen lighted by a smoky lamp. There was a woman sitting before the fire.

"Em," said the little creature who had let her in. "Em! It's a young lady." She turned to Laura. She said meaningly, "I'm 'er sister, miss. You'll excuse 'er, won't you?"

"Oh, but of course!" said Laura. "Please, please don't disturb her. I—I only want to leave—"

But at that moment the woman at the fire turned round. Her face, puffed up, red, with swollen eyes and swollen lips, looked terrible. She seemed as though she couldn't understand why Laura was there. What did it mean? Why was this stranger standing in the kitchen with a basket? What was it all about? And the poor face puckered up again.

"All right, my dear," said the other. "I'll thenk the young lady."

And again she began, "You'll excuse her, miss, I'm sure," and her face, swollen too, tried an oily smile.

Laura only wanted to get out, to get away. She was back in the passage. The door opened. She walked straight through into the bedroom, where the dead man was lying.

"You'd like a look at 'im, wouldn't you?" said Em's sister, and she brushed past Laura over to the bed. "Don't be afraid,

my lass,—" and now her voice sounded fond and sly, and fondly
she drew down the sheet—"'e looks a picture. There's nothing
to show. Come along, my dear."

Laura came.

There lay a young man, fast asleep—sleeping so soundly,
so deeply, that he was far, far away from them both. Oh, so remote, so peaceful. He was dreaming. Never wake him up again.
His head was sunk in the pillow, his eyes were closed; they were
blind under the closed eyelids. He was given up to his dream.
What did garden-parties and baskets and lace frocks matter to
him? He was far from all those things. He was wonderful, beautiful. While they were laughing and while the band was playing,
this marvel had come to the lane. Happy . . . happy. . . . All is well,
said that sleeping face. This is just as it should be. I am content.

But all the same you had to cry, and she couldn't go out of
the room without saying something to him. Laura gave a loud
childish sob.

"Forgive my hat," she said.

And this time she didn't wait for Em's sister. She found her
way out of the door, down the path, past all those dark people.
At the corner of the lane she met Laurie.

He stepped out of the shadow. "Is that you, Laura?"

"Yes."

"Mother was getting anxious. Was it all right?"

"Yes, quite. Oh, Laurie!" She took his arm, she pressed up
against him.

"I say, you're not crying, are you?" asked her brother.

Laura shook her head. She was.

Laurie put his arm round her shoulder. "Don't cry," he said
in his warm, loving voice. "Was it awful?"

"No," sobbed Laura. "It was simply marvellous. But, Laurie—" She stopped, she looked at her brother. "Isn't life," she
stammered, "isn't life—" But what life was she couldn't explain.
No matter. He quite understood.

"*Isn't* it, darling?" said Laurie.

MARGO JEFFERSON

Unreal Loyalties

$\mathcal{A}$S A WORD, "FREEDOM" IS FRIGHTENINGLY MALLEABLE. IT BE-comes a banner in war—unfurl it, and we are all supposed to cheer and go marching along in sanctimonious lockstep. But it justifies honorable struggles too: for freedom from servitude and slavery, freedom from poverty or persecution, freedom from terror and despair. And not a day goes by without our invoking the right to speak, write, and think freely.

In 1938, Virginia Woolf proposed one of the most exacting definitions I know. Asked what kind of freedom would advance the fight against fascism and its enduring allies, racism, colonialism, and sexism, she replied: "Freedom from unreal loyalties.... You must rid yourself of pride of nationality in the first place; also of religious pride, college pride, family pride, sex pride, and those unreal loyalties that spring from them." That's from *Three Guineas,* which along with the far more famous *A Room of One's Own* shows Woolf as a polemicist, a feminist with hard-won progressive politics. I say "hard-won" because so much has been made of Woolf's snobberies. I rarely read upper-middle-class writers who don't reveal snobberies of some kind, but I read plenty who don't bother to examine them, as Woolf did. This criticism is usually framed by the words "lady" or "genteel," which helps explain why so many of her male contemporaries are let off the hook.

Woolf's polemical style depends on surprise and strategic intimacy. She plays games, wears masks. She mixes public and private discourse. *A Room of One's Own* was based on lectures she gave to women students at Cambridge University in 1928. The book is a fantasia. History is improvised as she spins the tale of Shakespeare's lost sister. The secret motives of great men are fodder for gossip; hints of sexual desire and fear are everywhere. Teases veil serious themes. I'm not a famous novelist, Woolf says; I am like those women whose names float through the verses of old English ballads and disappear. Arch, perhaps, but the opening gambit in her warning against the temptations (ambition and greed) women will meet as they enter the professions.

There is nothing playful about *Three Guineas*. Economies were crashing when it came out. The war was starting. The anger Woolf had famously advised women writers to eschew in *A Room of One's Own*—anger distorted your vision, she said, even when your cause was just—blazed from every page, but artfully and cunningly. The book's three chapters take the form of letters. Letters and journals had always been available to women who could not or dared not publish. This time, though, Woolf writes as a famous author, a woman of importance being asked by a powerful man how to prevent the injustices that lead to war. Her answer begins with a relentless exhumation of injustice on the home front: England. The complacent world of Victorian gentlemen contained a domestic caste, she said. They were the ill-educated "daughters of educated men," who struggled against their fathers for the right to vote, attend universities, earn their living, and, with incomes of their own, develop opinions of their own. (As the university-deprived daughter of an eminent Victorian scholar, Woolf learned the survival tactics of this caste early on: flattery, submission, evasion, and the steady application of charm.)

The voices of the dead rise from these pages. This time their stories are harsh and factual, evidence presented in a court of world opinion. There are forty-three pages of footnotes, from employment statistics to speculations on the lives of Victorian maids. These daughters of educated men were an advance guard, Woolf says: "They were fighting the tyranny of the patriarchal state as you are fighting the tyranny of the fascist state." The new tyrant "is interfering now with your liberty, he is dictating how you shall live, he is making distinctions not merely between the sexes, but between the races. You are feeling in your own persons what your mothers felt when they were shut out, when they were shut up, because they were women. Now you are being shut out, you are being shut up, because you are Jews, because you are democrats, because of race, because of religion."

Woolf ends with a question that could not be more urgent. To what use do we put a history of injustice and oppression once we have won basic rights and privileges? She demands that women challenge any education that maintains "barriers of wealth and ceremony, of advertisement and competition"; any profession that measures success by greed and manipulation.

The daughters of educated men, she writes, were schooled by "poverty, chastity, derision" and the "lack of rights and privileges." Can those be translated into a manifesto for public life?

Poverty means "enough money to live upon . . . to buy that modicum of health, leisure, knowledge . . . that is needed for the full development of body and mind. But no more." Derision means "that you must refuse all methods of advertising merit. . . . Directly badges, orders or degrees are offered you, fling them back in the giver's face." Finally, she converts that dreary phrase, "lack of rights and privileges," into the valiant "freedom from unreal loyalties." It's a brilliant rhetorical stroke.

Now that *The Hours* has increased the sales of *Mrs. Dalloway*, it is worth noting that Woolf was already linking the "tyrannies and servilities" of private and public life in that great 1925 novel. Take the moment when the eminent psychiatrist, Sir William Bradshaw, advises the shattered war veteran Septimus Warren Smith to acquire a sense of proportion. "Worshiping proportion, Sir William not only prospered himself but made England prosper, secluded her lunatics, forbade childbirth, penalized despair, made it impossible for the unfit to propagate their views until they too shared his sense of proportion—his if they were men, Lady Bradshaw's if they were women (she embroidered, knitted, spent four nights out of seven at home with her son)."

But proportion has a "sister, less smiling, more formidable, a goddess even now engaged—in the heat and sands of India, the mud and swamp of Africa, the purlieus of London.... Conversion is her name and she feasts on the wills of the weakly, loving to impress, to impose, adoring her own features stamped on the face of the populace." Conversion "walks penitentially disguised as brotherly love through factories and parliaments; offers help, but desires power; smites out of her way roughly the dissentient, or dissatisfied; bestows her blessing on those who, looking upward, catch submissively from her eyes the light of their own."

APRIL 13, 2003
The New York Times Book Review

JAMES WOOD

Virginia Woolf's
Forgetful Selves

This and the three following essays were first presented as talks at a tribute to Virginia Woolf, sponsored by the PEN Forums Committee at Town Hall in New York City on March 9, 2000.

READERS EITHER WORSHIP OR DENIGRATE VIRGINIA WOOLF'S use of stream of consciousness. I will admit that there are times when her characters' mental ambling can seem frustratingly opaque, and I begin to grumble to myself about the soft metaphysics of English leisure.

But Woolf was a revolutionary, more even than Joyce in one respect, and precisely in the area of stream of consciousness. I believe that Woolf, with perhaps the example of the newly translated Chekhov in her mind, introduced absent-mindedness—in all senses of the phrase—to English fiction. Consider Woolf's most delicate treatment of absent-mindedness in *To the Lighthouse*. Readers will remember a lovely moment when Mrs. Ramsay, at dinner, thought well of her husband, and then a minute later felt "as if somebody had been praising her husband to her and their marriage, and she glowed all over without realizing that it was she herself who had praised him."

Thus, comically and lyrically, Mrs. Ramsay travels out of herself, forgets herself for a moment, and we experience this self-forgetfulness in the same way that Mrs. Ramsay does. An even finer passage occurs, I think, about twenty pages into the novel. For the first twenty pages, more or less, we have been seeing things through Mrs. Ramsay's drifting thoughts. She thinks about how much her son wants to go to the lighthouse; she is cross with Tansley for saying that the weather will not be good enough for the trip; she thinks a little about Tansley and her husband's earnest followers. We are then told that Mrs. Ramsay is sitting and looking out of the window at the lawn. She sees Augustus Carmichael, the poet, and she sees Lily Briscoe painting, and decides that Lily Briscoe is not really a serious artist. And suddenly, Mrs. Ramsay remembers that Lily is painting *her,* painting Mrs. Ramsay, and that "she was supposed to be keeping her head as much in the same position as possible for Lily's picture."

Now perhaps this doesn't seem like a very remarkable event; but consider the implications of what Woolf has written. Mrs. Ramsay has forgotten and only just remembered that she is at the center of Lily's painting. The remembrance is sudden to us too; it realigns the whole scene, for we realize that Mrs. Ramsay, just as she is actually at the center of Lily's portrait, is also actually at the center of this novel. Yet Mrs. Ramsay's slow forgetfulness, and ours too, has taken twenty pages to accumulate, twenty pages in which, in fact, Mrs. Ramsay *has* been at the center of the novel without realizing it until this moment. She has been at the center of the novel all along, and we have hardly noticed it, because seeing the world through her own drifting thought, we have inhabited her own invisibility. And we have *experienced* this self-forgetfulness, because it has been ours, as readers, too. It is not as if Woolf simply wrote: "Mrs. Ramsay forgot that she was at the center of the painting"; no, the entire preceding twenty pages has been our experience of her forgetting this.

Even so, you may say, this is a technical point, literary sleight-of-hand. But think of how Woolf thus revolutionizes the scope of what could be done with a certain kind of upper-class female character, an elegant mother and mistress of the house. Woolf is able to convert a cliché—the domestic absent-mindedness of a woman with too much time on her hands— into a ghostly ontology, whereby we discover ourselves in the process of forgetting ourselves. Mrs. Ramsay, we are told later on, dislikes anything that suggests that she has been sitting thinking. But that is precisely what we as readers have just done: we have seen Mrs. Ramsay sitting thinking, and she has seen herself in this mode, too. Mrs. Ramsay is the kind of woman, we're sure, who if asked what she was thinking about, would probably say "Nothing" and instantly get up to busy herself with some domestic task. But Woolf's delicate use of drifting thought has shown us that Mrs. Ramsay is never thinking of nothing, that we are always thinking of something, even if the thought is merely the process of forgetting something.

Return, one last time, to that sentence, "she was supposed to be keeping her head as much in the same position as possible for Lily's picture." Suddenly we realize that, in fact, Mrs. Ramsay's head has not been still, is never still. Yes, externally, it might have been as still as Lily Briscoe could want it, but inside her head nothing has been still, nothing has been "in the same position." She has been in the deepest sense absent-minded. In Woolf's novels, thought radiates outwards, as in a medieval town, from a beautifully neglected center. And it is we as readers who renovate this neglect as we read Woolf.

This, perhaps, was her greatest feminism. By endowing her female characters, like Mrs. Ramsay and Clarissa Dalloway, with truly random, drifting thought, she endowed them with a freedom which had generally been seen by society as an idleness, as nothing more than the irrelevant freedom of housebound women sitting thinking about nothing. And this is a dangerous literary innovation, because such random thought will seem to hostile critics no more than the literary analogue of that despised female idleness: all these women thinking about nothing, all these irrelevant thoughts. One still hears this about Woolf.

Yet that is the risk of random thought: that it will seem irrelevant. For when thought *is* truly random, then remembered detail has no metaphysical superiority, no privilege, over what has been forgotten. One of the reasons that random thought *is* random is that it is treading over what has been forgotten, over the corpses of thoughts. Thought then resembles the old fiendish punishment that used to be handed out in English boarding schools, in which the victim had to color in every other square on a piece of graph paper. There is no necessary difference between a colored square and a blank one.

The delicate question then becomes, what is the status of irrelevant thought? Is it remembered data or forgotten data? Is it the very definition of the self, or everything but the self? Are absent-mindedness and present-mindedness the same thing? Do Clarissa Dalloway and Mrs. Ramsay remember themselves? Do they know who they are? St. Augustine points out in the *Confessions* that memory is partly convincing yourself of what you already, really knew all along. We are always forgetting things until the moment when we actually remember them. And at that moment, are we really remembering them, or paying a kind of tribute to their forgettability? What does Mrs. Ramsay think she is worth? Worth remembering or only worth forgetting? Surely Mrs. Ramsay is real to us in part because she seems real to herself. She is real to herself but she does not know herself. In this way, Woolf turns female absent-mindedness into the most searching philosophy of the self, and we suffer with her heroines, who are suspended between forgetfulness and remembrance, between their fulfillment and their irrelevance.

SPRING 2001

*PEN America: A Journal
for Writers and Readers*

MARY GORDON

Bodies of Knowledge

THE WAVES IS VIRGINIA WOOLF'S MOST DIFFICULT BOOK. IT IS a difficult book by any standards, and its difficulty and its greatness are intertwined. Part of the difficulty is inherent in the form; there are six narrative voices, long sections separated by pure descriptions of the ocean, but only the loosest of narratives. It requires an attentiveness of reading that is sometimes exhausting. This is because *The Waves* is saturated by Woolf's own relentless observation, the quality of her seeing, the pure lyric intensity that drenches every sentence. The soil of this book is entirely porous; there are no dry spots that the mind's feet can skate or slide over. We must be with her at every moment, riding alongside her on the galloping horse of her rhythms, as Bernard gallops at the end, his lance couched, defying death. "It is all written against a background of death and the sea," Woolf says of this book in her diary. Death and the sea provide the background, but the subject is life, or life seen as consciousness.

The doubleness of anguish and exaltation is the body's own. For *The Waves* suggests that we learn who we are and what life is through the body. In his last soliloquy, Bernard, the summer up, recalls a moment from a childhood bath. "Mrs. Constable raised the sponge above her head, squeezed it, and out shot, right and left, all down the spine, arrows of sensation. And so, as long as we draw breath, for the rest of time, if we knock against a chair, a table, or a woman, we are pierced with arrows of sensation. Sometimes indeed when I pass a cottage with a light in the window where a child has been born, I could implore them not to squeeze the sponge over that new body." Sensation, consciousness bring gifts and also desolation when the gifts are taken back or so far obscured as to be inaccessible. "It seems we go on living," Rhoda notes. It is an exhausting and dangerous prospect, this living, taking place as it does against the backdrop of death. But there are moments of great beauty, great value, some of them in the company of friends. "We have proved, sitting eating, sitting talking, that we can add to the treasury of moments," Bernard says.

If we compare *The Waves* to two other great first-person narratives, *Notes from Underground* and *À la recherche du temps perdu,* we find in Woolf glimpses not only of joy but of life's goodness that the other writers nowhere provide. Certainly, Proust grants us moments of aesthetic bliss: the hawthorns, the sea at Balbec, the sonatas of Vinteul, the charms of Odette. But for Proust, human connection is a snare, a distraction from the important work of contemplation, apprehension, and creation. Dostoevsky's underground man finds the possibility of friendship risible to the point of nausea. Woolf, on the other hand, by the very nature of her structure, insists on the possibilities of human connection and indeed interpenetration. Bernard, who speaks for the other characters, is not sure whether he is himself or an entity made up of himself and his friends. A six-sided flower, as he calls it. Singularity may be a chimera; it is moments of union, moments only to be sure, that strike the spine with the piercing and enlivening arrows of sensation. And yet for some, like the character Rhoda, like Woolf herself, a suicide, these moments are not strong enough to make up for the ordeal, the horror of living.

In her diary, Woolf refers to the form of this novel as a "poem-play." If it is a play, it is a play with six characters: Bernard, Jinny, Neville, Susan, Rhoda, and Louis. Or perhaps it is a play with only one character having six sides. The plot is a series of variations of the story "This is who I am." As a poem (and it is important that it includes the entire text of one of the greatest English poems, "O Western Wind"), *The Waves* relies on images, images repeated, images with changes wrung upon them, as an essential way the I knows itself as the I. Each of the six characters bears within him- or herself an image that he or she carries from childhood through old age: for Bernard it is words that bubble up from the bottom of a saucepan, for Louis it is the great beast on the shore that stamps and stamps, for Jinny it is the body that puts forth a frill, for Susan the hard thing, her grief, her anger, that she screws up into a pocket handkerchief, for Neville it is the path of the Latin language throughout the sand, and boys eating bananas out of a paper sack, for Rhoda the petals that she rocks in her brown basin and the swallow who dips his wings in a pool at the end of the world. There are sentences in *The Waves* that have the lapidary quality of great lines of blank verse, sentences that lodge forever in the memory. I often find myself repeating sentences from *The Waves* at moments of stress. I hear Neville's "The reign of chaos is over, knives cut" when I have found my lost keys or discovered I have not in fact run out of toilet paper. Or all too often, in circumstances too obvious to be gone into, I hear Susan's words: "I shall be debased and hidebound by the bestial and beautiful passion of maternity. I shall push the fortunes of my children unscrupulously. I shall hate those who see their faults. I shall lie basely to help them." And there are passages whose beauty stops the heart: "The gold has faded between the trees and a slice of green lies behind them, elongated like the blade of a knife seen in dreams or some tapering island on which nobody sets foot."

In *The Waves,* Virginia Woolf came closest to fulfilling her aesthetic ideal. This ideal is a fiction in which the stuff of realistic fiction—money, class, social placement, the details of family connection—is notable for its absence, and attention is paid only to that which reveals the inner life. In her essay "Mr. Bennett and Mrs. Brown," in which she asserts that the inner life of the ordinary woman on the train, Mrs. Brown, is the true business of the modern novelist, she asserts her creed. "I was strongly tempted," she disingenuously says, "to manufacture a three-volume novel about the old lady's son and his adventures crossing the Atlantic and her daughter and how she keeps a milliner's shop in Westminster... though such stories seem to me the most dreary, irrelevant and humbugging affairs in the world. But if I had done that, I should have escaped the appalling effort of saying what I meant. And to have got at what I meant I would have had to go back and back, to experiment with one thing and another, to try this sentence and that, referring each sentence to my vision." This decision, of course, deprives the reader of many of the pleasures of fiction, even the experimental. We have none of Proust's delicious biting satire; we miss Dostoevsky's speculations about the nature of moral choice. But in focusing so intently upon the task of *The Waves,* Virginia Woolf triumphantly realized the goal she had set for herself in the privacy of her diary. "I want," she said, "to tell the truth and create something of beauty."

SPRING 2001
PEN America: A Journal for Writers and Readers

Invigorating Life

A ROOM OF ONE'S OWN MUST BE THE MOST POPULAR BOOK title that any author has ever written. Since its publication in 1929, Virginia Woolf's witty manifesto has not only become the mandatory reference for every feminist literary critic, but also has inspired the titles of scores of books on subjects very remote from Woolf's subject, the conditions of artistic creation. I did a quick search of the Princeton Library catalogue among books published merely since 1988, and found the following variants and homage: a place of one's own, a life of one's own, a profession of one's own; a field of one's own, a garden, a house, a studio, a school, a hut of one's own, and a mine of one's own (for women prospectors). There are books on a journey of one's own, a view, a faith, an art, and a style of one's own; and ominously, there are books on a doctor of one's own, a death of one's own, a corpse of one's own, and a courtroom of one's own. Someone has even written a book entitled *A Trumpet of One's Own.*

I think that Virginia Woolf, who was not in favor of tooting one's own horn, would have been astonished and amused by the fame of her title, and by the extraordinary influence of her book. *A Room of One's Own* had its beginnings in two lectures, or papers, on women and fiction she delivered at Newnham and Girton, the women's colleges of Cambridge University, in October 1928. In her diary, Woolf was more than usually ironic and self-critical about her performance: "Thank God," she wrote, "my long toil at the women's lecture is this moment ended. I am back from speaking at Girton, in floods of rain. Starved but valiant young women—that is my impression. Intelligent, eager, poor; and destined to become schoolmistresses in shoals. I blandly told them to drink wine and have a room of their own . . . I felt elderly and mature. And nobody respected me . . . Very little reverence or that sort of thing about." As she finished revisions on the book, she continued to be skeptical: "I have just set the last correction to *Women and Fiction* or *A Room of One's Own*. I shall never read it again. Good or bad? It has an uneasy life in it, I think: you feel the creature arching its back and galloping on, though as usual much is watery and flimsy and pitched in too high a voice." And on the eve of its publication, she predicted that it would not be well received: "the press will be kind & talk of its charm, & sprightliness; also I shall be attacked for a feminist and hinted at for a sapphist . . . I am afraid it will not be taken seriously." The night of publication she dreamed that she had a fatal heart disease that would kill her in six months, and woke up to find that *A Room of One's Own* was selling very well, and the Estonian Ambassador had asked her to lunch.

Of course Woolf's successors have taken *A Room of One's Own* very seriously indeed. In it, she had told the disrespectful young women of Cambridge that "a woman must have money and a room of her own if she is to write fiction." The room, moreover, must have a lock on the door. And the five hundred pounds, ideally, should be earned, although Woolf's narrator admits that hers is a legacy. The room is not just a material space, not a literal office or separate chamber: "Five hundred a year stands for the power to contemplate," Woolf explains. "A lock on the door means the power to think for oneself." Finally, she insists, financial independence and privacy doesn't mean separation or ghettoization or isolation: "When I ask you to earn money and have a room of your own, I am asking you to live in the presence of reality, an invigorating life."

As Woolf's details and images of starved young women hinted, that invigorating life should also include a wine cellar and a dining hall of one's own. It's amazing to read the attention this most famously anorexic of novelists pays to good food, as she contrasts the lavish cuisine of Trinity College — the men's college — with the beef, custard, and prunes of the women's college. "For one cannot think well," she notes, "one cannot love well, sleep well, if one has not dined well." And also, I suspect, she means, one cannot write well.

This section of the book made such an impression on me as a student that in 1973, when I first visited Cambridge University and had dinner at Trinity College, I noted the evening's menu in the yellowing margins of my paperback copy of *A Room of One's Own*: chef's salad, chicken Washington, new potatoes and peas, crème brûlée, crab on toast, followed by port, madeira, sauterne, claret, biscuits, cheese, fresh peaches, coffee and cigars, brandy and seltzer. How anyone wrote anything after such a dinner is still a mystery to me. Maybe there is something to be said for prunes and custard.

The part of the book most readers remember, I think, is Woolf's invocation of Judith Shakespeare, the sister of literary genius Shakespeare might have had, who would not have been able to become a great poet and playwright, but would have killed herself in despair. In her conclusion, Woolf called upon the women of 1928 to work to make possible that when Shakespeare's sister is born again, she shall be able to live and write her poetry. "If we live another century or so . . . and have five hundred a year each of us and rooms of our own; if we have the habit of freedom and the courage to write exactly what we think... then the opportunity will come and the dead poet who was Shakespeare's sister will put on the body which she has so often laid down. Drawing her life from the lives of the unknown who were her forerunners, as her brother did before her, she will be born."

As an American, I'm always struck by how much importance Woolf placed on the story of Shakespeare's sister, and on the coming of the great female literary messiah. Americans have not been so reverent, at least not American men. Herman Melville argued that to worship Shakespeare showed a want of gumption and proper democratic feeling. "This absolute and unconditional adoration of Shakespeare has grown to be a part of our Anglo-Saxon superstitions... what sort of belief is this for an American, a man who is bound to carry republican progressiveness into Literature as well as into Life?" Melville claimed that already in 1850, rather than a century in the future, "men not very much inferior to Shakespeare are... being born on the banks of the Ohio. And the day will come when you shall say, Who reads a book by an Englishman that is modern?"

Virginia Woolf was by no means a superstitious follower of received literary ideas, but she would not have been so confident about the future of *women's* writing. Perhaps it's independence or braggadocio that has made many brash American women readers of Woolf, including myself, so eager to update, democratize, modernize, and re-title *A Room of One's Own*. In 1977, Marilyn French's feminist novel, *The Women's Room,* seemed like a response to Woolf. In 1978, I wrote that if the room of one's own becomes a retreat, a feminine secession or escape from male power, logic, and violence, it can be a tomb. Alice Walker, in an essay called "One Child of One's Own," offered her own response to Woolf's prescription. And Camille Paglia announced that a room of one's own "was already too bourgeois for my subversive generation, whose brash rock spirit counsels: 'Get out of the house and keep on running. A *car* of one's own, the great equalizer, is more the mode of American Amazonism.'"

But whether in car or truck or SUV, we are still following Woolf's path. In her superb 1997 biography, Hermione Lee concludes that no critic can have the last word on Woolf: "Virginia Woolf's story is reformulated by each generation. She takes on the shape of difficult modernist preoccupied with questions of form, of comedian of manners, or neurotic highbrow aesthete, or inventive fantasist, or pernicious snob, or Marxist feminist, or historian of women's lives, or victim of abuse, or lesbian heroine, or cultural analyst, depending on who is reading her, and when, and in what context . . . and the debates she arouses—over madness, over modernism, over marriage"— over Shakespeare and his sister—"cannot be concluded and will go on being argued, well after this book is published." Women may be waiting around for Shakespeare's sister even longer than for Godot, but we'll each have a Woolf of our own.

SPRING 2001
*PEN America: A Journal
for Writers and Readers*

MICHAEL CUNNINGHAM

First Love

*M*RS. *DALLOWAY* IS THE FIRST GREAT BOOK I EVER READ. I WAS fifteen, a not very promising student at a not very good public high school in Southern California, where I read the books that I was made to read but thought of literature as a dying art form. One day I was out having a cigarette where we went to have cigarettes, and suddenly found myself standing beside the pirate queen of our school. She was beautiful and mean and smart, she had long red fingernails, and long straight hair. Fringe, pretty much everywhere. I found myself standing next to her, and I thought, "Uh oh, uh oh... Think fast, be suave, say something that will make her love you forever." So I said something that I thought then—and I think today—was very winning, about the poetry of Bob Dylan and Leonard Cohen. She was kind to me. She sucked in her entire Marlboro in one drag, but the ash didn't fall, and exhaled an immense cloud of smoke, and said, "Well, yes, they're very good, but how do you feel about T. S. Eliot and Virginia Woolf?"

Now, I wasn't completely illiterate—I had heard of T. S. Eliot and Virginia Woolf, and I knew Virginia Woolf was very tall and insane and lived in a lighthouse and jumped in the ocean, but I never expected I'd have to read either one of them. I went to the library, the Bookmobile, the little trailer where the books were. They didn't have any Eliot, but they did have one book of Woolf's, and it was *Mrs. Dalloway.* I took it out, and I took it home and read it, tried to read it, and I didn't know what was going on. In another way I did get it. I did get the depth and density, and the sentences, and it did turn on some little light inside my stupid skull.

Everybody who reads has a first book—maybe not the first book you read, but the first book that shows you what literature can be. Like a first kiss. And you read other books, you kiss other people, but especially for those who are romantically inclined, that first book stays with you. I felt wedded to *Mrs. Dalloway* in a way I've never felt about any other book. I finally, finally, finally grew up and wrote *The Hours,* in which I tried to take an existing work of great art and make another work of art out of it, the way a jazz musician might play improvisations on a great piece of music.

I learned so much from Woolf as a writer. I think what I learned most importantly was her conviction that the whole of human existence, while it is copiously contained in foreign wars and the death of kings, and the other big subjects for big novels, is also contained in every hour in the life of everybody, very much the way the blueprint for the whole organism is contained in every strand of its DNA. If you look with sufficient penetration, and sufficient art, at any hour in the life of anybody, you can crack it open. And get everything. Virginia Woolf understood that every character, no matter how minor, in a novel she wrote was visiting the novel, from a novel of his or her own, where he or she was the hero of another great tragic and comic tale.

SPRING 2001
*PEN America: A Journal
for Writers and Readers*

E. M. FORSTER

The Early Novels
of Virginia Woolf

Virginia Woolf and E. M. Forster, both artists working within the noted Bloomsbury Group, were tied together as practicing novelists, as critics who reviewed each other's work, and as friends with shared goals and visions. Here Forster writes a sketch of Virginia's early work in the hopes of introducing it to a wider audience.

I.

IT IS PROFOUNDLY CHARACTERISTIC OF THE ART OF VIRGINIA Woolf that when I decided to write about it and had planned a suitable opening paragraph, my fountain pen should disappear. Tiresome creature! It slipped through a pocket into a seam. I could pinch it, chivy it about, make holes in the coat lining, but a layer of tailor's stuffing prevented recovery. So near, and yet so far! Which is what one feels about her art. The pen is extricated in time, but during the struggle the opening paragraph has escaped; the words are here but the birds have flown; "opals and emeralds, they lie about the roots of turnips." It is far more difficult to catch her than it is for her to catch what she calls life—"life; London; this moment in June." Again and again she eludes, until the pen, getting restive, sets to work on its own and grinds out something like this, something totally false such as: "Mrs. Woolf is a talented but impressionistic writer, with little feeling for form and none for actuality." Rubbish. She has, among other achievements, made a definite contribution to the novelist's art. But how is this contribution to be stated? And how does she handle the ingredients of fiction—human beings, time, and space? Let us glance at her novels in the order of their composition.

The Voyage Out was published in 1915. It is a strange, tragic, inspired book whose scene is a South America not found on any map and reached by a boat which would not float on any sea, an America whose spiritual boundaries touch Xanadu and Atlantis. Hither, to a hotel, various English tourists repair, and the sketches of them are so lively and "life-like" that we expect a comedy of manners to result. Gradually a current sets in, a deep unrest. What are all these people doing—talking, eating, kissing, reading, being kind or unkind? What do they understand of each other or of themselves? What relations are possible between them? Two young men, bleak and honest intellectuals from Cambridge, ask the question; Rachel, an undeveloped girl, answers it. The uneasiness of society and its occasional panics take hold of her, and nothing can exorcise them, because it is her own desire to face the truth; nothing, not even love.

> They stood together in front of the looking-glass, and with a brush tried to make themselves look as if they had been feeling nothing all the morning, neither pain nor happiness. But it chilled them to see themselves in the glass, for instead of being vast and indivisible they were really very small and separate, the size of the glass leaving a large space for the reflection of other things.

Wedded bliss is promised her, but the voyage continues, the current deepens, carrying her between green banks of the jungle into disease and death. The closing chapters of the book are as poignant as anything in modern fiction, yet they arise naturally out of what has gone before. They are not an interruption but a fulfilment. Rachel has lost everything—for there is no hint of compensation beyond the grave—but she has not swerved from the course honesty marked out, she has not jabbered or pretended that human relationships are satisfactory. It is a noble book, so noble that a word of warning must be added: like all Virginia Woolf's work, it is not romantic, not mystic, not explanatory of the universe. By using a wrong tone of voice—over-stressing "South America" for instance—the critic might easily make it appear to be all these things, and perhaps waft it towards popular success! His honesty must equal the writer's; he is offered no ultimate good, but "life; London; this moment in June"; and it is his job to find out what the promise entails.

Will *Night and Day* help him? It is the simplest novel she has written, and to my mind the least successful. Very long, very careful, it condescends to many of the devices she so gaily derides in her essay on *Mr. Bennett and Mrs. Brown*. The two principal characters are equipped with houses and relatives which document their reality, they are screwed into Chelsea and Highgate as the case may be, and move from their bases to meet in the rooms and streets of a topographical metropolis. After misunderstandings, they marry, they are promised happiness. In view of what preceded it and of what is to follow, *Night and Day* seems to me a deliberate exercise in classicism. It contains all that has characterized English fiction for good or evil during the last hundred and fifty years—faith in personal relations, recourse to humorous side shows, insistence on petty social differences. Even the style has been normalized, and though the machinery is modern, the resultant form is as traditional as *Emma*. Surely the writer is using tools that don't belong to her. At all events she has never touched them again.

For, contemporary with this full length book, she made a
very different experiment, published two little — stories, sketches,
what is one to call them?—which show the direction in which
her genius has since moved. At last her sensitiveness finds full
play, and she is able to describe what she sees in her own words.
In *The Mark on the Wall* she sees a mark on the wall, wonders
what it is . . . and that is the entire story. In *Kew Gardens* she sees
men, sometimes looking at flowers, and flowers never looking at
men. And, in either case, she reports her vision impartially; she
strays forward, murmuring, wandering, falling asleep. Her style
trails after her, catching up grass and dust in its folds, and instead of the precision of the earlier writing we have something
more elusive than has yet been achieved in English. If a drowsy
and desultory person could also be a great artist he would talk
like this:

> Yellow and black, pink and snow white, shapes of
> all these colours, men, women and children were spot-
> ted for a second upon the horizon, and then, seeing the
> breadth of yellow that lay upon the grass, they wavered
> and sought shade beneath the trees, dissolving like drops
> of water in the yellow and green atmosphere, staining it
> faintly with red and blue. It seemed as if all gross and
> heavy bodies had sunk down in the heat motionless and
> lay huddled upon the ground, but their voices went
> wavering from them as if they were flames lolling from
> the thick waxen bodies of candles. Voices. Yes, voices.
> Wordless voices, breaking the silence suddenly with
> such depth of contentment, such passion of desire; or,
> in the voices of children, such freshness of surprise:
> breaking the silence? But there was no silence; all the
> time the motor omnibuses were turning their wheels
> and changing their gear; like a vast nest of Chinese
> boxes all of wrought steel turning ceaselessly one within

another the city murmured; on the top of which the voices cried aloud and the petals of myriads of flowers flashed their colours in the air.

The objection (or apparent objection) to this sort of writing is that it cannot say much or be sure of saying anything. It is an inspired breathlessness, a beautiful droning or gasping which trusts to luck, and can never express human relationships or the structure of society. So at least one would suppose, and that is why the novel of *Jacob's Room* (1922) comes as a tremendous surprise. The impossible has occurred. The style closely resembles that of *Kew Gardens.* The blobs of colour continue to drift past; but in their midst, interrupting their course like a closely sealed jar, rises the solid figure of a young man. In what sense Jacob is alive — in what sense any of Virginia Woolf's characters live — we have yet to determine. But that he exists, that he stands as does a monument is certain, and wherever he stands we recognize him for the same and are touched by his outline. The coherence of the book is even more amazing than its beauty. In the stream of glittering similes, unfinished sentences, hectic catalogues, unanchored proper names, we seem to be going nowhere. Yet the goal comes, the method and the matter prove to have been one, and looking back from the pathos of the closing scene we see for a moment the airy drifting atoms piled into a colonnade. The break with *Night and Day* and even with *The Voyage Out* is complete. A new type of fiction has swum into view, and it is none the less new because it has had a few predecessors — laborious, well-meaning, still-born books by up-to-date authors, which worked the gasp and the drone for all they were worth, and are unreadable.

Three years after *Jacob's Room* comes another novel in the same style, or slight modification of the style: *Mrs. Dalloway.* It is perhaps her masterpiece, but difficult, and I am not altogether sure about every detail, except when my fountain pen is in my hand. Here is London at all events—so much is certain, London chorusing with all its clocks and shops and sunlit parks, and writing texts with an aeroplane across God's heaven. Here is Clarissa Dalloway, elderly, kind, graceful, rather hard and superficial, and a terrible snob. How she loves London! And there is Septimus Warren Smith—she never meets him—a case of shell shock—very sad—who hears behind the chorus the voices of the dead singing, and sees his own apotheosis or damnation in the sky. That dreadful war! Sir William Bradshaw of Harley Street, himself in perfect health, very properly arranges for Septimus Warren Smith to go to a lunatic asylum. Septimus is ungrateful and throws himself out of the window. "Coward," cries the doctor, but is too late. News of which comes to Clarissa as she is giving an evening party. Does she likewise commit suicide? I thought she did the first time I read the book; not at my second reading, nor is the physical act important, for she is certainly left with the full knowledge—inside knowledge—of what suicide is. The societified lady and the obscure maniac are in a sense the same person. His foot has slipped through the gay surface on which she still stands—that is all the difference between them. She returns (it would seem) to her party and to the man she loves, and a hint of her new knowledge comes through to him as the London clock strikes three. Such apparently is the outline of this exquisite and superbly constructed book, and having made the outline one must rub it out at once. For emphasis is fatal to the understanding of this author's work. If we dared not overstress "South America" in *The Voyage Out,* still lighter must fall our touch on London here, still more disastrous would be the application to its shimmering fabric of mysticism, unity beneath multiplicity, twin souls. . . .

Why creeds and prayers and mackintoshes? when, thought Clarissa, that's the miracle, that's the mystery; that old lady, she meant, whom she could see going from chest of drawers to dressing-table. She could still see her. And the supreme mystery which Kilman might say she had solved, or Peter might say he had solved, but Clarissa didn't believe either of them had the ghost of an idea of solving was simply this: here is one room: there another. Did religion solve that, or love?

As far as her work has a message, it seems to be contained in the above paragraph. Here is one room, there another. Required like most writers to choose between the surface and the depths as the basis of her operations, she chooses the surface and then burrows in as far as she can.

2.

AFTER THIS GLANCE WE CAN BETTER UNDERSTAND HER EQUIP-ment, and realize that visual sensitiveness—in itself so slight a tool for a novelist—becomes in her case a productive force. How beautifully she sees! Look at "those churches, like shapes of grey paper, breasting the stream of the Strand," for instance. Or at "The flames were struggling through the wood and roaring up when, goodness knows where from, pails flung water in beautiful hollow shapes as of polished tortoiseshell; flung again and again; until the hiss was like a swarm of bees; and all the faces went out." How beautiful! Yet vision is only the frontier of her kingdom. Behind it lie other treasures; in particular the mind.

Her remarkable intellectual powers have nothing to do with common sense—masses of roses can be gathered at Christmas for instance, and the characters in one book need bear no resemblance to their namesakes in another. Nor is she much occupied in presenting clever men and women. What thrills her—for it starts as a thrill—is the actual working of a brain, especially of a youthful brain, and there are passages in *Jacob's Room* where the process becomes as physical as the raising of a hand. Moreover she reverences learning; it gives her disinterested pleasure, increases the natural nobility of her work.

Stone lies solid over the British Museum, as bone lies cool over the visions and heats of the brain. Only here the brain is Plato's brain and Shakespeare's; the brain has made pots and statues, great bulls and little jewels, and crossed the river of death this way and that incessantly, seeking some landing, now wrapping the body well for its long sleep; now laying a penny piece on the eyes; now turning the toes scrupulously to the East. Meanwhile Plato continues his dialogue; in spite of the rain; in spite of the cab whistles; in spite of the woman in the mews behind Great Ormond Street who has come home drunk and cries all night long, 'Let me in, let me in.'

The *Phaedrus* is very difficult. And so, when at length one reads straight ahead, falling into step, marching on becoming (so it seems) momentarily part of this rolling, imperturbable energy, which has driven darkness before it since Plato walked the Acropolis, it is impossible to see to the fire.

The dialogue draws to its close. Plato's argument is done. Plato's argument is stowed away in Jacob's mind, and for five minutes Jacob's mind continues alone, onwards, into the darkness. Then, getting up, he parted the curtains, and saw, with astonishing clearness, how the Springetts opposite had gone to bed; how it rained; how the Jews and the foreign woman, at the end of the street, stood by the pillar-box, arguing.

It is easy for a novelist to describe what a character thinks of; look at Mrs. Humphry Ward. But to convey the actual process of thinking is a creative feat, and I know of no one except Virginia Woolf who has accomplished it. Here at last thought, and the learning that is the result of thought, take their own high place upon the dais, exposed no longer to the patronage of the hostess or the jeers of the buffoon. Here Cambridge, with all its dons, is raised into the upper air and becomes a light for ships at sea, and Rachel, playing Bach upon a hotel piano, builds a momentary palace for the human mind.

But what of the subject that she regards as of the highest importance: human beings as a whole and as wholes? She tells us (in her essays) that human beings are the permanent material of fiction, that it is only the method of presenting them which changes and ought to change, that to capture their inner life presents a different problem to each generation of novelists; the great Victorians solved it in their way; the Edwardians shelved it by looking outwards at relatives and houses; the Georgians must solve it anew, and if they succeed a new age of fiction will begin. Has she herself succeeded? Do her own characters live?

I feel that they do live, but not continuously, whereas the characters of Tolstoy (let us say) live continuously. With her, the reader is in a state of constant approval. "Yes, that is right," he says, each time she implies something more about Jacob or Peter: "yes, that would be so: yes." Whereas in the case of Tolstoy approval is absent. We sink into André, into Nicolay Rostoff during the moments they come forth, and no more endorse the correctness of their functioning than we endorse our own. And the problem before her—the problem that she has set herself, and that certainly would inaugurate a new literature if solved—is to retain her own wonderful new method and form, and yet allow her readers to inhabit each character with Victorian thoroughness. Think how difficult this is. If you work in a storm of atoms and seconds, if your highest joy is "life; London; this moment in June" and your deepest mystery "here is one room; there another," then how can you construct your human beings so that each shall be not a movable monument but an abiding home, how can you build between them any permanent roads of love and hate? There was continuous life in the little hotel people of *The Voyage Out* because there was no innovation in the method. But Jacob in *Jacob's Room* is discontinuous, demanding — and obtaining — separate approval for everything he feels or does. And *Mrs. Dalloway?* There seems a slight change here, an approach towards character-construction in the Tolstoyan sense; Sir William Bradshaw, for instance, is uninterruptedly and embracingly evil. Any approach is significant, for it suggests that in future books she may solve the problem as a whole. She herself believes it can be done, and, with the exception of Joyce, she is the only writer of genius who is trying. All the other so-called innovators are (if not pretentious bunglers), merely innovators in subject matter and the praise we give them is of the kind we should accord to scientists. Their novels admit aeroplanes or bigamy, or give some fresh interpretation of the spirit of Norfolk or Persia, or at the most reveal some slight discovery about human nature. They do good work, because everything is subject matter for the novel, nothing ought to be ruled out on the ground that it is remote or indecent. But they do not advance the novelist's art. Virginia Woolf has already done that a little, and if she succeeds in her problem of rendering character, she will advance it enormously.

For English fiction, despite the variety of its content, has made little innovation in form between the days of Fielding and those of Arnold Bennett. It might be compared to a picture gallery, lit by windows placed at suitable intervals between the pictures. First come some portraits, then a window with a view say of Norfolk, then some more portraits and perhaps a still life, followed by a window with a view of Persia, then more portraits and perhaps a fancy piece, followed by a view of the universe. The pictures and the windows are infinite in number, so that every variety of experience seems assured, and yet there is one factor that never varies: namely the gallery itself; the gallery is always the same, and the reader always has the feeling that he is pacing along it, under the conditions of time and space that regulate his daily life. Virginia Woolf would do away with the sense

of pacing. The pictures and windows may remain if they can—
indeed the portraits must remain—but she wants to destroy the
gallery in which they are embedded and in its place build—
build what? Something more rhythmical. *Jacob's Room* suggests a
spiral whirling down to a point, *Mrs. Dalloway* a cathedral.

1925
from Abinger Harvest

DANIEL MENDELSOHN

Not Afraid of Virginia Woolf

Inspired by Michael Cunningham's Pulitzer Prize—winning novel of the same title, The Hours *was released in December of 2002 and directed by Stephen Daldry, based on a screenplay by David Hare. The film was nominated for nine Academy Awards, three Screen Actors Guild Awards, two Orange British Academy Film Awards, and a Writers Guild Award for Best Adapted Screenplay.*

I.

AT THE BEGINNING OF THE NOVEL IN QUESTION, IT IS A FINE June day in a great city, and a fifty-two-year-old woman named Clarissa goes shopping for flowers. She is giving a party that evening, and as she walks to the flower shop, a host of thoughts tumble through her mind. Not all of them are about her party. (Her party!) She worries, for instance, that her beautiful teen-aged daughter is in thrall to a humorless middle-aged woman who is, somehow her, Clarissa's, mortal enemy. (The woman's fierce ideological views make Clarissa feel slightly shabby in comparison; and indeed Clarissa supposes that she is, when all is said and done, quite "ordinary.") She is embarrassed to run into someone whom she hasn't invited; she has reveries about a long-ago summer in a house in the country when she and some friends indulged in illicit love affairs. (As she thinks these thoughts she is glimpsed by a neighbor who sternly, but not un-kindly, judges her looks: she has aged.) She thinks, often, about death. As she stands in the shop buying the flowers, there is commotion outside—a loud noise—and when Clarissa and the florist go to the window to see what it might be, they get a glimpse of a famous head emerging from a vehicle, someone everyone knows from the papers, from pictures.

The famous head, glimpsed from afar by curious, even prurient crowds, has been placed there by the author of this novel for the purpose of contrast. This head reminds us of the great world out there, and the values by which it measures things: fame, importance, power, rank, distinction—and hence stands in stark contrast to Clarissa's head, filled as it is with a quotidian, haphazard jumble of thoughts that are of no particular importance to anyone except Clarissa herself. Clarissa's life is meant, indeed, to be one of those existences, neither brilliant nor tragic, that moved Virginia Woolf, in *A Room of One's Own,* to ponder what the proper subject and style of an authentic women's literature might possibly be. The values of novels, she argued, reflect the values of life, which novels must mirror; and it was, furthermore, "obvious" that

> the values of women differ very often from the values which have been made by the other sex; naturally, this is so. Yet it is the masculine values that prevail. Speaking crudely, football and sport are "important"; the worship of fashion, the buying of clothes "trivial." And these values are inevitably transferred from life to fiction. This is an important book, the critic assumes, because it deals with war. This is an insignificant book because it deals with the feelings of women in a drawing-room. A scene in a battlefield is more important than a scene in a shop—everywhere and much more subtly the difference of value persists.

Part of the proper work of women's writing, Woolf suggested, was to recuperate for literature "these infinitely obscure lives

[that] remain to be recorded." Let men preoccupy themselves with "the great movements which, brought together, constitute the historian's view of the past." As Woolf grew as an artist, she experimented with ways to record and "bring . . . to life" another kind of experience altogether, one hitherto buried in the interstices of those great movements.

ONE WAY TO DO SO WAS, indeed, to focus on the concrete minutiae of women's everyday existences—everything that men's literature, by its very nature, overlooked, an omission that led to yet larger gaps and inaccuracies. "So much has been left out, unattempted," Woolf complained. "Almost without exception [women] are shown in their relation to men . . . not only seen by the other sex, but seen only in relation to the other sex." And so, she told the audiences of the lectures that would become *A Room of One's Own,*

> you must illumine your own soul with its profundities and its shallows, and its vanities and its generosities, and say what your beauty means to you or your plainness, and what is your relation to the everchanging and turning world of gloves and shoes and stuffs swaying up and down among the faint scents that come through chemists' bottles down arcades of dress material over a floor of pseudomarble.

That which men's literature dismissed as trivia must be taken up and forged into a new kind of literature that would suggest how great were the hidden worlds and movements in women's lives; such a literature was long overdue. "There is the girl behind the counter," she wrote toward the end of *A Room of One's Own.* "I would as soon have her true history as the hundred and fiftieth life of Napoleon or seventieth study of Keats and his use of Miltonic inversion which old Professor Z and his like are now inditing."

Hence Clarissa, with her random thoughts of flowers and parties and sewing and old love affairs: she is (for all the differences in social status) that girl, just as the famous head is a reminder of the other world, the world of great movements, of Napoleons and Miltons. And indeed the first great example of the literary project that Woolf advocates in *A Room of One's Own* was *Mrs. Dalloway,* first published in 1925, a few years before the essay in which she explicated that project.

And yet the novel I began this essay by describing is not, in fact, *Mrs. Dalloway.* Or, I should say, is not only *Mrs. Dalloway.* It is, rather, Michael Cunningham's *The Hours,* the 1999 Pulitzer Prize winner which is at once a homage to and an impersonation of the earlier work of fiction. (Woolf had long planned to call her novel "The Hours," but decided on *Mrs. Dalloway* in the end.) In it, three narratives about three women, each connected in some way to *Mrs. Dalloway,* are intertwined; in each of the three, numerous elements from Woolf's novel—characters, names, relationships, tiny details of phrasing, individual sentences, whole scenes (not least, the world-famous head poking momentarily from the big vehicle)—are reincarnated with almost obsessional devotion. But perhaps the most remarkable achievement of *The Hours* is to preserve Woolf's project—to avoid the banal ways in which male novelists often see women, either dramatizing them or trivializing them, and thereby making them more comfortable for consumption by men.

"THE DESIGN IS SO QUEER & so masterful," Woolf wrote in her journal, in June of 1923, of the book she was struggling to write; the same words, with additional overtones, could well be used of Cunningham's reinterpretation of it. Cunningham takes his Woolfian donnée and splits it into three narratives, each a kind of riff on some aspect of *Mrs. Dalloway.* Each takes place, as does *Mrs. Dalloway,* in the course of a single day: each focuses on the inner life of one woman. The sections called "Mrs. Dalloway," set in the 1990s, are about a lesbian book editor in New

York City named Clarissa Vaughan (whom her best friend and one-time lover, a poet now dying of AIDS, enjoys calling "Mrs. Dalloway"; she's giving a party to celebrate the prestigious literary award he's won). The sections called "Mrs. Brown," set in 1949, recount one fraught day in the life of an LA housewife, Laura Brown, who's torn between reading *Mrs. Dalloway* for the first time and planning a birthday party for her husband. And the "Mrs. Woolf" sections envision Virginia Woolf herself on a day in 1923 when she conceives how she might write *Mrs. Dalloway*. In each section, Cunningham ingeniously uses Woolf's novel as a template: like Woolf's Clarissa, each of his three heroines plans a party, has an unexpected visitor, escapes, in some sense, from the house, and tries to create something (a party, a cake, a book).

The central story is the story of Clarissa Vaughan, the woman whose preparations for a grand party, like those of Woolf's Clarissa Dalloway, are the vehicle for a stream-of-consciousness narrative that suggests a contemporary, wryly self-aware Everywoman: "an ordinary person (at this age, why bother trying to deny it?)." While this Clarissa prepares for her party, the dying poet, whose name is Richard (the given name of Mr. Dalloway, in Woolf's story) worsens: just as the Great War and the Spanish flu gave poignancy and weight to Clarissa Dalloway's musings about the essential goodness and beauty of everyday existence ("life; London; this moment in June"), so too does AIDS give substance to the similar thoughts of Cunningham's Clarissa ("What a thrill, what a shock, to be alive on a morning in June . . .").

Both Clarissas, for all that they are haunted by thoughts of death, are strong. In Cunningham's novel, as in Woolf's, it is the men surrounding the women who keep falling apart. In *Mrs. Dalloway*, Clarissa's old flame, Peter Walsh, disintegrates in tears when he shows up for an unexpected visit. (He's having an affair with a much younger married woman; sensible Clarissa knows she was right to refuse his offer of marriage, long ago.)

In a different part of town, meanwhile, the mad poet Septimus Smith disintegrates and flings himself from a window. Cunningham's novel reproduces these elements while updating them. His Clarissa lives in Greenwich Village with another woman, Sally (the name Woolf gave to the girl her Clarissa once kissed, long ago, in a country house); in his novel, it's an old flame of Richard's—his one-time lover, Louis—who shows up for an unexpected visit and, while Clarissa is preparing for the party, dissolves into tears. Like Woolf's Peter Walsh, Cunningham's Louis is foolish in love: he's having an affair with a male theater student who "does the most remarkable performance pieces about growing up white and gay in South Africa."

And in Cunningham's novel, too, it's a mad poet, Richard (to whom the author gives some of Septimus's lines: both characters believe they hear animals speaking ancient Greek), who kills himself toward the end of the book. In *A Room of One's Own,* Woolf hinted that behind the empire-building noise that men made, women were strong, too; that because of the patriarchal economy, their creations were more often than not children, households, families; but they did create, and could of course create art, too, if they had the means. It was just that no one had written of this strength, this creativity. In *Mrs. Dalloway,* she wrote of it—and of men's weakness; and in *The Hours,* Cunningham does too.

INDEED, THE OTHER two strands of Cunningham's tripartite narrative recapitulate this important if subtle motif of Woolf's story in various ways. His "Mrs. Woolf" section is a fantasy of what might have gone through Woolf's mind on the day that *Mrs. Dalloway* took shape. On that summer's day, she wakes up in Richmond (the suburb to which she and her husband, Leonard, had retreated for the sake of her fragile mental health), thinks about her book, entertains her sister, Vanessa Bell, and "Nessa"'s children to tea (they come unexpectedly early), and tries, unsuccessfully, to run off to London, whose noise and bustle she misses. (A frantic Leonard catches up with her outside the train station and fetches her home.) It is no easy or safe thing for a contemporary novelist to ventriloquize a great author who was a novelist herself, but Cunningham approaches his task with great delicacy—and no little erudition: much of the "Mrs. Woolf" section of his book is based on careful reading of Woolf's journals. The "escape" scene, for instance, is based on an episode that Woolf records in an October 15, 1923, diary entry.[1] Cunningham transforms it into a parable about Woolf's artistry, and her bravery—her yearning to have a full life out of which to create her art, whatever the risks.

But the real delight of the "Mrs. Woolf" portions of Cunningham's *The Hours* is its delicate, detailed, and sometimes witty suggestions about how Woolf might have come up with some of the material that appears in *Mrs. Dalloway*. In *The Hours*, Vanessa Bell's children find a dying bird in the garden, and the youngest, her daughter, Angelica Bell, makes an elaborate bier for it out of grass and roses. Peering at the tiny dead thing in its improbable nest, Virginia thinks to herself that "it could be a kind of hat. It could be the missing link between millinery and death." Readers of *Mrs. Dalloway* will remember that the wife of Septimus Smith is an Italian girl who makes hats; she is, indeed, making one just before her shell-shocked husband flings himself out the window. The hat-like bier gives Cunningham's Virginia an even more important idea: that it is not Clarissa who must die (she loves life, the world, too much), but the mad poet. "Clarissa," Virginia thinks, "is the bed in which the bride is laid." Clarissa's life, that is to say—and her

---

[1] "I felt it was intolerable to sit about, & must do the final thing, which was to go to London.... Saw men & women walking together; thought, you're safe & happy I'm an outcast; took my ticket; and 3 minutes to spare, & then, turning the corner of the station stairs, saw Leonard, coming along, bending rather, like a person walking very quick, in his mackintosh. He was rather cold & angry (as, perhaps was natural)."

love of life, the quotidian thoughts and feelings that suggest how good she finds life, and how strong she is—must be the surround, the context, in which the death of the poet, the young man, will stand out as anomalous, impossible to integrate, "other." Another way of putting this is that Virginia will do to her male characters what so many male authors do to their female characters.

IT IS THE THIRD of Cunningham's three women who has no clear referent in either *Mrs. Dalloway* or the life of its author. But this is not to say that Laura Brown, the housewife whose reading of Woolf's novel, one summer's day in 1949, transforms her life, has no basis in Woolf's work. In *A Room of One's Own,* Woolf wryly comments on the ironic way in which (as was the case in ancient Athens, she thinks; one recalls that she worked on her Greek every day) woman is "imaginatively"—i.e., in the works of male writers—"of the greatest importance," while being "completely insignificant" in real life. Hence what one must do to create a fully real woman is

> to think poetically and prosaically at one and the same moment, thus keeping in touch with fact—that she is Mrs. Martin, aged thirty-six, dressed in blue, wearing a black hat and brown shoes; but not losing sight of fiction either—that she is a vessel in which all sorts of spirits and forces are coursing and flashing perpetually.

In Cunningham's novel, Laura Brown is, in fact, just this combination of prose and poetry. Her life is an ostensibly ordinary one—her day consists of sending her husband Dan, a former war hero, off to work, and then baking a birthday cake for him with her little son Richie—but she is not, nor has she ever been, the homecoming queen type. Cunningham goes to considerable lengths to make sure we understand how starkly she stands out against her bland background, "the foreign-looking one with the dark, close-set eyes and the Roman nose," with her Polish maiden name and her passion for books. Privately Laura thinks she could be "brilliant" herself. Tormented by inner demons, seething with inchoate creativity, striking-looking, she is clearly meant to bring to mind Woolf herself; her tragedy, the author suggests, is that her time, culture, and circumstances provide no outlets for her lurking creativity other than domestic ones. Baking cakes, for instance: as Laura sets about her day's work, "she hopes to be as satisfied and as filled with anticipation as a writer putting down the first sentence."

It's really Laura who's the fulcrum of the novel, a hybrid of Clarissa, with her everyday bourgeois preoccupations, and Virginia, the dark, half-mad high priestess of art. And indeed, in the novel's deeply moving conclusion, we get to see how Laura is the bridge that connects Woolf, in 1923, to Clarissa Vaughan, in the 1990s: little Richie, it turns out, grows up to be Clarissa's friend Richard. It is Laura who, through her reading of Woolf (she flees to a hotel in order to finish the book in peace and quiet), understands that the life she's living is somehow terribly wrong for her: she feels she's going mad. And it is Laura who finds reserves of terrible strength to preserve her own sanity, her authentic self. By the end of *The Hours* she's decided to abandon her family after the birth of her second child; we learn later that she moves to Toronto, where she becomes a librarian—another position that places her midway, as it were, between literature and life. Throughout *The Hours,* as throughout *Mrs. Dalloway,* it's the women who are strong, who choose life, who survive.

AND SO CUNNINGHAM'S novel is a very interesting form of "adaptation" indeed: much more than being merely a clever repository of allusions to its model (although these are many and dazzling, and make *The Hours* a kind of scholarly treasure hunt for Woolf lovers), it transposes into a different key, as it were, the constituent elements of Woolf's novel, for the purposes of a serious literary investigation of large (and distinctively Woolfian) themes—the nature of creativity, the role of literature in life, the authentic feel of everyday living. Cunningham has, indeed, found just the right equivalents in today's world for many of the elements you find in *Mrs. Dalloway*. Take that famous head, for example—the apparition, in Woolf's book, that serves as symbol, in a way, for the world that is made by men, for men's literature and men's values—the great world, with its preoccupation with importance and fame and status. In Woolf's novel, people wonder who that briefly glimpsed head could belong to—"the Queen's, the Prince of Wales's, the Prime Minister's?" In Cunningham's book, the scene is replicated, but this time the VIPs come from a slightly different milieu. "Meryl Streep?" they wonder. "Vanessa Redgrave?"

By a bizarre coincidence that the author of *The Hours* cannot have foreseen, the invocation of Streep's and Redgrave's names invites us to consider another kind of adaptation altogether. As it happens, Vanessa Redgrave was the star of the film adaptation of *Mrs. Dalloway,* which appeared in 1998, the same year that Cunningham's novel was published; while Meryl Streep is the star of the film that seems poised to win this year's Best Picture Oscar, Stephen Daldry's recent adaptation of *The Hours.* Daldry's film is, like its model, a grave and beautiful work, and an affecting one, too; like its model, it goes to great lengths to suggest how literature can change the way we lead our lives. For those reasons, it deserves the acclaim it has gotten. And yet elements of the adaptation suggest that it has done to *The Hours* what *The Hours* would not do to *Mrs. Dalloway*.

2.

STEPHEN DALDRY'S FILM ADAPTATION OF CUNNINGHAM'S BOOK shows a good deal more visual imagination than did—which is to say, is a good deal more cinematic than was—his 2000 film *Billy Elliot,* a sentimental Cinderella fable about a working-class boy who dreams of becoming a ballet dancer. The new film is still, essentially, mainstream moviemaking; it saves its energies for communicating, as clearly as possible, the shape of its three narratives, which as in the book are interwoven, episode by episode. (You wouldn't want Daldry to make a film of *Mrs. Dalloway* itself. Indeed, the adaptation of Woolf's novel that starred Vanessa Redgrave, from a script by the actress Eileen Atkins, who played Woolf onstage in her *Vita and Virginia,* failed to convey the fragmented stream-of-consciousness that was Woolf's great achievement in the novel—her new way of "bringing to life" the experience of her ostensibly ordinary heroine.) And yet there are many effective, and affecting, visual touches that reproduce, in filmic terms, the tissues in Cunningham's novel that connect its three female figures. I am not talking here to much of the recurrent images—of eggs being broken, of flowers being placed in pots, of women kissing other women—that appear in each of the three narratives in the film, as I am of smaller but very telling touches, such as the ingenious cross-cutting between the Woolf, Vaughan, and Brown narratives. At the beginning of the film, when it is morning in all three worlds, we see Virginia bending down to wash her face; the head that rises up again to examine itself in the mirror is that of Meryl Streep, as Clarissa Vaughan.

Daldry and his screenwriter, David Hare, have, moreover, clearly thought hard about how to represent elements which, in the book, seem not to be of the highest importance, but which in the film convey the book's concerns in sometimes ravishing visual language. Early on in the novel's presentation of Laura Brown, Cunningham describes the young woman's feelings as she allows herself to be swept away by Woolf's fiction:

> She is taken by a wave of feeling, a sea-swell, that rises from under her breast and buoys her, floats her gently, as if she were a sea creature thrown back from the sand where it had beached itself.

Daldry and Hare transpose this minor moment to Laura's visit to the hotel, where it becomes an image that reminds us, in a complex way, just how "carried away" a woman can get by writing: in one of the film's most original moments (one spoiled, for the audience, by its inclusion in the theater trailers and television commercials for the film, which has resulted in a deadening of its impact in the theater), we see the pale, beautiful Julianne Moore, who plays Laura, lying on her hotel bed when suddenly the rushing waters of a river—the Ouse, surely—flood the room, buoying and then submerging her and the bed. It's just after the striking fantasy sequence involving the river waters that Laura realizes she can't kill herself. (In Daldry's film—but not in the book—the young mother has brought a number of bottles of prescription pills with her to the hotel, and we're meant to understand that she intends to take her life there.)

MORE OF A PROBLEM, inevitably, was the film's representation of Woolf herself. Much has been made of the prosthetic nose used to transform Nicole Kidman into Woolf for the purposes of the film, but while the fake nose has the virtue of making Kidman look less distractingly like an early-twenty-first-century movie star, it also coarsens the Woolf that we do see; the frumpy creature we see on screen, clumping around in a housedress, breathing heavily through a broad, flat, putty-colored nose, bears little resemblance to the fine-boned, strikingly delicate woman that you see in almost any photograph of Woolf, whose mother was a famous beauty, and who herself was memorably described by Nigel Nicolson, who knew her, as "always beautiful but never pretty."[2] Without the prosthesis, Kidman is pretty without being beautiful; with it, she is neither.

The physical appearance of the film's Woolf is only worth mentioning because it may be taken as a symbol of the ways in

---

[2]Nigel Nicolson, *Virginia Woolf* (Lipper/Viking, 2000), p. 4.

which the film's attempts to invoke Woolf herself, or her work, have the effect of flattening or misrepresenting her—not only Cunningham's carefully researched, if idiosyncratically reimagined, character, but also the real person. In Hare's script, for instance, Virginia announces that she's not going to kill off Mrs. Dalloway, as she'd originally intended; instead, she says, she's going to kill off the mad poet. (This is the bit that corresponds to Woolf's insight about the "bride of death" in the novel.) After Vanessa and the children have left, Leonard asks Virginia why she has to kill the poet. Because, Virginia announces, "someone has to die in order that the rest of us should value life more. The poet will die. The visionary." It is true that you can go back to *Mrs. Dalloway* and find there a climactic passage in which Clarissa Dalloway muses, on hearing of Septimus's suicide (it turns out that the young man's doctor is a guest at her party, and so she hears, as a piece of idle gossip, what has happened to him), that "she felt glad that he had done it; thrown it away. . . . He made her feel the beauty; made her feel the fun." But this is an implied comment on Clarissa, and how she thinks about things; the scene in the film, by contrast, suggests that it's a philosophical statement by Virginia Woolf herself: that poets must die so that the rest of us will appreciate the beauty of life, and so forth.

It is true that the film, like the book, focuses on a small sliver of Woolf's life: the moment in Richmond immediately prior to her return to London. But it is still a serious problem that little about this frumpy cinematic Woolf suggests just why she loves London so much; you get no sense of Woolf as the confident, gossip-loving queen of Bloomsbury, the vivid social figure, the amusing diarist, the impressively productive journalist expertly maneuvering her professional obligations—and relationships. (There's a lot more of the real Virginia Woolf in her Clarissa Dalloway than this film would ever lead you to believe.) If anything, the film's Woolf is just one half (if that much) of the real Woolf, and it's no coincidence that it's the half that satisfies a certain cultural fantasy, going back to early biographies of Sappho, about what creative women are like: distracted, isolated, doomed.

THERE ARE OTHER SHIFTS from the novel to the film that distort the female characters in Cunningham's book just as much, and to similar ends. It is strange, coming directly from the novel to Daldry's movie, to see the central element of Clarissa Vaughan's story—the unexpected visit from Richard's old lover Louis, who bursts into tears; a canny reincarnation of the scene in *Mrs. Dalloway* in which Clarissa's old flame Peter Walsh comes to see her and weeps uncontrollably—turned inside out. For in the film, it's Clarissa who goes to pieces in front of Louis. "I don't know what's happening," Meryl Streep says as she stands in her kitchen, cooking for her party. "I seem to be unraveling. . . . Explain to me why this is happening. . . . It's just too much." Her voice, as she says these lines, cracks on the verge of hysteria. Cunningham's (and Woolf's) book places Clarissa at the center of her story: she is the subject of ruminations about objects that are male—surprisingly weak or emotionally fractured males. Daldry and Hare's film may look as if it's putting Clarissa at the center of her story—Streep's the star, after all, or one of the three gifted stars—but what the makers of the film are doing, it occurs to you, is exactly what Woolf worried that men did in their fictional representations of women: seeing women from the perspective of men.

In the film these men include, indeed, not only Louis, who in the scene just mentioned sympathetically comforts the helpless Clarissa, but Richard too. In Cunningham's novel, there's a passing moment in which Clarissa Vaughan ruefully thinks to herself that she is "trivial, endlessly trivial" (she's fretting because Sally, a producer of documentaries, hasn't invited her along to lunch with a gay movie star); but in the film, she's worried what *Richard* thinks. "He gives me that look to say 'your life is trivial, you are trivial,'" Streep says, her voice quavering. For Hare and Daldry, a woman's story must, it seems, involve the spectacle of women in danger of losing their self-possession in front of their men. An old-fashioned "woman's drama," that is to say.

This is even clearer in the Laura Brown portions of the film. Gone are Laura's darkness, her hidden "brilliance," her foreign looks and last name: here, she is transformed into the exceedingly fair Julianne Moore, who has made a name for herself in a number of films about outwardly perfect young women who are losing their inner balance (as in this year's *Far from Heaven,* and the 1995 film *Safe*). But to make Laura into a prom queen inverts the delicate dynamic of the novel—the structure that makes you aware of Laura's latent poetic qualities, her latent similarities to Woolf. In the book, her madness is that of a poet who has not found a voice; in the film, she's yet another Fifties housewife whose immaculate exterior conceals deep, inchoate dissatisfactions. (I found it interesting that in the film, the date for the Mrs. Brown sections has been move from 1949, as in Cunningham's novel, to 1951; I suspect it's because the latter dovetails better with our own cultural clichés about the repressed Fifties. Laura's maiden name has been changed, too, from Zielski, as it is in the book, to McGrath.) And in the film, we should remember, Laura goes to the hotel for the day not to read, but to commit suicide, whereas in the novel the idea of self-annihilation occurs to her only once she's in the hotel, and then only fleetingly.[3]

And so this Laura, rather than being unusual and complex, is closer to a cliché of domestic repression than she is to Cunningham's character. No wonder that, in a key scene in the film—one that gives away its creators' prejudices, you suspect—this Laura gets *Mrs. Dalloway* so wrong. When she has a

---

[3]That Laura may have more dire intentions is possibly suggested by an abstruse literary allusion on Cunningham's part that has nothing to do with Woolf. Laura checks in to Room 19 at the Normandy Hotel—the same room and hotel where the heroine of Doris Lessing's story "To Room Nineteen" commits suicide.

visit from her neighbor Kitty (whose vibrancy and seeming good health are intended by Cunningham to suggest those of Vanessa Bell, whom the real Virginia Woolf thought "the most complete human being of us all"), Kitty—clearly not a great reader—asks about the copy of *Mrs. Dalloway* she sees lying on the kitchen counter. Laura replies by describing it as a story about a woman who's giving a party and "maybe because she's confident everyone thinks she's fine, but she isn't."

The problem is that Woolf's Clarissa *is* fine; as are Cunningham's Clarissa and his Woolf, and even his Laura, three women who understand, in their different ways, that, as Clarissa Vaughan realizes on the last page of the novel, "it is, in fact, great good fortune" to be alive. "Everyone thinks she's fine, but she isn't" is, on the other hand, a perfect description of Laura as she appears in this film: flawless, the American dream, on the outside, but unraveling on the inside. Which is to say, a character in a film we've seen many times.

AT THE CONCLUSION of *A Room of One's Own,* Woolf summed up her reasons for thinking that women should have a literature of their own: "The truth is, I often like women," she wrote. "I like their unconventionality. I like their subtlety. I like their anonymity. I like—but I must not run on in this way." I think Michael Cunningham likes women, too; his book's female characters are unconventional and subtle—the "anonymous" housewife more so, if anything, than the others. I also think that, at one level, the makers of the new film of Cunningham's book like women, too. Rarely has a mainstream film offered three more interesting roles for three more accomplished actresses, each of whom makes the most of an admittedly rare opportunity: there are moments—not least, a climactic encounter in Clarissa Vaughan's apartment between Clarissa's young daughter, Julia, and the now aged Laura Brown—that will make you cry. (I did.)

But I think these filmmakers like women in the way Virginia Woolf fears that male writers liked, and used, women: these female figures are, in the end, more conventional, less subtle than what either Cunningham or Woolf had in mind. They are, in other words, more like the women we already know from the books and films that men make about women: the self-destructive, glowering, mad poetess; the picture-perfect Fifties housewife slowly cracking up in her flawless mid-century modern décor; the contemporary lesbian frazzled by the effort of caring for her best friend with AIDS, a woman who goes to pieces on her kitchen floor while wearing rubber gloves.

Still, *The Hours* is a serious and moving film, one that achieves many of its goals; among other things, it will presumably have many, many more people reading *Mrs. Dalloway* than Woolf could ever have dreamed of. That is no mean accomplishment. Perhaps it was inevitable that, of all the elements you find in her great novel, the one that the film should have reproduced most successfully is Mrs. Dalloway's sense that what is truly strange, unconventional, and subtle must be sacrificed so the rest of us might feel the beauty, feel the fun.

MARCH 13, 2003
The New York Review of Books

SIGRID NUNEZ

On Rereading *Mrs. Dalloway*

*H*ERE IS MY COPY OF THE PAPERBACK EDITION OF *MRS. DAL-
loway* that I read for the first time more than thirty years ago. It
has my name in it because at that time I wrote my name in all
my books. Tucked inside the front cover is the stub from a ticket
to the play *Vita & Virginia* (Union Square Theatre, December
21, 1994), which I saw with a friend with whom I have since
fallen out. In that play the role of Vita Sackville-West was played
by Vanessa Redgrave, who was to play the role of Clarissa Dalloway in the movie version of *Mrs. Dalloway* that was made several years later. (The movie was a bore, the play great fun.) Also
tucked inside my copy of *Mrs. Dalloway* is a clipping from the
New York Times Book Review, which reprinted a letter from Vita
to Virginia dated Wednesday, December 1, 1926. ("Last night I
went to bed very early and read *Mrs. Dalloway*. It was a very curious sensation: I thought you were in the room———") It is a
letter that was clearly written under the influence of Woolf's
prose, and it is a love letter. My copy of *Mrs. Dalloway* has tiny
notches at the top of the spine; these were inflicted by Percival,

the very large brown-and-white rabbit I used to live with who had the awful habit of gnawing books. Every time I see such tooth marks (his taste was not limited to Woolf) I miss Percival; and, seeing the ticket stub, I miss my friend with whom I had the falling out and who, as it happens, once wrote a poem about that rabbit and his habit of gnawing books. No, I did not name the rabbit after the character in *The Waves*.

Mrs. Dalloway was the first novel by Virginia Woolf that I read. It would not be my favorite. *To the Lighthouse* and *The Waves* are better novels, and *Between the Acts* is her best. Around the same time I read *Mrs. Dalloway,* I also read *A Room of One's Own, A Writer's Diary,* and the Quentin Bell biography whose publication the year I graduated from college was drawing huge attention to Bloomsbury, to which, of course, much attention had been paid already. In those days of Women's Liberation, it meant a great deal that Woolf was a feminist. It mattered deeply that this indisputably first-rate mind had concerned itself with, among other things, what it meant not only to be a writer but also to be a woman and a woman writer. It mattered so much partly because so many contemporary women who were writers, including feminists, did not want that label "woman writer" pinned to their breast for any reason. (Still true.) And it mattered that she was not the kind of feminist who would *ever* give up reading men.

Long before reading *Mrs. Dalloway* I knew that I wanted to be a writer and that I wanted to write fiction. Now I thought I had discovered the kind of fiction I might try to write. To begin with, Woolf had broken certain rules that I had begun to find irksome. Here was proof that a novel—a great novel—could "show" nothing, in the conventional sense; could be all "tell." Repetition, rather than being something always conscientiously to avoid, could be used lavishly, to sublime effect. Plot could be forsaken, the development of character ignored. One day in the life of an ordinary middle-aged woman—thoughts of an intense, perceptive, sensitive mind—this in itself could make a narrative.

Form, style—beautiful sentences—were what mattered most. It was a revelation: A novel could be like a poem. Certainly, this was what Woolf was after in *Mrs. Dalloway,* and there was no doubt in my mind that she had succeeded. To read her as a young woman who hoped to write novels one day was to be a disciple. Everything I wrote during this time was some sort of feeble imitation of Woolf. And here is a question I don't remember ever asking myself: If the beauty of the writing was all that mattered, why should I have been hurt when people said of some story of mine, as they often did, It's beautifully written, *but...?*

Time passed. I read the other novels, I read the essays. Now came the years when the complete diaries and letters began to be published, and I read each new volume the moment it appeared, and I could hardly wait for the next one. There were long periods when I read so much Woolf and so hungrily that it often felt as though I were feeding off her as much as reading her. And many readers—writers especially, women writers above all—have fed off Woolf in this same way. With the publication of so much "life-writing," to use her own phrase for the genre (her favorite genre, according to her diary), the private world stood fully revealed. It was now possible to know more or less what Virginia Woolf had done almost every day of her adult life. It was possible to imagine that you knew her better than you knew your own friends. There was, most importantly, the detailed record of the painstaking efforts she put into her writing, the challenges she set herself with each new work, the depth and breadth of her reading, her formidable self-discipline, her stoical attitude toward criticism. And that she was not merely able to carry on but to triumph, over and over, her whole life long, despite bouts of psychosis and paralyzing depression, made her almost superhuman. She was a genius in art and a heroine in life. She was the Goddess of Literature. I was at her feet.

In the beginning I must have taken it for granted that everyone I admired—every writer, anyway—must love Woolf as I did, unconditionally. But it was not so among those I would meet just out of school, working at the *New York Review of Books*. I am talking about people whose opinions could not have been more important to me. Susan Sontag suggested that my passion for Woolf was something I would outgrow. Joseph Brodsky placed her well below such moderns as Proust and Joyce. Elizabeth Hardwick, with whom I had taken college courses in writing, published in the *Review* an essay, "Bloomsbury and Virginia Woolf," that came to the conclusion that "in a sense her novels aren't interesting." For Hardwick, this was "part of the risk of setting a goal in fiction, of having an idea about it, an abstract idea." Hardwick also had serious questions about the character Doris Kilman: "the object of the author's" (and not merely Mrs. Dalloway's) "insolent loathing." She accuses Woolf of "bad taste" and even sadism in her portrait of the embittered, perspiring, greedy, ugly-green-mackintosh-wearing, lower-class Kilman. "It doesn't matter to us that she hates a woman like Miss Kilman; we'd rather not be told."

I don't remember exactly when I read *Mrs. Dalloway* a second time. I know I had yet to accomplish anything as a writer myself, but by then a significant change had occurred in my life. Like Septimus Warren Smith, I had lost "a sense of proportion." I had had a total breakdown. I had been confined unwillingly to a quiet place (where it was no longer "You must rest in bed" but "You must take your medication"). Reading the novel for the second time, I remember thinking that, for all she knew what she was talking about, Woolf had not succeeded in making madness... *interesting*. By then I was also aware of the judgment of Louise Bogan, who records in one of her own journals her response to *A Writer's Diary*. Woolf is "a monster of egotism." And: "How I have always disliked *Mrs. Dalloway*, with its attempt to *care* for the poor young man." But Woolf did not "care," in the way I take Bogan to mean, about any of her characters. Bogan, who also suffered breakdowns and had experience of mental homes and psychiatrists, also disliked *Mrs. Dalloway* for "its hatred of doctors." Surely Holmes and Bradshaw, the

doctors who treat the psychologically damaged war veteran Septimus, are cartoon villains, indeed no more than targets for
Woolf's hatred and scorn, and surely it strains belief to have Dr.
Holmes cry "The coward!" at the moment Septimus has thrown
himself from a window to his death—and in the presence of the
victim's poor wife, no less. But much of *Mrs. Dalloway* strains
belief. We know that realism was not what Woolf was after. *Reality,* however, was a different matter. To dig beneath the surface,
to get at what lies behind the appearance of things, was always
her aim as a novelist, and we feel that she succeeds so well because so much of her writing has the ring of truth.

So: Here is my old copy with its two mementoes, ticket stub
and newspaper clipping. And what do I remember of this novel
I have read already twice? That it was one of the most beautiful
books I had ever read, that it gave me goose bumps, that it was
like no other book I had read, that it made me want to read
everything its author had written, that it made me want to write.
Some sentences had stayed with me from my first reading. The
famous opening: "Mrs. Dalloway said she would buy the flowers
herself." The famous last words: "For there she was." The early
description of Big Ben chiming—"The leaden circles dissolved
in the air"—which is repeated three more times in the book.
How people are often described as sitting or standing "upright"
or "very upright" or "perfectly upright." Punctuation: extravagant use of parentheses; semicolons where the reader might reasonably expect commas (doubtless to achieve the desired beat).
I remember all this. But Mrs. Dalloway? She does not live in
the memory the way many other literary characters do: Anna
Karenina, for example, or Daniel Deronda. It is the language I
remember (and wasn't this, after all, what the author said she
wanted?); it is the imagery (birds, skies, flowers, London gardens, London streets), the lovely, haunting cadences. And, always with Woolf, the death's-head showing through the fine
lace. Not the people, not what does or does not happen to
them, but the piercing beauty and sadness of the Woolfian vi-

sion is what lives on. It is like remembering a performance of Schubert.

I often thought I might someday write something about Woolf, and if I ever did it must be some kind of homage.

I had published two novels. I had read *Flush,* the least known of Woolf's novels, a mock biography of Elizabeth Barrett Browning's cocker spaniel. Remembering that the Woolfs had owned a pet monkey that had lived and traveled with them for several years in the 1930s, I made it the subject of a Life. Writing *Mitz: The Marmoset of Bloomsbury* meant many hours of rereading letters and diaries and researching other Bloomsbury documents. As it happened, the year I began doing this work was not a happy one for me; it was another period of personal upheaval, and retreating to the Bloomsbury sanctuary for a few hours each day was both a distraction and a solace.

Reading *Mrs. Dalloway* for the third and, I would say, probably the last time, I am struck by the book's artifice: specifically, the coincidences that bring Peter Walsh and Sally Seton, those major figures from Clarissa Dalloway's past—the two great loves of her life, neither of whom she has seen in years and both of whom just happen to be dominating her thoughts this very day—back to London, back into Clarissa's life, and, of course, to her party. And how the moment we see Septimus fling himself to his gruesome death we can be sure that some other character (it turns out to be Peter Walsh) will just happen to pass by, thinking some elevated thought (in this case, that the ambulance is "one of the triumphs of civilisation"). I don't recall being struck, much less troubled, by this kind of manipulation before (it is pure Woolf, after all). But there is something else that strikes and troubles me more, and it is this: moving constantly with the narrative from the mind of one character to another and, within the mind of each, back and forth in time as the character muses on his or her past, the present moment, or the future, why—no matter the character's age, sex, class, level of education, occupation, personality type, degree of sanity—why do I find these minds all more or less the same? This is true for the most part even of the very minor characters, such as Maisie Johnson ("only up from Edinburgh two days ago"), who happens to cross paths with Septimus and his wife in Regent's Park. In general (and not just in this novel), Woolf's characters tend to notice the same kind of things, to draw the same conclusions about what they see, and to be emotionally affected in the same way. All are obsessive and easily stirred. They all talk to themselves, usually with the same oracular blue streak; they all repeat little phrases such as "Fear no more" or "The death of the soul" or "It is the flesh." They are all highly susceptible to impressions; they are all terribly sensitive to nature; they all seem to have read Shelley and Shakespeare and Plato; they are all aesthetes; they are all mystics; they all have the same nostalgic relationship to the past; and they all use the same elaborate metaphors to interpret life and the human condition. Everyone is death-haunted, everyone is a poet, everyone is neurotic, everyone is a genius, everyone is Virginia Woolf.

And so, again and again, the reader has the uneasy feeling that the streams of thoughts sent gushing through the minds of the characters, from Mrs. Dalloway to Maisie Johnson, are too sophisticated for them. We do not believe these brilliant, original thoughts except as having come from the brilliant, original mind of the author. This might be less of a problem were the characters shown a little more from the outside, but Woolf will not give us this. It is strange. We know that she was a keen observer of other people, unusually perceptive about human nature and behavior (just read the letters); yet it is almost as if she were incapable of imagining any character that was not herself.

Perhaps one could argue that the language of consciousness is universal. Do not most people believe that all of us when we sleep, no matter how different we are, dream alike? Is there any reason to think we do not? Perhaps Woolf would argue that her goal (her duty, even) was to express her characters' inner lives as purely and eloquently and articulately as the characters themselves would express them, had they a novelist's gifts. Perhaps. But I remain unconvinced that people so various would wear such similar, interchangeable heads. If I have exaggerated above, it has not been by much, and on this reading it struck me full force: Mrs. Dalloway is not a character; she is a medium.

And not all the writing is good. "It was her punishment to see sink and disappear here a man, there a woman, in this profound darkness, and she forced to stand here in her evening dress. She had schemed; she had pilfered." (It is remarkable that no one has thought to initiate a bad Woolf contest, like the bad Hemingway contest.)

One more thing Louise Bogan disliked about *Mrs. Dalloway*: "Its frightful sentimentality." Bogan may have been thinking specifically of Woolf's romantic treatment of insanity, but the criticism could be made about much of this effusive book.

Flannery O'Connor thought Woolf had been compelled to use the novel as a laboratory. Elizabeth Hardwick calls Woolf "a theorist of fiction" and speaks admiringly of "the risk . . . of the bravest and most daring insistence that she would make something new." But for Bogan, Woolf "was not an innovator, in any true sense."

"Her work was the first definitive expression in the English novel of the whole, self-tortured modern consciousness, together with the precise idiom in which it does its thinking. . . . She masters her subject not by analyzing it from a strategic angle, but by achieving complete identity with it throughout."

Who else could these words be about but Virginia Woolf? Haven't we heard one version or another of them a hundred times? But, of course, these words were written not about Virginia Woolf but about Dorothy Richardson. They are the words of Wilson Follett, and they are quoted by Louise Bogan in a paper on women writers that she gave at Bennington College in 1962. And it is to Richardson, novelist and feminist, born the same year as Woolf and dying unknown sixteen years after Woolf's death, that Bogan awards the palm for true innovation, reminding us that it was Richardson who invented the stream-of-consciousness technique that Woolf was to use to such splendid effect.

Returning the much-read, rabbit-eaten *Mrs. Dalloway* to the bookshelf, I make a prediction: In future when I want to read Woolf, more likely I will go to the nonfiction.

And here is another hunch I have, not about the future but about the past. Had she wished to, in addition to her immortal achievements in other genres, Woolf could have written the greatest children's books of the age. There is much to suggest this, beginning, of course, with her extraordinary powers of imagination and verbal invention, the vividness and clarity of her prose, and the hushed, distilled quality that makes you bring the book a little closer to your nose. But there is also her love of animals, her high spirits, her playful and affectionate nature, her sense of comedy, the rocking-horse rhythm she sometimes gets into (*she rocks!*), her ability to cast a spell, and her child's sense of wonder about even the most ordinary things, which she herself never lost and which, with the generosity of the artist of genius, she keeps giving back to you. Of the thousands of letters Woolf wrote, some as beautiful as anything in her fiction, I do not love any one of them more than No. 3313, written to six-year-old Elaine Robson and quoted here in full.

> *I liked your poem and your story very much indeed. I have not seen a rabbit washing his ceiling but yesterday I saw a hare who was making a warm bed for his winter lodging in the marsh. He had just laid down a nice blanket made of thistledown when he saw me and ran away. His bed was quite hot, and I put a mushroom there for him to eat. The marsh is full of mushrooms. I wish you and Daddy and Mummie were all here to pick them and then we would cook them and have them for supper. I also saw a kingfisher. His bed is in the bank of the river but I have never found it. Sally has had a thorn in her paw and we have had to*

poultice it. At last the thorn came out and her paw is only as big as a penny bun. It was as big as a soup plate. Mitzi had a macaroon for breakfast this morning. When you are in London will you come to tea with us and make a binding for your lovely poem and story. Do you like writing prose or poetry best. This typewriter cannot spell and sometimes uses the wrong type. xxxxxx Uncle Leonard sends his love: Sally has just barked her love also and Mitz bit me in the ear which means she sends you her love too.

Your affectionate Aunt Virginia

JUNE 2003

DEBORAH EISENBERG

On *Mrs. Dalloway*

A RATHER UNREMARKABLE WOMAN SPENDS THE DAY PREPAR-
ing for the party she is to give that evening. Two old friends arrive unexpectedly in time for the party. At the party, the hostess
happens to learn that a stranger has committed suicide during
the course of the day. An unpromising set of suppositions for a
novel, you might think, if that's the way *Mrs. Dalloway* was described to you. You might expect something random, mundane,
and static, or else bloated and heavy with melodrama. But what
you would actually find, if you were to read it anyway, is something aerial, alive with motion and free of melodrama, a marvel
of tensile strength.

A novel has to carry us the length of its pages. And we are
generally accustomed to being moved along by a sequence of
related events that will culminate in an ending that is their sum
or result. If it is a good novel, this sequence will be convincing
or, at the least, plausible: "This" happened, and so, under the
circumstances, "This" was likely to occur. Or even: And so,

under the circumstances, absolutely nothing *but* "This" could have occurred.

A gripping narrative, though, can sometimes leave us a little uneasy. We feel: Yes, but—in the real world, the *truly* real world, does C *really* happen *because* of B? Does B *really* happen *because* of A? This is a matter that has, I gather, been mulled over quite a bit by various philosophers, and it troubles some of us less strictly cerebral people, too. We're fairly confident that one thing happens *after* another, but how deeply do we believe that one thing happens *because* of another? From time to time, wandering out around the frontiers of our consciousness, a suspicion overtakes us that this implicitly causal view of sequence, which is at the foundation of most novels and so habitual to our thinking, is nothing more than a conceptual expedient that gets us from moment to moment in daily life with a little peace of mind.

Though there are occasions when reading for sheer diversion will do nicely, at other times—when one's life feels not quite convincing, a little foggy, or inchoate—one picks up a book, vaguely in hopes of finding something solid and shapely, a missing piece of the puzzle. And on these occasions we're in no mood to waste time with expedients.

The (horrible) sensation of wasting time has less to do with the thing one is doing, whether it is playing computer solitaire or reading, than with the feeling that one is allocating one's resources poorly, the awareness that only a small part of ourselves is active. And reading a novel can dishearten us by making us feel how stark and mechanical, how insufficient, our customary unexamined causal view of behavior and events actually is. We think, if the formula is too thin and inadequate for a work of fiction, then how much more satisfactory can it be as a model for understanding our lives? And we feel that we have allowed ourselves to be duped by our own desire for an easy way to think about things. That such a view accounts for far too little is, in a work of fiction, most painfully evident.

In our spates of urgent reading, we look to fiction for insight. We want it *all* accounted for. We ask that the author dispose of the trash of our daily existence, the rinds and lint and chatter, and disclose the hidden world. We ask that the author arouse sleeping and neglected areas of our mind so that we may be receptive to this vision. At its most ardent and seeking, the desire to read fiction is a desire for an intense and mysterious encounter, a glimpse of the richness we believe to be lying beyond the fuzz and static — a brush with the essential.

A person is born and some time later dies; a certain number of things are bound to happen within those borders. We read for the fun of learning what things a life might encompass and also for the much more gratifying feeling that we are capable of understanding why those particular things fit together and what it is in them that springs from that particular life's core. No matter how noisy and passion-filled, no matter how antic or clever, no matter how "heartwarming" a work of fiction is, it will be no less tedious than the stack of bills waiting on the desk if it seems merely invented or assembled. And when we are reading for dear life, the book that fails to persuade us that its events are truly of a piece, that they have a profound, indubitable relationship to each other, goes sailing across the room; and we return to wasting time on our own terms.

Mrs. Dalloway is perhaps peerlessly brisk and easeful in the way it puts us in direct contact with the workings of the world. It seems to penetrate effortlessly through a thick mantle of incidentals, way down to the very plasma of human life and the mechanism that regulates it. And perhaps that is largely due to the fact that those causal relationships, which generally appear to be indispensable in relaying a story, are simply left out of the recipe here.

Was it inevitable, for example, that Clarissa would marry Richard rather than marrying Peter (or for that matter, running off with Sally Seton)? Maybe it was, given Clarissa's character and circumstances; but then again, maybe it wasn't. We aren't deeply concerned with that matter and neither is the book. What interests us is what *is,* not *why* it is or how it has come to be. And although Clarissa reflects on her choice of Richard casually in retrospect, and although on the whole her choice seems probably to have been a good one, we don't really examine it in order to evaluate it, we simply note that it was, in fact, a choice and enjoy its various emotional values. Clarissa's thoughts on her past engage us primarily because those are her thoughts today, they are part of the constantly modulating tone of the day, not because they offer any particular explanation. The nimbus of unrealized possibilities certainly gives depth to each personality and exchange, but the truly interesting fact of the matter is that Clarissa is married to Richard.

Furthermore, the book simply dispenses with our workaday assumptions in regard to priorities. Every moment of the day to which Woolf directs our attention arrives with an equal weight. Whether it is a moment that we ourselves—if we were observing the events—might automatically consider "trivial" (Clarissa entering a flower shop) or one that we would consider "significant" (Septimus's sudden, heartstopping lucidity as his wife trims a hat), each fragment of time comes to us here with the full status of human experience. Each thing that is thought, each thing that is done, is no more or less part of the composition of the day, just as no number, whether it is a big number or a small number, functions differently from any other. Even those of us who feel at times all but suffocated by Woolf's straight-faced portrait of London between the wars, with its rigid and barely conscious habits of empire and class, experience, for example, silly Hugh Whitbread's pursuit of his civic responsibilities as an element of life being lived that is equal in weight to all other elements of life being lived.

But if there is no strongly felt impress of causality or prioritization of events, something else is going to have to make the events in a novel cohere. In daily life we assume that coincidence, like causality, operates to join a certain number of things. But in a book, how much less convincing coincidence is than causality! Of course coincidences simply must squeak by in books now and then, but each one incurs a cost to credibility, and sometimes while we're reading, we really have to look the other way.

And yet, as we go through our days, we have a persistent intuition of living within something embracing and systemic, and we long to see it at work. We've all read books (and seen many movies) in which the author tosses an assortment of characters and episodes into the pot and then apparently just hopes for the best. Someone does X, for example, and some entirely other person does Y! How about *that,* we're evidently supposed to think; different things happen at *the very same time*—isn't *that* just the mystery of life!

Septimus, in the throes of manic grandiosity, believes that he is about to grasp the substance of this mystery, that it is encoded everywhere just awaiting his penetrating gaze. We feel wrenchingly the tragedy of this delusion. And yet, as we read *Mrs. Dalloway,* we grow convinced that we ourselves are actually being shown something of the mystery of life — an integral connection between things.

Woolf creates for us a world that consists entirely of relationships — a weave. This weave, the book's claim, is a different and more modest claim than Septimus's. Just as we are given to see in the book not *why* something has become but that it *has* become, we are given to see not *how* things are related but *that* they are.

Every bit of the book is active; everything is manifestly a moving part in a moving whole. And however we wish to describe Woolf's view of reality, *Mrs. Dalloway* is an organism, not a case being made; you can almost feel it breathe as you read. "What she liked was simply life," we are told of Clarissa as she justifies to herself her attention to her parties. And that's what the book likes, too. The hands of the clocks rotate, the leaden circles of Big Ben striking the hour dissolve. The spectators squint at the dissolving skywriting—its import (perhaps a different import to each) was just about to be disclosed! The buses flow through London carrying Clarissa's daughter as well as Clarissa at the age her daughter is now, and there is phantom water and glistening light everywhere. The sentences zing from here to there; they seem to have springs in them. We are simultaneously in London and at Bourton. We see Clarissa, her husband, and their friends in a middle age that incorporates their youth. We see Septimus's life shattering in the war, the fragments glittering in the light of the past and of the present.

Clarissa and the old woman she observes in the window contain one another. Clarissa and Septimus contain one another. Humanity appears now in one aspect, now in another. The planes of experience glide across each other, superimposing the characters in this situation or that. Everything shimmers, recombines, reflects. Death is the omnipresent background against which Woolf's map of the day glows vibrantly. Life strains against the gravitational force of death, toward its holdings, while death's lieutenants, the false healers Drs. Holmes and Bradshaw stalk among the living, sniffing out the wounded, throwing a freezing shadow over all the twinkling and rustling. It is successful and satisfied Clarissa who is privileged to choose the flowers, and it is ruined and anguished Septimus who is condemned to die, but these two strangers—their different sex, circumstances, class, and psyches notwithstanding—are connected to one another profoundly and intimately, even down to their shared lack of dexterity.

Mrs. Dalloway places its characters on a multidimensional grid whose powerful coordinates are spatial, temporal, and social. When one of the characters situated along these coordinates moves, we feel the entire, sensitive structure respond. It is the whole we see in each detail, the composition of the instant, today, right now. "Lolloping on the waves and braiding her tresses she seemed, having that gift still; to be;" Peter thinks, watching Clarissa move through her party, "to exist; to sum it all up in the moment as she passed . . ." And watching by Peter's side, we see Clarissa as he does and glimpse the great entity, too.

JUNE 2003

ELISSA SCHAPPELL

That Sort of Woman

"MRS. DALLOWAY SAID SHE WOULD BUY THE FLOWERS HERSELF."
I remember reading this line in college and thinking, "Oh wow, big deal." Judging from the margin notes I wrote in my copy of *Mrs. Dalloway* at the time —*Lesbian? Incredibly modern form for the time! War is hell.*—I didn't exactly immerse myself in the text. I wasn't interested in a book about class, and I was impatient with the drifting point of view, and anyway, I thought, I knew the sort of woman Mrs. Dalloway was. That was it, I knew what sort of woman Mrs. Dalloway was, and she didn't interest me one whit. I was nineteen, and Mrs. Dalloway seemed to me to be the very picture of a sort of woman I grew up with, the sort of woman I imagined occupying her hours with Junior League business, flower arranging, and all manner of gossip. The sort of woman who would swear until her teeth turned black that everything was fine, just fine, as she smiled at her husband's business associates and their wives, smiled at the neighbors, while balling up her own desires like a dirty napkin, all for the good of the family. The sort of woman who would, as

Clarissa Dalloway does, lament the tragedy of decorum that allows a suicide to be discussed openly at a party. I vowed that I would never be such a frivolous, ridiculous woman. In my mind women like Mrs. Dalloway had never suffered, had no private lives and no secrets.

The only part I liked, really liked, was the shell-shocked Septimus Smith fleeing the doctor he is sure is going to institutionalize him, throwing himself out the window of his home, and impaling himself on an iron fence. In my own adolescent and grandiose bouts of self-pity and depression I could imagine doing the same thing.

IN THE SUMMER of 1991 my husband and I rented a cottage in a tiny fishing village in the Alentejo region of Portugal. We'd gone there in the hopes of writing the elusive Great American Novel. Among the books I packed was *Mrs. Dalloway*. I hadn't meant to pack it. I meant to pack *The Waves*. *Mrs. Dalloway* had, through some act of fate, just ended up in my belongings.

When we first arrived in Portugal, I hadn't time to read much or, for that matter, write, because we spent the better part of our time exploring the coves along the beach and driving through the Portuguese countryside with its cork trees and lemon groves. After about a week, a friend came to visit. It came to pass that during the day he and my husband would leave early in the morning and go off and ride bikes together, disappearing for hours to return home sunburned and full of stories—the town with the chapel made completely of bones, a village that had a raven chained in the middle of the square. I was jealous of the time they spent together. They seemed to talk endlessly and effortlessly with each other, about art and politics and music, while I found myself resentful and sullen, sniping at my husband, the two of us falling into long periods of silence.

Come with us, they'd say sometimes, but I didn't. It was not just that I wasn't much of a rider; I knew they'd have more fun without me; they were asking me to be nice—which I couldn't bear—and anyway, I was going to write my book. I sat and I typed. I got up and went to the market. I bought bread and I bought cheese and I made pots of fish soup. I washed our clothes in the sink and hung them to dry outside on the line. I waited for the men to return. Was this what being a wife was?

Back in America I was a wife, sure, but I was a wife with friends, I was a writer, and a daughter, and a sister, and a friend, and, of course, a wife—but in Portugal what was I?

I was nothing. I was supposed to be a writer, but I wasn't writing anything worth a scratch. I was a daughter and a sister, but I couldn't see my family or speak to them much. I was supposed to be a friend, but after a month I began wearying of our friend's constant companionship and wanted him to leave.

I missed having big raucous dinner parties at our house. Parties fueled by cheap red wine and pot, parties that went on into the night with people sleeping over on couches and on the floor, then waking at noon and staying for pancakes. I missed feeling necessary in my friends' lives. I was not necessary to anyone, in any way here. Not even my husband, it seemed. I missed my friends, missed my family. My life was dull. Some afternoons I walked up along the cliffs and brought back eucalyptus and yellow flowers. I cut flowers from the garden outside our cottage—verbena, wild ginger, and the uncultivated pink roses, with their small hair-like thorns soft and red at the tip, their blossoms flat, uncomplicated, and full open.

I sat at the kitchen table and wrote badly for long hours, listening over and over again to tapes of music friends had made for me. I sat on the roof of our house and tried to read; I wanted something easy, something light, nothing that would challenge me to feel anything, so I picked up *Mrs. Dalloway,* annoyed that I had brought the wrong book. I opened it prepared to feel superior to dull old Mrs. Dalloway, with her arms full of sweet peas and her mending. I was prepared to feel very good about my life indeed.

From page one Mrs. Dalloway unnerved me. Yes, Clarissa was picking out flowers—didn't I pick flowers too? Didn't I take great comfort in them? As I read on, I came upon rose after rose—what did it mean? Hadn't I just that morning, upon seeing a new rose blooming at our gate, found it terribly symbolic that no matter how beautiful a thing is, it doesn't last?

Clarissa's husband, Richard Dalloway, disturbed me, too. Not that he was a bad sort, he wasn't. That was the problem; he was good and solid and kind. He loved Clarissa, he did, but he didn't seem to know his wife at all, and that terrified me. Did my husband, good, solid, and kind, know me? I had been his wife for almost two years, and yet there seemed to be times when I found myself thinking of another man, a man I'd loved in college—hadn't he known me far better? Hadn't he adored me in the same sort of bright and burning way it seemed Peter Walsh adored Clarissa?

He was younger than I, and he was naive, and I knew that we would not make a good match in the long run, but maybe we would have. Surely he wouldn't have left me day after day to go exploring with his friend. I had made a mistake marrying my husband whose reserve made it seem sometimes as though he didn't love me one bit. He was a man I'd fallen in love with in part because he'd never give his whole self to me, he'd never give me all that I wanted, he'd keep me curious and off guard. I wondered if he, like Richard Dalloway, ever looked at me and thought of saying I love you, but then didn't.

Clarissa had chosen Richard because in the most fundamental way he made sense.

Had I chosen my husband because he made sense? With no money, no ambition to make money or to take care of me, only to write and experience everything the world had to offer him—hadn't he been, perhaps, a bad choice? Or the very best choice?

As I reread *Mrs. Dalloway*, this time, freshly, as a wife, I wondered what toll wifedom had inflicted on me. Was I like

Sally, who went from the cigar-smoking, free-spirit nymph traipsing naked down the hall to retrieve her bath sponge to a dowager whose "voice was wrung of its old ravishing richness; her eyes not aglow as they used to be"? Was I being turned into some kind of creature?

When had I become the creature who waited at the door, waiting for the men to escort me out into the world? I was ashamed of myself.

As I continued to read, I found myself pulled into *Mrs. Dalloway,* the rhythmic language and sinewy transitions insinuating themselves into my consciousness. I had never until that time felt so infiltrated and inhabited by language, unnerved by the way Woolf moved like a breath from one character's point of view to another's—a woman stopping to ask for directions, a child running into the legs of a stranger, each passing the touch of consciousness from character to character.

Reading the words and hearing the voices wasn't unlike the experience I sometimes had of simultaneously holding many thoughts in my head at one time, of not being able to listen to just one singular voice for any length of time. It was a condition that had gotten worse since I arrived in Portugal. It was a condition that had gotten worse—though I didn't connect the two at the time—since I started drinking the locally made absinthe.

The allure of absinthe was threefold. One, its history; so many of the great writers and painters that I admired, from Verlaine and Wilde to van Gogh and Picasso, adored absinthe. Two, it was illegal in the United States. Three, better than any other alcohol I know, it created in me that most appealing state of languidness, dissolving muscle and mind so that I didn't really care what happened or didn't happen to me. So, while I enjoyed the way it made colors appear brighter and created halos around anything bright, the way it made the night sky itself seem to breathe like a giant beast crouched over me, I became hooked on absinthe because it allowed me to escape, the way that reading allowed me to escape.

I couldn't imagine Clarissa Dalloway ever drinking the way I did, though if she were to drink, absinthe might be just the thing. Unlike other alcohols absinthe didn't make me mean or weepy, I didn't want to dance on tables, and rarely did I say the wrong thing—all indispensable attributes in a cocktail.

What I did not realize at the time was that the thujone in the absinthe was exacerbating a seizure disorder I'd had since I was a child, but which I had given no thought to, thinking that everybody occasionally smelled things that weren't there, everyone occasionally got "stuck" in a position they couldn't seem to get out of. I took to spending long hours in bed just staring at a pattern of light shifting on the wall. My husband stood over me asking me what was wrong. There was *nothing whatever the matter* with me, I said. Isn't that what Dr. Holmes said to Septimus? Nothing a little fresh air and some distractions wouldn't cure. *Nothing whatever the matter with me, I'll be getting up in a moment,* I said rolling onto my side. What was I doing lying in bed?

I couldn't imagine Mrs. Dalloway lying in bed. She'd have no patience for me at all. When I sat up and read my book, I was disoriented by the prose, the way it slithered through my mind with all these voices on its back. I couldn't stop Rezia and the Drs. Holmes and Bradshaw from entering my mind. Couldn't stop lines like, *It could be possible that the world itself is without meaning* from sticking in my head. So I put it down.

IN MID-JULY we left Portugal for Berlin. Since the Wall had come down, there was much to see, a real cultural revolution going on, and we wanted to witness it. By this time I had started seeing rings around the sun and occasionally people's heads even when I wasn't drinking absinthe. I felt as though the air around me was elastic as a balloon, a membrane I could put my hand through. Occasionally I felt as though I was watching my life unfurl on film, the edge of my vision scratched up and bubbling like the tape had melted on to the bulb. The dark and jagged outline of a pine tree against the bright blue sky seemed violent. I would go into a state, a daze, sometimes for many minutes on end, as though the needle of my consciousness had gotten stuck in a groove. I couldn't speak though I could hear others around me speaking. I was unable to break out of this suspended animation, and after a while I didn't even try; I sank down into the nothing, knowing that I would eventually come back out.

Then one day I didn't.

When we arrived in Berlin it was gray and misty, and in my mind it never changed, although I know this isn't true. For a time we lived in a school dormitory in a rented room; then, when the moncy ran out, we squatted in an old building whose courtyard boasted a Wartburg sedan, crushed like an accordion and with bullet holes deep enough to swallow your index finger. We salvaged furniture out of the dumpsters and slept on old blankets that had been put out in the trash, we shared a filthy toilet with pale beleaguered-looking heroin addicts whom we usually only heard skittering like mice in the hall. Because there was no hot water, we ran the cold water we got at the gas station through an old coffeemaker we'd found on the street and bathed standing up in a bowl, soaping our bodies in full view of the open window to catch whatever warming sunlight there might be.

We had no money, I lost weight. I missed home. One night, drunk and exhausted, I snapped. I threatened to throw myself out the window. I wanted to jump. I wanted just to drop out of sight. I wanted to hit the ground and have my bones break. I wanted it to kill me. I wanted out. Septimus wasn't so crazy, he was just tired and scared.

I remember little from that time. The wail of a cricket echoing in the marble stairwell of the hotel we moved into until we could fly home; lying on the roof feeling pinned down by the sun that spun above my head like a fiery rope; the ice cream bar served to me at breakfast time on the plane. My husband whispering in my ear, holding my hand telling me he was going to get me back; my father having trouble unlocking the car door in the airport parking lot; my mother crying in the doctor's office when I told him I had wanted to kill myself, and still did.

Seeing my husband's face when I came out of a seizure or my parents' faces when I was deeply depressed, I would sometimes think in the voice of Dr. Holmes, *Didn't I have a duty to my husband? How unfair it was that I was scaring everybody like this.*

I remember my father cutting flowers for the house, for my room—irises and magnolias, dahlias and foxgloves. When I remember my father then, he is always coming in with flowers. Flowers, there were always flowers. How could I have laughed at Mrs. Dalloway selecting the flowers for her party? How delicate a task this was. How very, very important.

Later we moved back to New York City, and later to Brooklyn. Here, behind my Victorian-era brownstone, I have my own garden. It is a very English garden in some regards; the high fences are overgrown with ivy; pink and white climbing roses scale the back deck; fragrant honeysuckle and clematis vines lattice the trellis; and here and there appear patches of violets, snapdragons, bleeding hearts, and lavender. Every spring now for fifteen years, my husband and I throw a feast to celebrate the season; it has, as I have gone into my thirties, become a bit less pagan and more gustatory. I take joy in shopping for the supplies. I buy champagne, morels, and fiddlehead ferns and salad greens that get tossed with pansies and nasturtiums; I choose cheeses and sausages and shellfish for paella. Like Mrs. Dalloway I would trust no one to pick my flowers but myself. I enjoy sorting through the buckets of carnations and irises, daisies and hydrangeas. As I carry home my bouquets of butcher-wrapped flowers, parrot tulips and peonies, lilacs and lilies, I see people stare and smile.

A man asks, *Are you having a party?*

I am, I say, feeling slightly embarrassed. Here I am spending a week's salary on flowers and wine when children are starving in my city. Here I am, my head filled with recipes for cheese puffs and escargot while our government is taken over by a dictator.

Later, however, I am in the moment. As I see my friends arrive, entering my home and shucking off coats and wraps, I savor the bittersweet collision of past and present. My daughter, in conversation with her godfather, smiles at me across the room, while her little brother, at my hip, steals slices of orange dipped in chocolate. A woman I have recently become close with laughs. A man I love browns butter on the stove beside me, and I realize, staring into the face of a beautiful friend, that she is prettier for the lines around her eyes, and that, I too, am aging. As my husband goes out to call in the children's cat, I am filled with thankfulness. I would not have these children with another man—that other man I sometimes think about. I would not know what it was to be loved and necessary if it were not for these people in this room. Isn't that what Clarissa wanted? And so for a night, this is the most important thing to me, this party. It defines me and gives me shape, a past and a present, and perhaps a path to my future. For an evening the perfect party, the perfect dress, the perfect flowers, really do matter. I know what it's like to be that sort of woman.

JUNE 2003

VIRGINIA WOOLF

Mrs. Dalloway

*M*RS. DALLOWAY SAID SHE WOULD BUY THE FLOWERS HERSELF.

For Lucy had her work cut out for her. The doors would be taken off their hinges; Rumpelmayer's men were coming. And then, thought Clarissa Dalloway, what a morning—fresh as if issued to children on a beach.

What a lark! What a plunge! For so it had always seemed to her, when, with a little squeak of the hinges, which she could hear now, she had burst open the French windows and plunged at Bourton into the open air. How fresh, how calm, stiller than this of course, the air was in the early morning; like the flap of a wave; the kiss of a wave; chill and sharp and yet (for a girl of eighteen as she then was) solemn, feeling as she did, standing there at the open window, that something awful was about to happen; looking at the flowers, at the trees with the smoke winding off them and the rooks rising, falling; standing and looking until Peter Walsh said, "Musing among the vegetables?"—was that it?—"I prefer men to cauliflowers"—was that it? He must have said it at breakfast one morning when she had gone out on to the terrace—Peter Walsh. He would be back from India one of these days, June or July, she forgot which, for his letters were awfully dull; it was his sayings one remembered; his eyes, his pocket-knife, his smile, his grumpiness and, when millions of things had utterly vanished—how strange it was!—a few sayings like this about cabbages.

She stiffened a little on the kerb, waiting for Durtnall's van to pass. A charming woman, Scrope Purvis thought her (knowing her as one does know people who live next door to one in Westminster); a touch of the bird about her, of the jay, blue-green, light, vivacious, though she was over fifty, and grown very white since her illness. There she perched, never seeing him, waiting to cross, very upright.

For having lived in Westminster—how many years now? over twenty,—one feels even in the midst of the traffic, or waking at night, Clarissa was positive, a particular hush, or solemnity; an indescribable pause; a suspense (but that might be her heart, affected, they said, by influenza) before Big Ben strikes. There! Out it boomed. First a warning, musical; then the hour, irrevocable. The leaden circles dissolved in the air. Such fools we are, she thought, crossing Victoria Street. For Heaven only knows why one loves it so, how one sees it so, making it up, building it round one, tumbling it, creating it every moment afresh; but the veriest frumps, the most dejected of miseries sitting on doorsteps (drink their downfall) do the same; can't be dealt with, she felt positive, by Acts of Parliament for that very reason: they love life. In people's eyes, in the swing, tramp, and trudge; in the bellow and the uproar; the carriages, motor cars, omnibuses, vans, sandwich men shuffling and swinging; brass bands; barrel organs; in the triumph and the jingle and the strange high singing of some aeroplane overhead was what she loved; life; London; this moment of June.

For it was the middle of June. The War was over, except for some one like Mrs. Foxcroft at the Embassy last night eating her heart out because that nice boy was killed and now the old

Manor House must go to a cousin; or Lady Bexborough who opened a bazaar, they said, with the telegram in her hand, John, her favourite, killed; but it was over; thank Heaven—over. It was June. The King and Queen were at the Palace. And everywhere, though it was still so early, there was a beating, a stirring of galloping ponies, tapping of cricket bats; Lords, Ascot, Ranelagh and all the rest of it; wrapped in the soft mesh of the grey-blue morning air, which, as the day wore on, would unwind them, and set down on their lawns and pitches the bouncing ponies whose forefeet just struck the ground and up they sprung, the whirling young men, and laughing girls in their transparent muslins who, even now, after dancing all night, were taking their absurd woolly dogs for a run; and even now, at this hour, discreet old dowagers were shooting out in their motor cars on errands of mystery; and the shopkeepers were fidgeting in their windows with their paste and diamonds, their lovely old sea-green brooches in eighteenth-century settings to tempt Americans (but one must economise, not buy things rashly for Elizabeth), and she, too, loving it as she did with an absurd and faithful passion, being part of it, since her people were courtiers once in the time of the Georges, she, too, was going that very night to kindle and illuminate; to give her party. But how strange, on entering the Park, the silence; the mist; the hum; the slow-swimming happy ducks; the pouched birds waddling; and who should be coming along with his back against the Government buildings, most appropriately, carrying a despatch box stamped with the Royal Arms, who but Hugh Whitbread; her old friend Hugh—the admirable Hugh!

"Good-morning to you, Clarissa!" said Hugh, rather extravagantly, for they had known each other as children. "Where are you off to?"

"I love walking in London," said Mrs. Dalloway. "Really it's better than walking in the country."

They had just come up—unfortunately—to see doctors. Other people came to see pictures; go to the opera; take their daughters out; the Whitbreads came "to see doctors." Times without number Clarissa had visited Evelyn Whitbread in a nursing home. Was Evelyn ill again? Evelyn was a good deal out of sorts, said Hugh, intimating by a kind of pout or swell of his very well-covered, manly, extremely handsome, perfectly uphol-stered body (he was almost too well dressed always, but pre-sumably had to be, with his little job at Court) that his wife had some internal ailment, nothing serious, which, as an old friend, Clarissa Dalloway would quite understand without requiring him to specify. Ah yes, she did of course; what a nuisance; and felt very sisterly and oddly conscious at the same time of her hat. Not the right hat for the early morning, was that it? For Hugh always made her feel, as he bustled on, raising his hat rather extravagantly and assuring her that she might be a girl of eighteen, and of course he was coming to her party to-night, Evelyn absolutely insisted, only a little late he might be after the party at the Palace to which he had to take one of Jim's boys,— she always felt a little skimpy beside Hugh; schoolgirlish; but at-tached to him, partly from having known him always, but she did think him a good sort in his own way, though Richard was nearly driven mad by him, and as for Peter Walsh, he had never to this day forgiven her for liking him.

She could remember scene after scene at Bourton—Peter furious; Hugh not, of course, his match in any way, but still not a positive imbecile as Peter made out; not a mere barber's block. When his old mother wanted him to give up shooting or to take her to Bath he did it, without a word; he was really unselfish, and as for saying, as Peter did, that he had no heart, no brain, nothing but the manners and breeding of an English gentleman, that was only her dear Peter at his worst; and he could be intol-erable; he could be impossible; but adorable to walk with on a morning like this.

(June had drawn out every leaf on the trees. The mothers of Pimlico gave suck to their young. Messages were passing from the Fleet to the Admiralty. Arlington Street and Piccadilly seemed to chafe the very air in the Park and lift its leaves hotly, brilliantly, on waves of that divine vitality which Clarissa loved. To dance, to ride, she had adored all that.)

For they might be parted for hundreds of years, she and Peter; she never wrote a letter and his were dry sticks; but suddenly it would come over her, If he were with me now what would he say?—some days, some sights bringing him back to her calmly, without the old bitterness; which perhaps was the reward of having cared for people; they came back in the middle of St. James's Park on a fine morning—indeed they did. But Peter—however beautiful the day might be, and the trees and the grass, and the little girl in pink—Peter never saw a thing of all that. He would put on his spectacles, if she told him to; he would look. It was the state of the world that interested him; Wagner, Pope's poetry, people's characters eternally, and the defects of her own soul. How he scolded her! How they argued! She would marry a Prime Minister and stand at the top of a staircase; the perfect hostess he called her (she had cried over it in her bedroom), she had the makings of the perfect hostess, he said.

So she would still find herself arguing in St. James's Park, still making out that she had been right—and she had too—not to marry him. For in marriage a little licence, a little independence there must be between people living together day in day out in the same house; which Richard gave her, and she him. (Where was he this morning for instance? Some committee, she never asked what.) But with Peter everything had to be shared; everything gone into. And it was intolerable, and when it came to that scene in the little garden by the fountain, she had to break with him or they would have been destroyed, both of them ruined, she was convinced; though she had borne about with her for years like an arrow sticking in her heart the grief, the anguish; and then the horror of the moment when some one told her at a concert that he had married a woman met on the boat going to India! Never should she forget all that! Cold, heartless, a prude, he called her. Never could she understand how he cared. But those Indian women did presumably—silly, pretty, flimsy nincompoops. And she wasted her pity. For he was quite happy, he assured her—perfectly happy, though he had never done a thing that they talked of; his whole life had been a failure. It made her angry still.

She had reached the Park gates. She stood for a moment, looking at the omnibuses in Piccadilly.

She would not say of any one in the world now that they were this or were that. She felt very young; at the same time unspeakably aged. She sliced like a knife through everything; at the same time was outside, looking on. She had a perpetual sense, as she watched the taxi cabs, of being out, out, far out to sea and alone; she always had the feeling that it was very, very dangerous to live even one day. Not that she thought herself clever, or much out of the ordinary. How she had got through life on the few twigs of knowledge Fräulein Daniels gave them she could not think. She knew nothing; no language, no history; she scarcely read a book now, except memoirs in bed; and yet to her it was absolutely absorbing; all this; the cabs passing; and she would not say of Peter, she would not say of herself, I am this, I am that.

Her only gift was knowing people almost by instinct, she thought, walking on. If you put her in a room with some one, up went her back like a cat's; or she purred. Devonshire House, Bath House, the house with the china cockatoo, she had seen them all lit up once; and remembered Sylvia, Fred, Sally Seton—such hosts of people; and dancing all night; and the waggons plodding past to market; and driving home across the Park. She remembered once throwing a shilling into the Serpentine. But every one remembered; what she loved was this, here, now, in front of her; the fat lady in the cab. Did it matter then, she asked herself, walking towards Bond Street, did it matter that she must inevitably cease completely; all this must go on without her; did she resent it; or did it not become consoling to believe that death ended absolutely? but that somehow in the streets of Lon-

don, on the ebb and flow of things, here, there, she survived,
Peter survived, lived in each other, she being part, she was positive, of the trees at home; of the house there, ugly, rambling all
to bits and pieces as it was; part of people she had never met;
being laid out like a mist between the people she knew best,
who lifted her on their branches as she had seen the trees lift the
mist, but it spread ever so far, her life, herself. But what was she
dreaming as she looked into Hatchards' shop window? What
was she trying to recover? What image of white dawn in the
country, as she read in the book spread open:

> *Fear no more the heat o' the sun*
> *Nor the furious winter's rages.*

This late age of the world's experience had bred in them all, all
men and women, a well of tears. Tears and sorrows; courage and
endurance; a perfectly upright and stoical bearing. Think, for example, of the woman she admired most, Lady Bexborough,
opening the bazaar.

There were Jorrocks' *Jaunts and Jollities;* there were *Soapy
Sponge* and Mrs. Asquith's *Memoirs* and *Big Game Shooting in
Nigeria,* all spread open. Ever so many books there were; but
none that seemed exactly right to take to Evelyn Whitbread in
her nursing home. Nothing that would serve to amuse her and
make that indescribably dried-up little woman look, as Clarissa
came in, just for a moment cordial; before they settled down for
the usual interminable talk of women's ailments. How much she
wanted it—that people should look pleased as she came in,
Clarissa thought and turned and walked back towards Bond
Street, annoyed, because it was silly to have other reasons for
doing things. Much rather would she have been one of those
people like Richard who did things for themselves, whereas, she
thought, waiting to cross, half the time she did things not simply,
not for themselves; but to make people think this or that; perfect idiocy she knew (and now the policeman held up his hand)
for no one was ever for a second taken in. Oh if she could have

had her life over again! she thought, stepping on to the pavement, could have looked even differently!

She would have been, in the first place, dark like Lady Bexborough, with a skin of crumpled leather and beautiful eyes. She would have been, like Lady Bexborough, slow and stately; rather large; interested in politics like a man; with a country house; very dignified, very sincere. Instead of which she had a narrow pea-stick figure; a ridiculous little face, beaked like a bird's. That she held herself well was true; and had nice hands and feet; and dressed well, considering that she spent little. But often now this body she wore (she stopped to look at a Dutch picture), this body, with all its capacities, seemed nothing— nothing at all. She had the oddest sense of being herself invisible, unseen; unknown; there being no more marrying, no more having of children now, but only this astonishing and rather solemn progress with the rest of them, up Bond Street, this being Mrs. Dalloway; not even Clarissa any more; this being Mrs. Richard Dalloway.

Bond Street fascinated her; Bond Street early in the morning in the season; its flags flying; its shops; no splash; no glitter; one roll of tweed in the shop where her father had bought his suits for fifty years; a few pearls; salmon on an iceblock.

"That is all," she said, looking at the fishmonger's. "That is all," she repeated, pausing for a moment at the window of a glove shop where, before the War, you could buy almost perfect gloves. And her old Uncle William used to say a lady is known by her shoes and her gloves. He had turned on his bed one morning in the middle of the War. He had said, "I have had enough." Gloves and shoes; she had a passion for gloves; but her own daughter, her Elizabeth, cared not a straw for either of them.

Not a straw, she thought, going on up Bond Street to a shop where they kept flowers for her when she gave a party. Elizabeth really cared for her dog most of all. The whole house this morning smelt of tar. Still, better poor Grizzle than Miss Kilman; better distemper and tar and all the rest of it than sitting mewed in a stuffy bedroom with a prayer book! Better anything, she was inclined to say. But it might be only a phase, as Richard said, such as all girls go through. It might be falling in love. But why with Miss Kilman? who had been badly treated of course; one must make allowances for that, and Richard said she was very able, had a really historical mind. Anyhow they were inseparable, and Elizabeth, her own daughter, went to Communion; and how she dressed, how she treated people who came to lunch she did not care a bit, it being her experience that the religious ecstasy made people callous (so did causes); dulled their feelings, for Miss Kilman would do anything for the Russians, starved herself for the Austrians, but in private inflicted positive torture, so insensitive was she, dressed in a green mackintosh coat. Year in year out she wore that coat; she perspired; she was never in the room five minutes without making you feel her superiority, your inferiority; how poor she was; how rich you were; how she lived in a slum without a cushion or a bed or a rug or whatever it might be, all her soul rusted with that grievance sticking in it, her dismissal from school during the War—poor embittered unfortunate creature! For it was not her one hated but the idea of her, which undoubtedly had gathered in to itself a great deal that was not Miss Kilman; had become one of those spectres with which one battles in the night; one of those spectres who stand astride us and suck up half our life-blood, dominators and tyrants; for no doubt with another throw of the dice, had the black been uppermost and not the white, she would have loved Miss Kilman! But not in this world. No.

It rasped her, though, to have stirring about in her this brutal monster! to hear twigs cracking and feel hooves planted down in the depths of that leaf-encumbered forest, the soul; never to be content quite, or quite secure, for at any moment the brute would be stirring, this hatred, which, especially since her illness, had power to make her feel scraped, hurt in her spine; gave her physical pain, and made all pleasure in beauty, in friendship, in being well, in being loved and making her home delightful rock, quiver, and bend as if indeed there were a monster grubbing at the roots, as if the whole panoply of content were nothing but self love! this hatred!

Nonsense, nonsense! she cried to herself, pushing through the swing doors of Mulberry's the florists.

She advanced, light, tall, very upright, to be greeted at once by button-faced Miss Pym, whose hands were always bright red, as if they had been stood in cold water with the flowers.

There were flowers: delphiniums, sweet peas, bunches of lilac; and carnations, masses of carnations. There were roses; there were irises. Ah yes — so she breathed in the earthy garden sweet smell as she stood talking to Miss Pym who owed her help, and thought her kind, for kind she had been years ago; very kind, but she looked older, this year, turning her head from side to side among the irises and roses and nodding tufts of lilac with her eyes half closed, snuffing in, after the street uproar, the delicious scent, the exquisite coolness. And then, opening her eyes, how fresh like frilled linen clean from a laundry laid in wicker trays the roses looked; and dark and prim the red carnations, holding their heads up; and all the sweet peas spreading in their bowls, tinged violet, snow white, pale — as if it were the evening and girls in muslin frocks came out to pick sweet peas and roses after the superb summer's day, with its almost blue-black sky, its delphiniums, its carnations, its arum lilies was over; and it was the moment between six and seven when every flower — roses, carnations, irises, lilac — glows; white, violet, red, deep orange; every flower seems to burn by itself, softly, purely in the misty beds; and how she loved the grey-white moths spinning in and out, over the cherry pie, over the evening primroses!

And as she began to go with Miss Pym from jar to jar, choosing, nonsense, nonsense, she said to herself, more and more gently, as if this beauty, this scent, this colour, and Miss

Pym liking her, trusting her, were a wave which she let flow over her and surmount that hatred, that monster, surmount it all; and it lifted her up and up when—oh! a pistol shot in the street outside!

"Dear, those motor cars," said Miss Pym, going to the window to look, and coming back and smiling apologetically with her hands full of sweet peas, as if those motor cars, those tyres of motor cars, were all *her* fault.

THE VIOLENT EXPLOSION which made Mrs. Dalloway jump and Miss Pym go to the window and apologise came from a motor car which had drawn to the side of the pavement precisely opposite Mulberry's shop window. Passers-by who, of course, stopped and stared, had just time to see a face of the very greatest importance against the dove-grey upholstery, before a male hand drew the blind and there was nothing to be seen except a square of dove grey.

Yet rumours were at once in circulation from the middle of Bond Street to Oxford Street on one side, to Atkinson's scent shop on the other, passing invisibly, inaudibly, like a cloud, swift, veil-like upon hills, falling indeed with something of a cloud's sudden sobriety and stillness upon faces which a second before had been utterly disorderly. But now mystery had brushed them with her wing; they had heard the voice of authority; the spirit of religion was abroad with her eyes bandaged tight and her lips gaping wide. But nobody knew whose face had been seen. Was it the Prince of Wales's, the Queen's, the Prime Minister's? Whose face was it? Nobody knew.

Edgar J. Watkiss, with his roll of lead piping round his arm, said audibly, humorously of course: "The Proime Minister's kyar."

Septimus Warren Smith, who found himself unable to pass, heard him.

Septimus Warren Smith, aged about thirty, pale-faced, beak-nosed, wearing brown shoes and a shabby overcoat, with hazel eyes which had that look of apprehension in them which makes complete strangers apprehensive too. The world has raised its whip; where will it descend?

Everything had come to a standstill. The throb of the motor engines sounded like a pulse irregularly drumming through an entire body. The sun became extraordinarily hot because the motor car had stopped outside Mulberry's shop window; old ladies on the tops of omnibuses spread their black parasols; here a green, here a red parasol opened with a little pop. Mrs. Dalloway, coming to the window with her arms full of sweet peas, looked out with her little pink face pursed in enquiry. Every one looked at the motor car. Septimus looked. Boys on bicycles sprang off. Traffic accumulated. And there the motor car stood, with drawn blinds, and upon them a curious pattern like a tree, Septimus thought, and this gradual drawing together of everything to one centre before his eyes, as if some horror had come almost to the surface and was about to burst into flames, terrified him. The world wavered and quivered and threatened to burst into flames. It is I who am blocking the way, he thought. Was he not being looked at and pointed at; was he not weighted there, rooted to the pavement, for a purpose? But for what purpose?

"Let us go on, Septimus," said his wife, a little woman, with large eyes in a sallow pointed face; an Italian girl.

But Lucrezia herself could not help looking at the motor car and the tree pattern on the blinds. Was it the Queen in there — the Queen going shopping?

The chauffeur, who had been opening something, turning something, shutting something, got on to the box.

"Come on," said Lucrezia.

But her husband, for they had been married four, five years now, jumped, started, and said, "All right!" angrily, as if she had interrupted him.

People must notice; people must see. People, she thought, looking at the crowd staring at the motor car; the English people, with their children and their horses and their clothes, which she admired in a way; but they were "people" now, because Septimus had said, "I will kill myself"; an awful thing to say. Suppose they had heard him? She looked at the crowd. Help, help! she wanted to cry out to butchers' boys and women. Help! Only last autumn she and Septimus had stood on the Embankment wrapped in the same cloak and, Septimus reading a paper instead of talking, she had snatched it from him and laughed in the old man's face who saw them! But failure one conceals. She must take him away into some park.

"Now we will cross," she said.

She had a right to his arm, though it was without feeling. He would give her, who was so simple, so impulsive, only twenty-four, without friends in England, who had left Italy for his sake, a piece of bone.

The motor car with its blinds drawn and an air of inscrutable reserve proceeded towards Piccadilly, still gazed at, still ruffling the faces on both sides of the street with the same dark breath of veneration whether for Queen, Prince, or Prime Minister nobody knew. The face itself had been seen only once by three people for a few seconds. Even the sex was now in dispute. But there could be no doubt that greatness was seated within; greatness was passing, hidden, down Bond Street, removed only by a hand's-breadth from ordinary people who might now, for the first and last time, be within speaking distance of the majesty of England, of the enduring symbol of the state which will be known to curious antiquaries, sifting the ruins of time, when London is a grass-grown path and all those hurrying along the pavement this Wednesday morning are but bones with a few wedding rings mixed up in their dust and the gold stoppings of innumerable decayed teeth. The face in the motor car will then be known.

It is probably the Queen, thought Mrs. Dalloway, coming out of Mulberry's with her flowers; the Queen. And for a second she wore a look of extreme dignity standing by the flower

shop in the sunlight while the car passed at a foot's pace, with its
blinds drawn. The Queen going to some hospital; the Queen
opening some bazaar, thought Clarissa.

The crush was terrific for the time of day. Lords, Ascot,
Hurlingham, what was it? she wondered, for the street was
blocked. The British middle classes sitting sideways on the tops
of omnibuses with parcels and umbrellas, yes, even furs on a
day like this, were, she thought, more ridiculous, more unlike
anything there has ever been than one could conceive; and the
Queen herself held up; the Queen herself unable to pass.
Clarissa was suspended on one side of Brook Street; Sir John
Buckhurst, the old Judge on the other, with the car between
them (Sir John had laid down the law for years and liked a well-
dressed woman) when the chauffeur, leaning ever so slightly,
said or showed something to the policeman, who saluted and
raised his arm and jerked his head and moved the omnibus to
the side and the car passed through. Slowly and very silently it
took its way.

Clarissa guessed; Clarissa knew of course; she had seen
something white, magical, circular, in the footman's hand, a disc
inscribed with a name,— the Queen's, the Prince of Wales's, the
Prime Minister's?—which, by force of its own lustre, burnt its
way through (Clarissa saw the car diminishing, disappearing), to
blaze among candelabras, glittering stars, breasts stiff with oak
leaves, Hugh Whitbread and all his colleagues, the gentlemen of
England, that night in Buckingham Palace. And Clarissa, too,
gave a party. She stiffened a little; so she would stand at the top
of her stairs.

The car had gone, but it had left a slight ripple which flowed
through glove shops and hat shops and tailors' shops on both
sides of Bond Street. For thirty seconds all heads were inclined
the same way—to the window. Choosing a pair of gloves—
should they be to the elbow or above it, lemon or pale grey?—
ladies stopped; when the sentence was finished something had
happened. Something so trifling in single instances that no math-

ematical instrument, though capable of transmitting shocks in China, could register the vibration; yet in its fulness rather formidable and in its common appeal emotional; for in all the hat shops and tailors' shops strangers looked at each other and thought of the dead; of the flag; of Empire. In a public house in a back street a Colonial insulted the House of Windsor which led to words, broken beer glasses, and a general shindy, which echoed strangely across the way in the ears of girls buying white underlinen threaded with pure white ribbon for their weddings. For the surface agitation of the passing car as it sunk grazed something very profound.

Gliding across Piccadilly, the car turned down St. James's Street. Tall men, men of robust physique, well-dressed men with their tail-coats and their white slips and their hair raked back who, for reasons difficult to discriminate, were standing in the bow window of Brooks's with their hands behind the tails of their coats, looking out, perceived instinctively that greatness was passing, and the pale light of the immortal presence fell upon them as it had fallen upon Clarissa Dalloway. At once they stood even straighter, and removed their hands, and seemed ready to attend their Sovereign, if need be, to the cannon's mouth, as their ancestors had done before them. The white busts and the little tables in the background covered with copies of the *Tatler* and syphons of soda water seemed to approve; seemed to indicate the flowing corn and the manor houses of England; and to return the frail hum of the motor wheels as the walls of a whispering gallery return a single voice expanded and made sonorous by the might of a whole cathedral. Shawled Moll Pratt with her flowers on the pavement wished the dear boy well (it was the Prince of Wales for certain) and would have tossed the price of a pot of beer—a bunch of roses—into St. James's Street out of sheer light-heartedness and contempt of poverty had she not seen the constable's eye upon her, discouraging an old Irishwoman's loyalty. The sentries at St. James's saluted; Queen Alexandra's policeman approved.

A small crowd meanwhile had gathered at the gates of Buckingham Palace. Listlessly, yet confidently, poor people all of them, they waited; looked at the Palace itself with the flag flying; at Victoria, billowing on her mound, admired her shelves of running water, her geraniums; singled out from the motor cars in the Mall first this one, then that; bestowed emotion, vainly, upon commoners out for a drive; recalled their tribute to keep it unspent while this car passed and that; and all the time let rumour accumulate in their veins and thrill the nerves in their thighs at the thought of Royalty looking at them; the Queen bowing; the Prince saluting; at the thought of the heavenly life divinely bestowed upon Kings; of the equerries and deep curtsies; of the Queen's old doll's house; of Princess Mary married to an Englishman, and the Prince — ah! the Prince! who took wonderfully, they said, after old King Edward, but was ever so much slimmer. The Prince lived at St. James's; but he might come along in the morning to visit his mother.

So Sarah Bletchley said with her baby in her arms, tipping her foot up and down as though she were by her own fender in Pimlico, but keeping her eyes on the Mall, while Emily Coates ranged over the Palace windows and thought of the housemaids, the innumerable housemaids, the bedrooms, the innumerable bedrooms. Joined by an elderly gentleman with an Aberdeen terrier, by men without occupation, the crowd increased. Little Mr. Bowley, who had rooms in the Albany and was sealed with wax over the deeper sources of life but could be unsealed suddenly, inappropriately, sentimentally, by this sort of thing — poor women waiting to see the Queen go past — poor women, nice little children, orphans, widows, the War — tut-tut — actually had tears in his eyes. A breeze flaunting ever so warmly down the Mall through the thin trees, past the bronze heroes, lifted some flag flying in the British breast of Mr. Bowley and he raised his hat as the car turned into the Mall and held it high as the car approached; and let the poor mothers of Pimlico press close to him, and stood very upright. The car came on.

Suddenly Mrs. Coates looked up into the sky. The sound of an aeroplane bored ominously into the ears of the crowd. There it was coming over the trees, letting out white smoke from behind, which curled and twisted, actually writing something! making letters in the sky! Every one looked up.

Dropping dead down the aeroplane soared straight up, curved in a loop, raced, sank, rose, and whatever it did, wherever it went, out fluttered behind it a thick ruffled bar of white smoke which curled and wreathed upon the sky in letters. But what letters? A C was it? an E, then an L? Only for a moment did they lie still; then they moved and melted and were rubbed out up in the sky, and the aeroplane shot further away and again, in a fresh space of sky, began writing a K, an E, a Y perhaps?

"Glaxo," said Mrs. Coates in a strained, awe-stricken voice, gazing straight up, and her baby, lying stiff and white in her arms, gazed straight up.

"Kreemo," murmured Mrs. Bletchley, like a sleepwalker. With his hat held out perfectly still in his hand, Mr. Bowley gazed straight up. All down the Mall people were standing and looking up into the sky. As they looked the whole world became perfectly silent, and a flight of gulls crossed the sky, first one gull leading, then another, and in this extraordinary silence and peace, in this pallor, in this purity, bells struck eleven times, the sound fading up there among the gulls.

The aeroplane turned and raced and swooped exactly where it liked, swiftly, freely, like a skater—

"That's an E," said Mrs. Bletchley—or a dancer—

"It's toffee," murmured Mr. Bowley—(and the car went in at the gates and nobody looked at it), and shutting off the smoke, away and away it rushed, and the smoke faded and as-sembled itself round the broad white shapes of the clouds.

It had gone; it was behind the clouds. There was no sound. The clouds to which the letters E, G, or L had attached them-selves moved freely, as if destined to cross from West to East on a mission of the greatest importance which would never be revealed, and yet certainly so it was—a mission of the greatest importance. Then suddenly, as a train comes out of a tunnel, the aeroplane rushed out of the clouds again, the sound boring into the ears of all people in the Mall, in the Green Park, in Piccadilly, in Regent Street, in Regent's Park, and the bar of smoke curved behind and it dropped down, and it soared up and wrote one letter after another—but what word was it writing?

Lucrezia Warren Smith, sitting by her husband's side on a seat in Regent's Park in the Broad Walk, looked up.

"Look, look, Septimus!" she cried. For Dr. Holmes had told her to make her husband (who had nothing whatever seriously the matter with him but was a little out of sorts) take an interest in things outside himself.

So, thought Septimus, looking up, they are signalling to me. Not indeed in actual words; that is, he could not read the language yet; but it was plain enough, this beauty, this exquisite beauty, and tears filled his eyes as he looked at the smoke words languishing and melting in the sky and bestowing upon him in their inexhaustible charity and laughing goodness one shape after another of unimaginable beauty and signalling their intention to provide him, for nothing, for ever, for looking merely, with beauty, more beauty! Tears ran down his cheeks.

It was toffee; they were advertising toffee, a nursemaid told Rezia. Together they began to spell t . . . o . . . f . . .

"K . . . R . . ." said the nursemaid, and Septimus heard her say "Kay Arr" close to his ear, deeply, softly, like a mellow organ, but with a roughness in her voice like a grasshopper's, which rasped his spine deliciously and sent running up into his brain waves of sound which, concussing, broke. A marvellous discovery indeed—that the human voice in certain atmospheric conditions (for one must be scientific, above all scientific) can quicken trees into life! Happily Rezia put her hand with a tremendous weight on his knee so that he was weighted down, transfixed, or the excitement of the elm trees rising and falling, rising and falling with all their leaves alight and the colour thinning and thickening from blue to the green of a hollow wave, like plumes on horses' heads, feathers on ladies', so proudly they rose and fell, so superbly, would have sent him mad. But he would not go mad. He would shut his eyes; he would see no more.

But they beckoned; leaves were alive; trees were alive. And the leaves being connected by millions of fibres with his own body, there on the seat, fanned it up and down; when the branch stretched he, too, made that statement. The sparrows fluttering, rising, and falling in jagged fountains were part of the pattern; the white and blue, barred with black branches. Sounds made harmonies with premeditation; the spaces between them were as significant as the sounds. A child cried. Rightly far away a horn sounded. All taken together meant the birth of a new religion—

"Septimus!" said Rezia. He started violently. People must notice.

"I am going to walk to the fountain and back," she said.

For she could stand it no longer. Dr. Holmes might say there was nothing the matter. Far rather would she that he were dead! She could not sit beside him when he stared so and did not see her and made everything terrible; sky and tree, children playing, dragging carts, blowing whistles, falling down; all were terrible. And he would not kill himself; and she could tell no one. "Septimus has been working too hard"—that was all she could say to her own mother. To love makes one solitary, she thought. She could tell nobody, not even Septimus now, and looking back, she saw him sitting in his shabby overcoat alone, on the seat, hunched up, staring. And it was cowardly for a man to say he would kill himself, but Septimus had fought; he was brave; he was not Septimus now. She put on her lace collar. She put on her new hat and he never noticed; and he was happy without her. Nothing could make her happy without him! Nothing! He was selfish. So men are. For he was not ill. Dr. Holmes said there was nothing the matter with him. She spread her hand before her. Look! Her wedding ring slipped—she had grown so thin. It was she who suffered—but she had nobody to tell.

Far was Italy and the white houses and the room where her sisters sat making hats, and the streets crowded every evening with people walking, laughing out loud, not half alive like people here, huddled up in Bath chairs, looking at a few ugly flowers stuck in pots!

"For you should see the Milan gardens," she said aloud. But to whom?

There was nobody. Her words faded. So a rocket fades. Its sparks, having grazed their way into the night, surrender to it, dark descends, pours over the outlines of houses and towers; bleak hillsides soften and fall in. But though they are gone, the night is full of them; robbed of colour, blank of windows, they exist more ponderously, give out what the frank daylight fails to transmit—the trouble and suspense of things conglomerated there in the darkness; huddled together in the darkness; reft of the relief which dawn brings when, washing the walls white and grey, spotting each windowpane, lifting the mist from the fields, showing the red brown cows peacefully grazing, all is once more decked out to the eye; exists again. I am alone; I am alone! she cried, by the fountain in Regent's Park (staring at the Indian and his cross), as perhaps at midnight, when all boundaries are lost, the country reverts to its ancient shape, as the Romans saw it, lying cloudy, when they landed, and the hills had no names and rivers wound they knew not where—such was her darkness; when suddenly, as if a shelf were shot forth and she stood on it, she said how she was his wife, married years ago in Milan, his wife, and would never, never tell that he was mad! Turning, the shelf fell; down, down she dropped. For he was gone, she thought—gone, as he threatened, to kill himself—to throw himself under a cart! But no; there he was; still sitting alone on the seat, in his shabby overcoat, his legs crossed, staring, talking aloud.

Men must not cut down trees. There is a God. (He noted such revelations on the backs of envelopes.) Change the world. No one kills from hatred. Make it known (he wrote it down). He waited. He listened. A sparrow perched on the railing opposite chirped Septimus, Septimus, four or five times over and went on, drawing its notes out, to sing freshly and piercingly in Greek words how there is no crime and, joined by another sparrow, they sang in voices prolonged and piercing in Greek words, from trees in the meadow of life beyond a river where the dead walk, how there is no death.

There was his hand; there the dead. White things were assembling behind the railings opposite. But he dared not look. Evans was behind the railings!

"What are you saying?" said Rezia suddenly, sitting down by him.

Interrupted again! She was always interrupting.

Away from people—they must get away from people, he said (jumping up), right away over there, where there were chairs beneath a tree and the long slope of the park dipped like a length of green stuff with a ceiling cloth of blue and pink smoke high above, and there was a rampart of far irregular houses hazed in smoke, the traffic hummed in a circle, and on the right, dun-coloured animals stretched long necks over the Zoo palings, barking, howling. There they sat down under a tree.

"Look," she implored him, pointing at a little troop of boys carrying cricket stumps, and one shuffled, spun round on his heel and shuffled, as if he were acting a clown at the music hall.

"Look," she implored him, for Dr. Holmes had told her to make him notice real things, go to a music hall, play cricket—that was the very game, Dr. Holmes said, a nice out-of-door game, the very game for her husband.

"Look," she repeated.

Look the unseen bade him, the voice which now communicated with him who was the greatest of mankind, Septimus, lately taken from life to death, the Lord who had come to renew society, who lay like a coverlet, a snow blanket smitten only by the sun, for ever unwasted, suffering for ever, the scapegoat, the eternal sufferer, but he did not want it, he moaned, putting from him with a wave of his hand that eternal suffering, that eternal loneliness.

"Look," she repeated, for he must not talk aloud to himself out of doors.

"Oh look," she implored him. But what was there to look at? A few sheep. That was all.

The way to Regent's Park Tube station— could they tell her the way to Regent's Park Tube station—Maisie Johnson wanted to know. She was only up from Edinburgh two days ago.

"Not this way—over there!" Rezia exclaimed, waving her aside, lest she should see Septimus.

Both seemed queer, Maisie Johnson thought. Everything seemed very queer. In London for the first time, come to take up a post at her uncle's in Leadenhall Street, and now walking through Regent's Park in the morning, this couple on the chairs gave her quite a turn; the young woman seeming foreign, the man looking queer; so that should she be very old she would still remember and make it jangle again among her memories how she had walked through Regent's Park on a fine summer's morning fifty years ago. For she was only nineteen and had got her way at last, to come to London; and now how queer it was, this couple she had asked the way of, and the girl started and jerked her hand, and the man—he seemed awfully odd; quarrelling, perhaps; parting for ever, perhaps; something was up, she knew; and now all these people (for she returned to the Broad Walk), the stone basins, the prim flowers, the old men and women, invalids most of them in Bath chairs—all seemed, after Edinburgh, so queer. And Maisie Johnson, as she joined that gently trudging, vaguely gazing, breeze-kissed company— squirrels perching and preening, sparrow fountains fluttering for crumbs, dogs busy with the railings, busy with each other, while the soft warm air washed over them and lent to the fixed unsurprised gaze with which they received life something whimsical and mollified—Maisie Johnson positively felt she must cry Oh! (For that young man on the seat had given her quite a turn. Something was up, she knew.)

Horror! horror! she wanted to cry. (She had left her people; they had warned her what would happen.)

Why hadn't she stayed at home? she cried, twisting the knob of the iron railing.

That girl, thought Mrs. Dempster (who saved crusts for the squirrels and often ate her lunch in Regent's Park), don't know a thing yet; and really it seemed to her better to be a little stout, a little slack, a little moderate in one's expectations. Percy drank. Well, better to have a son, thought Mrs. Dempster. She had had a hard time of it, and couldn't help smiling at a girl like that. You'll get married, for you're pretty enough, thought Mrs. Dempster. Get married, she thought, and then you'll know. Oh, the cooks, and so on. Every man has his ways. But whether I'd have chosen quite like that if I could have known, thought Mrs. Dempster, and could not help wishing to whisper a word to Maisie Johnson; to feel on the creased pouch of her worn old face the kiss of pity. For it's been a hard life, thought Mrs. Dempster. What hadn't she given to it? Roses; figure; her feet too. (She drew the knobbed lumps beneath her skirt.)

Roses, she thought sardonically. All trash, m'dear. For really, what with eating, drinking, and mating, the bad days and good, life had been no mere matter of roses, and what was more, let me tell you, Carrie Dempster had no wish to change her lot with any woman's in Kentish Town! But, she implored, pity. Pity, for the loss of roses. Pity she asked of Maisie Johnson, standing by the hyacinth beds.

Ah, but that aeroplane! Hadn't Mrs. Dempster always longed to see foreign parts? She had a nephew, a missionary. It soared and shot. She always went on the sea at Margate, not out o' sight of land, but she had no patience with women who were afraid of water. It swept and fell. Her stomach was in her mouth. Up again. There's a fine young feller aboard of it, Mrs. Dempster wagered, and away and away it went, fast and fading, away and away the aeroplane shot; soaring over Greenwich and all the masts; over the little island of grey churches, St. Paul's and the rest till, on either side of London, fields spread out and dark brown woods where adventurous thrushes hopping boldly, glancing quickly, snatched the snail and tapped him on a stone, once, twice, thrice.

Away and away the aeroplane shot, till it was nothing but a bright spark; an aspiration; a concentration; a symbol (so it seemed to Mr. Bentley, vigorously rolling his strip of turf at Greenwich) of man's soul; of his determination, thought Mr. Bentley, sweeping round the cedar tree, to get outside his body, beyond his house, by means of thought, Einstein, speculation, mathematics, the Mendelian theory—away the aeroplane shot.

Then, while a seedy-looking nondescript man carrying a leather bag stood on the steps of St. Paul's Cathedral, and hesitated, for within was what balm, how great a welcome, how many tombs with banners waving over them, tokens of victories not over armies, but over, he thought, that plaguy spirit of truth seeking which leaves me at present without a situation, and more than that, the cathedral offers company, he thought, invites you to membership of a society; great men belong to it; martyrs have died for it; why not enter in, he thought, put this leather bag stuffed with pamphlets before an altar, a cross, the symbol of something which has soared beyond seeking and questing and knocking of words together and has become all spirit, disembodied, ghostly—why not enter in? he thought and while he hesitated out flew the aeroplane over Ludgate Circus.

It was strange; it was still. Not a sound was to be heard above the traffic. Unguided it seemed; sped of its own free will.

And now, curving up and up, straight up, like something mounting in ecstasy, in pure delight, out from behind poured white smoke looping, writing a T, an O, an F.

"WHAT ARE THEY LOOKING AT?" said Clarissa Dalloway to the maid who opened her door.

The hall of the house was cool as a vault. Mrs. Dalloway raised her hand to her eyes, and, as the maid shut the door to, and she heard the swish of Lucy's skirts, she felt like a nun who has left the world and feels fold round her the familiar veils and the response to old devotions. The cook whistled in the kitchen. She heard the click of the typewriter. It was her life, and, bending her head over the hall table, she bowed beneath the influence, felt blessed and purified, saying to herself, as she took the pad with the telephone message on it, how moments like this are buds on the tree of life, flowers of darkness they are, she thought (as if some lovely rose had blossomed for her eyes only); not for a moment did she believe in God; but all the more, she thought, taking up the pad, must one repay in daily life to servants, yes, to dogs and canaries, above all to Richard her husband, who was the foundation of it—of the gay sounds, of the green lights, of the cook even whistling, for Mrs. Walker was Irish and whistled all day long—one must pay back from this secret deposit of exquisite moments, she thought, lifting the pad, while Lucy stood by her, trying to explain how.

"Mr. Dalloway, ma'am"—

Clarissa read on the telephone pad, "Lady Bruton wishes to know if Mr. Dalloway will lunch with her to-day."

"Mr. Dalloway, ma'am, told me to tell you he would be lunching out."

"Dear!" said Clarissa, and Lucy shared as she meant her to her disappointment (but not the pang); felt the concord between them; took the hint; thought how the gentry love; gilded her own future with calm; and, taking Mrs. Dalloway's parasol, handled it like a sacred weapon which a Goddess, having acquitted herself honourably in the field of battle, sheds, and placed it in the umbrella stand.

"Fear no more," said Clarissa. Fear no more the heat o' the sun; for the shock of Lady Bruton asking Richard to lunch without her made the moment in which she had stood shiver, as a plant on the river-bed feels the shock of a passing oar and shivers: so she rocked: so she shivered.

Millicent Bruton, whose lunch parties were said to be extraordinarily amusing, had not asked her. No vulgar jealousy could separate her from Richard. But she feared time itself, and read on Lady Bruton's face, as if it had been a dial cut in impassive stone, the dwindling of life; how year by year her share was sliced; how little the margin that remained was capable any longer of stretching, of absorbing, as in the youthful years, the colours, salts, tones of existence, so that she filled the room she entered, and felt often as she stood hesitating one moment on the threshold of her drawing-room, an exquisite suspense, such as might stay a diver before plunging while the sea darkens and brightens beneath him, and the waves which threaten to break, but only gently split their surface, roll and conceal and encrust as they just turn over the weeds with pearl.

She put the pad on the hall table. She began to go slowly upstairs, with her hand on the bannisters, as if she had left a party, where now this friend now that had flashed back her face, her voice; had shut the door and gone out and stood alone, a single figure against the appalling night, or rather, to be accurate, against the stare of this matter-of-fact June morning; soft with the glow of rose petals for some, she knew, and felt it, as she paused by the open staircase window which let in blinds flapping, dogs barking, let in, she thought, feeling herself suddenly shrivelled, aged, breastless, the grinding, blowing, flowering of the day, out of doors, out of the window, out of her body and brain which now failed, since Lady Bruton, whose lunch parties were said to be extraordinarily amusing, had not asked her.

Like a nun withdrawing, or a child exploring a tower, she went upstairs, paused at the window, came to the bathroom. There was the green linoleum and a tap dripping. There was an emptiness about the heart of life; an attic room. Women must put off their rich apparel. At midday they must disrobe. She pierced the pin-cushion and laid her feathered yellow hat on the bed. The sheets were clean, tight stretched in a broad white band from side to side. Narrower and narrower would her bed be. The candle was half burnt down and she had read deep in Baron Marbot's *Memoirs.* She had read late at night of the retreat from Moscow. For the House sat so long that Richard insisted, after her illness, that she must sleep undisturbed. And really she preferred to read of the retreat from Moscow. He knew it. So the room was an attic; the bed narrow; and lying there reading, for she slept badly, she could not dispel a virginity preserved through childbirth which clung to her like a sheet. Lovely in girlhood, suddenly there came a moment—for example on the river beneath the woods at Clieveden—when, through some contraction of this cold spirit, she had failed him. And then at Constantinople, and again and again. She could see what she lacked. It was not beauty; it was not mind. It was something central which permeated; something warm which broke up surfaces and rippled the cold contact of man and woman, or of women together. For *that* she could dimly perceive. She resented it, had a scruple picked up Heaven knows where, or, as she felt, sent by Nature (who is invariably wise); yet she could not resist sometimes yielding to the charm of a woman, not a girl, of a woman confessing, as to her they often did, some scrape, some folly. And whether it was pity, or their beauty, or that she was older, or some accident—like a faint scent, or a violin next door (so strange is the power of sounds at certain moments), she did undoubtedly then feel what men felt. Only for a moment; but it was enough. It was a sudden revelation, a tinge like a blush which one tried to check and then, as it spread, one yielded to its expansion, and rushed to the farthest verge and there quivered and felt the world come closer, swollen with some astonishing significance, some pressure of rapture, which split its thin skin and gushed and poured with an extraordinary alleviation over the cracks and sores! Then, for that moment, she had seen an illumination; a match burning in a crocus; an inner meaning almost expressed. But the close withdrew; the hard softened. It was over—the moment. Against such moments (with women too) there contrasted (as she laid her hat down) the bed and Baron Marbot and the candle half-burnt. Lying awake, the floor creaked; the lit house was suddenly darkened, and if she raised her head she could just hear the click of the handle released as gently as possible by Richard, who slipped upstairs in his socks and then, as often as not, dropped his hot-water bottle and swore! How she laughed!

But this question of love (she thought, putting her coat away), this falling in love with women. Take Sally Seton; her relation in the old days with Sally Seton. Had not that, after all, been love?

She sat on the floor—that was her first impression of Sally—she sat on the floor with her arms round her knees, smoking a cigarette. Where could it have been? The Mannings? The Kinloch-Jones's? At some party (where, she could not be certain), for she had a distinct recollection of saying to the man she was with, "Who is *that*?" And he had told her, and said that Sally's parents did not get on (how that shocked her—that one's parents should quarrel!). But all that evening she could not take her eyes off Sally. It was an extraordinary beauty of the kind she most admired, dark, large-eyed, with that quality which, since she hadn't got it herself, she always envied—a sort of abandonment, as if she could say anything, do anything; a quality much commoner in foreigners than in Englishwomen. Sally always said she had French blood in her veins, an ancestor had been with Marie Antoinette, had his head cut off, left a ruby ring. Perhaps that summer she came to stay at Bourton, walking in quite unexpectedly without a penny in her pocket, one night after dinner, and upsetting poor Aunt Helena to such an extent that she never forgave her. There had been some quarrel at home. She literally hadn't a penny that night when she came to them—had pawned a brooch to come down. She had rushed off in a passion. They sat up till all hours of the night talking. Sally it was who made her feel, for the first time, how sheltered the life at Bourton was. She knew nothing about sex—nothing about social problems. She had once seen an old man who had dropped dead in a field—she had seen cows just after their calves were born. But Aunt Helena never liked discussion of anything (when Sally gave her William Morris, it had to be wrapped in brown paper). There they sat, hour after hour, talking in her bedroom at the top of the house, talking about life, how they were to reform the world. They meant to found a society to abolish private property, and actually had a letter written, though not sent out. The ideas were Sally's, of course—but very soon she was just as excited—read Plato in bed before breakfast; read Morris; read Shelley by the hour.

Sally's power was amazing, her gift, her personality. There was her way with flowers, for instance. At Bourton they always had stiff little vases all the way down the table. Sally went out, picked hollyhocks, dahlias—all sorts of flowers that had never been seen together—cut their heads off, and made them swim on the top of water in bowls. The effect was extraordinary—coming in to dinner in the sunset. (Of course Aunt Helena thought it wicked to treat flowers like that.) Then she forgot her sponge, and ran along the passage naked. That grim old housemaid, Ellen Atkins, went about grumbling—"Suppose any of the gentlemen had seen?" Indeed she did shock people. She was untidy, Papa said.

The strange thing, on looking back, was the purity, the integrity, of her feeling for Sally. It was not like one's feeling for a man. It was completely disinterested, and besides, it had a quality which could only exist between women, between women just grown up. It was protective, on her side; sprang from a sense of being in league together, a presentiment of something that was bound to part them (they spoke of marriage always as a catastrophe), which led to this chivalry, this protective feeling which was much more on her side than Sally's. For in those days she was completely reckless; did the most idiotic things out of bravado; bicycled round the parapet on the terrace; smoked cigars. Absurd, she was—very absurd. But the charm was overpowering, to her at least, so that she could remember standing in her bedroom at the top of the house holding the hot-water can in her hands and saying aloud, "She is beneath this roof. . . . She is beneath this roof!"

No, the words meant absolutely nothing to her now. She could not even get an echo of her old emotion. But she could remember going cold with excitement, and doing her hair in a kind of ecstasy (now the old feeling began to come back to her, as she took out her hairpins, laid them on the dressing-table, began to do her hair), with the rooks flaunting up and down in the pink evening light, and dressing, and going downstairs, and feeling as she crossed the hall "if it were now to die 'twere now to be most happy." That was her feeling—Othello's feeling, and she felt it, she was convinced, as strongly as Shakespeare meant Othello to feel it, all because she was coming down to dinner in a white frock to meet Sally Seton!

She was wearing pink gauze—was that possible? She *seemed,* anyhow, all light, glowing, like some bird or air ball that has flown in, attached itself for a moment to a bramble. But nothing is so strange when one is in love (and what was this except being in love?) as the complete indifference of other people. Aunt Helena just wandered off after dinner; Papa read the paper. Peter Walsh might have been there, and old Miss Cummings; Joseph Breitkopf certainly was, for he came every summer, poor old man, for weeks and weeks, and pretended to read German with her, but really played the piano and sang Brahms without any voice.

All this was only a background for Sally. She stood by the fireplace talking, in that beautiful voice which made everything she said sound like a caress, to Papa, who had begun to be attracted rather against his will (he never got over lending her one of his books and finding it soaked on the terrace), when suddenly she said, "What a shame to sit indoors!" and they all went out on to the terrace and walked up and down. Peter Walsh and Joseph Breitkopf went on about Wagner. She and Sally fell a little behind. Then came the most exquisite moment of her whole life passing a stone urn with flowers in it. Sally stopped; picked a flower; kissed her on the lips. The whole world might have turned upside down! The others disappeared; there she was alone with Sally. And she felt that she had been given a present, wrapped up, and told just to keep it, not to look at it— a diamond, something infinitely precious, wrapped up, which, as they walked (up and down, up and down), she uncovered, or the radiance burnt through, the revelation, the religious feeling!— when old Joseph and Peter faced them:

"Star-gazing?" said Peter.

It was like running one's face against a granite wall in the darkness! It was shocking; it was horrible!

Not for herself. She felt only how Sally was being mauled already, maltreated; she felt his hostility; his jealousy; his determination to break into their companionship. All this she saw as one sees a landscape in a flash of lightning—and Sally (never had she admired her so much!) gallantly taking her way unvanquished. She laughed. She made old Joseph tell her the names of the stars, which he liked doing very seriously. She stood there: she listened. She heard the names of the stars.

"Oh this horror!" she said to herself, as if she had known all along that something would interrupt, would embitter her moment of happiness.

Yet, after all, how much she owed to him later. Always when she thought of him she thought of their quarrels for some reason—because she wanted his good opinion so much, perhaps. She owed him words: "sentimental," "civilised"; they started up every day of her life as if he guarded her. A book was sentimental; an attitude to life sentimental. "Sentimental," perhaps she was to be thinking of the past. What would he think, she wondered, when he came back?

That she had grown older? Would he say that, or would she see him thinking when he came back, that she had grown older? It was true. Since her illness she had turned almost white.

Laying her brooch on the table, she had a sudden spasm, as if, while she mused, the icy claws had had the chance to fix in her. She was not old yet. She had just broken into her fifty-second year. Months and months of it were still untouched. June, July, August! Each still remained almost whole, and, as if to catch the falling drop, Clarissa (crossing to the dressing-table) plunged into the very heart of the moment, transfixed it, there—the moment of this June morning on which was the pressure of all the other mornings, seeing the glass, the dressing-table, and all the bottles afresh, collecting the whole of her at one point (as she looked into the glass), seeing the delicate pink face of the woman who was that very night to give a party; of Clarissa Dalloway; of herself.

How many million times she had seen her face, and always with the same imperceptible contraction! She pursed her lips when she looked in the glass. It was to give her face point. That was her self—pointed; dartlike; definite. That was her self when some effort, some call on her to be her self, drew the parts together, she alone knew how different, how incompatible and composed so for the world only into one centre, one diamond, one woman who sat in her drawing-room and made a meeting-point, a radiancy no doubt in some dull lives, a refuge for the lonely to come to, perhaps; she had helped young people, who were grateful to her; had tried to be the same always, never showing a sign of all the other sides of her—faults, jealousies, vanities, suspicions, like this of Lady Bruton not asking her to lunch; which, she thought (combing her hair finally), is utterly base! Now, where was her dress?

Her evening dresses hung in the cupboard. Clarissa, plunging her hand into the softness, gently detached the green dress and carried it to the window. She had torn it. Some one had trod on the skirt. She had felt it give at the Embassy party at the top among the folds. By artificial light the green shone, but lost its colour now in the sun. She would mend it. Her maids had too much to do. She would wear it to-night. She would take her silks, her scissors, her—what was it?—her thimble, of course, down into the drawing-room, for she must also write, and see that things generally were more or less in order.

Strange, she thought, pausing on the landing, and assembling that diamond shape, that single person, strange how a mistress knows the very moment, the very temper of her house! Faint sounds rose in spirals up the well of the stairs; the swish of a mop; tapping; knocking; a loudness when the front door opened; a voice repeating a message in the basement; the chink of silver on a tray; clean silver for the party. All was for the party.

(And Lucy, coming into the drawing-room with her tray held out, put the giant candlesticks on the mantelpiece, the silver casket in the middle, turned the crystal dolphin towards the clock. They would come; they would stand; they would talk in the mincing tones which she could imitate, ladies and gentlemen. Of all, her mistress was loveliest—mistress of silver, of linen, of china, for the sun, the silver, doors off their hinges, Rumpelmayer's men, gave her a sense, as she laid the paper-knife on the inlaid table, of something achieved. Behold! Behold! she said, speaking to her old friends in the baker's shop, where she had first seen service at Caterham, prying into the glass. She was Lady Angela, attending Princess Mary, when in came Mrs. Dalloway.)

"Oh Lucy," she said, "the silver does look nice!"

"And how," she said, turning the crystal dolphin to stand straight, "how did you enjoy the play last night?" "Oh, they had to go before the end!" she said. "They had to be back at ten!"

she said. "So they don't know what happened," she said. "That does seem hard luck," she said (for her servants stayed later, if they asked her). "That does seem rather a shame," she said, taking the old bald-looking cushion in the middle of the sofa and putting it in Lucy's arms, and giving her a little push, and crying:

"Take it away! Give it to Mrs. Walker with my compliments! Take it away!" she cried.

And Lucy stopped at the drawing-room door, holding the cushion, and said, very shyly, turning a little pink, Couldn't she help to mend that dress?

But, said Mrs. Dalloway, she had enough on her hands already, quite enough of her own to do without that.

"But, thank you, Lucy, oh, thank you," said Mrs. Dalloway, and thank you, thank you, she went on saying (sitting down on the sofa with her dress over her knees, her scissors, her silks), thank you, thank you, she went on saying in gratitude to her servants generally for helping her to be like this, to be what she wanted, gentle, generous-hearted. Her servants liked her. And then this dress of hers—where was the tear? and now her needle to be threaded. This was a favourite dress, one of Sally Parker's, the last almost she ever made, alas, for Sally had now retired, living at Ealing, and if ever I have a moment, thought Clarissa (but never would she have a moment any more), I shall go and see her at Ealing. For she was a character, thought Clarissa, a real artist. She thought of little out-of-the-way things; yet her dresses were never queer. You could wear them at Hatfield; at Buckingham Palace. She had worn them at Hatfield; at Buckingham Palace.

Quiet descended on her, calm, content, as her needle, drawing the silk smoothly to its gentle pause, collected the green folds together and attached them, very lightly, to the belt. So on a summer's day waves collect, overbalance, and fall; collect and fall; and the whole world seems to be saying "that is all" more and more ponderously, until even the heart in the body which lies in the sun on the beach says too, That is all. Fear no more, says the heart. Fear no more, says the heart, committing its burden to some sea, which sighs collectively for all sorrows, and renews, begins, collects, lets fall. And the body alone listens to the passing bee; the wave breaking; the dog barking, far away barking and barking.

"Heavens, the front-door bell!" exclaimed Clarissa, staying her needle. Roused, she listened.

"Mrs. Dalloway will see me," said the elderly man in the hall. "Oh yes, she will see *me*," he repeated, putting Lucy aside very benevolently, and running upstairs ever so quickly. "Yes, yes, yes," he muttered as he ran upstairs. "She will see me. After five years in India, Clarissa will see me."

"Who can—what can," asked Mrs. Dalloway (thinking it was outrageous to be interrupted at eleven o'clock on the morning of the day she was giving a party), hearing a step on the stairs. She heard a hand upon the door. She made to hide her dress, like a virgin protecting chastity, respecting privacy. Now the brass knob slipped. Now the door opened, and in came — for a single second she could not remember what he was called! so surprised she was to see him, so glad, so shy, so utterly taken aback to have Peter Walsh come to her unexpectedly in the morning! (She had not read his letter.)

"And how are you?" said Peter Walsh, positively trembling; taking both her hands; kissing both her hands. She's grown older, he thought, sitting down. I shan't tell her anything about it, he thought, for she's grown older. She's looking at me, he thought, a sudden embarrassment coming over him, though he had kissed her hands. Putting his hand into his pocket, he took out a large pocket-knife and half opened the blade.

Exactly the same, thought Clarissa; the same queer look; the same check suit; a little out of the straight his face is, a little thinner, dryer, perhaps, but he looks awfully well, and just the same.

"How heavenly it is to see you again!" she exclaimed. He had his knife out. That's so like him, she thought.

He had only reached town last night, he said; would have to

go down into the country at once; and how was everything, how was everybody—Richard? Elizabeth?

"And what's all this?" he said, tilting his pen-knife towards her green dress.

He's very well dressed, thought Clarissa; yet he always criticises *me*.

Here she is mending her dress; mending her dress as usual, he thought; here she's been sitting all the time I've been in India; mending her dress; playing about; going to parties; running to the House and back and all that, he thought, growing more and more irritated, more and more agitated, for there's nothing in the world so bad for some women as marriage, he thought; and politics; and having a Conservative husband, like the admirable Richard. So it is, so it is, he thought, shutting his knife with a snap.

"Richard's very well. Richard's at a Committee," said Clarissa.

And she opened her scissors, and said, did he mind her just finishing what she was doing to her dress, for they had a party that night?

"Which I shan't ask you to," she said. "My dear Peter!" she said.

But it was delicious to hear her say that—my dear Peter! Indeed, it was all so delicious—the silver, the chairs; all so delicious!

Why wouldn't she ask him to her party? he asked.

Now of course, thought Clarissa, he's enchanting! perfectly enchanting! Now I remember how impossible it was ever to make up my mind—and why did I make up my mind—not to marry him? she wondered, that awful summer?

"But it's so extraordinary that you should have come this morning!" she cried, putting her hands, one on top of another, down on her dress.

"Do you remember," she said, "how the blinds used to flap at Bourton?"

"They did," he said; and he remembered breakfasting alone, very awkwardly, with her father; who had died; and he had not written to Clarissa. But he had never got on well with old Parry, that querulous, weak-kneed old man, Clarissa's father, Justin Parry.

"I often wish I'd got on better with your father," he said.

"But he never liked any one who—our friends," said Clarissa; and could have bitten her tongue for thus reminding Peter that he had wanted to marry her.

Of course I did, thought Peter; it almost broke my heart too, he thought; and was overcome with his own grief, which rose like a moon looked at from a terrace, ghastly beautiful with light from the sunken day. I was more unhappy than I've ever been since, he thought. And as if in truth he were sitting there on the terrace he edged a little towards Clarissa; put his hand out; raised it; let it fall. There above them it hung, that moon. She too seemed to be sitting with him on the terrace, in the moonlight.

"Herbert has it now," she said. "I never go there now," she said.

Then, just as happens on a terrace in the moonlight, when one person begins to feel ashamed that he is already bored, and yet as the other sits silent, very quiet, sadly looking at the moon, does not like to speak, moves his foot, clears his throat, notices some iron scroll on a table leg, stirs a leaf, but says nothing—so Peter Walsh did now. For why go back like this to the past? he thought. Why make him think of it again? Why make him suffer, when she had tortured him so infernally? Why?

"Do you remember the lake?" she said, in an abrupt voice, under the pressure of an emotion which caught her heart, made the muscles of her throat stiff, and contracted her lips in a spasm as she said "lake." For she was a child, throwing bread to the ducks, between her parents, and at the same time a grown woman coming to her parents who stood by the lake, holding her life in her arms which, as she neared them, grew larger and larger in her arms, until it became a whole life, a complete life, which she put down by them and said, "This is what I have made of it! This!" And what had she made of it? What, indeed? sitting there sewing this morning with Peter.

She looked at Peter Walsh; her look, passing through all that time and that emotion, reached him doubtfully; settled on him tearfully; and rose and fluttered away, as a bird touches a branch and rises and flutters away. Quite simply she wiped her eyes.

"Yes," said Peter. "Yes, yes, yes," he said, as if she drew up to the surface something which positively hurt him as it rose. Stop! Stop! he wanted to cry. For he was not old; his life was not over; not by any means. He was only just past fifty. Shall I tell her, he thought, or not? He would like to make a clean breast of it all. But she is too cold, he thought; sewing, with her scissors; Daisy would look ordinary beside Clarissa. And she would think me a failure, which I am in their sense, he thought; in the Dalloways' sense. Oh yes, he had no doubt about that; he was a failure, compared with all this—the inlaid table, the mounted paper-knife, the dolphin and the candlesticks, the chair-covers and the old valuable English tinted prints—he was a failure! I detest the smugness of the whole affair, he thought; Richard's doing, not Clarissa's; save that she married him. (Here Lucy came into the room, carrying silver, more silver, but charming, slender, graceful she looked, he thought, as she stooped to put it down.) And this has been going on all the time! he thought; week after week; Clarissa's life; while I—he thought; and at once everything seemed to radiate from him; journeys; rides; quarrels; adventures; bridge parties; love affairs; work; work, work! and he took out his knife quite openly—his old horn-handled knife which Clarissa could swear he had had these thirty years—and clenched his fist upon it.

What an extraordinary habit that was, Clarissa thought; always playing with a knife. Always making one feel, too, frivolous; empty-minded; a mere silly chatterbox, as he used. But I too, she thought, and, taking up her needle, summoned, like a Queen whose guards have fallen sleep and left her unprotected (she had been quite taken aback by this visit—it had upset her) so that any one can stroll in and have a look at her where she lies with the brambles curving over her, summoned to her help the things she did; the things she liked; her husband; Elizabeth; her self, in short, which Peter hardly knew now, all to come about her and beat off the enemy.

"Well, and what's happened to you?" she said. So before a battle begins, the horses paw the ground; toss their heads; the light shines on their flanks; their necks curve. So Peter Walsh and Clarissa, sitting side by side on the blue sofa, challenged each other. His powers chafed and tossed in him. He assembled from different quarters all sorts of things; praise; his career at Oxford; his marriage, which she knew nothing whatever about; how he had loved; and altogether done his job.

"Millions of things!" he exclaimed, and, urged by the assembly of powers which were now charging this way and that and giving him the feeling at once frightening and extremely exhilarating of being rushed through the air on the shoulders of people he could no longer see, he raised his hands to his forehead.

Clarissa sat very upright; drew in her breath.

"I am in love," he said, not to her however, but to some one raised up in the dark so that you could not touch her but must lay your garland down on the grass in the dark.

"In love," he repeated, now speaking rather dryly to Clarissa Dalloway; "in love with a girl in India." He had deposited his garland. Clarissa could make what she would of it.

"In love!" she said. That he at his age should be sucked under in his little bow-tie by that monster! And there's no flesh on his neck; his hands are red; and he's six months older than I am! her eye flashed back to her; but in her heart she felt, all the same, he is in love. He has that, she felt; he is in love.

But the indomitable egotism which for ever rides down the hosts opposed to it, the river which says on, on, on; even though, it admits, there may be no goal for us whatever, still on, on; this indomitable egotism charged her cheeks with colour; made her look very young; very pink; very bright-eyed as she sat with her dress upon her knee, and her needle held to the end of green silk, trembling a little. He was in love! Not with her. With some younger woman, of course.

"And who is she?" she asked.

Now this statue must be brought from its height and set down between them.

"A married woman, unfortunately," he said; "the wife of a Major in the Indian Army."

And with a curious ironical sweetness he smiled as he placed her in this ridiculous way before Clarissa.

(All the same, he is in love, thought Clarissa.)

"She has," he continued, very reasonably, "two small children; a boy and a girl; and I have come over to see my lawyers about the divorce."

There they are! he thought. Do what you like with them, Clarissa! There they are! And second by second it seemed to him that the wife of the Major in the Indian Army (his Daisy) and her two small children became more and more lovely as Clarissa looked at them; as if he had set light to a grey pellet on a plate and there had risen up a lovely tree in the brisk sea-salted air of their intimacy (for in some ways no one understood him, felt with him, as Clarissa did)—their exquisite intimacy.

She flattered him; she fooled him, thought Clarissa; shaping the woman, the wife of the Major in the Indian Army, with three strokes of a knife. What a waste! What a folly! All his life long Peter had been fooled like that; first getting sent down from Oxford; next marrying the girl on the boat going out to India; now the wife of a Major in the Indian Army—thank Heaven she had refused to marry him! Still, he was in love; her old friend, her dear Peter, he was in love.

"But what are you going to do?" she asked him. Oh the lawyers and solicitors, Messrs. Hooper and Grateley of Lincoln's

Inn, they were going to do it, he said. And he actually pared his nails with his pocket-knife.

For Heaven's sake, leave your knife alone! she cried to herself in irrepressible irritation; it was his silly unconventionality, his weakness; his lack of the ghost of a notion what any on else was feeling that annoyed her, had always annoyed her; and now at his age, how silly!

I know all that, Peter thought; I know what I'm up against, he thought, running his finger along the blade of his knife, Clarissa and Dalloway and all the rest of them; but I'll show Clarissa—and then to his utter surprise, suddenly thrown by those uncontrollable forces thrown through the air, he burst into tears; wept; wept without the least shame, sitting on the sofa, the tears running down his cheeks.

And Clarissa had leant forward, taken his hand, drawn him to her, kissed him,—actually had felt his face on hers before she could down the brandishing of silver flashing—plumes like pampas grass in a tropic gale in her breast, which, subsiding, left her holding his hand, patting his knee and, feeling as she sat back extraordinarily at her ease with him and light-hearted, all in a clap it came over her, If I had married him, this gaiety would have been mine all day!

It was all over for her. The sheet was stretched and the bed narrow. She had gone up into the tower alone and left them blackberrying in the sun. The door had shut, and there among the dust of fallen plaster and the litter of birds' nests how distant the view had looked, and the sounds came thin and chill (once on Leith Hill, she remembered), and Richard, Richard! she cried, as a sleeper in the night starts and stretches a hand in the dark for help. Lunching with Lady Bruton, it came back to her. He has left me; I am alone for ever, she thought, folding her hands upon her knee.

Peter Walsh had got up and crossed to the window and stood with his back to her, flicking a bandanna handkerchief from side to side. Masterly and dry and desolate he looked, his thin shoulder-blades lifting his coat slightly; blowing his nose violently. Take me with you, Clarissa thought impulsively, as if he were starting directly upon some great voyage; and then, next moment, it was as if the five acts of a play that had been very exciting and moving were now over and she had lived a lifetime in them and had run away, had lived with Peter, and it was now over.

Now it was time to move, and, as a woman gathers her things together, her cloak, her gloves, her opera-glasses, and gets up to go out of the theatre into the street, she rose from the sofa and went to Peter.

And it was awfully strange, he thought, how she still had the power, as she came tinkling, rustling, still had the power as she came across the room, to make the moon, which he detested, rise at Bourton on the terrace in the summer sky.

"Tell me," he said, seizing her by the shoulders. "Are you happy, Clarissa? Does Richard——"

The door opened.

"Here is my Elizabeth," said Clarissa, emotionally, histrionically, perhaps.

"How d'y do?" said Elizabeth coming forward.

The sound of Big Ben striking the half-hour stuck out between them with extraordinary vigour, as if a young man, strong, indifferent, inconsiderate, were swinging dumb-bells this way and that.

"Hullo, Elizabeth!" cried Peter, stuffing his handkerchief into his pocket, going quickly to her, saying "Good-bye, Clarissa" without looking at her, leaving the room quickly, and running downstairs and opening the hall door.

"Peter! Peter!" cried Clarissa, following him out on to the landing. "My party to-night! Remember my party to-night!" she cried, having to raise her voice against the roar of the open air, and, overwhelmed by the traffic and the sound of all the clocks striking, her voice crying "Remember my party to-night!"

sounded frail and thin and very far away as Peter Walsh shut the door.

REMEMBER MY PARTY, remember my party, said Peter Walsh as he stepped down the street, speaking to himself rhythmically, in time with the flow of the sound, the direct downright sound of Big Ben striking the half-hour. (The leaden circles dissolved in the air.) Oh these parties, he thought; Clarissa's parties. Why does she give these parties, he thought. Not that he blamed her or this effigy of a man in a tail-coat with a carnation in his button-hole coming towards him. Only one person in the world could be as he was, in love. And there he was, this fortunate man, himself, reflected in the plate-glass window of a motor-car manufacturer in Victoria Street. All India lay behind him; plains, mountains; epidemics of cholera; a district twice as big as Ireland; decisions he had come to alone — he, Peter Walsh; who was now really for the first time in his life, in love. Clarissa had grown hard, he thought; and a trifle sentimental into the bargain, he suspected, looking at the great motor-cars capable of doing — how many miles on how many gallons? For he had a turn for mechanics; had invented a plough in his district, had ordered wheel-barrows from England, but the coolies wouldn't use them, all of which Clarissa knew nothing whatever about.

The way she said "Here is my Elizabeth!" — that annoyed him. Why not "Here's Elizabeth" simply? It was insincere. And Elizabeth didn't like it either. (Still the last tremors of the great booming voice shook the air round him; the half-hour; still early; only half-past eleven still.) For he understood young people; he liked them. There was always something cold in Clarissa, he thought. She had always, even as a girl, a sort of timidity, which in middle age becomes conventionality, and then it's all up, it's all up, he thought, looking rather drearily into the glassy depths, and wondering whether by calling at that hour he had annoyed her; overcome with shame suddenly at having been a fool; wept; been emotional; told her everything, as usual, as usual.

As a cloud crosses the sun, silence falls on London; and falls on the mind. Effort ceases. Time flaps on the mast. There we stop; there we stand. Rigid, the skeleton of habit alone upholds the human frame. Where there is nothing, Peter Walsh said to himself; feeling hollowed out, utterly empty within. Clarissa refused me, he thought. He stood there thinking, Clarissa refused me.

Ah, said St. Margaret's, like a hostess who comes into her drawing-room on the very stroke of the hour and finds her guests there already. I am not late. No, it is precisely half-past eleven, she says. Yet, though she is perfectly right, her voice, being the voice of the hostess, is reluctant to inflict its individuality. Some grief for the past holds it back; some concern for the present. It is half-past eleven, she says, and the sound of St. Margaret's glides into the recesses of the heart and buries itself in ring after ring of sound, like something alive which wants to confide itself, to disperse itself, to be, with a tremor of delight, at rest—like Clarissa herself, thought Peter Walsh, coming down the stairs on the stroke of the hour in white. It is Clarissa herself, he thought, with a deep emotion, and an extraordinarily clear, yet puzzling, recollection of her, as if this bell had come into the room years ago, where they sat at some moment of great intimacy, and had gone from one to the other and had left, like a bee with honey, laden with the moment. But what room? What moment? And why had he been so profoundly happy when the clock was striking? Then, as the sound of St. Margaret's languished, he thought, She has been ill, and the sound expressed languor and suffering. It was her heart, he remembered; and the sudden loudness of the final stroke tolled for death that surprised in the midst of life, Clarissa failing where she stood, in her drawing room. No! No! he cried. She is not dead! I am not old, he cried, and marched up Whitehall, as if there rolled down to him, vigorous, unending, his future.

He was not old, or set, or dried in the least. As for caring what they said of him—the Dalloways, the Whitbreads, and their set, he cared not a straw—not a straw (though it was true he would have, some time or other, to see whether Richard couldn't help him to some job). Striding, staring, he glared at the statue of the Duke of Cambridge. He had been sent down from Oxford—true. He had been a Socialist, in some sense a failure—true. Still the future of civilisation lies, he thought, in the hands of young men like that; of young men such as he was, thirty years ago; with their love of abstract principles; getting books sent out to them all the way from London to a peak in the Himalayas; reading science; reading philosophy. The future lies in the hands of young men like that, he thought.

A patter like the patter of leaves in a wood came from behind, and with it a rustling, regular thudding sound, which as it overtook him drummed his thoughts, strict in step, up Whitehall, without his doing. Boys in uniform, carrying guns, marched with their eyes ahead of them, marched, their arms stiff, and on their faces an expression like the letters of a legend written round the base of a statue praising duty, gratitude, fidelity, love of England.

It is, thought Peter Walsh, beginning to keep step with them, a very fine training. But they did not look robust. They were weedy for the most part, boys of sixteen, who might, to-morrow, stand behind bowls of rice, cakes of soap on counters. Now they wore on them unmixed with sensual pleasure or daily preoccupations the solemnity of the wreath which they had fetched from Finsbury Pavement to the empty tomb. They had taken their vow. The traffic respected it; vans were stopped.

I can't keep up with them, Peter Walsh thought, as they marched up Whitehall, and sure enough, on they marched, past him, past every one, in their steady way, as if one will worked legs and arms uniformly, and life, with its varieties, its irreticences, had been laid under a pavement of monuments and wreaths and drugged into a stiff yet staring corpse by discipline. One had to respect it; one might laugh; but one had to respect it, he thought. There they go, thought Peter Walsh, pausing at the edge of the pavement; and all the exalted statues, Nelson, Gordon, Havelock, the black, the spectacular images of great soldiers stood looking ahead of them, as if they too had made the same renunciation (Peter Walsh felt he too had made it, the great renunciation), trampled under the same temptations, and achieved at length a marble stare. But the stare Peter Walsh did not want for himself in the least; though he could respect it in others. He could respect it in boys. They don't know the troubles of the flesh yet, he thought, as the marching boys disappeared in the direction of the Strand—all that I've been through, he thought, crossing the road, and standing under Gordon's statue, Gordon whom as a boy he had worshipped; Gordon standing lonely with one leg raised and his arms crossed,—poor Gordon, he thought.

And just because nobody yet knew he was in London, except Clarissa, and the earth, after the voyage, still seemed an island to him, the strangeness of standing alone, alive, unknown, at half-past eleven in Trafalgar Square overcame him. What is it? Where am I? And why, after all, does one do it? he thought, the divorce seeming all moonshine. And down his mind went flat as a marsh, and three great emotions bowled over him; understanding; a vast philanthropy; and finally, as if the result of the others, an irrepressible, exquisite delight; as if inside his brain by another hand strings were pulled, shutters moved, and he, having nothing to do with it, yet stood at the opening of endless avenues, down which if he chose he might wander. He had not felt so young for years.

He had escaped! was utterly free — as happens in the downfall of habit when the mind, like an unguarded flame, bows and bends and seems about to blow from its holding. I haven't felt so young for years! thought Peter, escaping (only of course for an hour or so) from being precisely what he was, and feeling like a child who runs out of doors, and sees, as he runs, his old nurse waving at the wrong window. But she's extraordinarily attractive, he thought, as, walking across Trafalgar Square in the direction of the Haymarket, came a young woman who, as she passed Gordon's statue, seemed, Peter Walsh thought (susceptible as he was), to shed veil after veil, until she became the very woman he had always had in mind; young, but stately; merry, but discreet; black, but enchanting.

Straightening himself and stealthily fingering his pocket-knife he started after her to follow this woman, this excitement, which seemed even with its back turned to shed on him a light which connected them, which singled him out, as if the random uproar of the traffic had whispered through hollowed hands his name, not Peter, but his private name which he called himself in his own thoughts. "You," she said, only "you," saying it with her white gloves and her shoulders. Then the thin long cloak which the wind stirred as she walked past Dent's shop in Cockspur Street blew out with an enveloping kindness, a mournful tenderness, as of arms that would open and take the tired—

But she's not married; she's young; quite young, thought Peter, the red carnation he had seen her wear as she came across Trafalgar Square burning again in his eyes and making her lips red. But she waited at the kerbstone. There was a dignity about her. She was not worldly, like Clarissa; not rich, like Clarissa. Was she, he wondered as she moved, respectable? Witty, with a lizard's flickering tongue, he thought (for one must invent, must allow oneself a little diversion), a cool waiting wit, a darting wit; not noisy.

She moved; she crossed; he followed her. To embarrass her was the last thing he wished. Still if she stopped he would say "Come and have an ice," he would say, and she would answer, perfectly simply, "Oh yes."

But other people got between them in the street, obstructing him, blotting her out. He pursued; she changed. There was colour in her cheeks; mockery in her eyes; he was an adventurer, reckless, he thought, swift, daring, indeed (landed as he was last night from India) a romantic buccaneer, careless of all these damned proprieties, yellow dressing-gowns, pipes, fishing-rods, in the shop windows; and respectability and evening parties and spruce old men wearing white slips beneath their waistcoats. He was a buccaneer. On and on she went, across Piccadilly, and up Regent Street, ahead of him, her cloak, her gloves, her shoulders combining with the fringes and the laces and the feather boas in the windows to make the spirit of finery and whimsy which dwindled out of the shops on to the pavement, as the light of a lamp goes wavering at night over hedges in the darkness.

Laughing and delightful, she had crossed Oxford Street and Great Portland Street and turned down one of the little streets, and now, and now, the great moment was approaching, for now she slackened, opened her bag, and with one look in his direction, but not at him, one look that bade farewell, summed up the whole situation and dismissed it triumphantly, for ever, had fitted her key, opened the door, and gone! Clarissa's voice saying, Remember my party, Remember my party, sang in his ears. The house was one of those flat red houses with hanging flower-baskets of vague impropriety. It was over.

Well, I've had my fun; I've had it, he thought, looking up at the swinging baskets of pale geraniums. And it was smashed to atoms—his fun, for it was half made up, as he knew very well; invented, this escapade with the girl; made up, as one makes up the better part of life, he thought—making oneself up; making her up; creating an exquisite amusement, and something more. But odd it was, and quite true; all this one could never share— it smashed to atoms.

He turned; went up the street, thinking to find somewhere to sit, till it was time for Lincoln's Inn—for Messrs. Hooper and Grateley. Where should he go? No matter. Up the street, then, towards Regent's Park. His boots on the pavement struck out "no matter"; for it was early, still very early.

It was a splendid morning too. Like the pulse of a perfect heart, life struck straight through the streets. There was no fumbling—no hesitation. Sweeping and swerving, accurately, punctually, noiselessly, there, precisely at the right instant, the motor-car stopped at the door. The girl, silk-stockinged, feathered, evanescent, but not to him particularly attractive (for he had had his fling), alighted. Admirable butlers, tawny chow dogs, halls laid in black and white lozenges with white blinds blowing, Peter saw through the opened door and approved of. A splendid achievement in its own way, after all, London; the season; civilisation. Coming as he did from a respectable Anglo-Indian family which for at least three generations had administered the affairs of a continent (it's strange, he thought, what a sentiment I have about that, disliking India, and empire, and army as he did), there were moments when civilisation, even of this sort, seemed dear to him as a personal possession; moments of pride in England; in butlers; chow dogs; girls in their security. Ridiculous enough, still there it is, he thought. And the doctors and men of business and capable women all going about their business, punctual, alert, robust, seemed to him wholly admirable, good fellows, to whom one would entrust one's life, companions in the art of living, who would see one through. What with one thing and another, the show was really very tolerable; and he would sit down in the shade and smoke.

There was Regent's Park. Yes. As a child he had walked in Regent's Park—odd, he thought, how the thought of childhood keeps coming back to me—the result of seeing Clarissa, perhaps; for women live much more in the past than we do, he thought. They attach themselves to places; and their fathers—a woman's always proud of her father. Bourton was a nice place, a very nice place, but I could never get on with the old man, he thought. There was quite a scene one night—an argument about something or other, what, he could not remember. Politics presumably.

Yes, he remembered Regent's Park; the long straight walk; the little house where one bought air-balls to the left; an absurd statue with an inscription somewhere or other. He looked for an empty seat. He did not want to be bothered (feeling a little drowsy as he did) by people asking him the time. An elderly grey nurse, with a baby asleep in its perambulator—that was the best he could do for himself; sit down at the far end of the seat by that nurse.

She's a queer-looking girl, he thought, suddenly remembering Elizabeth as she came into the room and stood by her mother. Grown big; quite grown-up, not exactly pretty; handsome rather; and she can't be more than eighteen. Probably she doesn't get on with Clarissa. "There's my Elizabeth"—that sort of thing—why not "Here's Elizabeth" simply?—trying to make out, like most mothers, that things are what they're not. She trusts to her charm too much, he thought. She overdoes it.

The rich benignant cigar smoke eddied coolly down his throat; he puffed it out again in rings which breasted the air bravely for a moment; blue, circular—I shall try and get a word alone with Elizabeth to-night, he thought—then began to wobble into hour-glass shapes and taper away; odd shapes they take, he thought. Suddenly he closed his eyes, raised his hand with an effort, and threw away the heavy end of his cigar. A great brush swept smooth across his mind, sweeping across it moving branches, children's voices, the shuffle of feet, and people passing, and humming traffic, rising and falling traffic. Down, down he sank into the plumes and feathers of sleep, sank, and was muffled over.

THE GREY NURSE resumed her knitting as Peter Walsh, on the hot seat beside her, began snoring. In her grey dress, moving her hands indefatigably yet quietly, she seemed like the champion of the rights of sleepers, like one of those spectral presences which rise in twilight in woods made of sky and branches. The solitary traveller, haunter of lanes, disturber of ferns, and devastator of great hemlock plants, looking up, suddenly sees the giant figure at the end of the ride.

By conviction an atheist perhaps, he is taken by surprise with moments of extraordinary exaltation. Nothing exists outside us except a state of mind, he thinks; a desire for solace, for relief, for something outside these miserable pigmies, these feeble, these ugly, these craven men and women. But if he can conceive of her, then in some sort she exists, he thinks, and advancing down the path with his eyes upon sky and branches he rapidly endows them with womanhood; sees with amazement how grave they become; how majestically, as the breeze stirs them, they dispense with a dark flutter of the leaves charity, comprehension, absolution, and then, flinging themselves suddenly aloft, confound the piety of their aspect with a wild carouse.

Such are the visions which proffer great cornucopias full of fruit to the solitary traveller, or murmur in his ear like sirens lolloping away on the green sea waves, or are dashed in his face like bunches of roses, or rise to the surface like pale faces which fishermen flounder through floods to embrace.

Such are the visions which ceaselessly float up, pace beside, put their faces in front of, the actual thing; often overpowering the solitary traveller and taking away from him the sense of the earth, the wish to return, and giving him for substitute a general peace, as if (so he thinks as he advances down the forest ride) all this fever of living were simplicity itself; and myriads of things merged in one thing; and this figure, made of sky and branches as it is, had risen from the troubled sea (he is elderly, past fifty now) as a shape might be sucked up out of the waves to shower down from her magnificent hands compassion, comprehension, absolution. So, he thinks, may I never go back to the lamplight; to the sitting-room; never finish my book; never knock out my pipe; never ring for Mrs. Turner to clear away; rather let me walk straight on to this great figure, who will, with a toss of her head, mount me on her streamers and let me blow to nothingness with the rest.

Such are the visions. The solitary traveller is soon beyond the wood; and there, coming to the door with shaded eyes, possibly to look for his return, with hands raised, with white apron blowing, is an elderly woman who seems (so powerful is this infirmity) to seek, over a desert, a lost son; to search for a rider destroyed; to be the figure of the mother whose sons have been killed in the battles of the world. So, as the solitary traveller advances down the village street where the women stand knitting and the men dig in the garden, the evening seems ominous; the figures still; as if some august fate, known to them, awaited without fear, were about to sweep them into complete annihilation.

Indoors among ordinary things, the cupboard, the table, the window-sill with its geraniums, suddenly the outline of the land-lady, bending to remove the cloth, becomes soft with light, an adorable emblem which only the recollection of cold human contacts forbids us to embrace. She takes the marmalade; she shuts it in the cupboard.

"There is nothing more to-night, sir?"

But to whom does the solitary traveller make reply?

So THE ELDERLY NURSE knitted over the sleeping baby in Regent's Park. So Peter Walsh snored.

He woke with extreme suddenness, saying to himself, "The death of the soul."

"Lord, Lord!" he said to himself out loud, stretching and opening his eyes. "The death of the soul." The words attached themselves to some scene, to some room, to some past he had been dreaming of. It became clearer; the scene, the room, the past he had been dreaming of.

It was at Bourton that summer, early in the 'nineties, when he was so passionately in love with Clarissa. There were a great many people there, laughing and talking, sitting round a table after tea and the room was bathed in yellow light and full of cigarette smoke. They were talking about a man who had married his housemaid, one of the neighbouring squires, he had forgotten his name. He had married his housemaid, and she had been brought to Bourton to call—an awful visit it had been. She was absurdly over-dressed, "like a cockatoo," Clarissa had said, imitating her, and she never stopped talking. On and on she went, on and on. Clarissa imitated her. Then somebody said—Sally Seton it was—did it make any real difference to one's feelings to know that before they'd married she had had a baby? (In those days, in mixed company, it was a bold thing to say.) He could see Clarissa now, turning bright pink; somehow contracting; and saying, "Oh, I shall never be able to speak to her again!" Whereupon the whole party sitting round the tea-table seemed to wobble. It was very uncomfortable.

He hadn't blamed her for minding the fact, since in those days a girl brought up as she was, knew nothing, but it was her manner that annoyed him; timid; hard; something arrogant; unimaginative; prudish. "The death of the soul." He had said that instinctively, ticketing the moment as he used to do—the death of her soul.

Every one wobbled; every one seemed to bow, as she spoke, and then to stand up different. He could see Sally Seton, like a child who has been in mischief, leaning forward, rather flushed, wanting to talk, but afraid, and Clarissa did frighten people. (She was Clarissa's greatest friend, always about the place, totally unlike her, an attractive creature, handsome, dark, with the reputation in those days of great daring and he used to give her cigars, which she smoked in her bedroom. She had either been engaged to somebody or quarrelled with her family and old Parry disliked them both equally, which was a great bond.) Then Clarissa, still with an air of being offended with them all, got up, made some excuse, and went off, alone. As she opened the door, in came that great shaggy dog which ran after sheep. She flung herself upon him, went into raptures. It was as if she said to Peter—it was all aimed at him, he knew—"I know you thought me absurd about that woman just now; but see how extraordinarily sympathetic I am; see how I love my Rob!"

They had always this queer power of communicating without words. She knew directly he criticised her. Then she would do something quite obvious to defend herself, like this fuss with the dog—but it never took him in, he always saw through

Clarissa. Not that he said anything, of course; just sat looking glum. It was the way their quarrels often began.

She shut the door. At once be became extremely depressed. It all seemed useless—going on being in love; going on quarrelling; going on making it up, and he wandered off alone, among outhouses, stables, looking at the horses. (The place was quite a humble one; the Parrys were never very well off; but there were always grooms and stable-boys about—Clarissa loved riding—and an old coachman—what was his name?—an old nurse, old Moody, old Goody, some such name they called her, whom one was taken to visit in a little room with lots of photographs, lots of bird-cages.)

It was an awful evening! He grew more and more gloomy, not about that only; about everything. And he couldn't see her; couldn't explain to her; couldn't have it out. There were always people about—she'd go on as if nothing had happened. That was the devilish part of her—this coldness, this woodenness, something very profound in her, which he had felt again this morning talking to her; an impenetrability. Yet Heaven knows he loved her. She had some queer power of fiddling on one's nerves, turning one's nerves to fiddle-strings, yes.

He had gone in to dinner rather late, from some idiotic idea of making himself felt, and had sat down by old Miss Parry—Aunt Helena—Mr. Parry's sister, who was supposed to preside. There she sat in her white Cashmere shawl, with her head against the window—a formidable old lady, but kind to him, for he had found her some rare flower, and she was a great botanist, marching off in thick boots with a black collecting-box slung between her shoulders. He sat down beside her, and couldn't speak. Everything seemed to race past him; he just sat there, eating. And then half-way through dinner he made himself look across at Clarissa for the first time. She was talking to a young man on her right. He had a sudden revelation. "She will marry that man," he said to himself. He didn't even know his name.

For of course it was that afternoon, that very afternoon, that Dalloway had come over; and Clarissa called him "Wickham"; that was the beginning of it all. Somebody had brought him over; and Clarissa got his name wrong. She introduced him to everybody as Wickham. At last he said "My name is Dalloway!"—that was his first view of Richard—a fair young man, rather awkward, sitting on a deck-chair, and blurting out "My name is Dalloway!" Sally got hold of it; always after that she called him "My name is Dalloway!"

He was a prey to revelations at that time. This one—that she would marry Dalloway—was blinding—overwhelming at the moment. There was a sort of—how could he put it?—a sort of ease in her manner to him; something maternal; something gentle. They were talking about politics. All through dinner he tried to hear what they were saying.

Afterwards he could remember standing by old Miss Parry's chair in the drawing-room. Clarissa came up, with her perfect manners, like a real hostess, and wanted to introduce him to some one—spoke as if they had never met before, which enraged him. Yet even then he admired her for it. He admired her courage; her social instinct; he admired her power of carrying things through. "The perfect hostess," he said to her, whereupon she winced all over. But he meant her to feel it. He would have done anything to hurt her after seeing her with Dalloway. So she left him. And he had a feeling that they were all gathered together in a conspiracy against him—laughing and talking—behind his back. There he stood by Miss Parry's chair as though he had been cut out of wood, he talking about wild flowers. Never, never had he suffered so infernally! He must have forgotten even to pretend to listen; at last he woke up; he saw Miss Parry looking rather disturbed, rather indignant, with her prominent eyes fixed. He almost cried out that he couldn't attend because he was in Hell! People began going out of the room. He heard them talking about fetching cloaks; about its being cold on the water, and so on. They were going boating on the lake by moonlight—one of Sally's mad ideas. He could hear her describing the moon. And they all went out. He was left quite alone.

"Don't you want to go with them?" said Aunt Helena—old Miss Parry!—she had guessed. And he turned round and there was Clarissa again. She had come back to fetch him. He was overcome by her generosity—her goodness.

"Come along," she said. "They're waiting."

He had never felt so happy in the whole of his life! Without a word they made it up. They walked down to the lake. He had twenty minutes of perfect happiness. Her voice, her laugh, her dress (something floating, white, crimson), her spirit, her adventurousness; she made them all disembark and explore the island; she startled a hen; she laughed; she sang. And all the time, he knew perfectly well, Dalloway was falling in love with her; she was falling in love with Dalloway; but it didn't seem to matter. Nothing mattered. They sat on the ground and talked—he and Clarissa. They went in and out of each other's minds without any effort. And then in a second it was over. He said to himself as they were getting into the boat, "She will marry that man," dully, without any resentment; but it was an obvious thing. Dalloway would marry Clarissa.

Dalloway rowed them in. He said nothing. But somehow as they watched him start, jumping on to his bicycle to ride twenty miles through the woods, wobbling off down the drive, waving his hand and disappearing, he obviously did feel, instinctively, tremendously, strongly, all that; the night; the romance; Clarissa. He deserved to have her.

For himself, he was absurd. His demands upon Clarissa (he could see it now) were absurd. He asked impossible things. He made terrible scenes. She would have accepted him still, perhaps, if he had been less absurd. Sally thought so. She wrote him all that summer long letters; how they had talked of him; how she had praised him, how Clarissa burst into tears! It was an extraordinary summer—all letters, scenes, telegrams—arriving at

Bourton early in the morning, hanging about till the servants were up; appalling *tête-à-têtes* with old Mr. Parry at breakfast; Aunt Helena formidable but kind; Sally sweeping him off for talks in the vegetable garden; Clarissa in bed with headaches.

The final scene, the terrible scene which he believed had mattered more than anything in the whole of his life (it might be an exaggeration—but still so it did seem now) happened at three o'clock in the afternoon of a very hot day. It was a trifle that led up to it—Sally at lunch saying something about Dalloway, and calling him "My name is Dalloway"; whereupon Clarissa suddenly stiffened, coloured, in a way she had, and rapped out sharply, "We've had enough of that feeble joke." That was all; but for him it was precisely as if she had said, "I'm only amusing myself with you; I've an understanding with Richard Dalloway." So he took it. He had not slept for nights. "It's got to be finished one way or the other," he said to himself. He sent a note to her by Sally asking her to meet him by the fountain at three. "Something very important has happened," he scribbled at the end of it.

The fountain was in the middle of a little shrubbery, far from the house, with shrubs and trees all round it. There she came, even before the time, and they stood with the fountain between them, the spout (it was broken) dribbling water incessantly. How sights fix themselves upon the mind! For example, the vivid green moss.

She did not move. "Tell me the truth, tell me the truth," he kept on saying. He felt as if his forehead would burst. She seemed contracted, petrified. She did not move. "Tell me the truth," he repeated, when suddenly that old man Breitkopf popped his head in carrying the *Times*; stared at them; gaped; and went away. They neither of them moved. "Tell me the truth," he repeated. He felt that he was grinding against something physically hard; she was unyielding. She was like iron, like flint, rigid up the backbone. And when she said, "It's no use. It's no use. This is the end"—after he had spoken for hours, it seemed, with the tears running down his cheeks—it was as if she had hit him in the face. She turned, she left him, went away.

"Clarissa!" he cried. "Clarissa!" But she never came back. It was over. He went away that night. He never saw her again.

IT WAS AWFUL, he cried, awful, awful!

Still, the sun was hot. Still, one got over things. Still, life had a way of adding day to day. Still, he thought, yawning and beginning to take notice—Regent's Park had changed very little since he was a boy, except for the squirrels—still, presumably there were compensations—when little Elise Mitchell, who had been picking up pebbles to add to the pebble collection which she and her brother were making on the nursery mantelpiece, plumped her handful down on the nurse's knee and scudded off again full tilt into a lady's legs. Peter Walsh laughed out.

But Lucrezia Warren Smith was saying to herself, It's wicked; why should I suffer? she was asking, as she walked down the broad path. No; I can't stand it any longer, she was saying, having left Septimus, who wasn't Septimus any longer, to say hard, cruel, wicked things, to talk to himself, to talk to a dead man, on the seat over there; when the child ran full tilt into her, fell flat, and burst out crying.

That was comforting rather. She stood her upright, dusted her frock, kissed her.

But for herself she had done nothing wrong; she had loved Septimus; she had been happy; she had had a beautiful home, and there her sisters lived still, making hats. Why should *she* suffer?

The child ran straight back to its nurse, and Rezia saw her scolded, comforted, taken up by the nurse who put down her knitting, and the kind-looking man gave her his watch to blow open to comfort her—but why should *she* be exposed? Why not left in Milan? Why tortured? Why?

Slightly waved by tears the broad path, the nurse, the man in grey, the perambulator, rose and fell before her eyes. To be rocked by this malignant torturer was her lot. But why? She was like a bird sheltering under the thin hollow of a leaf, who blinks at the sun when the leaf moves; starts at the crack of a dry twig. She was exposed; she was surrounded by the enormous trees, vast clouds of an indifferent world, exposed; tortured; and why should she suffer? Why?

She frowned; she stamped her foot. She must go back again to Septimus since it was almost time for them to be going to Sir William Bradshaw. She must go back and tell him, go back to him sitting there on the green chair under the tree, talking to himself, or to that dead man Evans, whom she had only seen once for a moment in the shop. He had seemed a nice quiet man; a great friend of Septimus's, and he had been killed in the War. But such things happen to every one. Every one has friends who were killed in the War. Every one gives up something when they marry. She had given up her home. She had come to live here, in this awful city. But Septimus let himself think about horrible things, as she could too, if she tried. He had grown stranger and stranger. He said people were talking behind the bedroom walls. Mrs. Filmer thought it odd. He saw things too—he had seen an old woman's head in the middle of a fern. Yet he could be happy when he chose. They went to Hampton Court on top of a bus, and they were perfectly happy. All the little red and yellow flowers were out on the grass, like floating lamps he said, and talked and chattered and laughed, making up stories. Suddenly he said, "Now we will kill ourselves," when they were standing by the river, and he looked at it with a look which she had seen in his eyes when a train went by, or an omnibus—a look as if something fascinated him; and she felt he was going from her and she caught him by the arm. But going home he was perfectly quiet—perfectly reasonable. He would argue with her about killing themselves; and explain how wicked people were; how he could see them making up lies as they passed in the street. He knew all their thoughts, he said; he knew everything. He knew the meaning of the world, he said.

Then when they got back he could hardly walk. He lay on the sofa and made her hold his hand to prevent him from falling down, down, he cried, into the flames! and saw faces laughing at him, calling him horrible disgusting names, from the walls, and hands pointing round the screen. Yet they were quite alone. But he began to talk aloud, answering people, arguing, laughing, crying, getting very excited and making her write things down. Perfect nonsense it was; about death; about Miss Isabel Pole. She could stand it no longer. She would go back.

She was close to him now, could see him staring at the sky, muttering, clasping his hands. Yet Dr. Holmes said there was nothing the matter with him. What then had happened—why had he gone, then, why, when she sat by him, did he start, frown at her, move away, and point at her hand, take her hand, look at it terrified?

Was it that she had taken off her wedding ring? "My hand has grown so thin," she said. "I have put it in my purse," she told him.

He dropped her hand. Their marriage was over, he thought, with agony, with relief. The rope was cut; he mounted; he was free, as it was decreed that he, Septimus, the lord of men, should be free; alone (since his wife had thrown away her wedding ring; since she had left him), he, Septimus, was alone, called forth in advance of the mass of men to hear the truth, to learn the meaning, which now at last, after all the toils of civilisation—Greeks, Romans, Shakespeare, Darwin, and now himself—was to be given whole to.... "To whom?" he asked aloud. "To the Prime Minister," the voices which rustled above his head replied. The supreme secret must be told to the Cabinet; first that trees are alive; next there is no crime; next love, universal love, he muttered, gasping, trembling, painfully drawing out these profound truths which needed, so deep were they, so difficult, an immense effort to speak out, but the world was entirely changed by them for ever.

No crime; love; he repeated, fumbling for his card and pencil, when a Skye terrier snuffed his trousers and he started in an agony of fear. It was turning into a man! He could not watch it happen! It was horrible, terrible to see a dog become a man! At once the dog trotted away.

Heaven was divinely merciful, infinitely benignant. It spared him, pardoned his weakness. But what was the scientific explanation (for one must be scientific above all things)? Why could he see through bodies, see into the future, when dogs will become men? It was the heat wave presumably, operating upon a brain made sensitive by eons of evolution. Scientifically speaking, the flesh was melted off the world. His body was macerated until only the nerve fibres were left. It was spread like a veil upon a rock.

He lay back in his chair, exhausted but upheld. He lay resting, waiting, before he again interpreted, with effort, with agony, to mankind. He lay very high, on the back of the world. The earth thrilled beneath him. Red flowers grew through his flesh; their stiff leaves rustled by his head. Music began clanging against the rocks up here. It is a motor horn down in the street, he muttered; but up here it cannoned from rock to rock, divided, met in shocks of sound which rose in smooth columns (that music should be visible was a discovery) and became an anthem, an anthem twined round now by a shepherd boy's piping (That's an old man playing a penny whistle by the public-house, he muttered) which, as the boy stood still came bubbling from his pipe, and then, as he climbed higher, made its exquisite plaint while the traffic passed beneath. This boy's elegy is played among the traffic, thought Septimus. Now he withdraws up into the snows, and roses hang about him—the thick red roses which grow on my bedroom wall, he reminded himself. The music stopped. He has his penny, he reasoned it out, and has gone on to the next public-house.

But he himself remained high on his rock, like a drowned sailor on a rock. I leant over the edge of the boat and fell down, he thought. I went under the sea. I have been dead, and yet am now alive, but let me rest still; he begged (he was talking to himself again—it was awful, awful!); and as, before waking, the voices of birds and the sound of wheels chime and chatter in a queer harmony, grow louder and louder and the sleeper feels himself drawing to the shores of life, so he felt himself drawing towards life, the sun growing hotter, cries sounding louder, something tremendous about to happen.

He had only to open his eyes; but a weight was on them; a fear. He strained; he pushed; he looked; he saw Regent's Park before him. Long streamers of sunlight fawned at his feet. The trees waved, brandished. We welcome, the world seemed to say; we accept; we create. Beauty, the world seemed to say. And as if to prove it (scientifically) wherever he looked at the houses, at the railings, at the antelopes stretching over the palings, beauty sprang instantly. To watch a leaf quivering in the rush of air was an exquisite joy. Up in the sky swallows swooping, swerving, flinging themselves in and out, round and round, yet always with perfect control as if elastics held them; and the flies rising and falling; and the sun spotting now this leaf, now that, in mockery, dazzling it with soft gold in pure good temper; and now and again some chime (it might be a motor horn) tinkling divinely on the grass stalks—all of this, calm and reasonable as it was, made out of ordinary things as it was, was the truth now; beauty, that was the truth now. Beauty was everywhere.

"It is time," said Rezia.

The word "time" split its husk; poured its riches over him; and from his lips fell like shells, like shavings from a plane, without his making them, hard, white, imperishable words, and flew to attach themselves to their places in an ode to Time; an immortal ode to Time. He sang. Evans answered from behind the tree. The dead were in Thessaly, Evans sang, among the orchids. There they waited till the War was over, and now the dead, now Evans himself—

"For God's sake don't come!" Septimus cried out. For he could not look upon the dead.

But the branches parted. A man in grey was actually walking towards them. It was Evans! But no mud was on him; no wounds; he was not changed. I must tell the whole world, Septimus cried, raising his hand (as the dead man in the grey suit came nearer), raising his hand like some colossal figure who has lamented the fate of man for ages in the desert alone with his hands pressed to his forehead, furrows of despair on his cheeks, and now sees light on the desert's edge which broadens and strikes the iron-black figure (and Septimus half rose from his chair), and with legions of men prostrate behind him he, the giant mourner, receives for one moment on his face the whole —

"But I am so unhappy, Septimus," said Rezia trying to make him sit down.

The millions lamented; for ages they had sorrowed. He would turn round, he would tell them in a few moments, only a few moments more, of this relief, of this joy, of this astonishing revelation —

"The time, Septimus," Rezia repeated. "What is the time?"

He was talking, he was starting, this man must notice him. He was looking at them.

"I will tell you the time," said Septimus, very slowly, very drowsily, smiling mysteriously. As he sat smiling at the dead man in the grey suit the quarter struck — the quarter to twelve.

And that is being young, Peter Walsh thought as he passed them. To be having an awful scene — the poor girl looked absolutely desperate — in the middle of the morning. But what was it about, he wondered, what had the young man in the overcoat been saying to her to make her look like that; what awful fix had they got themselves into, both to look so desperate as that on a fine summer morning? The amusing thing about coming back to England, after five years, was the way it made, anyhow the first days, things stand out as if one had never seen them before; lovers squabbling under a tree; the domestic family life of the parks. Never had he seen London look so enchanting — the

softness of the distances; the richness; the greenness; the civilisation, after India, he thought, strolling across the grass.

This susceptibility to impressions had been his undoing no
doubt. Still at his age he had, like a boy or a girl even, these alternations of mood; good days, bad days, for no reason whatever, happiness from a pretty face, downright misery at the sight
of a frump. After India of course one fell in love with every
woman one met. There was a freshness about them; even the
poorest dressed better than five years ago surely; and to his eye
the fashions had never been so becoming; the long black cloaks;
the slimness; the elegance; and then the delicious and apparently
universal habit of paint. Every woman, even the most respectable, had roses blooming under glass; lips cut with a knife;
curls of Indian ink; there was design, art, everywhere; a change
of some sort had undoubtedly taken place. What did the young
people think about? Peter Walsh asked himself.

Those five years—1918 to 1923—had been, he suspected,
somehow very important. People looked different. Newspapers
seemed different. Now for instance there was a man writing
quite openly in one of the respectable weeklies about water-
closets. That you couldn't have done ten years ago—written
quite openly about water-closets in a respectable weekly. And
then this taking out a stick of rouge, or a powder-puff and making up in public. On board ship coming home there were lots of
young men and girls—Betty and Bertie he remembered in particular—carrying on quite openly; the old mother sitting and
watching them with her knitting, cool as a cucumber. The girl
would stand still and powder her nose in front of every one.
And they weren't engaged; just having a good time; no feelings
hurt on either hide. As hard as nails she was—Betty What'shername—; but a thorough good sort. She would make a very
good wife at thirty—she would marry when it suited her to
marry; marry some rich man and live in a large house near
Manchester.

Who was it now who had done that? Peter Walsh asked himself, turning into the Broad Walk,—married a rich man and lived in a large house near Manchester? Somebody who had written him a long, gushing letter quite lately about "blue hydrangeas." It was seeing blue hydrangeas that made her think of him and the old days—Sally Seton, of course! It was Sally Seton—the last person in the world one would have expected to marry a rich man and live in a large house near Manchester, the wild, the daring, the romantic Sally!

But of all that ancient lot, Clarissa's friends—Whitbreads, Kinderleys, Cunninghams, Kinloch-Jones's—Sally was probably the best. She tried to get hold of things by the right end anyhow. She saw through Hugh Whitbread anyhow—the admirable Hugh—when Clarissa and the rest were at his feet.

"The Whitbreads?" he could hear her saying. "Who are the Whitbreads? Coal merchants. Respectable tradespeople.'

Hugh she detested for some reason. He thought of nothing but his own appearance, she said. He ought to have been a Duke. He would be certain to marry one of the Royal Princesses. And of course Hugh had the most extraordinary, the most natural, the most sublime respect for the British aristocracy of any human being he had ever come across. Even Clarissa had to own that. Oh, but he was such a dear, so unselfish, gave up shooting to please his old mother—remembered his aunts' birthdays, and so on.

Sally, to do her justice, saw through all that. One of the things he remembered best was an argument one Sunday morning at Bourton about women's rights (that antediluvian topic), when Sally suddenly lost her temper, flared up, and told Hugh that he represented all that was most detestable in British middle-class life. She told him that she considered him responsible for the state of "those poor girls in Piccadilly"—Hugh, the perfect gentleman, poor Hugh!—never did a man look more horrified! She did it on purpose she said afterwards (for they used to get together in the vegetable garden and compare notes). "He's read nothing, thought nothing, felt nothing," he could hear her saying in that very emphatic voice which carried so much farther than she knew. The stable-boys had more life in them than Hugh, she said. He was a perfect specimen of the public school type, she said. No country but England could have produced him. She was really spiteful, for some reason; had some grudge against him. Something had happened—he forgot what—in the smoking-room. He had insulted her—kissed her? Incredible! Nobody believed a word against Hugh of course. Who could? Kissing Sally in the smoking-room! If it had been some Honourable Edith or Lady Violet, perhaps; but not that ragamuffin Sally without a penny to her name, and a father or a mother gambling at Monte Carlo. For all the people he had ever met Hugh was the greatest snob—the most obsequious—no, he didn't cringe exactly. He was too much of a prig for that. A first-rate valet was the obvious comparison—somebody who walked behind carrying suit cases; could be trusted to send telegrams—indispensable to hostesses. And he'd found his job—married his Honourable Evelyn; got some little post at Court, looked after the King's cellars, polished the Imperial shoe-buckles, went about in knee-breeches and lace ruffles. How remorseless life is! A little job at Court!

He had married this lady, the Honourable Evelyn, and they lived hereabouts, so he thought (looking at the pompous houses overlooking the Park), for he had lunched there once in a house which had, like all Hugh's possessions, something that no other house could possibly have—linen cupboards it might have been. You had to go and look at them—you had to spend a great deal of time always admiring whatever it was—linen cupboards, pillow-cases, old oak furniture, pictures, which Hugh had picked up for an old song. But Mrs. Hugh sometimes gave the show away. She was one of those obscure mouse-like little women who admire big men. She was almost negligible. Then suddenly she would say something quite unexpected—something sharp. She had the relics of the grand manner perhaps. The steam coal was a little too strong for her—it made the atmosphere thick. And so there they lived, with their linen cupboards and their old masters and their pillow-cases fringed with real lace at the rate of five or ten thousand a year presumably, while he, who was two years older than Hugh, cadged for a job.

At fifty-three he had to come and ask them to put him into some secretary's office, to find him some usher's job teaching little boys Latin, at the beck and call of some mandarin in an office, something that brought in five hundred a year; for if he married Daisy, even with his pension, they could never do on less. Whitbread could do it presumably; or Dalloway. He didn't mind what he asked Dalloway. He was a thorough good sort; a bit limited; a bit thick in the head; yes; but a thorough good sort. Whatever he took up he did in the same matter-of-fact sensible way; without a touch of imagination, without a spark of brilliancy, but with the inexplicable niceness of his type. He ought to have been a country gentleman—he was wasted on politics. He was at his best out of doors, with horses and dogs—how good he was, for instance, when that great shaggy dog of Clarissa's got caught in a trap and had its paw half torn off, and Clarissa turned faint and Dalloway did the whole thing; bandaged, made splints; told Clarissa not to be a fool. That was what she liked him for perhaps—that was what she needed. "Now, my dear, don't be a fool. Hold this—fetch that," all the time talking to the dog as if it were a human being.

But how could she swallow all that stuff about poetry? How could she let him hold forth about Shakespeare? Seriously and solemnly Richard Dalloway got on his hind legs and said that no decent man ought to read Shakespeare's sonnets because it was like listening at keyholes (besides the relationship was not one that he approved). No decent man ought to let his wife visit a deceased wife's sister. Incredible! The only thing to do was to pelt him with sugared almonds—it was at dinner. But Clarissa sucked it all in; thought it so honest of him; so independent of him; Heaven knows if she didn't think him the most original mind she'd ever met!

That was one of the bonds between Sally and himself. There was a garden where they used to walk, a walled-in place, with rose-bushes and giant cauliflowers—he could remember Sally tearing off a rose, stopping to exclaim at the beauty of the cabbage leaves in the moonlight (it was extraordinary how vividly it all came back to him, things he hadn't thought of for years), while she implored him, half laughing of course, to carry off Clarissa, to save her from the Hughs and the Dalloways and all the other "perfect gentlemen" who would "stifle her soul" (she wrote reams of poetry in those days), make a mere hostess of her, encourage her worldliness. But one must do Clarissa justice. She wasn't going to marry Hugh anyhow. She had a perfectly clear notion of what she wanted. Her emotions were all on the surface. Beneath, she was very shrewd—a far better judge of character than Sally, for instance, and with it all, purely feminine; with that extraordinary gift, that woman's gift, of making a world of her own wherever she happened to be. She came into a room; she stood, as he had often seen her, in a doorway with lots of people round her. But it was Clarissa one remembered. Not that she was striking; not beautiful at all; there was nothing picturesque about her; she never said anything specially clever; there she was, however; there she was.

No, no, no! He was not in love with her any more! He only felt, after seeing her that morning, among her scissors and silks, making ready for the party, unable to get away from the thought of her; she kept coming back and back like a sleeper jolting against him in a railway carriage; which was not being in love, of course; it was thinking of her, criticising her, starting again, after thirty years, trying to explain her. The obvious thing to say of her was that she was worldly; cared too much for rank and society and getting on in the world—which was true in a sense; she had admitted it to him. (You could always get her to own up if you took the trouble; she was honest.) What she would say was that she hated frumps, fogies, failures, like himself presumably; thought people had no right to slouch about with their hands in their pockets; must do something, be something; and these great swells, these Duchesses, these hoary old Countesses one met in her drawing-room, unspeakably remote as he felt them to be from anything that mattered a straw, stood for something real to her. Lady Bexborough, she said once, held herself upright (so did Clarissa herself; she never lounged in any sense of the word; she was straight as a dart, a little rigid in fact). She said they had a kind of courage which the older she grew the more she respected. In all this there was a great deal of Dalloway, of course; a great deal of the public-spirited, British Empire, tariff-reform, governing-class spirit, which had grown on her, as it tends to do. With twice his wits, she had to see things through his eyes—one of the tragedies of married life. With a mind of her own, she must always be quoting Richard—as if one couldn't know to a tittle what Richard thought by reading the *Morning Post* of a morning! These parties for example were all for him, or for her idea of him (to do Richard justice he would have been happier farming in Norfolk). She made her drawing-room a sort of meeting-place; she had a genius for it. Over and over again he had seen her take some raw youth, twist him, turn him, wake him up; set him going. Infinite numbers of dull people conglomerated round her of course. But odd unexpected people turned up; an artist sometimes; sometimes a writer; queer fish in that atmosphere. And behind it all was that network of visiting, leaving cards, being kind to people; running about with bunches of flowers, little presents; So-and-so was going to France—must have an air-cushion; a real drain on her strength; all that interminable traffic that women of her sort keep up; but she did it genuinely, from a natural instinct.

Oddly enough, she was one of the most thorough-going sceptics he had ever met, and possibly (this was a theory he used to make up to account for her, so transparent in some ways, so inscrutable in others), possibly she said to herself, As we are a doomed race, chained to a sinking ship (her favourite reading as a girl was Huxley and Tyndall, and they were fond of these nautical metaphors), as the whole thing is a bad joke, let us, at any rate, do our part; mitigate the sufferings of our fellow-prisoners (Huxley again); decorate the dungeon with flowers and air-cushions; be as decent as we possibly can. Those ruffians, the Gods, shan't have it all their own way,—her notion being that the Gods, who never lost a chance of hurting, thwarting and spoiling human lives were seriously put out if, all the same, you behaved like a lady. That phase came directly after Sylvia's death—that horrible affair. To see your own sister killed by a falling tree (all Justin Parry's fault—all his carelessness) before your very eyes, a girl too on the verge of life, the most gifted of them, Clarissa always said, was enough to turn one bitter. Later she wasn't so positive perhaps; she thought there were no Gods; no one was to blame; and so she evolved this atheist's religion of doing good for the sake of goodness.

And of course she enjoyed life immensely. It was her nature to enjoy (though goodness only knows, she had her reserves; it was a mere sketch, he often felt, that even he, after all these years, could make of Clarissa). Anyhow there was no bitterness in her; none of that sense of moral virtue which is so repulsive in good women. She enjoyed practically everything. If you walked with her in Hyde Park now it was a bed of tulips, now a child in a perambulator, now some absurd little drama she made up on the spur of the moment. (Very likely, she would have talked to those lovers, if she had thought them unhappy.) She had a sense of comedy that was really exquisite, but she needed people, always people, to bring it out, with the inevitable result that she frittered her time away, lunching, dining, giving these incessant parties of hers, talking nonsense, sayings things she didn't mean, blunting the edge of her mind, losing her discrimination. There she would sit at the head of the table taking infinite pains with some old buffer who might be useful to Dalloway—they knew the most appalling bores in Europe—or in came Elizabeth and everything must give way to *her*. She was at a High School, at the inarticulate stage last time he was over, a round-eyed, pale-faced girl, with nothing of her mother in her, a silent stolid creature, who took it all as a matter of course, let her mother make a fuss of her, and then said "May I go now?" like a child of four; going off, Clarissa explained, with that mixture of amusement and pride which Dalloway himself seemed to rouse in her, to play hockey. And now Elizabeth was "out," presumably; thought him an old fogy, laughed at her mother's friends. Ah well, so be it. The compensation of growing old, Peter Walsh thought, coming out of Regent's Park, and holding his hat in hand, was simply this; that the passions remain as strong as ever, but one has gained—at last!—the power which adds the supreme flavour to existence,— the power of taking hold of experience, of turning it round, slowly, in the light.

A terrible confession it was (he put his hat on again), but now, at the age of fifty three one scarcely needed people any more. Life itself, every moment of it, every drop of it, here, this instant, now, in the sun, in Regent's Park, was enough. Too much indeed. A whole lifetime was too short to bring out, now that one had acquired the power, the full flavour; to extract every ounce of pleasure, every shade of meaning; which both were so much more solid than they used to be, so much less personal. It was impossible that he should ever suffer again as Clarissa had made him suffer. For hours at a time (pray God that one might say these things without being overheard!), for hours and days he never thought of Daisy.

Could it be that he was in love with her then, remembering the misery, the torture, the extraordinary passion of those days? It was a different thing altogether—a much pleasanter thing— the truth being, of course, that now *she* was in love with *him*. And that perhaps was the reason why, when the ship actually sailed, he felt an extraordinary relief, wanted nothing so much as to be alone; was annoyed to find all her little attentions—cigars, notes, a rug for the voyage—in his cabin. Every one if they were honest would say the same; one doesn't want people after fifty; one doesn't want to go on telling women they are pretty; that's what most men of fifty would say, Peter Walsh thought, if they were honest.

But then these astonishing accesses of emotion—bursting into tears this morning, what was all that about? What could Clarissa have thought of him? thought him a fool presumably, not for the first time. It was jealousy that was at the bottom of it— jealousy which survives every other passion of mankind, Peter Walsh thought, holding his pocket-knife at arm's length. She had been meeting Major Orde, Daisy said in her last letter; said it on purpose he knew; said it to make him jealous; he could see her wrinkling her forehead as she wrote, wondering what she could say to hurt him; and yet it made no difference; he was furious! All this pother of coming to England and seeing lawyers wasn't to marry her, but to prevent her from marrying anybody else. That was what tortured him, that was what came over him when he saw Clarissa so calm, so cold, so intent on her dress or whatever it was; realising what she might have spared him, what she had re-duced him to—a whimpering, snivelling old ass. But women, he thought, shutting his pocket-knife, don't know what passion is. They don't know the meaning of it to men. Clarissa was as cold as an icicle. There she would sit on the sofa by his side, let him take her hand, give him one kiss—Here he was at the crossing.

A sound interrupted him; a frail quivering sound, a voice bubbling up without direction, vigour, beginning or end, run-ning weakly and shrilly and with an absence of all human mean-ing into

ee um fah um so
foo swee too eem oo—

the voice of no age or sex, the voice of an ancient spring spout-ing from the earth; which issued, just opposite Regent's Park Tube station from a tall quivering shape, like a funnel, like a rusty pump, like a wind-beaten tree for ever barren of leaves which lets the wind run up and down its branches singing

ee um fah um so
foo swee too eem oo

and rocks and creaks and moans in the eternal breeze.

Through all ages—when the pavement was grass, when it was swamp, through the age of tusk and mammoth, through the age of silent sunrise, the battered woman—for she wore a skirt—with her right hand exposed, her left clutching at her side, stood singing of love—love which has lasted a million years, she sang, love which prevails, and millions of years ago, her lover, who had been dead these centuries, had walked, she crooned, with her in May; but in the course of ages, long as summer days, and flaming, she remembered, with nothing but red asters, he had gone; death's enormous sickle had swept those tremendous hills, and when at last she laid her hoary and immensely aged head on the earth, now become a mere cinder of ice, she implored the Gods to lay by her side a bunch of purple heather, there on her high burial place which the last rays of the last sun caressed; for then the pageant of the universe would be over.

As the ancient song bubbled up opposite Regent's Park Tube station still the earth seemed green and flowery; still, though it issued from so rude a mouth, a mere hole in the earth, muddy too, matted with root fibres and tangled grasses, still the old bubbling burbling song, soaking through the knotted roots of infinite ages, and skeletons and treasure, streamed away in rivulets over the pavement and all along the Marylebone Road, and down towards Euston, fertilising, leaving a damp stain.

Still remembering how once in some primeval May she had walked with her lover, this rusty pump, this battered old woman with one hand exposed for coppers the other clutching her side, would still be there in ten million years, remembering how once she had walked in May, where the sea flows now, with whom it did not matter—he was a man, oh yes, a man who had loved her. But the passage of ages had blurred the clarity of that ancient May day; the bright petalled flowers were hoar and silver frosted; and she no longer saw, when she implored him (as she did now quite clearly) "look in my eyes with thy sweet eyes intently," she no longer saw brown eyes, black whiskers or sunburnt face but only a looming shape, a shadow shape, to which, with the bird-like freshness of the very aged she still twittered "give me your hand and let me press it gently" (Peter Walsh couldn't help giving the poor creature a coin as he stepped into his taxi), "and if some one should see, what matter they?" she demanded; and her fist clutched at her side, and she smiled, pocketing her shilling, and all peering inquisitive eyes seemed blotted out, and the passing generations—the pavement was crowded with bustling middle-class people—vanished, like leaves, to be trodden under, to be soaked and steeped and made mould of by that eternal spring—

> *ee um fah um so*
> *foo swee too eem oo*

"Poor old woman," said Rezia Warren Smith, waiting to cross.

Oh poor old wretch!

Suppose it was a wet night? Suppose one's father, or somebody who had known one in better days had happened to pass, and saw one standing there in the gutter? And where did she sleep at night?

Cheerfully, almost gaily, the invincible thread of sound wound up into the air like the smoke from a cottage chimney, winding up clean beech trees and issuing in a tuft of blue smoke among the topmost leaves. "And if some one should see, what matter they?"

Since she was so unhappy, for weeks and weeks now, Rezia

had given meanings to things that happened, almost felt some-times that she must stop people in the street, if they looked good, kind people, just to say to them "I am unhappy"; and this old woman singing in the street "if some one should see, what matter they?" made her suddenly quite sure that everything was going to be right. They were going to Sir William Bradshaw; she thought his name sounded nice; he would cure Septimus at once. And then there was a brewer's cart, and the grey horses had upright bristles of straw in their tails; there were newspaper placards. It was a silly, silly dream, being unhappy.

So they crossed, Mr. and Mrs. Septimus Warren Smith, and was there, after all, anything to draw attention to them, anything to make a passer-by suspect here is a young man who carries in him the greatest message in the world, and is, moreover, the hap-piest man in the world, and the most miserable? Perhaps they walked more slowly than other people, and there was something hesitating, trailing, in the man's walk, but what more natural for a clerk, who has not been in the West End on a weekday at this hour for years, than to keep looking at the sky, looking at this, that and the other, as if Portland Place were a room he had come into when the family are away, the chandeliers being hung in hol-land bags, and the caretaker, as she lets in long shafts of dusty light upon deserted, queer-looking armchairs, lifting one corner of the long blinds, explains to the visitors what a wonderful place it is; how wonderful, but at the same time, he thinks, as he looks at chairs and tables, how strange.

To look at, he might have been a clerk, but of the better sort; for he wore brown boots; his hands were educated; so, too, his profile — his angular, big-nosed, intelligent, sensitive profile; but not his lips altogether, for they were loose; and his eyes (as eyes tend to be), eyes merely; hazel, large; so that he was, on the whole, a border case, neither one thing nor the other, might end with a house at Purley and a motor car, or continue renting apartments in back streets all his life; one of those half-educated, self-educated men whose education is all learnt from books borrowed from public libraries, read in the evening after the day's work, on the advice of well-known authors consulted by letter.

As for the other experiences, the solitary ones, which people go through alone, in their bedrooms, in their offices, walking the fields and the streets of London, he had them; had left home, a mere boy, because of his mother; she lied; because he came down to tea for the fiftieth time with his hands unwashed; because he could see no future for a poet in Stroud; and so, making a confidant of his little sister, had gone to London leaving an absurd note behind him, such as great men have written, and the world has read later when the story of their struggles has become famous.

London has swallowed up many millions of young men called Smith; thought nothing of fantastic Christian names like Septimus with which their parents have thought to distinguish them. Lodging off the Euston Road, there were experiences, again experiences, such as change a face in two years from a pink innocent oval to a face lean, contracted, hostile. But of all this what could the most observant of friends have said except what a gardener says when he opens the conservatory door in the morning and finds a new blossom on his plant:—It has flowered; flowered from vanity, ambition, idealism, passion, loneliness, courage, laziness, the usual seeds, which all muddled up (in a room off the Euston Road), made him shy, and stammering, made him anxious to improve himself, made him fall in love with Miss Isabel Pole, lecturing in the Waterloo Road upon Shakespeare.

Was he not like Keats? she asked; and reflected how she might give him a taste of *Antony and Cleopatra* and the rest; lent him books; wrote him scraps of letters; and lit in him such a fire as burns only once in a lifetime, without heat, flickering a red gold flame infinitely ethereal and insubstantial over Miss Pole; *Antony and Cleopatra;* and the Waterloo Road. He thought her beautiful, believed her impeccably wise; dreamed of her, wrote poems to her, which, ignoring the subject, she corrected in red ink; he saw her, one summer evening, walking in a green dress in a square. "It has flowered," the gardener might have said, had he opened the door; had he come in, that is to say, any night about this time, and found him writing; found him tearing up his writing; found him finishing a masterpiece at three o'clock in the morning and running out to pace the streets, and visiting churches, and fasting one day, drinking another, devouring Shakespeare, Darwin, *The History of Civilisation,* and Bernard Shaw.

Something was up, Mr. Brewer knew; Mr. Brewer, managing clerk at Sibleys and Arrowsmiths, auctioneers, valuers, land and estate agents; something was up, he thought, and, being paternal with his young men, and thinking very highly of Smith's abilities, and prophesying that he would, in ten or fifteen years, succeed to the leather arm-chair in the inner room under the skylight with the deed-boxes round him, "if he keeps his health," said Mr. Brewer, and that was the danger—he looked weakly; advised football, invited him to supper and was seeing his way to consider recommending a rise of salary, when something happened which threw out many of Mr. Brewer's calculations, took away his ablest young fellows, and eventually, so prying and insidious were the fingers of the European War, smashed a plaster cast of Ceres, ploughed a hole in the geranium beds, and utterly ruined the cook's nerves at Mr. Brewer's establishment at Muswell Hill.

Septimus was one of the first to volunteer. He went to France to save an England which consisted almost entirely of Shakespeare's plays and Miss Isabel Pole in a green dress walking in a square. There in the trenches the change which Mr. Brewer desired when he advised football was produced instantly; he developed manliness; he was promoted; he drew the attention, indeed the affection of his officer, Evans by name. It was a case of two dogs playing on a hearth-rug; one worrying a paper screw, snarling, snapping, giving a pinch, now and then, at the old dog's ear; the other lying somnolent, blinking at the fire, raising a paw, turning and growling good-temperedly. They had to be together, share with each other, fight with each other, quarrel with each other. But when Evans (Rezia who had only seen him once called him "a quiet man," a sturdy red-haired man, undemonstrative in the company of women), when Evans was killed, just before the Armistice, in Italy, Septimus, far from showing any emotion or recognising that here was the end of a friendship, congratulated himself upon feeling very little and very reasonably. The War had taught him. It was sublime. He had gone through the whole show, friendship, European War, death, had won promotion, was still under thirty and was bound to survive. He was right there. The last shells missed him. He watched them explode with indifference. When peace came he was in Milan, billeted in the house of an innkeeper with a courtyard, flowers in tubs, little tables in the open, daughters making hats, and to Lucrezia, the younger daughter, he became engaged one evening when the panic was on him—that he could not feel.

For now that it was all over, truce signed, and the dead buried, he had, especially in the evening, these sudden thunderclaps of fear. He could not feel. As he opened the door of the room where the Italian girls sat making hats, he could see them; could hear them; they were rubbing wires among coloured beads in saucers; they were turning buckram shapes this way and that; the table was all strewn with feathers, spangles, silks, ribbons; scissors were rapping on the table; but something failed him; he could not feel. Still, scissors rapping, girls laughing, hats being made protected him; he was assured of safety; he had a refuge. But he could not sit there all night. There were moments of waking in the early morning. The bed was falling; he was falling. Oh for the scissors and the lamplight and the buckram shapes! He asked Lucrezia to marry him, the younger of the two, the gay, the frivolous, with those little artist's fingers that she would hold up and say "It is all in them." Silk, feathers, what not were alive to them.

"It is the hat that matters most," she would say, when they walked out together. Every hat that passed, she would examine; and the cloak and the dress and the way the woman held herself. Ill-dressing, over-dressing she stigmatised, not savagely, rather with impatient movements of the hands, like those of a painter who puts from him some obvious well-meant glaring imposture; and then, generously, but always critically, she would welcome a shopgirl who had turned her little bit of stuff gallantly, or praise, wholly, with enthusiastic and professional understanding, a French lady descending from her carriage, in chinchilla, robes, pearls.

"Beautiful!" she would murmur, nudging Septimus, that he might see. But beauty was behind a pane of glass. Even taste (Rezia liked ices, chocolates, sweet things) had no relish to him. He put down his cup on the little marble table. He looked at people outside; happy they seemed, collecting in the middle of the street, shouting, laughing, squabbling over nothing. But he could not taste, he could not feel. In the teashop among the tables and the chattering waiters the appalling fear came over him—he could not feel. He could reason; he could read, Dante for example, quite easily ("Septimus, do put down your book," said Rezia, gently shutting the *Inferno*), he could add up his bill; his brain was perfect; it must be the fault of the world then— that he could not feel.

"The English are so silent," Rezia said. She liked it, she said. She respected these Englishmen, and wanted to see London, and the English horses, and the tailor-made suits, and could remember hearing how wonderful the shops were, from an Aunt who had married and lived in Soho.

It might be possible, Septimus thought, looking at England from the train window, as they left Newhaven; it might be possible that the world itself is without meaning.

At the office they advanced him to a post of considerable responsibility. They were proud of him; he had won crosses. "You have done your duty; it is up to us—" began Mr. Brewer;

and could not finish, so pleasurable was his emotion. They took admirable lodgings off the Tottenham Court Road.

Here he opened Shakespeare once more. That boy's business of the intoxication of language—*Antony and Cleopatra*—had shrivelled utterly. How Shakespeare loathed humanity—the putting on of clothes, the getting of children, the sordidity of the mouth and the belly! This was now revealed to Septimus; the message hidden in the beauty of words. The secret signal which one generation passes, under disguise, to the next is loathing, hatred, despair. Dante the same. Aeschylus (translated) the same. There Rezia sat at the table trimming hats. She trimmed hats for Mrs. Filmer's friends; she trimmed hats by the hour. She looked pale, mysterious, like a lily, drowned, under water, he thought.

"The English are so serious," she would say, putting her arms round Septimus, her cheek against his.

Love between man and woman was repulsive to Shakespeare. The business of copulation was filth to him before the end. But, Rezia said, she must have children. They had been married five years.

They went to the Tower together; to the Victoria and Albert Museum; stood in the crowd to see the King open Parliament. And there were the shops—hat shops, dress shops, shops with leather bags in the window, where she would stand staring. But she must have a boy.

She must have a son like Septimus, she said. But nobody could be like Septimus; so gentle; so serious; so clever. Could she not read Shakespeare too? Was Shakespeare a difficult author? she asked.

One cannot bring children into a world like this. One cannot perpetuate suffering, or increase the breed of these lustful animals, who have no lasting emotions, but only whims and vanities, eddying them now this way, now that.

He watched her snip, shape, as one watches a bird hop, flit in the grass, without daring to move a finger. For the truth is (let her ignore it) that human beings have neither kindness, nor faith, nor charity beyond what serves to increase the pleasure of the moment. They hunt in packs. Their packs scour the desert and vanish screaming into the wilderness. They desert the fallen. They are plastered over with grimaces. There was Brewer at the office, with his waxed moustache, coral tie-pin, white slip, and pleasurable emotions—all coldness and clamminess within,— his geraniums ruined in the War—his cook's nerves destroyed; or Amelia What'shername, handing round cups of tea punctu- ally at five—a leering, sneering obscene little harpy; and the Toms and Berties in their starched shirt fronts oozing thick drops of vice. They never saw him drawing pictures of them naked at their antics in his notebook. In the street, vans roared past him; brutality blared out on placards; men were trapped in mines; women burnt alive; and once a maimed file of lunatics being exercised or displayed for the diversion of the populace (who laughed aloud), ambled and nodded and grinned past him, in the Tottenham Court Road, each half apologetically, yet tri- umphantly, inflicting his hopeless woe. And would *he* go mad?

At tea Rezia told him that Mrs. Filmer's daughter was ex- pecting a baby. *She* could not grow old and have no children! She was very lonely, she was very unhappy! She cried for the first time since they were married. Far away he heard her sob- bing; he heard it accurately, he noticed it distinctly; he compared it to a piston thumping. But he felt nothing.

His wife was crying, and he felt nothing; only each time she sobbed in this profound, this silent, this hopeless way, he de- scended another step into the pit.

At last, with a melodramatic gesture which he assumed me- chanically and with complete consciousness of its insincerity, he dropped his head on his hands. Now he had surrendered; now other people must help him. People must be sent for. He gave in.

Nothing could rouse him. Rezia put him to bed. She sent for a doctor—Mrs. Filmer's Dr. Holmes. Dr. Holmes examined him. There was nothing whatever the matter, said Dr. Holmes.

Oh, what a relief! What a kind man, what a good man! thought Rezia. When he felt like that he went to the Music Hall, said Dr. Holmes. He took a day off with his wife and played golf. Why not try two tabloids of bromide dissolved in a glass of water at bedtime? These old Bloomsbury houses, said Dr. Holmes, tapping the wall, are often full of very fine panelling, which the landlords have the folly to paper over. Only the other day, visiting a patient, Sir Somebody Something in Bedford Square—

So there was no excuse; nothing whatever the matter, except the sin for which human nature had condemned him to death; that he did not feel. He had not cared when Evans was killed; that was worst; but all the other crimes raised their heads and shook their fingers and jeered and sneered over the rail of the bed in the early hours of the morning at the prostrate body which lay realising its degradation; how he had married his wife without loving her; had lied to her; seduced her; outraged Miss Isabel Pole, and was so pocked and marked with vice that women shuddered when they saw him in the street. The verdict of human nature on such a wretch was death.

Dr. Holmes came again. Large, fresh coloured, handsome, flicking his boots, looking in the glass, he brushed it all aside— headaches, sleeplessness, fears, dreams—nerve symptoms and nothing more, he said. If Dr. Holmes found himself even half a pound below eleven stone six, he asked his wife for another plate of porridge at breakfast. (Rezia would learn to cook porridge.) But, he continued, health is largely a matter in our own control. Throw yourself into outside interests; take up some hobby. He opened Shakespeare—*Antony and Cleopatra*; pushed Shakespeare aside. Some hobby, said Dr. Holmes, for did he not owe his own excellent health (and he worked as hard as any man in London) to the fact that he could always switch off from his patients on to old furniture? And what a very pretty comb, if he might say so, Mrs. Warren Smith was wearing!

When the damned fool came again, Septimus refused to see him. Did he indeed? said Dr. Holmes, smiling agreeably. Really he had to give that charming little lady, Mrs. Smith, a friendly push before be could get past her into her husband's bedroom.

"So you're in a funk," he said agreeably, sitting down by his patient's side. He had actually talked of killing himself to his wife, quite a girl, a foreigner, wasn't she? Didn't that give her a very odd idea of English husbands? Didn't one owe perhaps a duty to one's wife? Wouldn't it be better to do something instead of lying in bed? For he had had forty years' experience behind him; and Septimus could take Dr. Holmes's word for it—there was nothing whatever the matter with him. And next time Dr. Holmes came he hoped to find Smith out of bed and not making that charming little lady his wife anxious about him.

Human nature, in short, was on him—the repulsive brute, with the blood-red nostrils. Holmes was on him. Dr. Holmes came quite regularly every day. Once you stumble, Septimus wrote on the back of a postcard, human nature is on you. Holmes is on you. Their only chance was to escape, without letting Holmes know; to Italy—anywhere, anywhere, away from Dr. Holmes.

But Rezia could not understand him. Dr. Holmes was such a kind man. He was so interested in Septimus. He only wanted to help them, he said. He had four little children and he had asked her to tea, she told Septimus.

So he was deserted. The whole world was clamouring: Kill yourself, kill yourself, for our sakes. But why should he kill himself for their sakes? Food was pleasant; the sun hot; and this killing oneself, how does one set about it, with a table knife, uglily, with floods of blood,—by sucking a gaspipe? He was too weak; he could scarcely raise his hand. Besides, now that he was quite alone, condemned, deserted, as those who are about to die are alone, there was a luxury in it, an isolation full of sublimity; a freedom which the attached can never know. Holmes had won of course; the brute with the red nostrils had won. But even Holmes himself could not touch this last relic straying on the edge of the world, this outcast, who gazed back at the inhabited regions, who lay, like a drowned sailor, on the shore of the world.

It was at that moment (Rezia gone shopping) that the great revelation took place. A voice spoke from behind the screen. Evans was speaking. The dead were with him.

"Evans, Evans!" he cried.

Mr. Smith was talking aloud to himself, Agnes the servant girl cried to Mrs. Filmer in the kitchen. "Evans, Evans," he had said as she brought in the tray. She jumped, she did. She scuttled downstairs.

And Rezia came in, with her flowers, and walked across the room, and put the roses in a vase, upon which the sun struck directly, and it went laughing, leaping round the room.

She had had to buy the roses, Rezia said, from a poor man in the street. But they were almost dead already, she said, arranging the roses.

So there was a man outside; Evans presumably; and the roses, which Rezia said were half dead, had been picked by him in the fields of Greece. "Communication is health; communication is happiness, communication—" he muttered.

"What are you saying, Septimus?" Rezia asked, wild with terror, for he was talking to himself.

She sent Agnes running for Dr. Holmes. Her husband, she said, was mad. He scarcely knew her.

"You brute! You brute!" cried Septimus, seeing human nature, that is Dr. Holmes, enter the room.

"Now what's all this about?" said Dr. Holmes in the most amiable way in the world. "Talking nonsense to frighten your wife?" But he would give him something to make him sleep. And if they were rich people, said Dr. Holmes, looking ironically round the room, by all means let them go to Harley Street; if they had no confidence in him, said Dr. Holmes, looking not quite so kind.

It was precisely twelve o'clock; twelve by Big Ben; whose stroke was wafted over the northern part of London; blent with that of other clocks, mixed in a thin ethereal way with the clouds and wisps of smoke, and died up there among the seagulls— twelve o'clock struck as Clarissa Dalloway laid her green dress on her bed, and the Warren Smiths walked down Harley Street. Twelve was the hour of their appointment. Probably, Rezia thought, that was Sir William Bradshaw's house with the grey motor car in front of it. The leaden circles dissolved in the air.

Indeed it was—Sir William Bradshaw's motor car; low, powerful, grey with plain initials interlocked on the panel, as if the pomps of heraldry were incongruous, this man being the ghostly helper, the priest of science; and, as the motor car was grey, so to match its sober suavity, grey furs, silver grey rugs were heaped in it, to keep her ladyship warm while she waited. For often Sir William would travel sixty miles or more down into the country to visit the rich, the afflicted, who could afford the very large fee which Sir William very properly charged for his advice. Her ladyship waited with the rugs about her knees an hour or more, leaning back, thinking sometimes of the patient, sometimes, excusably, of the wall of gold, mounting minute by minute while she waited; the wall of gold that was mounting between them and all shifts and anxieties (she had borne them bravely; they had had their struggles) until she felt wedged on a calm ocean, where only spice winds blow; respected, admired, envied, with scarcely anything left to wish for, though she regretted her stoutness; large dinner-parties every Thursday night to the profession; an occasional bazaar to be opened; Royalty greeted; too little time, alas, with her husband, whose work grew and grew; a boy doing well at Eton; she would have liked a daughter too; interests she had, however, in plenty; child welfare; the after-care of the epileptic, and photography, so that if there was a church building, or a church decaying, she bribed the sexton, got the key and took photographs, which were scarcely to be distinguished from the work of professionals, while she waited.

Sir William himself was no longer young. He had worked very hard; he had won his position by sheer ability (being the son of a shopkeeper); loved his profession; made a fine figure-head at ceremonies and spoke well—all of which had by the time he was knighted given him a heavy look, a weary look (the stream of patients being so incessant, the responsibilities and privileges of his profession so onerous), which weariness, to-gether with his grey hairs, increased the extraordinary distinc-tion of his presence and gave him the reputation (of the utmost importance in dealing with nerve cases) not merely of lightning skill, and almost infallible accuracy in diagnosis but of sympathy; tact; understanding of the human soul. He could see the first moment they came into the room (the Warren Smiths they were called); he was certain directly he saw the man; it was a case of extreme gravity. It was a case of complete breakdown—com-plete physical and nervous breakdown, with every symptom in an advanced stage, he ascertained in two or three minutes (writ-ing answers to questions, murmured discreetly, on a pink card).

How long had Dr. Holmes been attending him?

Six weeks.

Prescribed a little bromide? Said there was nothing the mat-ter? Ah yes (those general practitioners! thought Sir William. It took half his time to undo their blunders. Some were irreparable).

"You served with great distinction in the War?"

The patient repeated the word "war" interrogatively.

He was attaching meanings to words of a symbolical kind. A serious symptom, to be noted on the card.

"The War?" the patient asked. The European War—that little shindy of schoolboys with gunpowder? Had he served with distinction? He really forgot. In the War itself he had failed.

"Yes, he served with the greatest distinction," Rezia assured the doctor; "he was promoted."

"And they have the very highest opinion of you at your of-fice?" Sir William murmured, glancing at Mr. Brewer's very gen-erously worded letter. "So that you have nothing to worry you, no financial anxiety, nothing?"

He had committed an appalling crime and been condemned to death by human nature.

"I have—I have," he began, "committed a crime—"

"He has done nothing wrong whatever," Rezia assured the doctor. If Mr. Smith would wait, said Sir William, he would speak to Mrs. Smith in the next room. Her husband was very seriously ill, Sir William said. Did he threaten to kill himself?

Oh, he did, she cried. But he did not mean it, she said. Of course not. It was merely a question of rest, said Sir William; of rest, rest, rest; a long rest in bed. There was a delightful home down in the country where her husband would be perfectly looked after. Away from her? she asked. Unfortunately, yes; the people we care for most are not good for us when we are ill. But he was not mad, was he? Sir William said he never spoke of "madness"; he called it not having a sense of proportion. But her husband did not like doctors. He would refuse to go there. Shortly and kindly Sir William explained to her the state of the case. He had threatened to kill himself. There was no alternative. It was a question of law. He would lie in bed in a beautiful house in the country. The nurses were admirable. Sir William would visit him once a week. If Mrs. Warren Smith was quite sure she had no more questions to ask—he never hurried his patients—they would return to her husband. She had nothing more to ask—not of Sir William.

So they returned to the most exalted of mankind; the criminal who faced his judges; the victim exposed on the heights; the fugitive; the drowned sailor; the poet of the immortal ode; the Lord who had gone from life to death; to Septimus Warren Smith, who sat in the arm-chair under the skylight staring at a photograph of Lady Bradshaw in Court dress, muttering messages about beauty.

"We have had our little talk," said Sir William.

"He says you are very, very ill," Rezia cried.

"We have been arranging that you should go into a home," said Sir William.

"One of Holmes's homes?" sneered Septimus.

The fellow made a distasteful impression. For there was in Sir William, whose father had been a tradesman, a natural respect for breeding and clothing, which shabbiness nettled; again, more profoundly, there was in Sir William, who had never had time for reading, a grudge, deeply buried, against cultivated people who came into his room and intimated that doctors, whose profession is a constant strain upon all the highest faculties, are not educated men.

"One of *my* homes, Mr. Warren Smith," he said, "where we will teach you to rest."

And there was just one thing more.

He was quite certain that when Mr. Warren Smith was well he was the last man in the world to frighten his wife. But he had talked of killing himself.

"We all have our moments of depression," said Sir William.

Once you fall, Septimus repeated to himself, human nature is on you. Holmes and Bradshaw are on you. They scour the desert. They fly screaming into the wilderness. The rack and the thumbscrew are applied. Human nature is remorseless.

"Impulses came upon him sometimes?" Sir William asked, with his pencil on a pink card.

That was his own affair, said Septimus.

"Nobody lives for himself alone," said Sir William, glancing at the photograph of his wife in Court dress.

"And you have a brilliant career before you," said Sir William. There was Mr. Brewer's letter on the table. "An exceptionally brilliant career."

But if he confessed? If he communicated? Would they let him off then, his torturers?

"I—I—" he stammered.

But what was his crime? He could not remember it.

"Yes?" Sir William encouraged him. (But it was growing late.)

Love, trees, there is no crime—what was his message?

He could not remember it.

"I—I—" Septimus stammered.

"Try to think as little about yourself as possible," said Sir William kindly. Really, he was not fit to be about.

Was there anything else they wished to ask him? Sir William would make all arrangements (he murmured to Rezia) and he would let her know between five and six that evening he murmured.

"Trust everything to me," he said, and dismissed them.

Never, never had Rezia felt such agony in her life! She had asked for help and been deserted! He had failed them! Sir William Bradshaw was not a nice man.

The upkeep of that motor car alone cost him quite a lot, said Septimus, when they got out into the street.

She clung to his arm. They had been deserted.

But what more did she want?

To his patients he gave three-quarters of an hour; and if in this exacting science which has to do with what, after all, we know nothing about—the nervous system, the human brain—a doctor loses his sense of proportion, as a doctor he fails. Health we must have; and health is proportion; so that when a man comes into your room and says he is Christ (a common delusion), and has a message, as they mostly have, and threatens, as they often do, to kill himself, you invoke proportion; order rest in bed; rest in solitude; silence and rest; rest without friends, without books, without messages; six months' rest; until a man who went in weighing seven stone six comes out weighing twelve.

Proportion, divine proportion, Sir William's goddess, was acquired by Sir William walking hopsitals, catching salmon, begetting one son in Harley Street by Lady Bradshaw, who caught salmon herself and took photographs scarcely to be distinguished from the work of professionals. Worshipping proportion, Sir William not only prospered himself but made England prosper, secluded her lunatics, forbade childbirth, penalised despair, made it impossible for the unfit to propagate their views until they, too, shared his sense of proportion—his, if they were men, Lady Bradshaw's if they were women (she embroidered, knitted, spent four nights out of seven at home with her son), so that not only did his colleagues respect him, his subordinates fear him, but the friends and relations of his patients felt for him the keenest gratitude for insisting that these prophetic Christs and Christesses, who prophesied the end of the world, or the advent of God, should drink milk in bed, as Sir William ordered; Sir William with his thirty years' experience of these kinds of cases, and his infallible instinct, this is madness, this sense; in fact, his sense of proportion.

But Proportion has a sister, less smiling, more formidable, a Goddess even now engaged—in the heat and sands of India, the mud and swamp of Africa, the purlieus of London, wherever in short the climate or the devil tempts men to fall from the true belief which is her own—is even now engaged in dashing down shrines, smashing idols, and setting up in their place her own stern countenance. Conversion is her name and she feasts on the wills of the weakly, loving to impress, to impose, adoring her own features stamped on the face of the populace. At Hyde Park Corner on a tub she stands preaching; shrouds herself in white and walks penitentially disguised as brotherly love through factories and parliaments; offers help, but desires power; smites out of her way roughly the dissentient, or dissatisfied; bestows her blessing on those who, looking upward, catch submissively from her eyes the light of their own. This lady too (Rezia Warren Smith divined it) had her dwelling in Sir William's heart, though concealed, as she mostly is, under some plausible disguise; some venerable name; love, duty, self sacrifice. How he would work—how toil to raise funds, propagate reforms, initiate institutions! But conversion, fastidious Goddess, loves blood better than brick, and feasts most subtly on the human will. For example, Lady Bradshaw. Fifteen years ago she had gone under. It was nothing you could put your finger on; there had been no scene, no snap; only the slow sinking, water-logged, of her will into his. Sweet was her smile, swift her submission; dinner in Harley Street, numbering eight or nine courses, feeding ten or fifteen guests of the professional classes, was smooth and urbane. Only as the evening wore on a very slight dulness, or uneasiness perhaps, a nervous twitch, fumble, stumble and confusion indicated, what it was really painful to believe—that the poor lady lied. Once, long ago, she had caught salmon freely: now, quick to minister to the craving which lit her husband's eye so oilily for dominion, for power, she cramped, squeezed, pared, pruned, drew back, peeped through; so that without knowing precisely what made the evening disagreeable, and caused this pressure on the top of the head (which might well be imputed to the professional conversation, or the fatigue of a great doctor whose life, Lady Bradshaw said, "is not his own but his patients'") disagreeable it was: so that guests, when the clock struck ten, breathed in the air of Harley Street even with rapture; which relief, however, was denied to his patients.

There in the grey room, with the pictures on the wall, and the valuable furniture, under the ground glass skylight, they learnt the extent of their transgressions; huddled up in armchairs, they watched him go through, for their benefit, a curious exercise with the arms, which he shot out, brought sharply back to his hip, to prove (if the patient was obstinate) that Sir William was master of his own actions, which the patient was not. There some weakly broke down; sobbed, submitted; others, inspired by Heaven knows what intemperate madness, called Sir William to his face a damnable humbug; questioned, even more impiously, life itself. Why live? they demanded. Sir William replied that life was good. Certainly Lady Bradshaw in ostrich feathers hung over the mantelpiece, and as for his income it was quite twelve thousand a year. But to us, they protested, life has given no such bounty. He acquiesced. They lacked a sense of proportion. And perhaps, after all, there is no God? He shrugged his shoulders. In short, this living or not living is an affair of our own? But there they were mistaken. Sir William had a friend in Surrey where they taught, what Sir William frankly admitted was a difficult art—a sense of proportion. There were, moreover, family affection; honour; courage; and a brilliant career. All of these had in Sir William a resolute champion. If they failed him, he had to support police and the good of society, which, he remarked very quietly, would take care, down in Surrey, that these unsocial impulses, bred more than anything by the lack of good blood, were held in control. And then stole out from her hiding-place and mounted her throne that Goddess whose lust is to override opposition, to stamp indelibly in the sanctuaries of others the image of herself. Naked, defenceless, the exhausted, the friendless received the impress of Sir William's will. He swooped; he devoured. He shut people up. It was this combination of decision and humanity that endeared Sir William so greatly to the relations of his victims.

But Rezia Warren Smith cried, walking down Harley Street, that she did not like that man.

Shredding and slicing, dividing and subdividing, the clocks of Harley Street nibbled at the June day, counselled submission, upheld authority, and pointed out in chorus the supreme advantages of a sense of proportion, until the mound of time was so far diminished that a commercial clock, suspended above a shop in Oxford Street, announced, genially and fraternally, as if it were a pleasure to Messrs. Rigby and Lowndes to give the information gratis, that it was half-past one.

Looking up, it appeared that each letter of their names stood for one of the hours; subconsciously one was grateful to Rigby and Lowndes for giving one time ratified by Greenwich; and this gratitude (so Hugh Whitbread ruminated, dallying there in front of the shop window), naturally took the form later of buying off Rigby and Lowndes socks or shoes. So he ruminated. It was his habit. He did not go deeply. He brushed surfaces; the dead languages, the living, life in Constantinople, Paris, Rome; riding, shooting, tennis, it had been once. The malicious asserted that he now kept guard at Buckingham Palace, dressed in silk stockings and knee-breeches, over what nobody knew. But he did it extremely efficiently. He had been afloat on the cream of English society for fifty-five years. He had known Prime Ministers. His affections were understood to be deep. And if it were true that he had not taken part in any of the great movements of the time or held important office, one or two humble reforms stood to his credit; an improvement in public shelters was one; the protection of owls in Norfolk another; servant girls had reason to be grateful to him; and his name at the end of letters to the *Times,* asking for funds, appealing to the public to protect, to preserve, to clear up litter, to abate smoke, and stamp out immorality in parks, commanded respect.

A magnificent figure he cut too, pausing for a moment (as the sound of the half hour died away) to look critically, magisterially, at socks and shoes; impeccable, substantial, as if he beheld the world from a certain eminence, and dressed to match; but realised the obligations which size, wealth, health, entail, and observed punctiliously even when not absolutely necessary, little courtesies, old-fashioned ceremonies which gave a quality to his manner, something to imitate, something to remember him by, for he would never lunch, for example, with Lady Bruton, whom he had known these twenty years, without bringing her in his outstretched hand a bunch of carnations and asking Miss Brush, Lady Bruton's secretary, after her brother in South Africa, which, for some reason, Miss Brush, deficient though she was in every attribute of female charm, so much resented that she said "Thank you, he's doing very well in South Africa," when, for half a dozen years, he had been doing badly in Portsmouth.

Lady Bruton herself preferred Richard Dalloway, who arrived at the next moment. Indeed they met on the doorstep.

Lady Bruton preferred Richard Dalloway of course. He was made of much finer material. But she wouldn't let them run down her poor dear Hugh. She could never forget his kindness—he had been really remarkably kind—she forgot precisely upon what occasion. But he had been—remarkably kind. Anyhow, the difference between one man and another does not amount to much. She had never seen the sense of cutting people up, as Clarissa Dalloway did—cutting them up and sticking them together again; not at any rate when one was sixty-two. She took Hugh's carnations with her angular grim smile. There was nobody else coming, she said. She had got them there on false pretences, to help her out of a difficulty—

"But let us eat first," she said.

And so there began a soundless and exquisite passing to and fro through swing doors of aproned white-capped maids, handmaidens not of necessity, but adepts in a mystery or grand deception practised by hostesses in Mayfair from one-thirty to two, when, with a wave of the hand, the traffic ceases, and there rises instead this profound illusion in the first place about the food—how it is not paid for; and then that the table spreads itself voluntarily with glass and silver, little mats, saucers of red fruit; films of brown cream mask turbot; in casseroles severed chickens swim; coloured, undomestic, the fire burns; and with the wine and the coffee (not paid for) rise jocund visions before musing eyes; gently speculative eyes; eyes to whom life appears musical, mysterious; eyes now kindled to observe genially the beauty of the red carnations which Lady Bruton (whose movements were always angular) had laid beside her plate, so that Hugh Whitbread, feeling at peace with the entire universe and at the same time completely sure of his standing, said, resting his fork.

"Wouldn't they look charming against your lace?"

Miss Brush resented this familiarity intensely. She thought him an underbred fellow. She made Lady Bruton laugh.

Lady Bruton raised the carnations, holding them rather stiffly with much the same attitude with which the General held the scroll in the picture behind her; she remained fixed, tranced. Which was she now, the General's great-grand-daughter? great-great-grand-daughter? Richard Dalloway asked himself. Sir

Roderick, Sir Miles, Sir Talbot—that was it. It was remarkable how in that family the likeness persisted in the women. She should have been a general of dragoons herself. And Richard would have served under her, cheerfully; he had the greatest respect for her; he cherished these romantic views about well-set-up old women of pedigree, and would have liked, in his good-humoured way, to bring some young hot-heads of his acquaintance to lunch with her; as if a type like hers could be bred of amiable tea-drinking enthusiasts! He knew her country. He knew her people. There was a vine, still bearing, which either Lovelace or Herrick—she never read a word of poetry herself, but so the story ran—had sat under. Better wait to put before them the question that bothered her (about making an appeal to the public; if so, in what terms and so on), better wait until they have had their coffee, Lady Bruton thought; and so laid the carnations down beside her plate.

"How's Clarissa?" she asked abruptly.

Clarissa always said that Lady Bruton did not like her. Indeed, Lady Bruton had the reputation of being more interested in politics than people; of talking like a man; of having had a finger in some notorious intrigue of the eighties, which was now beginning to be mentioned in memoirs. Certainly there was an alcove in her drawing-room, and a table in that alcove, and a photograph upon that table of General Sir Talbot Moore, now deceased, who had written there (one evening in the eighties) in Lady Bruton's presence, with her cognisance, perhaps advice, a telegram ordering the British troops to advance upon an historical occasion. (She kept the pen and told the story.) Thus, when she said in her offhand way "How's Clarissa?" husbands had difficulty in persuading their wives and indeed, however devoted, were secretly doubtful themselves, of her interest in women who often got in their husbands' way, prevented them from accepting posts abroad, and had to be taken to the seaside in the middle of the session to recover from influenza. Nevertheless her inquiry, "How's Clarissa?" was known by women infallibly, to be a signal from a well-wisher, from an almost silent companion, whose utterances (half a dozen perhaps in the course of a lifetime) signified recognition of some feminine comradeship which went beneath masculine lunch parties and united Lady Bruton and Mrs. Dalloway, who seldom met, and appeared when they did meet indifferent and even hostile, in a singular bond.

"I met Clarissa in the Park this morning," said Hugh Whitbread, diving into the casserole, anxious to pay himself this little tribute, for he had only to come to London and he met everybody at once; but greedy, one of the greediest men she had ever known, Milly Brush thought, who observed men with unflinching rectitude, and was capable of everlasting devotion, to her own sex in particular, being knobbed, scraped, angular, and entirely without feminine charm.

"D'you know who's in town?" said Lady Bruton suddenly bethinking her. "Our old friend, Peter Walsh."

They all smiled. Peter Walsh! And Mr. Dalloway was genuinely glad, Milly Brush thought; and Mr. Whitbread thought only of his chicken.

Peter Walsh! All three, Lady Bruton, Hugh Whitbread, and Richard Dalloway, remembered the same thing—how passionately Peter had been in love; been rejected; gone to India; come a cropper; made a mess of things; and Richard Dalloway had a very great liking for the dear old fellow too. Milly Brush saw that; saw a depth in the brown of his eyes; saw him hesitate; consider; which interested her, as Mr. Dalloway always interested her, for what was he thinking, she wondered, about Peter Walsh?

That Peter Walsh had been in love with Clarissa; that he would go back directly after lunch and find Clarissa; that he would tell her, in so many words, that he loved her. Yes, he would say that.

Milly Brush once might almost have fallen in love with these silences; and Mr. Dalloway was always so dependable; such a gentleman too. Now, being forty, Lady Bruton had only to nod, or turn her head a little abruptly, and Milly Brush took the signal, however deeply she might be sunk in these reflections of a detached spirit, of an uncorrupted soul whom life could not bamboozle, because life had not offered her a trinket of the slightest value; not a curl, smile, lip, cheek, nose; nothing whatever; Lady Bruton had only to nod, and Perkins was instructed to quicken the coffee.

"Yes; Peter Walsh has come back," said Lady Bruton. It was vaguely flattering to them all. He had come back, battered, unsuccessful, to their secure shores. But to help him, they reflected, was impossible; there was some flaw in his character. Hugh Whitbread said one might of course mention his name to So-and-so. He wrinkled lugubriously, consequentially, at the thought of the letters he would write to the heads of Government offices about "my old friend, Peter Walsh," and so on. But it wouldn't lead to anything—not to anything permanent, because of his character.

"In trouble with some woman," said Lady Bruton. They had all guessed that *that* was at the bottom of it.

"However," said Lady Bruton, anxious to leave the subject, "we shall hear the whole story from Peter himself."

(The coffee was very slow in coming.)

"The address?" murmured Hugh Whitbread; and there was at once a ripple in the grey tide of service which washed round Lady Bruton day in, day out, collecting, intercepting, enveloping her in a fine tissue which broke concussions, mitigated interruptions, and spread round the house in Brook Street a fine net where things lodged and were picked out accurately, instantly, by grey-haired Perkins, who had been with Lady Bruton these thirty years and now wrote down the address; handed it to Mr. Whitbread, who took out his pocketbook, raised his eyebrows, and slipping it in among documents of the highest importance, said that he would get Evelyn to ask him to lunch.

(They were waiting to bring the coffee until Mr. Whitbread had finished.)

Hugh was very slow, Lady Bruton thought. He was getting fat, she noticed. Richard always kept himself in the pink of condition. She was getting impatient; the whole of her being was setting positively, undeniably, domineeringly brushing aside all this unnecessary trifling (Peter Walsh and his affairs) upon that subject which engaged her attention, and not merely her attention, but that fibre which was the ramrod of her soul, that essential part of her without which Millicent Bruton would not have been Millicent Bruton; that project for emigrating young people of both sexes born of respectable parents and setting them up with a fair prospect of doing well in Canada. She exaggerated. She had perhaps lost her sense of proportion. Emigration was not to others the obvious remedy, the sublime conception. It was not to them (not to Hugh, or Richard, or even to devoted Miss Brush) the liberator of the pent egotism, which a strong martial woman, well nourished, well descended, of direct impulses, downright feelings, and little introspective power (broad and simple—why could not every one be broad and simple? she asked) feels rise within her, once youth is past, and must eject upon some object—it may be Emigration, it may be Emancipation; but whatever it be, this object round which the essence of her soul is daily secreted, becomes inevitably prismatic, lustrous, half looking-glass, half precious stone; now carefully hidden in case people should sneer at it; now proudly displayed. Emigration had become, in short, largely Lady Bruton.

But she had to write. And one letter to the *Times,* she used to say to Miss Brush, cost her more than to organise an expedition to South Africa (which she had done in the war). After a morning's battle beginning, tearing up, beginning again, she used to feel the futility of her own womanhood as she felt it on no other occasion, and would turn gratefully to the thought of Hugh Whitbread who possessed—no one could doubt it—the art of writing letters to the *Times.*

A being so differently constituted from herself, with such a command of language; able to put things as editors like them put; had passions which one could not call simply greed. Lady Bruton often suspended judgement upon men in deference to the mysterious accord in which they, but no woman, stood to the laws of the universe; knew how to put things; knew what was said; so that if Richard advised her, and Hugh wrote for her, she was sure of being somehow right. So she let Hugh eat his soufflé; asked after poor Evelyn; waited until they were smoking, and then said.

"Milly, would you fetch the papers?"

And Miss Brush went out, came back; laid papers on the table; and Hugh produced his fountain pen; his silver fountain pen, which had done twenty years' service, he said, unscrewing the cap. It was still in perfect order; he had shown it to the makers; there was no reason, they said, why it should ever wear out; which was somehow to Hugh's credit, and to the credit of the sentiments which his pen expressed (so Richard Dalloway felt) as Hugh began carefully writing capital letters with rings round them in the margin, and thus marvellously reduced Lady Bruton's tangles to sense, to grammar such as the editor of the *Times,* Lady Bruton felt, watching the marvellous transformation, must respect. Hugh was slow. Hugh was pertinacious. Richard said one must take risks. Hugh proposed modifications in deference to people's feelings, which, he said rather tartly when Richard laughed, "had to be considered," and read out "how, therefore, we are of opinion that the times are ripe ... the superfluous youth of our ever-increasing population ... what we owe to the dead ..." which Richard thought all stuffing and bunkum, but no harm in it, of course, and Hugh went on drafting sentiments in alphabetical order of the highest nobility, brushing the cigar ash from his waistcoat, and summing up now and then the progress they had made until, finally, he read out the draft of a letter which Lady Bruton felt certain was a masterpiece. Could her own meaning sound like that?

Hugh could not guarantee that the editor would put it in; but he would be meeting somebody at luncheon.

Whereupon Lady Bruton, who seldom did a graceful thing, stuffed all Hugh's carnations into the front of her dress, and flinging her hands out called him "My Prime Minister!" What she would have done without them both she did not know. They rose. And Richard Dalloway strolled off as usual to have a look at the General's portrait, because he meant, whenever he had a moment of leisure, to write a history of Lady Bruton's family.

And Millicent Bruton was very proud of her family. But they could wait, they could wait, she said, looking at the picture; meaning that her family, of military men, administrators, admirals, had been men of action, who had done their duty; and Richard's first duty was to his country, but it was a fine face, she said; and all the papers were ready for Richard down at Aldmixton whenever the time came; the Labour Government she meant. "Ah, the news from India!" she cried.

And then, as they stood in the hall taking yellow gloves from the bowl on the malachite table and Hugh was offering Miss Brush with quite unnecessary courtesy some discarded ticket or other compliment, which she loathed from the depths of her heart and blushed brick red, Richard turned to Lady Bruton, with his hat in his hand, and said.

"We shall see you at our party to-night?" whereupon Lady Bruton resumed the magnificence which letter-writing had shattered. She might come; or she might not come. Clarissa had wonderful energy. Parties terrified Lady Bruton. But then, she was getting old. So she intimated, standing at her doorway; handsome; very erect; while her chow stretched behind her, and Miss Brush disappeared into the background with her hands full of papers.

And Lady Bruton went ponderously, majestically, up to her room, lay, one arm extended, on the sofa. She sighed, she snored, not that she was asleep, only drowsy and heavy, drowsy and heavy, like a field of clover in the sunshine this hot June day, with the bees going round and about and the yellow butterflies.

Always she went back to those fields down in Devonshire, where she had jumped the brooks on Patty, her pony, with Mortimer and Tom, her brothers. And there were the dogs; there were the rats; there were her father and mother on the lawn under the trees, with the tea-things out, and the beds of dahlias, the hollyhocks, the pampas grass; and they, little wretches, always up to some mischief! stealing back through the shrubbery, so as not to be seen, all bedraggled from some roguery. What old nurse used to say about her frocks!

Ah dear, she remembered—it was Wednesday in Brook Street. Those kind good fellows, Richard Dalloway, Hugh Whitbread, had gone this hot day through the streets whose growl came up to her lying on the sofa. Power was hers, position, income. She had lived in the forefront of her time. She had had good friends; known the ablest men of her day. Murmuring London flowed up to her, and her hand, lying on the sofa back, curled upon some imaginary baton such as her grandfathers might have held, holding which she seemed, drowsy and heavy, to be commanding battalions marching to Canada, and those good fellows walking across London, that territory of theirs, that little bit of carpet, Mayfair.

And they went further and further from her, being attached to her by a thin thread (since they had lunched with her) which would stretch and stretch, get thinner and thinner as they walked across London; as if one's friends were attached to one's body, after lunching with them, by a thin thread, which (as she dozed there) became hazy with the sound of bells, striking the hour or ringing to service, as a single spider's thread is blotted with rain-drops, and, burdened, sags down. So she slept.

And Richard Dalloway and Hugh Whitbread hesitated at the corner of Conduit Street at the very moment that Millicent Bruton, lying on the sofa, let the thread snap; snored. Contrary winds buffeted at the street corner. They looked in at a shop window; they did not wish to buy or to talk but to part, only with contrary winds buffeting the street corner, with some sort of lapse in the tides of the body, two forces meeting in a swirl, morning and afternoon, they paused. Some newspaper placard went up in the air, gallantly, like a kite at first, then paused, swooped, fluttered; and a lady's veil hung. Yellow awnings trembled. The speed of the morning traffic slackened, and single carts rattled carelessly down half-empty streets. In Norfolk, of which Richard Dalloway was half thinking, a soft warm wind blew back the petals; confused the waters; ruffled the flowering grasses. Haymakers, who had pitched beneath hedges to sleep away the morning toil, parted curtains of green blades; moved trembling globes of cow parsley to see the sky; the blue, the steadfast, the blazing summer sky.

Aware that he was looking at a silver two-handled Jacobean mug, and that Hugh Whitbread admired condescendingly with airs of connoisseurship a Spanish necklace which he thought of asking the price of in case Evelyn might like it—still Richard was torpid; could not think or move. Life had thrown up this wreckage; shop windows full of coloured paste, and one stood stark with the lethargy of the old, stiff with the rigidity of the old, looking in. Evelyn Whitbread might like to buy this Spanish necklace—so she might. Yawn he must. Hugh was going into the shop.

"Right you are!" said Richard, following.

Goodness knows he didn't want to go buying necklaces with Hugh. But there are tides in the body. Morning meets afternoon. Borne like a frail shallop on deep, deep floods, Lady Bruton's great-grandfather and his memoir and his campaigns in North America were whelmed and sunk. And Millicent Bruton too. She went under. Richard didn't care a straw what became of Emigration; about that letter, whether the editor put it in or not. The necklace hung stretched between Hugh's admirable fingers. Let him give it to a girl, if he must buy jewels— any girl, any girl in the street. For the worthlessness of this life did strike Richard pretty forcibly—buying necklaces for Evelyn. If he'd had a boy he'd have said, Work, work. But he had his Elizabeth; he adored his Elizabeth.

"I should like to see Mr. Dubonnet," said Hugh in his curt worldly way. It appeared that this Dubonnet had the measurements of Mrs. Whitbread's neck, or, more strangely still, knew her views upon Spanish jewellery and the extent of her possessions in that line (which Hugh could not remember). All of which seemed to Richard Dalloway awfully odd. For he never gave Clarissa presents, except a bracelet two or three years ago, which had not been a success. She never wore it. It pained him to remember that she never wore it. And as a single spider's thread after wavering here and there attaches itself to the point of a leaf, so Richard's mind, recovering from its lethargy, set now on his wife, Clarissa, whom Peter Walsh had loved so passionately; and Richard had had a sudden vision of her there at luncheon; of himself and Clarissa; of their life together; and he drew the tray of old jewels towards him, and taking up first this brooch then that ring, "How much is that?" he asked, but doubted his own taste. He wanted to open the drawing-room door and come in holding out something; a present for Clarissa. Only what? But Hugh was on his legs again. He was unspeakably pompous. Really, after dealing here for thirty-five years he was not going to be put off by a mere boy who did not know his business. For Dubonnet, it seemed, was out, and Hugh would not buy anything until Mr. Dubonnet chose to be in; at which the youth flushed and bowed his correct little bow. It was all perfectly correct. And yet Richard couldn't have said that to save his life! Why these people stood that damned insolence he could not conceive. Hugh was becoming an intolerable ass. Richard Dalloway could not stand more than an hour of his society. And, flicking his bowler hat by way of farewell, Richard turned at the corner of Conduit Street eager, yes, very eager, to travel that spider's thread of attachment between himself and Clarissa; he would go straight to her, in Westminster.

But he wanted to come in holding something. Flowers? Yes, flowers, since he did not trust his taste in gold; any number of flowers, roses, orchids, to celebrate what was, reckoning things as you will, an event; this feeling about her when they spoke of Peter Walsh at luncheon; and they never spoke of it; not for years had they spoken of it; which, he thought, grasping his red and white roses together (a vast bunch in tissue paper), is the greatest mistake in the world. The time comes when it can't be said; one's too shy to say it, he thought, pocketing his sixpence or two of change, setting off with his great bunch held against his body to Westminster to say straight out in so many words (whatever she might think of him), holding out his flowers, "I love you." Why not? Really it was a miracle thinking of the War, and thousands of poor chaps, with all their lives before them, shovelled together, already half forgotten; it was a miracle. Here he was walking across London to say to Clarissa in so many words that he loved her. Which one never does say, he thought. Partly one's lazy; partly one's shy. And Clarissa—it was difficult to think of her; except in starts, as at luncheon, when he saw her quite distinctly; their whole life. He stopped at the crossing; and repeated—being simple by nature, and undebauched, because he had tramped, and shot; being pertinacious and dogged, having championed the downtrodden and followed his instincts in the House of Commons; being preserved in his simplicity yet at the same time grown rather speechless, rather stiff—he repeated that it was a miracle that he should have married Clarissa; a miracle—his life had been a miracle, he thought; hesitating to cross. But it did make his blood boil to see little creatures of five or six crossing Piccadilly alone. The police ought to have stopped the traffic at once. He had no illusions about the London police. Indeed, he was collecting evidence of their malpractices; and those costermongers, not allowed to stand their barrows in the streets; and prostitutes, good Lord, the fault wasn't in them, nor in young men either, but in our detestable social system and so forth; all of which he considered, could be seen considering, grey, dogged, dapper, clean, as he walked across the Park to tell his wife that he loved her.

For he would say it in so many words, when he came into the room. Because it is a thousand pities never to say what one feels, he thought, crossing the Green Park and observing with pleasure how in the shade of the trees whole families, poor families, were sprawling; children kicking up their legs; sucking milk; paper bags thrown about, which could easily be picked up (if people objected) by one of those fat gentlemen in livery; for he was of opinion that every park, and every square, during the summer months should be open to children (the grass of the park flushed and faded, lighting up the poor mothers of Westminster and their crawling babies, as if a yellow lamp were moved beneath). But what could be done for female vagrants like that poor creature, stretched on her elbow (as if she had flung herself on the earth, rid of all ties, to observe curiously, to speculate boldly, to consider the whys and the wherefores, impudent, loose-lipped, humorous), he did not know. Bearing his flowers like a weapon, Richard Dalloway approached her; intent he passed her; still there was time for a spark between them— she laughed at the sight of him, he smiled good-humouredly, considering the problem of the female vagrant; not that they would ever speak. But he would tell Clarissa that he loved her, in so many words. He had, once upon a time, been jealous of Peter Walsh; jealous of him and Clarissa. But she had often said to him that she had been right not to marry Peter Walsh; which, knowing Clarissa, was obviously true; she wanted support. Not that she was weak; but she wanted support.

As for Buckingham Palace (like an old prima donna facing the audience all in white) you can't deny it a certain dignity, he considered, nor despise what does, after all, stand to millions of people (a little crowd was waiting at the gate to see the King drive out) for a symbol, absurd though it is; a child with a box of bricks could have done better, he thought; looking at the memorial to Queen Victoria (whom he could remember in her horn spectacles driving through Kensington), its white mound, its billowing motherliness; but he liked being ruled by the descendant of Horsa; he liked continuity; and the sense of handing on the traditions of the past. It was a great age in which to have lived. Indeed, his own life was a miracle; let him make no mistake about it; here he was, in the prime of life, walking to his house in Westminster to tell Clarissa that he loved her. Happiness is this, he thought.

It is this, he said, as he entered Dean's Yard. Big Ben was beginning to strike, first the warning, musical; then the hour, irrevocable. Lunch parties waste the entire afternoon, he thought, approaching his door.

The sound of Big Ben flooded Clarissa's drawing-room, where she sat, ever so annoyed, at her writing-table; worried; annoyed. It was perfectly true that she had not asked Ellie Henderson to her party; but she had done it on purpose. Now Mrs. Marsham wrote "she had told Ellie Henderson she would ask Clarissa—Ellie so much wanted to come."

But why should she invite all the dull women in London to her parties? Why should Mrs. Marsham interfere? And there was Elizabeth closeted all this time with Doris Kilman. Anything more nauseating she could not conceive. Prayer at this hour with that woman. And the sound of the bell flooded the room with its melancholy wave; which receded, and gathered itself together to fall once more, when she heard, distractingly, something fumbling, something scratching at the door. Who at this hour? Three, good Heavens! Three already! For with overpowering directness and dignity the clock struck three; and she heard nothing else; but the door handle slipped round and in came Richard! What a surprise! In came Richard, holding out flowers. She had failed him, once at Constantinople; and Lady Bruton, whose lunch parties were said to be extraordinarily amusing, had not asked her. He was holding out flowers— roses, red and white roses. (But he could not bring himself to say he loved her; not in so many words.)

But how lovely, she said, taking his flowers. She understood; she understood without his speaking; his Clarissa. She put them in vases on the mantelpiece. How lovely they looked! she said. And was it amusing, she asked? Had Lady Bruton asked after her? Peter Walsh was back. Mrs. Marsham had written. Must she ask Ellie Henderson? That woman Kilman was upstairs.

"But let us sit down for five minutes," said Richard.

It all looked so empty. All the chairs were against the wall. What had they been doing? Oh, it was for the party; no, he had not forgotten, the party. Peter Walsh was back. Oh yes; she had had him. And he was going to get a divorce; and he was in love with some woman out there. And he hadn't changed in the slightest. There she was, mending her dress....

"Thinking of Bourton," she said.

"Hugh was at lunch," said Richard. She had met him too! Well, he was getting absolutely intolerable. Buying Evelyn neck-laces; fatter than ever; an intolerable ass.

"And it came over me 'I might have married you,'" she said, thinking of Peter sitting there in his little bow-tie; with that knife, opening it, shutting it. "Just as he always was, you know."

They were talking about him at lunch, said Richard. (But he could not tell her he loved her. He held her hand. Happiness is this, he thought.) They had been writing a letter to the *Times* for Millicent Bruton. That was about all Hugh was fit for.

"And our dear Miss Kilman?" he asked. Clarissa thought the roses absolutely lovely; first bunched together; now of their own accord starting apart.

"Kilman arrives just as we've done lunch," she said. "Elizabeth turns pink. They shut themselves up. I suppose they're praying."

Lord! He didn't like it; but these things pass over if you let them.

"In a mackintosh with an umbrella," said Clarissa.

He had not said "I love you"; but he held her hand. Happiness is this, is this, he thought.

"But why should I ask all the dull women in London to my parties?" said Clarissa. And if Mrs. Marsham gave a party, did *she* invite her guests?

"Poor Ellie Henderson," said Richard—it was a very odd thing how much Clarissa minded about her parties, he thought.

But Richard had no notion of the look of a room. However—what was he going to say?

If she worried about these parties he would not let her give them. Did she wish she had married Peter? But he must go.

He must be off, he said, getting up. But he stood for a moment as if he were about to say something; and she wondered what? Why? There were the roses.

"Some Committee?" she asked, as he opened the door.

"Armenians," he said; or perhaps it was "Albanians."

And there is a dignity in people; a solitude; even between husband and wife a gulf; and that one must respect, thought Clarissa, watching him open the door; for one would not part with it oneself, or take it, against his will, from one's husband, without losing one's independence, one's self-respect—something, after all, priceless.

He returned with a pillow and a quilt.

"An hour's complete rest after luncheon," he said. And he went.

How like him! He would go on saying "An hour's complete rest after luncheon" to the end of time, because a doctor had ordered it once. It was like him to take what doctors said literally; part of his adorable, divine simplicity, which no one had to the same extent; which made him go and do the thing while she and Peter frittered their time away bickering. He was already halfway to the House of Commons, to his Armenians, his Albanians, having settled her on the sofa, looking at his roses. And people would say, "Clarissa Dalloway is spoilt." She cared much more for her roses than for the Armenians. Hunted out of existence, maimed, frozen, the victims of cruelty and injustice (she had heard Richard say so over and over again)—no, she could feel nothing for the Albanians, or was it the Armenians? but she loved her roses (didn't that help the Armenians?)—the only flowers she could bear to see cut. But Richard was already at the House of Commons; at his Committee, having settled all her difficulties. But no; alas, that was not true. He did not see the reasons against asking Ellie Henderson. She would do it, of course, as he wished it. Since he had brought the pillows, she would lie down.... But—but—why did she suddenly feel, for no reason that she could discover, desperately unhappy? As a person who has dropped some grain of pearl or diamond into the grass and parts the tall blades very carefully, this way and that, and searches here and there vainly, and at last spies it there at the roots, so she went through one thing and another; no, it was not Sally Seton saying that Richard would never be in the Cabinet because he had a second-class brain (it came back to her); no, she did not mind that; nor was it to do with Elizabeth either and Doris Kilman; those were facts. It was a feeling, some unpleasant feeling, earlier in the day perhaps; something that Peter had said, combined with some depression of her own, in her bedroom, taking off her hat; and what Richard had said had added to it, but what had he said? There were his roses. Her parties! That was it! Her parties! Both of them criticised her very unfairly, laughed at her very unjustly, for her parties. That was it! That was it!

Well, how was she going to defend herself? Now that she knew what it was, she felt perfectly happy. They thought, or Peter at any rate thought, that she enjoyed imposing herself; liked to have famous people about her; great names; was simply a snob in short. Well, Peter might think so. Richard merely thought it foolish of her to like excitement when she knew it was bad for her heart. It was childish, he thought. And both were quite wrong. What she liked was simply life.

"That's what I do it for," she said, speaking aloud, to life.

Since she was lying on the sofa, cloistered, exempt, the presence of this thing which she felt to be so obvious became physically existent; with robes of sound from the street, sunny, with hot breath, whispering, blowing out the blinds. But suppose Peter said to her, "Yes, yes, but your parties—what's the sense of your parties?" all she could say was (and nobody could be expected to understand): They're an offering; which sounded horribly vague. But who was Peter to make out that life was all plain sailing?—Peter always in love, always in love with the wrong woman? What's your love? she might say to him. And she knew his answer; how it is the most important thing in the world and no woman possibly understood it. Very well. But could any man understand what she meant either? about life? She could not imagine Peter or Richard taking the trouble to give a party for no reason whatever.

But to go deeper, beneath what people said (and these judgements, how superficial, how fragmentary they are!) in her own mind now, what did it mean to her, this thing she called life? Oh, it was very queer. Here was So-and-so in South Kensington; some one up in Bayswater; and somebody else, say, in Mayfair. And she felt quite continuously a sense of their existence; and she felt what a waste; and she felt what a pity; and she felt if only they could be brought together; so she did it. And it was an offering; to combine, to create; but to whom?

An offering for the sake of offering, perhaps. Anyhow, it was her gift. Nothing else had she of the slightest importance; could not think, write, even play the piano. She muddled Armenians and Turks; loved success; hated discomfort; must be liked; talked oceans of nonsense: and to this day, ask her what the Equator was, and she did not know.

All the same, that one day should follow another; Wednesday, Thursday, Friday, Saturday; that one should wake up in the morning; see the sky; walk in the park; meet Hugh Whitbread; then suddenly in came Peter; then these roses; it was enough. After that, how unbelievable death was!—that it must end; and no one in the whole world would know how she had loved it all; how, every instant...

The door opened. Elizabeth knew that her mother was resting. She came in very quietly. She stood perfectly still. Was it that some Mongol had been wrecked on the coast of Norfolk (as Mrs. Hilbery said), had mixed with the Dalloway ladies, perhaps, a hundred years ago? For the Dalloways, in general, were fair-haired; blue-eyed; Elizabeth, on the contrary, was dark; had Chinese eyes in a pale face; an Oriental mystery; was gentle, considerate, still. As a child, she had had a perfect sense of humour; but now at seventeen, why, Clarissa could not in the least understand, she had become very serious; like a hyacinth, sheathed in glossy green, with buds just tinted, a hyacinth which has had no sun.

She stood quite still and looked at her mother; but the door was ajar, and outside the door was Miss Kilman, as Clarissa knew; Miss Kilman in her mackintosh, listening to whatever they said.

Yes, Miss Kilman stood on the landing, and wore a mackintosh; but had her reasons. First, it was cheap; second, she was over forty; and did not, after all, dress to please. She was poor, moreover; degradingly poor. Otherwise she would not be taking jobs from people like the Dalloways; from rich people, who liked to be kind. Mr. Dalloway, to do him justice, had been kind. But Mrs. Dalloway had not. She had been merely condescending. She came from the most worthless of all classes—the rich, with a smattering of culture. They had expensive things everywhere; pictures, carpets, lots of servants. She considered that she had a perfect right to anything that the Dalloways did for her.

She had been cheated. Yes, the word was no exaggeration, for surely a girl has a right to some kind of happiness? And she had never been happy, what with being so clumsy and so poor. And then, just as she might have had a chance at Miss Dolby's school, the War came; and she had never been able to tell lies. Miss Dolby thought she would be happier with people who shared her views about the Germans. She had had to go. It was true that the family was of German origin; spelt the name Kiehlman in the eighteenth century; but her brother had been killed. They turned her out because she would not pretend that the Germans were all villains—when she had German friends, when the only happy days of her life had been spent in Germany! And after all, she could read history. She had had to take whatever she could get. Mr. Dalloway had come across her working for the Friends. He had allowed her (and that was really generous of him) to teach his daughter history. Also she did a little Extension lecturing and so on. Then Our Lord had come to her (and here she always bowed her head). She had seen the light two years and three months ago. Now she did not envy women like Clarissa Dalloway; she pitied them.

She pitied and despised them from the bottom of her heart, as she stood on the soft carpet, looking at the old engraving of a little girl with a muff. With all this luxury going on, what hope was there for a better state of things? Instead of lying on a sofa—"My mother is resting," Elizabeth had said—she should have been in a factory; behind a counter; Mrs. Dalloway and all the other fine ladies!

Bitter and burning, Miss Kilman had turned in to a church two years three months ago. She had heard the Rev. Edward Whittaker preach; the boys sing; had seen the solemn lights descend, and whether it was the music, or the voices (she herself when alone in the evening found comfort in a violin; but the sound was excruciating; she had no ear), the hot and turbulent feelings which boiled and surged in her had been assuaged as she sat there, and she had wept copiously, and gone to call on Mr. Whittaker at his private house in Kensington. It was the hand of God, he said. The Lord had shown her the way. So now, whenever the hot and painful feelings boiled within her, this hatred of Mrs. Dalloway, this grudge against the world, she thought of God. She thought of Mr. Whittaker. Rage was succeeded by calm. A sweet savour filled her veins, her lips parted, and, standing formidable upon the landing in her mackintosh, she looked with steady and sinister serenity at Mrs. Dalloway, who came out with her daughter.

Elizabeth said she had forgotten her gloves. That was because Miss Kilman and her mother hated each other. She could not bear to see them together. She ran upstairs to find her gloves.

But Miss Kilman did not hate Mrs. Dalloway. Turning her large gooseberry-coloured eyes upon Clarissa, observing her small pink face, her delicate body, her air of freshness and fashion, Miss Kilman felt, Fool! Simpleton! You who have known neither sorrow nor pleasure; who have trifled your life away! And there rose in her an overmastering desire to overcome her; to unmask her. If she could have felled her it would have eased her. But it was not the body; it was the soul and its mockery that she wished to subdue; make feel her mastery. If only she could make her weep; could ruin her; humiliate her; bring her to her knees crying, You are right! But this was God's will, not Miss Kilman's. It was to be a religious victory. So she glared; so she glowered.

Clarissa was really shocked. This a Christian—this woman! This woman had taken her daughter from her! She in touch with invisible presences! Heavy, ugly, commonplace, without kindness or grace, she knew the meaning of life!

"You are taking Elizabeth to the Stores?" Mrs. Dalloway said.

Miss Kilman said she was. They stood there. Miss Kilman was not going to make herself agreeable. She had always earned her living. Her knowledge of modern history was thorough in the extreme. She did out of her meagre income set aside so much for causes she believed in; whereas this woman did nothing, believed nothing; brought up her daughter—but here was Elizabeth, rather out of breath, the beautiful girl.

So they were going to the Stores. Odd it was, as Miss Kilman stood there (and stand she did, with the power and taciturnity of some prehistoric monster armoured for primeval warfare), how, second by second, the idea of her diminished, how hatred (which was for ideas, not people) crumbled, how she lost her malignity, her size, became second by second merely Miss Kilman, in a mackintosh, whom Heaven knows Clarissa would have liked to help.

At this dwindling of the monster, Clarissa laughed. Saying good-bye, she laughed.

Off they went together, Miss Kilman and Elizabeth, downstairs.

With a sudden impulse, with a violent anguish, for this woman was taking her daughter from her, Clarissa leant over the bannisters and cried out, "Remember the party! Remember our party to-night!"

But Elizabeth had already opened the front door; there was a van passing; she did not answer.

Love and religion! thought Clarissa, going back into the drawing-room, tingling all over. How detestable, how detestable they are! For now that the body of Miss Kilman was not before her, it overwhelmed her—the idea. The cruelest things in the world, she thought, seeing them clumsy, hot, domineering, hypocritical, eavesdropping, jealous, infinitely cruel and unscrupulous, dressed in a mackintosh coat, on the landing; love and religion. Had she ever tried to convert any one herself? Did she not wish everybody merely to be themselves? And she watched out of the window the old lady opposite climbing upstairs. Let her climb upstairs if she wanted to; let her stop; then let her, as Clarissa had often seen her, gain her bedroom, part her curtains, and disappear again into the background. Somehow one respected that—that old woman looking out of the window, quite unconscious that she was being watched. There was something solemn in it—but love and religion would destroy that, whatever it was, the privacy of the soul. The odious Kilman would destroy it. Yet it was a sight that made her want to cry.

Love destroyed too. Everything that was fine, everything that was true went. Take Peter Walsh now. There was a man, charming, clever, with ideas about everything. If you wanted to know about Pope, say, or Addison, or just to talk nonsense, what people were like, what things meant, Peter knew better than any one. It was Peter who had helped her; Peter who had lent her books. But look at the women he loved—vulgar, trivial, commonplace. Think of Peter in love—he came to see her after all these years, and what did he talk about? Himself. Horrible passion! she thought. Degrading passion! she thought, thinking of Kilman and her Elizabeth walking to the Army and Navy Stores.

Big Ben struck the half-hour.

How extraordinary it was, strange, yes, touching, to see the old lady (they had been neighbours ever so many years) move away from the window, as if she were attached to that sound, that string. Gigantic as it was, it had something to do with her. Down, down, into the midst of ordinary things the finger fell making the moment solemn. She was forced, so Clarissa tried to follow her as she turned and disappeared, and could still just see her white cap moving at the back of the bedroom. She was still there moving about at the other end of the room. Why creeds and prayers and mackintoshes? when, thought Clarissa, that's the miracle, that's the mystery; that old lady, she meant, whom she could see going from chest of drawers to dressing-table. She could still see her. And the supreme mystery which Kilman might say she had solved, or Peter might say he had solved, but Clarissa didn't believe either of them had the ghost of an idea of solving, was simply this: here was one room; there another. Did religion solve that, or love?

Love—but here the other clock, the clock which always struck two minutes after Big Ben, came shuffling in with its lap full of odds and ends, which it dumped down as if Big Ben were all very well with his majesty laying down the law, so solemn, so

just, but she must remember all sorts of little things besides—
Mrs. Marsham, Ellie Henderson, glasses for ices—all sorts of
little things came flooding and lapping and dancing in on the
wake of that solemn stroke which lay flat like a bar of gold on
the sea. Mrs. Marsham, Ellie Henderson, glasses for ices. She
must telephone now at once.

Volubly, troublously, the late clock sounded, coming in on
the wake of Big Ben, with its lap full of trifles. Beaten up, broken up by the assault of carriages, the brutality of vans, the eager
advance of myriads of angular men, of flaunting women, the
domes and spires of offices and hospitals, the last relics of this
lap full of odds and ends seemed to break, like the spray of an
exhausted wave, upon the body of Miss Kilman standing still in
the street for a moment to mutter "It is the flesh."

It was the flesh that she must control. Clarissa Dalloway had
insulted her. That she expected. But she had not triumphed; she
had not mastered the flesh. Ugly, clumsy, Clarissa Dalloway had
laughed at her for being that; and had revived the fleshly desires,
for she minded looking as she did beside Clarissa. Nor could
she talk as she did. But why wish to resemble her? Why? She despised Mrs. Dalloway from the bottom of her heart. She was not
serious. She was not good. Her life was a tissue of vanity and de-
ceit. Yet Doris Kilman had been overcome. She had, as a matter
of fact, very nearly burst into tears when Clarissa Dalloway
laughed at her. "It is the flesh, it is the flesh," she muttered (it
being her habit to talk aloud) trying to subdue this turbulent and
painful feeling as she walked down Victoria Street. She prayed
to God. She could not help being ugly; she could not afford to
buy pretty clothes. Clarissa Dalloway had laughed—but she
would concentrate her mind upon something else until she had
reached the pillar-box. At any rate she had got Elizabeth. But
she would think of something else; she would think of Russia;
until she reached the pillar-box.

How nice it must be, she said, in the country, struggling, as
Mr. Whittaker had told her, with that violent grudge against the

world which had scorned her, sneered at her, cast her off, beginning with this indignity—the infliction of her unlovable body which people could not bear to see. Do her hair as she might, her forehead remained like an egg, bald, white. No clothes suited her. She might buy anything. And for a woman, of course, that meant never meeting the opposite sex. Never would she come first with any one. Sometimes lately it had seemed to her that, except for Elizabeth, her food was all that she lived for; her comforts; her dinner, her tea; her hot-water bottle at night. But one must fight; vanquish; have faith in God. Mr. Whittaker had said she was there for a purpose. But no one knew the agony! He said, pointing to the crucifix, that God knew. But why should she have to suffer when other women, like Clarissa Dalloway, escaped? Knowledge comes through suffering, said Mr. Whittaker.

She had passed the pillar box, and Elizabeth had turned into the cool brown tobacco department of the Army and Navy Stores while she was still muttering to herself what Mr. Whittaker had said about knowledge coming through suffering and the flesh. "The flesh," she muttered.

What department did she want? Elizabeth interrupted her.

"Petticoats," she said abruptly, and stalked straight on to the lift.

Up they went. Elizabeth guided her this way and that; guided her in her abstraction as if she had been a great child, an unwieldy battleship. There were the petticoats, brown, decorous, striped, frivolous, solid, flimsy; and she chose, in her abstraction, portentously, and the girl serving thought her mad.

Elizabeth rather wondered, as they did up the parcel, what Miss Kilman was thinking. They must have their tea, said Miss Kilman, rousing, collecting herself. They had their tea.

Elizabeth rather wondered whether Miss Kilman could be hungry. It was her way of eating, eating with intensity, then looking, again and again, at a plate of sugared cakes on the table next them; then, when a lady and a child sat down and the child took the cake, could Miss Kilman really mind it? Yes, Miss Kilman did mind it. She had wanted that cake — the pink one. The pleasure of eating was almost the only pure pleasure left her, and then to be baffled even in that!

When people are happy, they have a reserve, she had told Elizabeth, upon which to draw, whereas she was like a wheel without a tyre (she was fond of such metaphors), jolted by every pebble, so she would say staying on after the lesson standing by the fire-place with her bag of books, her "satchel," she called it, on a Tuesday morning, after the lesson was over. And she talked too about the War. After all, there were people who did not think the English invariably right. There were books. There were meetings. There were other points of view. Would Elizabeth like to come with her to listen to So-and-so (a most extraordinary looking old man)? Then Miss Kilman took her to some church in Kensington and they had tea with a clergyman. She had lent her books. Law, medicine, politics, all professions are open to women of your generation, said Miss Kilman. But for herself, her career was absolutely ruined and was it her fault? Good gracious, said Elizabeth, no.

And her mother would come calling to say that a hamper had come from Bourton and would Miss Kilman like some flowers? To Miss Kilman she was always very, very nice, but Miss Kilman squashed the flowers all in a bunch, and hadn't any small talk, and what interested Miss Kilman bored her mother, and Miss Kilman and she were terrible together; and Miss Kilman swelled and looked very plain. But then Miss Kilman was frightfully clever. Elizabeth had never thought about the poor. They lived with everything they wanted,—her mother had breakfast in bed every day; Lucy carried it up; and she liked old women because they were Duchesses, and being descended from some Lord. But Miss Kilman said (one of those Tuesday mornings when the lesson was over), "My grandfather kept an oil and colour shop in Kensington." Miss Kilman made one feel so small.

Miss Kilman took another cup of tea. Elizabeth, with her oriental bearing, her inscrutable mystery, sat perfectly upright; no, she did not want anything more. She looked for her gloves—her white gloves. They were under the table. Ah, but she must not go! Miss Kilman could not let her go! this youth, that was so beautiful, this girl, whom she genuinely loved! Her large hand opened and shut on the table.

But perhaps it was a little flat somehow, Elizabeth felt. And really she would like to go.

But said Miss Kilman, "I've not quite finished yet."

Of course, then, Elizabeth would wait. But it was rather stuffy in here.

"Are you going to the party to-night?" Miss Kilman said. Elizabeth supposed she was going; her mother wanted her to go. She must not let parties absorb her, Miss Kilman said, fingering the last two inches of a chocolate éclair.

She did not much like parties, Elizabeth said. Miss Kilman opened her mouth, slightly projected her chin, and swallowed down the last inches of the chocolate éclair, then wiped her fingers, and washed the tea round in her cup.

She was about to split asunder, she felt. The agony was so terrific. If she could grasp her, if she could clasp her, if she could make her hers absolutely and forever and then die; that was all she wanted. But to sit here, unable to think of anything to say; to see Elizabeth turning against her; to be felt repulsive even by her—it was too much; she could not stand it. The thick fingers curled inwards.

"I never go to parties," said Miss Kilman, just to keep Elizabeth from going. "People don't ask me to parties"—and she knew as she said it that it was this egotism that was her undoing; Mr. Whittaker had warned her; but she could not help it. She had suffered so horribly. "Why should they ask me?" she said. "I'm plain, I'm unhappy." She knew it was idiotic. But it was all those people passing—people with parcels who despised her, who made her say it. However, she was Doris Kilman. She had her degree. She was a woman who had made her way in the world. Her knowledge of modern history was more than respectable.

"I don't pity myself," she said. "I pity"—she meant to say "your mother" but no, she could not, not to Elizabeth. "I pity other people," she said, "more."

Like some dumb creature who has been brought up to a gate for an unknown purpose, and stands there longing to gallop away, Elizabeth Dalloway sat silent. Was Miss Kilman going to say anything more?

"Don't quite forget me," said Doris Kilman; her voice quivered. Right away to the end of the field the dumb creature galloped in terror.

The great hand opened and shut.

Elizabeth turned her head. The waitress came. One had to pay at the desk, Elizabeth said, and went off, drawing out, so Miss Kilman felt, the very entrails in her body, stretching them as she crossed the room, and then, with a final twist, bowing her head very politely, she went.

She had gone. Miss Kilman sat at the marble table among the éclairs, stricken once, twice, thrice by shocks of suffering. She had gone. Mrs. Dalloway had triumphed. Elizabeth had gone. Beauty had gone, youth had gone.

So she sat. She got up, blundered off among the little tables, rocking slightly from side to side, and somebody came after her with her petticoat, and she lost her way, and was hemmed in by trunks specially prepared for taking to India; next got among the accouchement sets, and baby linen; through all the commodities of the world, perishable and permanent, hams, drugs, flowers, stationery, variously smelling, now sweet, now sour she lurched; saw herself thus lurching with her hat askew, very red in the face, full length in a looking-glass; and at last came out into the street.

The tower of Westminster Cathedral rose in front of her, the habitation of God. In the midst of the traffic, there was the habitation of God. Doggedly she set off with her parcel to that other sanctuary, the Abbey, where, raising her hands in a tent before her face, she sat beside those driven into shelter too; the variously assorted worshippers, now divested of social rank, almost of sex, as they raised their hands before their faces; but once they removed them, instantly reverent, middle class, English men and women, some of them desirous of seeing the wax works.

But Miss Kilman held her tent before her face. Now she was deserted; now rejoined. New worshippers came in from the street to replace the strollers, and still, as people gazed round and shuffled past the tomb of the Unknown Warrior, still she barred her eyes with her fingers and tried in this double darkness, for the light in the Abbey was bodiless, to aspire above the vanities, the desires, the commodities, to rid herself both of hatred and of love. Her hands twitched. She seemed to struggle. Yet to others God was accessible and the path to Him smooth. Mr. Fletcher, retired, of the Treasury, Mrs. Gorham, widow of the famous K.C., approached Him simply, and having done their praying, leant back, enjoyed the music (the organ pealed sweetly), and saw Miss Kilman at the end of the row, praying, praying, and, being still on the threshold of their underworld, thought of her sympathetically as a soul haunting the same territory; a soul cut out of immaterial substance; not a woman, a soul.

But Mr. Fletcher had to go. He had to pass her, and being himself neat as a new pin, could not help being a little distressed by the poor lady's disorder; her hair down; her parcel on the floor. She did not at once let him pass. But, as he stood gazing about him, at the white marbles, grey window panes, and accumulated treasures (for he was extremely proud of the Abbey), her largeness, robustness, and power as she sat there shifting her knees from time to time (it was so rough the approach to her God—so tough her desires) impressed him, as they had impressed Mrs. Dalloway (she could not get the thought of her out of her mind that afternoon), the Rev. Edward Whittaker, and Elizabeth too.

And Elizabeth waited in Victoria Street for an omnibus. It was so nice to be out of doors. She thought perhaps she need not go home just yet. It was so nice to be out in the air. So she would get on to an omnibus. And already, even as she stood there, in her very well cut clothes, it was beginning.... People were beginning to compare her to poplar trees, early dawn, hyacinths, fawns, running water, and garden lilies, and it made her life a burden to her, for she so much preferred being left alone to do what she liked in the country, but they would compare her to lilies, and she had to go to parties, and London was so dreary compared with being alone in the country with her father and the dogs.

Buses swooped, settled, were off—garish caravans, glistening with red and yellow varnish. But which should she get on to? She had no preferences. Of course, she would not push her way. She inclined to be passive. It was expression she needed, but her eyes were fine, Chinese, oriental, and, as her mother said, with such nice shoulders and holding herself so straight, she was always charming to look at; and lately, in the evening especially, when she was interested, for she never seemed excited, she looked almost beautiful, very stately, very serene. What could she be thinking? Every man fell in love with her, and she was really awfully bored. For it was beginning. Her mother could see that—the compliments were beginning. That she did not care more about it—for instance for her clothes—sometimes worried Clarissa, but perhaps it was as well with all those puppies and guinea pigs about having distemper, and it gave her a charm. And now there was this odd friendship with Miss Kilman. Well, thought Clarissa about three o'clock in the morning, reading Baron Marbot for she could not sleep, it proves she has a heart.

Suddenly Elizabeth stepped forward and most competently boarded the omnibus, in front of everybody. She took a seat on top. The impetuous creature—a pirate—started forward, sprang away; she had to hold the rail to steady herself, for a pirate it was, reckless, unscrupulous, bearing down ruthlessly, circumventing dangerously, boldly snatching a passenger, or ignoring a passenger, squeezing eel-like and arrogant in between, and then rushing insolently all sails spread up Whitehall. And did Elizabeth give one thought to poor Miss Kilman who loved her without jealousy, to whom she had been a fawn in the open, a moon in a glade? She was delighted to be free. The fresh air was so delicious. It had been so stuffy in the Army and Navy Stores. And now it was like riding, to be rushing up Whitehall; and to each movement of the omnibus the beautiful body in the fawn-coloured coat responded freely like a rider, like the figure-head of a ship, for the breeze slightly disarrayed her; the heat gave her cheeks the pallor of white painted wood; and her fine eyes, having no eyes to meet, gazed ahead, blank, bright, with the staring incredible innocence of sculpture.

It was always talking about her own sufferings that made Miss Kilman so difficult. And was she right? If it was being on committees and giving up hours and hours every day (she hardly ever saw him in London) that helped the poor, her father did that, goodness knows,—if that was what Miss Kilman meant about being a Christian; but it was so difficult to say. Oh, she would like to go a little further. Another penny was it to the Strand? Here was another penny then. She would go up the Strand.

She liked people who were ill. And every profession is open to the women of your generation, said Miss Kilman. So she might be a doctor. She might be a farmer. Animals are often ill. She might own a thousand acres and have people under her. She would go and see them in their cottages. This was Somerset House. One might be a very good farmer—and that, strangely enough though Miss Kilman had her share in it, was almost entirely due to Somerset House. It looked so splendid, so serious, that great grey building. And she liked the feeling of people working. She liked those churches, like shapes of grey paper, breasting the stream of the Strand. It was quite different here from Westminster, she thought, getting off at Chancery Lane. It was so serious; it was so busy. In short, she would like to have a profession. She would become a doctor, a farmer, possibly go into Parliament, if she found it necessary, all because of the Strand.

The feet of those people busy about their activities, hands putting stone to stone, minds eternally occupied not with trivial chatterings (comparing women to poplars—which was rather exciting, of course, but very silly), but with thoughts of ships, of business, of law, of administration, and with it all so stately (she was in the Temple), gay (there was the river), pious (there was the Church), made her quite determined, whatever her mother might say, to become either a farmer or a doctor. But she was, of course, rather lazy.

And it was much better to say nothing about it. It seemed so silly. It was the sort of thing that did sometimes happen, when one was alone—buildings without architects' names, crowds of people coming back from the city having more power than single clergymen in Kensington, than any of the books Miss Kilman had lent her, to stimulate what lay slumbrous, clumsy, and shy on the mind's sandy floor to break surface, as a child suddenly stretches its arms; it was just that, perhaps, a sigh, a stretch of the arms, an impulse, a revelation, which has its effects for ever, and then down again it went to the sandy floor. She must go home. She must dress for dinner. But what was the time?—where was a clock?

She looked up Fleet Street. She walked just a little way towards St. Paul's, shyly, like some one penetrating on tiptoe, exploring a strange house by night with a candle, on edge lest the owner should suddenly fling wide his bedroom door and ask her business, nor did she dare wander off into queer alleys, tempting bye-streets, any more than in a strange house open doors which might be bedroom doors, or sitting-room doors, or lead straight to the larder. For no Dalloways came down the Strand daily; she was a pioneer, a stray, venturing, trusting.

In many ways, her mother felt, she was extremely immature, like a child still, attached to dolls, to old slippers; a perfect baby; and that was charming. But then, of course, there was in the Dalloway family the tradition of public service. Abbesses, principals, head mistresses, dignitaries, in the republic of women—without being brilliant, any of them, they were that. She penetrated a little further in the direction of St. Paul's. She liked the geniality, sisterhood, motherhood, brotherhood of this uproar. It seemed to her good. The noise was tremendous; and suddenly there were trumpets (the unemployed) blaring, rattling about in the uproar; military music; as if people were marching; yet had they been dying—had some woman breathed her last and whoever was watching, opening the window of the room where she had just brought off that act of supreme dignity, looked down on Fleet Street, that uproar, that military music would have come triumphing up to him, consolatory, indifferent.

It was not conscious. There was no recognition in it of one's fortune, or fate, and for that very reason even to those dazed with watching for the last shivers of consciousness on the faces of the dying, consoling. Forgetfulness in people might wound, their ingratitude corrode, but this voice, pouring endlessly, year in year out, would take whatever it might be; this vow; this van; this life; this procession, would wrap them all about and carry them on, as in the rough stream of a glacier the ice holds a splinter of bone, a blue petal, some oak trees, and rolls them on.

But it was later than she thought. Her mother would not like her to be wandering off alone like this. She turned back down the Strand.

A puff of wind (in spite of the heat, there was quite a wind) blew a thin black veil over the sun and over the Strand. The faces faded; the omnibuses suddenly lost their glow. For although the clouds were of mountainous white so that one could fancy hacking hard chips off with a hatchet, with broad golden slopes, lawns of celestial pleasure gardens, on their flanks, and had all the appearance of settled habitations assembled for the conference of gods above the world, there was a perpetual movement among them. Signs were interchanged, when, as if to fulfil some scheme arranged already, now a summit dwindled, now a whole block of pyramidal size which had kept its station inalterably advanced into the midst or gravely led the procession to fresh anchorage. Fixed though they seemed at their posts, at rest in perfect unanimity, nothing could be fresher, freer, more sensitive superficially than the snow-white or gold-kindled surface; to change, to go, to dismantle the solemn assemblage was immediately possible; and in spite of the grave fixity, the accumulated robustness and solidity, now they struck light to the earth, now darkness.

Calmly and competently, Elizabeth Dalloway mounted the Westminster omnibus.

Going and coming, beckoning, signalling, so the light and shadow which now made the wall grey, now the bananas bright yellow, now made the Strand grey, now made the omnibuses bright yellow, seemed to Septimus Warren Smith lying on the sofa in the sitting-room; watching the watery gold glow and fade with the astonishing sensibility of some live creature on the roses, on the wall-paper. Outside the trees dragged their leaves like nets through the depths of the air; the sound of water was in the room and through the waves came the voices of birds singing. Every power poured its treasures on his head, and his hand lay there on the back of the sofa, as he had seen his hand lie when he was bathing, floating, on the top of the waves, while far away on shore he heard dogs barking and barking far away. Fear no more, says the heart in the body; fear no more.

He was not afraid. At every moment Nature signified by some laughing hint like that gold spot which went round the wall—there, there, there—her determination to show, by brandishing her plumes, shaking her tresses, flinging her mantle this way and that, beautifully, always beautifully, and standing close up to breathe through her hollowed hands Shakespeare's words, her meaning.

Rezia, sitting at the table twisting a hat in her hands, watched him; saw him smiling. He was happy then. But she could not bear to see him smiling. It was not marriage; it was not being one's husband to look strange like that, always to be starting, laughing, sitting hour after hour silent, or clutching her and telling her to write. The table drawer was full of those writings; about war; about Shakespeare; about great discoveries; how there is no death. Lately he had become excited suddenly for no reason (and both Dr. Holmes and Sir William Bradshaw said excitement was the worst thing for him), and waved his hands and cried out that he knew the truth! He knew everything! That man, his friend who was killed, Evans, had come, he said. He was singing behind the screen. She wrote it down just as he spoke it. Some things were very beautiful; others sheer nonsense. And he was always stopping in the middle, changing his mind; wanting to add something; hearing something new; listening with his hand up.

But she heard nothing.

And once they found the girl who did the room reading one of these papers in fits of laughter. It was a dreadful pity. For that made Septimus cry out about human cruelty—how they tear each other to pieces. The fallen, he said, they tear to pieces. "Holmes is on us," he would say, and he would invent stories about Holmes; Holmes eating porridge; Holmes reading Shakespeare—making himself roar with laughter or rage, for Dr. Holmes seemed to stand for something horrible to him. "Human nature," he called him. Then there were the visions. He was drowned, he used to say, and lying on a cliff with the gulls screaming over him. He would look over the edge of the sofa down into the sea. Or he was hearing music. Really it was only a barrel organ or some man crying in the street. But "Lovely!" he used to cry, and the tears would run down his cheeks, which was to her the most dreadful thing of all, to see a man like Septimus, who had fought, who was brave, crying. And he would lie listening until suddenly he would cry that he was falling down,

down into the flames! Actually she would look for flames, it was so vivid. But there was nothing. They were alone in the room. It was a dream, she would tell him and so quiet him at last, but sometimes she was frightened too. She sighed as she sat sewing.

Her sigh was tender and enchanting, like the wind outside a wood in the evening. Now she put down her scissors; now she turned to take something from the table. A little stir, a little crinkling, a little tapping built up something on the table there, where she sat sewing. Through his eyelashes he could see her blurred outline; her little black body; her face and hands; her turning movements at the table, as she took up a reel, or looked (she was apt to lose things) for her silk. She was making a hat for Mrs. Filmer's married daughter, whose name was—he had forgotten her name.

"What is the name of Mrs. Filmer's married daughter?" he asked.

"Mrs. Peters," said Rezia. She was afraid it was too small, she said, holding it before her. Mrs. Peters was a big woman; but she did not like her. It was only because Mrs. Filmer had been so good to them. "She gave me grapes this morning," she said—that Rezia wanted to do something to show that they were grateful. She had come into the room the other evening and found Mrs. Peters, who thought they were out, playing the gramophone.

"Was it true?" he asked. She was playing the gramophone? Yes; she had told him about it at the time; she had found Mrs. Peters playing the gramophone.

He began, very cautiously, to open his eyes, to see whether a gramophone was really there. But real things—real things were too exciting. He must be cautious. He would not go mad. First he looked at the fashion papers on the lower shelf, then, gradually at the gramophone with the green trumpet. Nothing could be more exact. And so, gathering courage, he looked at the sideboard; the plate of bananas; the engraving of Queen Victoria and the Prince Consort; at the mantelpiece, with the jar of roses. None of these things moved. All were still; all were real.

"She is a woman with a spiteful tongue," said Rezia.

"What does Mr. Peters do?" Septimus asked.

"Ah," said Rezia, trying to remember. She thought Mrs. Filmer had said that he travelled for some company. "Just now he is in Hull," she said.

"Just now!" She said that with her Italian accent. She said that herself. He shaded his eyes so that he might see only a little of her face at a time, first the chin, then the nose, then the forehead, in case it were deformed, or had some terrible mark on it. But no, there she was, perfectly natural, sewing, with the pursed lips that women have, the set, the melancholy expression, when sewing. But there was nothing terrible about it, he assured himself, looking a second time, a third time at her face, her hands, for what was frightening or disgusting in her as she sat there in broad daylight, sewing? Mrs. Peters had a spiteful tongue. Mr. Peters was in Hull. Why then rage and prophesy? Why fly scourged and outcast? Why be made to tremble and sob by the clouds? Why seek truths and deliver messages when Rezia sat sticking pins into the front of her dress, and Mr. Peters was in Hull? Miracles, revelations, agonies, loneliness, falling through the sea, down, down into the flames, all were burnt out, for he had a sense, as he watched Rezia trimming the straw hat for Mrs. Peters, of a coverlet of flowers.

"It's too small for Mrs. Peters," said Septimus.

For the first time for days he was speaking as he used to do! Of course it was—absurdly small, she said. But Mrs. Peters had chosen it.

He took it out of her hands. He said it was an organ grinder's monkey's hat.

How it rejoiced her that! Not for weeks had they laughed like this together, poking fun privately like married people. What she meant was that if Mrs. Filmer had come in, or Mrs. Peters or anybody they would not have understood what she and Septimus were laughing at.

"There," she said, pinning a rose to one side of the hat. Never had she felt so happy! Never in her life!

But that was still more ridiculous, Septimus said. Now the poor woman looked like a pig at a fair, (Nobody ever made her laugh as Septimus did.)

What had she got in her work-box? She had ribbons and beads, tassels, artificial flowers. She tumbled them out on the table. He began putting odd colours together—for though he had no fingers, could not even do up a parcel, he had a wonderful eye, and often he was right, sometimes absurd, of course, but sometimes wonderfully right.

"She shall have a beautiful hat!" he murmured, taking up this and that, Rezia kneeling by his side, looking over his shoulder. Now it was finished—that is to say the design; she must stitch it together. But she must be very, very careful, he said, to keep it just as he had made it.

So she sewed. When she sewed, he thought, she made a sound like a kettle on the hob; bubbling, murmuring, always busy, her strong little pointed fingers pinching and poking; her needle flashing straight. The sun might go in and out, on the tassels, on the wallpaper, but he would wait, he thought, stretching out his feet, looking at his ringed sock at the end of the sofa; he would wait in this warm place, this pocket of still air, which one comes on at the edge of a wood sometimes in the evening, when, because of a fall in the ground, or some arrangement of the trees (one must be scientific above all, scientific), warmth lingers, and the air buffets the cheek like the wing of a bird.

"There it is," said Rezia, twirling Mrs. Peters' hat on the tips of her fingers. "That'll do for the moment. Later..." her sentence bubbled away drip, drip, drip, like a contented tap left running.

It was wonderful. Never had he done anything which made

him feel so proud. It was so real, it was so substantial, Mrs. Peters' hat.

"Just look at it," he said.

Yes, it would always make her happy to see that hat. He had become himself then, he had laughed then. They had been alone together. Always she would like that hat.

He told her to try it on.

"But I must look so queer!" she cried, running over to the glass and looking first this side then that. Then she snatched it off again, for there was a tap at the door. Could it be Sir William Bradshaw? Had he sent already?

No! it was only the small girl with the evening paper.

What always happened, then happened—what happened every night of their lives. The small girl sucked her thumb at the door; Rezia went down on her knees; Rezia cooed and kissed; Rezia got a bag of sweets out of the table drawer. For so it always happened. First one thing, then another. So she built it up, first one thing and then another. Dancing, skipping, round and round the room they went. He took the paper. Surrey was all out, he read. There was a heat wave. Rezia repeated: Surrey was all out. There was a heat wave, making it part of the game she was playing with Mrs. Filmer's grandchild, both of them laughing, chattering at the same time, at their game. He was very tired. He was very happy. He would sleep. He shut his eyes. But directly he saw nothing the sounds of the game became fainter and stranger and sounded like the cries of people seeking and not finding, and passing further and further away. They had lost him!

He started up in terror. What did he see? The plate of bananas on the sideboard. Nobody was there (Rezia had taken the child to its mother. It was bedtime). That was it: to be alone forever. That was the doom pronounced in Milan when he came into the room and saw them cutting out buckram shapes with their scissors; to be alone forever.

He was alone with the sideboard and the bananas. He was alone, exposed on this bleak eminence, stretched out—but not on a hill-top; not on a crag; on Mrs. Filmer's sitting-room sofa. As for the visions, the faces, the voices of the dead, where were they? There was a screen in front of him, with black bulrushes and blue swallows. Where he had once seen mountains, where he had seen faces, where he had seen beauty, there was a screen.

"Evans!" he cried. There was no answer. A mouse had squeaked, or a curtain rustled. Those were the voices of the dead. The screen, the coal-scuttle, the sideboard remained to him. Let him then face the screen, the coal-scuttle and the sideboard... but Rezia burst into the room chattering.

Some letter had come. Everybody's plans were changed. Mrs. Filmer would not be able to go to Brighton after all. There was no time to let Mrs. Williams know, and really Rezia thought it very, very annoying, when she caught sight of the hat and thought... perhaps... she... might just make a little.... Her voice died out in contented melody.

"Ah, damn!" she cried (it was a joke of theirs, her swearing), the needle had broken. Hat, child, Brighton, needle. She built it up; first one thing, then another, she built it up, sewing.

She wanted him to say whether by moving the rose she had improved the hat. She sat on the end of the sofa.

They were perfectly happy now, she said, suddenly, putting the hat down. For she could say anything to him now. She could say whatever came into her head. That was almost the first thing she had felt about him, that night in the café when he had come in with his English friends. He had come in, rather shyly, looking round him, and his hat had fallen when he hung it up. That she could remember. She knew he was English, though not one of the large Englishmen her sister admired, for he was always thin; but he had a beautiful fresh colour; and with his big nose, his bright eyes, his way of sitting a little hunched made her think, she had often told him, of a young hawk, that first evening she saw him, when they were playing dominoes, and he had come in—of a young hawk; but with her he was always very gentle. She had never seen him wild or drunk, only suffering sometimes through this terrible war, but even so, when she came in, he would put it all away. Anything, anything in the whole world, any little bother with her work, anything that struck her to say she would tell him, and he understood at once. Her own family even were not the same. Being older than she was and being so clever—how serious he was, wanting her to read Shakespeare before she could even read a child's story in English!—being so much more experienced, he could help her. And she too could help him.

But this hat now. And then (it was getting late) Sir William Bradshaw.

She held her hands to her head, waiting for him to say did he like the hat or not, and as she sat there, waiting, looking down, he could feel her mind, like a bird, falling from branch to branch, and always alighting, quite rightly; he could follow her mind, as she sat there in one of those loose lax poses that came to her naturally and, if he should say anything, at once she smiled, like a bird alighting with all its claws firm upon the bough.

But he remembered Bradshaw said, "The people we are most fond of are not good for us when we are ill." Bradshaw said, he must be taught to rest. Bradshaw said they must be separated.

"Must," "must," why "must"? What power had Bradshaw over him? "What right has Bradshaw to say 'must' to me?" he demanded.

"It is because you talked of killing yourself," said Rezia. (Mercifully, she could now say anything to Septimus.)

So he was in their power! Holmes and Bradshaw were on him! The brute with the red nostrils was snuffing into every secret place! "Must" it could say! Where were his papers? the things he had written?

She brought him his papers, the things he had written, things she had written for him. She tumbled them out on to the sofa. They looked at them together. Diagrams, designs, little men and women brandishing sticks for arms, with wings—were they?—on their backs; circles traced round shillings and six-pences—the suns and stars; zigzagging precipices with moun-taineers ascending roped together, exactly like knives and forks; sea pieces with little faces laughing out of what might perhaps be waves: the map of the world. Burn them! he cried. Now for his writings; how the dead sing behind rhododendron bushes; odes to Time; conversations with Shakespeare; Evans, Evans, Evans—his messages from the dead; do not cut down trees; tell the Prime Minister. Universal love: the meaning of the world. Burn them! he cried.

But Rezia laid her hands on them. Some were very beauti-ful, she thought. She would tie them up (for she had no enve-lope) with a piece of silk.

Even if they took him, she said, she would go with him. They could not separate them against their wills, she said.

Shuffling the edges straight, she did up the papers, and tied the parcel almost without looking, sitting beside him, he thought, as if all her petals were about her. She was a flowering tree; and through her branches looked out the face of a lawgiver, who had reached a sanctuary where she feared no one; not Holmes; not Bradshaw; a miracle, a triumph, the last and great-est. Staggering he saw her mount the appalling staircase, laden with Holmes and Bradshaw, men who never weighed less than eleven stone six, who sent their wives to Court, men who made ten thousand a year and talked of proportion; who different in their verdicts (for Holmes said one thing, Bradshaw another), yet judges they were; who mixed the vision and the sideboard; saw nothing clear, yet ruled, yet inflicted. "Must" they said. Over them she triumphed.

"There!" she said. The papers were tied up. No one should get at them. She would put them away.

And, she said, nothing should separate them. She sat down beside him and called him by the name of that hawk or crow which being malicious and a great destroyer of crops was precisely like him. No one could separate them, she said.

Then she got up to go into the bedroom to pack their things, but hearing voices downstairs and thinking that Dr. Holmes had perhaps called, ran down to prevent him coming up.

Septimus could hear her talking to Holmes on the staircase.

"My dear lady, I have come as a friend," Holmes was saying.

"No. I will not allow you to see my husband," she said.

He could see her, like a little hen, with her wings spread barring his passage. But Holmes persevered.

"My dear lady, allow me . . ." Holmes said, putting her aside (Holmes was a powerfully built man).

Holmes was coming upstairs. Holmes would burst open the door. Holmes would say "In a funk, eh?" Holmes would get him. But no; not Holmes; not Bradshaw. Getting up rather unsteadily, hopping indeed from foot to foot, he considered Mrs Filmer's nice clean bread knife with "Bread" carved on the handle. Ah, but one mustn't spoil that. The gas fire? But it was too late now. Holmes was coming. Razors he might have got, but Rezia, who always did that sort of thing, had packed them. There remained only the window, the large Bloomsbury-lodging house window, the tiresome, the troublesome, and rather melodramatic business of opening the window and throwing himself out. It was their idea of tragedy, not his or Rezia's (for she was with him). Holmes and Bradshaw like that sort of thing. (He sat on the sill.) But he would wait till the very last moment. He did not want to die. Life was good. The sun hot. Only human beings—what did *they* want? Coming down the staircase opposite an old man stopped and stared at him. Holmes was at the door. "I'll give it you!" he cried, and flung himself vigorously, violently down on to Mrs. Filmer's area railings.

"The coward!" cried Dr. Holmes, bursting the door open. Rezia ran to the window, she saw; she understood. Dr. Holmes and Mrs. Filmer collided with each other. Mrs. Filmer flapped her apron and made her hide her eyes in the bedroom. There was a great deal of running up and down stairs. Dr. Holmes came in—white as a sheet, shaking all over, with a glass in his hand. She must be brave and drink something, he said (What was it? Something sweet), for her husband was horribly mangled, would not recover consciousness, she must not see him, must be spared as much as possible, would have the inquest to go through, poor young woman. Who could have foretold it? A sudden impulse, no one was in the least to blame (he told Mrs. Filmer). And why the devil he did it, Dr. Holmes could not conceive.

It seemed to her as she drank the sweet stuff that she was opening long windows, stepping out into some garden. But where? The clock was striking—one, two, three: how sensible the sound was; compared with all this thumping and whispering; like Septimus himself. She was falling asleep. But the clock went on striking, four, five, six and Mrs. Filmer waving her apron (they wouldn't bring the body in here, would they?) seemed part of that garden; or a flag. She had once seen a flag slowly rippling out from a mast when she stayed with her aunt at Venice. Men killed in battle were thus saluted, and Septimus had been through the War. Of her memories, most were happy.

She put on her hat, and ran through cornfields—where could it have been?—on to some hill, somewhere near the sea, for there were ships, gulls, butterflies, they sat on a cliff. In London too, there they sat, and, half dreaming, came to her through the bedroom door, rain falling, whisperings, stirrings among dry corn, the caress of the sea, as it seemed to her, hollowing them in its arched shell and murmuring to her laid on shore, strewn she felt, like flying flowers over some tomb.

"He is dead," she said, smiling at the poor old woman who guarded her with her honest light-blue eyes fixed on the door. (They wouldn't bring him in here, would they?) But Mrs. Filmer pooh-poohed. Oh no, oh no! They were carrying him away now. Ought she not to be told? Married people ought to be together, Mrs. Filmer thought. But they must do as the doctor said.

"Let her sleep," said Dr. Holmes, feeling her pulse. She saw the large outline of his body standing dark against the window. So that was Dr. Holmes.

ONE OF THE TRIUMPHS of civilisation, Peter Walsh thought. It is one of the triumphs of civilisation, as the light high bell of the ambulance sounded. Swiftly, cleanly the ambulance sped to the hospital, having picked up instantly, humanely, some poor devil; some one hit on the head, struck down by disease, knocked over perhaps a minute or so ago at one of these crossings, as might happen to oneself. That was civilisation. It struck him coming back from the East—the efficiency, the organisation, the communal spirit of London. Every cart or carriage of its own accord drew aside to let the ambulance pass. Perhaps it was morbid; or was it not touching rather, the respect which they showed this ambulance with its victim inside—busy men hurrying home yet instantly bethinking them as it passed of some wife; or presumably how easily it might have been them there, stretched on a shelf with a doctor and a nurse.... Ah, but thinking became morbid, sentimental, directly one began conjuring up doctors, dead bodies; a little glow of pleasure, a sort of lust too over the visual impression warned one not to go on with that sort of thing any more—fatal to art, fatal to friendship. True. And yet, thought Peter Walsh, as the ambulance turned the corner though the light high bell could be heard down the next street and still farther as it crossed the Tottenham Court Road, chiming constantly, it is the privilege of loneliness; in privacy one may do as one chooses. One might weep if no one saw. It had been his undoing—this susceptibility—in Anglo-Indian society; not weeping at the right time, or laughing either. I have that in me, he thought standing by the pillar-box, which could now dissolve in tears. Why, Heaven knows. Beauty of some sort probably, and the weight of the day, which beginning with that visit to Clarissa had exhausted him with its heat, its intensity, and the drip, drip, of one impression after another down into that cellar where they stood, deep, dark, and no one would ever know. Partly for that reason, its secrecy, complete and inviolable, he had found life like an unknown garden, full of turns and corners, surprising, yes; really it took one's breath away, these moments; there coming to him by the pillar-box opposite the British Museum one of them, a moment, in which things came together; this ambulance; and life and death. It was as if he were sucked up to some very high roof by that rush of emotion and the rest of him, like a white shell-sprinkled beach, left bare. It had been his undoing in Anglo-Indian society—this susceptibility.

Clarissa once, going on top of an omnibus with him somewhere, Clarissa superficially at least, so easily moved, now in despair, now in the best of spirits, all aquiver in those days and such good company, spotting queer little scenes, names, people from the top of a bus, for they used to explore London and bring back bags full of treasures from the Caledonian market—Clarissa had a theory in those days—they had heaps of theories, always theories, as young people have. It was to explain the feeling they had of dissatisfaction; not knowing people; not being known. For how could they know each other? You met every day; then not for six months, or years. It was unsatisfactory, they agreed, how little one knew people. But she said, sitting on the bus going up Shaftesbury Avenue, she felt herself everywhere; not "here, here, here"; and she tapped the back of the seat; but everywhere. She waved her hand, going up Shaftesbury Avenue. She was all that. So that to know her, or any one, one must seek out the people who completed them; even the places. Odd affinities she had with people she had never spoken to, some woman in the street, some man behind a counter—even trees, or barns. It ended in a transcendental theory which, with her horror of death, allowed her to believe, or say that she believed (for all her scepticism), that since our apparitions, the part of us which appears, are so momentary compared with the other, the unseen part of us, which spreads wide, the unseen might survive, be recovered somehow attached to this person or that, or even haunting certain places after death . . . perhaps—perhaps.

Looking back over that long friendship of almost thirty years her theory worked to this extent. Brief, broken, often painful as their actual meetings had been what with his absences and interruptions (this morning, for instance, in came Elizabeth, like a long-legged colt, handsome, dumb, just as he was beginning to talk to Clarissa) the effect of them on his life was immeasurable. There was a mystery about it. You were given a sharp, acute, uncomfortable grain—the actual meeting; horribly painful as often as not; yet in absence, in the most unlikely places, it would flower out, open, shed its scent, let you touch, taste, look about you, get the whole feel of it and understanding, after years of lying lost. Thus she had come to him; on board ship; in the Himalayas; suggested by the oddest things (so Sally Seton, generous, enthusiastic goose! thought of *him* when she saw blue hydrangeas). She had influenced him more than any person he had ever known. And always in this way coming before him without his wishing it, cool, lady-like, critical; or ravishing, romantic, recalling some field or English harvest. He saw her most often in the country, not in London. One scene after another at Bourton. . . .

He had reached his hotel. He crossed the hall, with its mounds of reddish chairs and sofas, its spike-leaved, withered-looking plants. He got his key off the hook. The young lady handed him some letters. He went upstairs—he saw her most often at Bourton, in the late summer, when he stayed there for a week, or fortnight even, as people did in those days. First on top of some hill there she would stand, hands clapped to her hair, her cloak blowing out, pointing, crying to them—she saw the Severn beneath. Or in a wood, making the kettle boil—very ineffective with her fingers; the smoke curtseying, blowing in their faces; her little pink face showing through; begging water from an old woman in a cottage, who came to the door to watch them go. They walked always; the others drove. She was bored driving, disliked all animals, except that dog. They tramped miles along roads. She would break off to get her bearings, pilot him back across country; and all the time they argued, discussed poetry, discussed people, discussed politics (she was a Radical then); never noticing a thing except when she stopped, cried out at a view or a tree, and made him look with her; and so on again, through stubble fields, she walking ahead, with a flower for her aunt, never tired of walking for all her delicacy; to drop down on Bourton in the dusk. Then, after dinner, old Breitkopf would open the piano and sing without any voice, and they would lie sunk in arm-chairs, trying not to laugh, but always breaking down and laughing laughing — laughing at nothing. Breitkopf was supposed not to see. And then in the morning, flirting up and down like a wagtail in front of the house. . . .

Oh it was a letter from her! This blue envelope; that was her hand. And he would have to read it. Here was another of those meetings, bound to be painful! To read her letter needed the devil of an effort. "How heavenly it was to see him. She must tell him that." That was all.

But it upset him. It annoyed him. He wished she hadn't written it. Coming on top of his thoughts, it was like a nudge in the ribs. Why couldn't she let him be? After all, she had married Dalloway, and lived with him in perfect happiness all these years.

These hotels are not consoling places. Far from it. Any number of people had hung up their hats on those pegs. Even the flies, if you thought of it, had settled on other people's noses. As for the cleanliness which hit him in the face, it wasn't cleanliness, so much as bareness, frigidity; a thing that had to be. Some arid matron made her rounds at dawn sniffing, peering, causing blue-nosed maids to scour, for all the world as if the next visitor were a joint of meat to be served on a perfectly clean platter. For sleep, one bed; for sitting in, one arm-chair; for cleaning one's teeth and shaving one's chin, one tumbler, one looking-glass. Books, letters, dressing-gown, slipped about

on the impersonality of the horsehair like incongruous imperti-
nences. And it was Clarissa's letter that made him see all this.
"Heavenly to see you. She must say so!" He folded the paper;
pushed it away; nothing would induce him to read it again!

To get that letter to him by six o'clock she must have sat
down and written it directly he left her; stamped it; sent somebody to the post. It was, as people say, very like her. She was
upset by his visit. She had felt a great deal; had for a moment,
when she kissed his hand, regretted, envied him even, remembered possibly (for he saw her look it) something he had
said—how they would change the world if she married him
perhaps; whereas, it was this; it was middle age; it was medioc-
rity; then forced herself with her indomitable vitality to put all
that aside, there being in her a thread of life which for tough-
ness, endurance, power to overcome obstacles, and carry her
triumphantly through he had never known the like of. Yes; but
there would come a reaction directly he left the room. She
would be frightfully sorry for him; she would think what in the
world she could do to give him pleasure (short always of the one
thing) and he could see her with the tears running down her
cheeks going to her writing-table and dashing off that one line
which he was to find greeting him. . . . "Heavenly to see you!"
And she meant it.

Peter Walsh had now unlaced his boots.

But it would not have been a success, their marriage. The
other thing, after all, came so much more naturally.

It was odd; it was true; lots of people felt it. Peter Walsh,
who had done just respectably, filled the usual posts adequately,
was liked, but thought a little cranky, gave himself airs—it was
odd that *he* should have had, especially now that his hair was
grey, a contented look; a look of having reserves. It was this that
made him attractive to women who liked the sense that he was
not altogether manly. There was something unusual about him,
or something behind him. It might be that he was bookish—
never came to see you without taking up the book on the table

(he was now reading, with his bootlaces trailing on the floor); or that he was a gentleman, which showed itself in the way he knocked the ashes out of his pipe, and in his manners of course to women. For it was very charming and quite ridiculous how easily some girl without a grain of sense could twist him round her finger. But at her own risk. That is to say, though he might be ever so easy, and indeed with his gaiety and good-breeding fascinating to be with, it was only up to a point. She said something—no, no; he saw through that. He wouldn't stand that—no, no. Then he could shout and rock and hold his sides together over some joke with men. He was the best judge of cooking in India. He was a man. But not the sort of man one had to respect—which was a mercy; not like Major Simmons, for instance; not in the least like that, Daisy thought, when, in spite of her two small children, she used to compare them.

He pulled off his boots. He emptied his pockets. Out came with his pocket-knife a snapshot of Daisy on the verandah; Daisy all in white, with a fox-terrier on her knee; very charming, very dark; the best he had ever seen of her. It did come, after all so naturally; so much more naturally than Clarissa. No fuss. No bother. No finicking and fidgeting. All plain sailing. And the dark, adorably pretty girl on the verandah exclaimed (he could hear her). Of course, of course she would give him everything! she cried (she had no sense of discretion) everything he wanted! she cried, running to meet him, whoever might be looking. And she was only twenty-four. And she had two children. Well, well!

Well indeed he had got himself into a mess at his age. And it came over him when he woke in the night pretty forcibly. Suppose they did marry? For him it would be all very well, but what about her? Mrs. Burgess, a good sort and no chatterbox, in whom he had confided, thought this absence of his in England, ostensibly to see lawyers might serve to make Daisy reconsider, think what it meant. It was a question of her position, Mrs. Burgess said; the social barrier; giving up her children. She'd be a widow with a past one of these days, draggling about in the suburbs, or more likely, indiscriminate (you know, she said, what such women get like, with too much paint). But Peter Walsh pooh-poohed all that. He didn't mean to die yet. Anyhow she must settle for herself; judge for herself, he thought, padding about the room in his socks, smoothing out his dress-shirt, for he might go to Clarissa's party, or he might go to one of the Halls, or he might settle in and read an absorbing book written by a man he used to know at Oxford. And if he did retire, that's what he'd do—write books. He would go to Oxford and poke about in the Bodleian. Vainly the dark, adorably pretty girl ran to the end of the terrace; vainly waved her hand; vainly cried she didn't care a straw what people said. There he was, the man she thought the world of, the perfect gentleman, the fascinating, the distinguished (and his age made not the least difference to her), padding about a room in an hotel in Bloomsbury, shaving, washing, continuing, as he took up cans, put down razors, to poke about in the Bodleian, and get at the truth about one or two little matters that interested him. And he would have a chat with whoever it might be, and so come to disregard more and more precise hours for lunch, and miss engagements, and when Daisy asked him, as she would, for a kiss, a scene, fail to come up to the scratch (though he was genuinely devoted to her)—in short it might be happier, as Mrs. Burgess said, that she should forget him, or merely remember him as he was in August 1922, like a figure standing at the cross roads at dusk, which grows more and more remote as the dog-cart spins away, carrying her securely fastened to the back seat, though her arms are out-stretched, and as she sees the figure dwindle and disappear still she cries out how she would do anything in the world, anything, anything, anything. . . .

He never knew what people thought. It became more and more difficult for him to concentrate. He become absorbed; he became busied with his own concerns; now surly, now gay; de-pendent on women, absent-minded, moody, less and less able (so he thought as he shaved) to understand why Clarissa couldn't simply find them a lodging and be nice to Daisy; introduce her. And then he could just—just do what? just haunt and hover (he was at the moment actually engaged in sorting out various keys, papers), swoop and taste, be alone, in short, sufficient to himself; and yet nobody of course was more dependent upon others (he buttoned his waistcoat); it had been his undoing. He could not keep out of smoking-rooms, liked colonels, liked golf, liked bridge, and above all women's society, and the fineness of their companionship, and their faithfulness and audacity and greatness in loving which though it had its drawbacks seemed to him (and the dark, adorably pretty face was on top of the envelopes) so wholly admirable, so splendid a flower to grow on the crest of human life, and yet he could not come up to the scratch, being always apt to see round things (Clarissa had sapped something in him permanently), and to tire very easily of mute devotion and to want variety in love, though it would make him furious if Daisy loved anybody else, furious! for he was jealous, uncontrollably jealous by temperament. He suffered tortures! But where was his knife; his watch; his seals, his notecase, and Clarissa's letter which he would not read again but liked to think of, and Daisy's photograph? And now for dinner.

They were eating.

Sitting at little tables round vases, dressed or not dressed, with their shawls and bags laid beside them, with their air of false composure, for they were not used to so many courses at dinner, and confidence, for they were able to pay for it, and strain, for they had been running about London all day shopping, sightseeing; and their natural curiosity, for they looked round and up as the nice-looking gentleman in horn-rimmed spectacles came in, and their good nature, for they would have been glad to do any little service, such as lend a time-table or impart useful information, and their desire, pulsing in them, tugging at them subterraneously, somehow to establish connections if it were only a birthplace (Liverpool, for example) in common or friends of the same name; with their furtive glances, odd silences, and sudden withdrawals into family jocularity and isolation; there they sat eating dinner when Mr. Walsh came in and took his seat at a little table by the curtain.

It was not that he said anything, for being solitary he could only address himself to the waiter; it was his way of looking at the menu, of pointing his forefinger to a particular wine, of hitching himself up to the table, of addressing himself seriously, not gluttonously to dinner, that won him their respect; which, having to remain unexpressed for the greater part of the meal, flared up at the table where the Morrises sat when Mr. Walsh was heard to say at the end of the meal, "Bartlett pears." Why he should have spoken so moderately yet firmly, with the air of a disciplinarian well within his rights which are founded upon justice, neither young Charles Morris, nor old Charles, neither Miss Elaine nor Mrs. Morris knew. But when he said, "Bartlett pears," sitting alone at his table, they felt that he counted on their support in some lawful demand; was champion of a cause which immediately became their own, so that their eyes met his eyes sympathetically, and when they all reached the smoking-room simultaneously, a little talk between them became inevitable.

It was not very profound—only to the effect that London was crowded; had changed in thirty years; that Mr. Morris preferred Liverpool; that Mrs. Morris had been to the Westminster flower-show, and that they had all seen the Prince of Wales. Yet, thought Peter Walsh, no family in the world can compare with the Morrises; none whatever; and their relations to each other are perfect, and they don't care a hang for the upper classes, and they like what they like, and Elaine is training for the family business, and the boy has won a scholarship at Leeds, and the old lady (who is about his own age) has three more children at home; and they have two motor cars, but Mr. Morris still mends the boots on Sunday: it is superb, it is absolutely superb, thought Peter Walsh, swaying a little backwards and forwards with his liqueur glass in his hand among the hairy red chairs and ashtrays, feeling very well pleased with himself, for the Morrises liked him. Yes, they liked a man who said, "Bartlett pears." They liked him, he felt.

He would go to Clarissa's party. (The Morrises moved off; but they would meet again.) He would go to Clarissa's party, because he wanted to ask Richard what they were doing in India—the conservative duffers. And what's being acted? And music. . . . Oh yes, and mere gossip.

For this is the truth about our soul, he thought, our self, who fish-like inhabits deep seas and plies among obscurities threading her way between the boles of giant weeds, over sun-flickered spaces and on and on into gloom, cold, deep, inscrutable; suddenly she shoots to the surface and sports on the wind-wrinkled waves; that is, has a positive need to brush, scrape, kindle herself, gossiping. What did the Government mean—Richard Dalloway would know—to do about India?

Since it was a very hot night and the paper boys went by with placards proclaiming in huge red letters that there was a heat-wave, wicker chairs were placed on the hotel steps and there, sipping, smoking, detached gentlemen sat. Peter Walsh sat there. One might fancy that day, the London day, was just beginning. Like a woman who had slipped off her print dress and white apron to array herself in blue and pearls, the day changed, put off stuff, took gauze, changed to evening, and with the same sigh of exhilaration that a woman breathes, tumbling petticoats on the floor, it too shed dust, heat, colour; the traffic thinned; motor cars, tinkling, darting, succeeded the lumber of vans; and here and there among the thick foliage of the squares an intense light hung. I resign, the evening seemed to say, as it paled and faded above the battlements and prominences, moulded, pointed, of hotel, flat, and block of shops, I fade, she was beginning, I disappear, but London would have none of it, and rushed her bayonets into the sky, pinioned her, constrained her to partnership in her revelry.

For the great revolution of Mr. Willett's summer time had taken place since Peter Walsh's last visit to England. The pro-

longed evening was new to him. It was inspiriting, rather. For as
the young people went by with their despatch-boxes, awfully
glad to be free, proud too, dumbly, of stepping this famous
pavement, joy of a kind, cheap, tinselly, if you like, but all the
same rapture, flushed their faces. They dressed well too; pink
stockings; pretty shoes. They would now have two hours at the
pictures. It sharpened, it refined them, the yellow-blue evening
light; and on the leaves in the square shone lurid, livid—they
looked as if dipped in sea water—the foliage of a submerged
city. He was astonished by the beauty; it was encouraging too,
for where the returned Anglo-Indian sat by rights (he knew
crowds of them) in the Oriental Club biliously summing up the
ruin of the world, here was he, as young as ever; envying young
people their summer time and the rest of it, and more than sus-
pecting from the words of a girl, from a housemaid's laughter—
intangible things you couldn't lay your hands on—that shift
in the whole pyramidal accumulation which in his youth had
seemed immovable. On top of them it had pressed; weighed
them down, the women especially, like those flowers Clarissa's
Aunt Helena used to press between sheets of grey blotting-
paper with Littré's dictionary on top, sitting under the lamp
after dinner. She was dead now. He had heard of her, from
Clarissa, losing the sight of one eye. It seemed so fitting—one
of nature's masterpieces—that old Miss Parry should turn to
glass. She would die like some bird in a frost gripping her perch.
She belonged to a different age, but being so entire, so complete, would always stand up on the horizon, stone-white,
eminent, like a lighthouse marking some past stage on this adventurous, long, long voyage, this interminable (he felt for a
copper to buy a paper and read about Surrey and Yorkshire—
he had held out that copper millions of times. Surrey was all out
once more)—this interminable life. But cricket was no mere
game. Cricket was important. He could never help reading
about cricket. He read the scores in the stop press first, then
how it was a hot day; then about a murder case. Having done

things millions of times enriched them, though it might be said
to take the surface off. The past enriched, and experience, and
having cared for one or two people, and so having acquired the
power which the young lack, of cutting short, doing what one
likes, not caring a rap what people say and coming and going
without any very great expectations (he left his paper on the
table and moved off), which however (and he looked for his hat
and coat) was not altogether true of him, not to-night, for here
he was starting to go to a party, at his age, with the belief upon
him that he was about to have an experience. But what?

Beauty anyhow. Not the crude beauty of the eye. It was not
beauty pure and simple—Bedford Place leading into Russell
Square. It was straightness and emptiness of course; the symme-
try of a corridor; but it was also windows lit up, a piano, a gramophone sounding; a sense of pleasure-making hidden, but now
and again emerging when, through the uncurtained window, the
window left open, one saw parties sitting over tables, young
people slowly circling, conversations between men and women,
maids idly looking out (a strange comment theirs, when work
was done), stockings drying on top ledges, a parrot, a few plants.
Absorbing, mysterious, of infinite richness, this life. And in the
large square where the cabs shot and swerved so quick, there
were loitering couples, dallying, embracing, shrunk up under the
shower of a tree; that was moving; so silent, so absorbed, that
one passed, discreetly, timidly, as if in the presence of some sacred ceremony to interrupt which would have been impious.
That was interesting. And so on into the flare and glare.

His light overcoat blew open, he stepped with indescribable
idiosyncrasy, leant a little forward, tripped, with his hands behind his back and his eyes still a little hawklike; he tripped
through London, towards Westminster, observing.

Was everybody dining out, then? Doors were being opened
here by a footman to let issue a high-stepping old dame, in
buckled shoes, with three purple ostrich feathers in her hair.

Doors were being opened for ladies wrapped like mummies in shawls with bright flowers on them, ladies with bare heads. And in respectable quarters with stucco pillars through small front gardens lightly swathed with combs in their hair (having run up to see the children), women came; men waited for them, with their coats blowing open, and the motor started. Everybody was going out. What with these doors being opened, and the descent and the start, it seemed as if the whole of London were embarking in little boats moored to the bank, tossing on the waters, as if the whole place were floating off in carnival. And Whitehall was skated over, silver beaten as it was, skated over by spiders, and there was a sense of midges round the arc lamps; it was so hot that people stood about talking. And here in Westminster was a retired Judge, presumably, sitting four square at his house door dressed all in white. An Anglo-Indian presumably.

And here a shindy of brawling women, drunken women; here only a policeman and looming houses, high houses, domed houses, churches, parliaments, and the hoot of a steamer on the river, a hollow misty cry. But it was her street, this, Clarissa's; cabs were rushing round the corner, like water round the piers of a bridge, drawn together, it seemed to him because they bore people going to her party, Clarissa's party.

The cold stream of visual impressions failed him now as if the eye were a cup that overflowed and let the rest run down its china walls unrecorded. The brain must wake now. The body must contract now, entering the house, the lighted house, where the door stood open, where the motor cars were standing, and bright women descending: the soul must brave itself to endure. He opened the big blade of his pocket-knife.

LUCY CAME RUNNING full tilt downstairs, having just nipped in to the drawing-room to smooth a cover, to straighten a chair, to pause a moment and feel whoever came in must think how clean, how bright, how beautifully cared for, when they saw the beautiful silver, the brass fire-irons, the new chair-covers, and the curtains of yellow chintz: she appraised each; heard a roar of voices; people already coming up from dinner; she must fly!

The Prime Minister was coming, Agnes said: so she had heard them say in the dining-room, she said, coming in with a tray of glasses. Did it matter, did it matter in the least, one Prime Minister more or less? It made no difference at this hour of the night to Mrs. Walker among the plates, saucepans, cullenders, frying-pans, chicken in aspic, ice-cream freezers, pared crusts of bread, lemons, soup tureens, and pudding basins which, however hard they washed up in the scullery seemed to be all on top of her, on the kitchen table, on chairs, while the fire blared and roared, the electric lights glared, and still supper had to be laid. All she felt was, one Prime Minister more or less made not a scrap of difference to Mrs. Walker.

The ladies were going upstairs already, said Lucy; the ladies were going up, one by one, Mrs. Dalloway walking last and almost always sending back some message to the kitchen, "My love to Mrs. Walker," that was it one night. Next morning they would go over the dishes—the soup, the salmon; the salmon, Mrs. Walker knew, as usual underdone, for she always got nervous about the pudding and left it to Jenny; so it happened, the salmon was always underdone. But some lady with fair hair and silver ornaments had said, Lucy said, about the entrée, was it really made at home? But it was the salmon that bothered Mrs. Walker, as she spun the plates round and round, and pulled in dampers and pulled out dampers; and there came a burst of laughter from the dining-room; a voice speaking; then another burst of laughter—the gentlemen enjoying themselves when the ladies had gone. The tokay, said Lucy runfling in. Mr. Dalloway had sent for the tokay, from the Emperor's cellars, the Imperial Tokay.

It was borne through the kitchen. Over her shoulder Lucy reported how Miss Elizabeth looked quite lovely; she couldn't take her eyes off her; in her pink dress, wearing the necklace Mr.

Dalloway had given her. Jenny must remember the dog, Miss Elizabeth's fox-terrier, which, since it bit, had to be shut up and might, Elizabeth thought, want something. Jenny must remember the dog. But Jenny was not going upstairs with all those people about. There was a motor at the door already! There was a ring at the bell—and the gentlemen still in the dining-room, drinking tokay!

There, they were going upstairs; that was the first to come, and now they would come faster and faster, so that Mrs. Parkinson (hired for parties) would leave the hall door ajar, and the hall would be full of gentlemen waiting (they stood waiting, sleeking down their hair) while the ladies took their cloaks off in the room along the passage; where Mrs. Barnet helped them, old Ellen Barnet, who had been with the family for forty years, and came every summer to help the ladies, and remembered mothers when they were girls, and though very unassuming did shake hands; said "milady" very respectfully, yet had a humorous way with her, looking at the young ladies, and ever so tactfully helping Lady Lovejoy, who had some trouble with her underbodice. And they could not help feeling, Lady Lovejoy and Miss Alice, that some little privilege in the matter of brush and comb, was awarded them having known Mrs. Barnet— "thirty years, milady," Mrs. Barnet supplied her. Young ladies did not use to rouge, said Lady Lovejoy, when they stayed at Bourton in the old days. And Miss Alice didn't need rouge, said Mrs. Barnet, looking at her fondly. There Mrs. Barnet would sit, in the cloakroom, patting down the furs, smoothing out the Spanish shawls, tidying the dressing-table, and knowing perfectly well, in spite of the furs and the embroideries, which were nice ladies, which were not. The dear old body, said Lady Lovejoy, mounting the stairs, Clarissa's old nurse.

And then Lady Lovejoy stiffened. "Lady and Miss Lovejoy," she said to Mr. Wilkins (hired for parties). He had an admirable manner, as he bent and straightened himself, bent and straightened himself and announced with perfect impartiality "Lady and Miss Lovejoy... Sir John and Lady Needham... Miss Weld... Mr. Walsh." His manner was admirable; his family life must be irreproachable, except that it seemed impossible that a being with greenish lips and shaven cheeks could ever have blundered into the nuisance of children.

"How delightful to see you!" said Clarissa. She said it to every one. How delightful to see you! She was at her worst— effusive, insincere. It was a great mistake to have come. He should have stayed at home and read his book, thought Peter Walsh; should have gone to a music hall; he should have stayed at home, for he knew no one.

Oh dear, it was going to be a failure; a complete failure, Clarissa felt it in her bones as dear old Lord Lexham stood there apologising for his wife who had caught cold at the Buckingham Palace garden party. She could see Peter out of the tail of her eye, criticising her, there, in that corner. Why, after all, did she do these things? Why seek pinnacles and stand drenched in fire? Might it consume her anyhow! Burn her to cinders! Better anything, better brandish one's torch and hurl it to earth than taper and dwindle away like some Ellie Henderson! It was extraordinary how Peter put her into these states just by coming and standing in a corner. He made her see herself; exaggerate. It was idiotic. But why did he come, then, merely to criticise? Why always take, never give? Why not risk one's one little point of view? There he was wandering off, and she must speak to him. But she would not get the chance. Life was that—humiliation, renunciation. What Lord Lexham was saying was that his wife would not wear her furs at the garden party because "my dear, you ladies are all alike"—Lady Lexham being seventy-five at least! It was delicious, how they petted each other, that old couple. She did like old Lord Lexham. She did think it mattered, her party, and it made her feel quite sick to know that it was all going wrong, all falling flat. Anything, any explosion, any horror was better than people wandering aimlessly, standing in a bunch

at a corner like Ellie Henderson, not even caring to hold themselves upright.

Gently the yellow curtain with all the birds of Paradise blew
out and it seemed as if there were a flight of wings into the
room, right out, then sucked back. (For the windows were
open.) Was it draughty, Ellie Henderson wondered? She was
subject to chills. But it did not matter that she should come
down sneezing tomorrow; it was the girls with their naked
shoulders she thought of, being trained to think of others by an
old father, an invalid, late vicar of Bourton, but he was dead
now; and her chills never went to her chest, never. It was the
girls she thought of, the young girls with their bare shoulders,
she herself having always been a wisp of a creature, with her
thin hair and meagre profile; though now, past fifty, there was
beginning to shine through some mild beam, something purified into distinction by years of self-abnegation but obscured
again, perpetually, by her distressing gentility, her panic fear,
which arose from three hundred pounds' income, and her
weaponless state (she could not earn a penny) and it made her
timid, and more and more disqualified year by year to meet well-
dressed people who did this sort of thing every night of the season, merely telling their maids "I'll wear so and so," whereas
Ellie Henderson ran out nervously and bought cheap pink flowers, half a dozen, and then threw a shawl over her old black
dress. For her invitation to Clarissa's party had come at the last
moment. She was not quite happy about it. She had a sort of
feeling that Clarissa had not meant to ask her this year.

Why should she? There was no reason really, except that
they had always known each other. Indeed, they were cousins.
But naturally they had rather drifted apart, Clarissa being so
sought after. It was an event to her, going to a party. It was quite
a treat just to see the lovely clothes. Wasn't that Elizabeth,
grown up, with her hair done in the fashionable way, in the pink
dress? Yet she could not be more than seventeen. She was very,

very handsome. But girls when they first came out didn't seem to wear white as they used. (She must remember everything to tell Edith.) Girls wore straight frocks, perfectly tight, with skirts well above the ankles. It was not becoming, she thought.

So, with her weak eyesight, Ellie Henderson craned rather forward, and it wasn't so much she who minded not having any one to talk to (she hardly knew anybody there), for she felt that they were all such interesting people to watch; politicians presumably; Richard Dalloway's friends; but it was Richard himself who felt that he could not let the poor creature go on standing there all the evening by herself.

"Well, Ellie, and how's the world treating *you?*" he said in his genial way, and Ellie Henderson, getting nervous and flushing and feeling that it was extraordinarily nice of him to come and talk to her, said that many people really felt the heat more than the cold.

"Yes, they do," said Richard Dalloway. "Yes."

But what more did one say?

"Hullo, Richard," said somebody, taking him by the elbow, and, good Lord, there was old Peter, old Peter Walsh. He was delighted to see him—ever so pleased to see him! He hadn't changed a bit. And off they went together walking right across the room, giving each other little pats, as if they hadn't met for a long time, Ellie Henderson thought, watching them go, certain she knew that man's face. A tall man, middle aged, rather fine eyes, dark, wearing spectacles, with a look of John Burrows. Edith would be sure to know.

The curtain with its flight of birds of Paradise blew out again. And Clarissa saw—she saw Ralph Lyon beat it back, and go on talking. So it wasn't a failure after all! it was going to be all right now—her party. It had begun. It had started. But it was still touch and go. She must stand there for the present. People seemed to come in a rush.

Colonel and Mrs. Garrod . . . Mr. Hugh Whitbread . . . Mr. Bowley . . . Mrs. Hilbery . . . Lady Mary Maddox . . . Mr. Quin . . .

intoned Wilkin. She had six or seven words with each, and they went on, they went into the rooms; into something now, not nothing, since Ralph Lyon had beat back the curtain.

And yet for her own part, it was too much of an effort. She was not enjoying it. It was too much like being—just anybody, standing there; anybody could do it, yet this anybody she did a little admire, couldn't help feeling that she had, anyhow, made this happen, that it marked a stage, this post that she felt herself to have become, for oddly enough she had quite forgotten what she looked like, but felt herself a stake driven in at the top of her stairs. Every time she gave a party she had this feeling of being something not herself, and that every one was unreal in one way; much more real in another. It was, she thought, partly their clothes, partly being taken out of their ordinary ways, partly the background, it was possible to say things you couldn't say anyhow else, things that needed an effort; possible to go much deeper. But not for her; not yet anyhow.

"How delightful to see you!" she said. Dear old Sir Harry! He would know every one.

And what was so odd about it was the sense one had as they came up the stairs one after another, Mrs. Mount and Celia, Herbert Ainsty, Mrs. Dakers—oh and Lady Bruton!

"How awfully good of you to come!" she said, and she meant it—it was odd how standing there one felt them going on, going on, some quite old, some...

What name? Lady Rosseter? But who on earth was Lady Rosseter?

"Clarissa!" That voice! It was Sally Seton! Sally Seton! after all these years! She loomed through a mist. For she hadn't looked like *that,* Sally Seton, when Clarissa grasped the hot water can, to think of her under this roof, under this roof! Not like that!

All on top of each other, embarrassed, laughing, words tumbled out—passing through London; heard from Clara Haydon; what a chance of seeing you! So I thrust myself in—without an invitation. . . .

One might put down the hot water can quite composedly. The lustre had gone out of her. Yet it was extraordinary to see her again, older, happier, less lovely. They kissed each other, first this cheek then that, by the drawing-room door, and Clarissa turned, with Sally's hand in hers, and saw her rooms full, heard the roar of voices, saw the candlesticks, the blowing curtains, and the roses which Richard had given her.

"I have five enormous boys," said Sally.

She had the simplest egotism, the most open desire to be thought first always, and Clarissa loved her for being still like that. "I can't believe it!" she cried, kindling all over with pleasure at the thought of the past.

But alas, Wilkins; Wilkins wanted her; Wilkins was emitting in a voice of commanding authority as if the whole company must be admonished and the hostess reclaimed from frivolity, one name:

"The Prime Minister," said Peter Walsh.

The Prime Minister? Was it really? Ellie Henderson marvelled. What a thing to tell Edith!

One couldn't laugh at him. He looked so ordinary. You might have stood him behind a counter and bought biscuits—poor chap, all rigged up in gold lace. And to be fair, as he went his rounds, first with Clarissa then with Richard escorting him, he did it very well. He tried to look somebody. It was amusing to watch. Nobody looked at him. They just went on talking, yet it was perfectly plain that they all knew, felt to the marrow of their bones, this majesty passing; this symbol of what they all stood for, English society. Old Lady Bruton, and she looked very fine too, very stalwart in her lace, swam up, and they withdrew into a little room which at once became spied upon, guarded, and a sort of stir and rustle rippled through every one, openly: the Prime Minister!

Lord, lord, the snobbery of the English! thought Peter Walsh, standing in the corner. How they loved dressing up in gold lace and doing homage! There! That must be, by Jove it was, Hugh Whitbread, snuffing round the precincts of the great, grown rather fatter, rather whiter, the admirable Hugh!

He looked always as if he were on duty, thought Peter, a privileged, but secretive being, hoarding secrets which he would die to defend, though it was only some little piece of tittle-tattle dropped by a court footman, which would be in all the papers to-morrow. Such were his rattles, his baubles, in playing with which he had grown white, come to the verge of old age, enjoying the respect and affection of all who had the privilege of knowing this type of the English public school man. Inevitably one made up things like that about Hugh; that was his style; the style of those admirable letters which Peter had read thousands of miles across the sea in the *Times,* and had thanked God he was out of that pernicious hubble-bubble if it were only to hear baboons chatter and coolies beat their wives. An olive-skinned youth from one of the Universities stood obsequiously by. Him he would patronise, initiate, teach how to get on. For he liked nothing better than doing kindnessses, making the hearts of old ladies palpitate with the joy of being thought of in their age, their affliction, thinking themselves quite forgotten, yet here was dear Hugh driving up and spending an hour talking of the past, remembering trifles, praising the homemade cake, though Hugh might eat cake with a Duchess any day of his life, and, to look at him, probably did spend a good deal of time in that agreeable occupation. The All-judging, the All-merciful, might excuse. Peter Walsh had no mercy. Villains there must be, and God knows the rascals who get hanged for battering the brains of a girl out in a train do less harm on the whole than Hugh Whitbread and his kindness. Look at him now, on tiptoe, dancing forward, bowing and scraping, as the Prime Minister and Lady Bruton emerged, intimating for all the world to see that he was privileged to say something, something private, to Lady Bruton as she passed. She stopped. She wagged her fine old head. She was thanking him presumably for some piece of servility. She had her toadies, minor officials in Government offices who ran about putting through little jobs on her behalf, in return for which she gave them luncheon. But she derived from the eighteenth century. She was all right.

And now Clarissa escorted her Prime Minister down the room, prancing, sparkling, with the stateliness of her grey hair. She wore ear-rings, and a silver-green mermaid's dress. Lolloping on the waves and braiding her tresses she seemed, having that gift still; to be; to exist; to sum it all up in the moment as she passed; turned, caught her scarf in some other woman's dress, unhitched it, laughed, all with the most perfect ease and air of a creature floating in its element. But age had brushed her; even as a mermaid might behold in her glass the setting sun on some very clear evening over the waves. There was a breath of tenderness; her severity, her prudery, her woodenness were all warmed through now, and she had about her as she said good-bye to the thick gold-laced man who was doing his best, and good luck to him, to look important, an inexpressible dignity; an exquisite cordiality; as if she wished the whole world well, and must now, being on the very verge and rim of things, take her leave. So she made him think. (But he was not in love.)

Indeed, Clarissa felt, the Prime Minister had been good to come. And, walking down the room with him, with Sally there and Peter there and Richard very pleased, with all those people rather inclined, perhaps, to envy, she had felt that intoxication of the moment, that dilatation of the nerves of the heart itself till it seemed to quiver, steeped, upright;—yes, but after all it was what other people felt, that; for, though she loved it and felt it tingle and sting, still these semblances, these triumphs (dear old Peter, for example, thinking her so brilliant), had a hollowness; at arm's length they were, not in the heart; and it might be that she was growing old but they satisfied her no longer as they used; and suddenly, as she saw the Prime Minister go down the stairs, the gilt rim of the Sir Joshua picture of the little girl with a muff brought back Kilman with a rush; Kilman her enemy.

That was satisfying; that was real. Ah, how she hated her—hot, hypocritical, corrupt; with all that power; Elizabeth's seducer; the woman who had crept in to steal and defile (Richard would say, What nonsense!). She hated her: she loved her. It was enemies one wanted, not friends—not Mrs. Durrant and Clara, Sir William and Lady Bradshaw, Miss Truelock and Eleanor Gibson (whom she saw coming upstairs). They must find her if they wanted her. She was for the party!

There was her old friend Sir Harry.

"Dear Sir Harry!" she said, going up to the fine old fellow who had produced more bad pictures than any other two Academicians in the whole of St. John's Wood (they were always of cattle, standing in sunset pools absorbing moisture, or signifying, for he had a certain range of gesture, by the raising of one foreleg and the toss of the antlers, "the Approach of the Stranger"—all his activities, dining out, racing, were founded on cattle standing absorbing moisture in sunset pools).

"What are you laughing at?" she asked him. For Willie Titcomb and Sir Harry and Herbert Ainsty were all laughing. But no. Sir Harry could not tell Clarissa Dalloway (much though he liked her; of her type he thought her perfect, and threatened to paint her) his stories of the music hall stage. He chaffed her about her party. He missed his brandy. These circles, he said, were above him. But he liked her; respected her, in spite of her damnable, difficult upper-class refinement, which made it impossible to ask Clarissa Dalloway to sit on his knee. And up came that wandering will-o'-the wisp, that vagulous phosphorescence, old Mrs. Hilbery, stretching her hands to the blaze of his laughter (about the Duke and the Lady), which, as she heard it across the room, seemed to reassure her on a point which sometimes bothered her if she woke early in the morning and did not like to call her maid for a cup of tea; how it is certain we must die.

"They won't tell us their stories," said Clarissa.

"Dear Clarissa!" exclaimed Mrs. Hilbery. She looked to-night, she said, so like her mother as she first saw her walking in a garden in a grey hat.

And really Clarissa's eyes filled with tears. Her mother, walking in a garden! But alas, she must go.

For there was Professor Brierly, who lectured on Milton, talking to little Jim Hutton (who was unable even for a party like this to compass both tie and waistcoat or make his hair lie flat), and even at this distance they were quarrelling, she could see. For Professor Brierly was a very queer fish. With all those degrees, honours, lectureships between him and the scribblers he suspected instantly an atmosphere not favourable to his queer compound; his prodigious learning and timidity; his wintry charm without cordiality; his innocence blent with snobbery; he quivered if made conscious by a lady's unkempt hair, a youth's boots, of an underworld, very creditable doubtless, of rebels, of ardent young people; of would-be geniuses, and intimated with a little toss of the head, with a sniff—Humph!—the value of moderation; of some slight training in the classics in order to appreciate Milton. Professor Brierly (Clarissa could see) wasn't hitting it off with little Jim Hutton (who wore red socks, his black being at the laundry) about Milton. She interrupted.

She said she loved Bach. So did Hutton. That was the bond between them, and Hutton (a very bad poet) always felt that Mrs. Dalloway was far the best of the great ladies who took an interest in art. It was odd how strict she was. About music she was purely impersonal. She was rather a prig. But how charming to look at! She made her house so nice if it weren't for her Professors. Clarissa had half a mind to snatch him off and set him down at the piano in the back room. For he played divinely.

"But the noise!" she said. "The noise!"

"The sign of a successful party." Nodding urbanely, the Professor stepped delicately off.

"He knows everything in the whole world about Milton," said Clarissa.

"Does he indeed?" said Hutton, who would imitate the Professor throughout Hampstead; the Professor on Milton; the Professor on moderation; the Professor stepping delicately off.

But she must speak to that couple, said Clarissa, Lord Gayton and Nancy Blow.

Not that *they* added perceptibly to the noise of the party. They were not talking (perceptibly) as they stood side by side by the yellow curtains. They would soon be off elsewhere, together; and never had very much to say in any circumstances. They looked; that was enough. They looked so clean, so sound, she with an apricot bloom of powder and paint, but he scrubbed, rinsed, with the eyes of a bird, so that no ball could pass him or stroke surprise him. He struck, he leapt, accurately, on the spot. Ponies' mouths quivered at the end of his reins. He had his honours, ancestral monuments, banners hanging in the church at home. He had his duties; his tenants; a mother and sisters; had been all day at Lords, and that was what they were talking about—cricket, cousins, the movies—when Mrs. Dalloway came up. Lord Gayton liked her most awfully. So did Miss Blow. She had such charming manners.

"It is angelic—it is delicious of you to have come!" she said. She loved Lords; she loved youth, and Nancy, dressed at enormous expense by the greatest artists in Paris, stood there looking as if her body had merely put forth, of its own accord, a green frill.

"I had meant to have dancing," said Clarissa.

For the young people could not talk. And why should they? Shout, embrace, swing, be up at dawn; carry sugar to ponies; kiss and caress the snouts of adorable chows; and then all tingling and streaming, plunge and swim. But the enormous resources of the English language, the power it bestows, after all, of communicating feelings (at their age, she and Peter would have been arguing all the evening), was not for them. They would solidify young. They would be good beyond measure to the people on the estate, but alone, perhaps, rather dull.

"What a pity!" she said. "I had hoped to have dancing."

It was so extraordinarily nice of them to have come! But talk of dancing! The rooms were packed.

There was old Aunt Helena in her shawl. Alas, she must leave them—Lord Gayton and Nancy Blow. There was old Miss Parry, her aunt.

For Miss Helena Parry was not dead: Miss Parry was alive. She was past eighty. She ascended staircases slowly with a stick. She was placed in a chair (Richard had seen to it). People who had known Burma in the 'seventies were always led up to her. Where had Peter got to? They used to be such friends. For at the mention of India, or even Ceylon, her eyes (only one was glass) slowly deepened, became blue, beheld, not human beings—she had no tender memories, no proud illusions about Viceroys, Generals, Mutinies—it was orchids she saw, and mountain passes and herself carried on the backs of coolies in the 'sixties over solitary peaks; or descending to uproot orchids (startling blossoms, never beheld before) which she painted in water-colour; an indomitable Englishwoman, fretful if disturbed by the War, say, which dropped a bomb at her very door, from her deep meditation over orchids and her own figure journeying in the 'sixties in India—but here was Peter.

"Come and talk to Aunt Helena about Burma," said Clarissa.

And yet he had not had a word with her all the evening!

"We will talk later," said Clarissa, leading him up to Aunt Helena, in her white shawl, with her stick.

"Peter Walsh," said Clarissa.

That meant nothing.

Clarissa had asked her. It was tiring; it was noisy; but Clarissa had asked her. So she had come. It was a pity that they lived in London—Richard and Clarissa. If only for Clarissa's health it would have been better to live in the country. But Clarissa had always been fond of society.

"He has been in Burma," said Clarissa.

Ah. She could not resist recalling what Charles Darwin had said about her little book on the orchids of Burma.

(Clarissa must speak to Lady Bruton.)

No doubt it was forgotten now, her book on the orchids of Burma, but it went into three editions before 1870, she told Peter. She remembered him now. He had been at Bourton (and he had left her, Peter Walsh remembered, without a word in the drawing-room that night when Clarissa had asked him to come boating).

"Richard so much enjoyed his lunch party," said Clarissa to Lady Bruton.

"Richard was the greatest possible help," Lady Bruton replied. "He helped me to write a letter. And how are you?"

"Oh, perfectly well!" said Clarissa. (Lady Bruton detested illness in the wives of politicians.)

"And there's Peter Walsh!" said Lady Bruton (for she could never think of anything to say to Clarissa; though she liked her. She had lots of fine qualities; but they had nothing in common—she and Clarissa. It might have been better if Richard had married a woman with less charm, who would have helped him more in his work. He had lost his chance of the Cabinet). "There's Peter Walsh!" she said, shaking hands with that agreeable sinner, that very able fellow who should have made a name for himself but hadn't (always in difficulties with women), and, of course, old Miss Parry. Wonderful old lady!

Lady Bruton stood by Miss Parry's chair, a spectral grenadier, draped in black, inviting Peter Walsh to lunch; cordial; but without small talk, remembering nothing whatever about the flora or fauna of India. She had been there, of course; had stayed with three Viceroys; thought some of the Indian civilians uncommonly fine fellows; but what a tragedy it was— the state of India! The Prime Minister had just been telling her (old Miss Parry huddled up in her shawl, did not care what the Prime Minister had just been telling her), and Lady Bruton would like to have Peter Walsh's opinion, he being fresh from the centre, and she would get Sir Sampson to meet him, for really it prevented her from sleeping at night, the folly of it, the wickedness she might say, being a soldier's daughter. She was an old woman now, not good for much. But her house, her servants, her good friend Milly Brush—did he remember her?— were all there only asking to be used if—if they could be of help, in short. For she never spoke of England, but this isle of men, this dear, dear land, was in her blood (without reading Shakespeare), and if ever a woman could have worn the helmet and shot the arrow, could have led troops to attack, ruled with indomitable justice barbarian hordes and lain under a shield noseless in a church, or made a green grass mound on some primeval hillside, that woman was Millicent Bruton. Debarred by her sex and some truancy, too, of the logical faculty (she found it impossible to write a letter to the *Times*), she had the thought of Empire always at hand, and had acquired from her association with that armoured goddess her ramrod bearing, her robustness of demeanour, so that one could not figure her even in death parted from the earth or roaming territories over which, in some spiritual shape, the Union Jack had ceased to fly. To be not English even among the dead—no, no! Impossible!

But was it Lady Bruton (whom she used to know)? Was it Peter Walsh grown grey? Lady Rosseter asked herself (who had been Sally Seton). It was old Miss Parry certainly—the old aunt who used to be so cross when she stayed at Bourton. Never should she forget running along the passage naked, and being sent for by Miss Parry! And Clarissa! oh Clarissa! Sally caught her by the arm.

Clarissa stopped beside them.

"But I can't stay," she said. "I shall come later. Wait," she said, looking at Peter and Sally. They must wait, she meant, until all these people had gone.

"I shall come back," she said, looking at her old friends,

Sally and Peter, who were shaking hands, and Sally, remembering the past no doubt, was laughing.

But her voice was wrung of its old ravishing richness; her eyes not aglow as they used to be, when she smoked cigars, when she ran down the passage to fetch her sponge bag, without a stitch of clothing on her, and Ellen Atkins asked, What if the gentlemen had met her? But everybody forgave her. She stole a chicken from the larder because she was hungry in the night; she smoked cigars in her bedroom; she left a priceless book in the punt. But everybody adored her (except perhaps Papa). It was her warmth; her vitality—she would paint, she would write. Old women in the village never to this day forgot to ask after "your friend in the red cloak who seemed so bright." She accused Hugh Whitbread, of all people (and there he was, her old friend Hugh, talking to the Portuguese Ambassador), of kissing her in the smoking-room to punish her for saying that women should have votes. Vulgar men did, she said. And Clarissa remembered having to persuade her not to denounce him at family prayers—which she was capable of doing with her daring, her recklessness, her melodramatic love of being the centre of everything and creating scenes, and it was bound, Clarissa used to think, to end in some awful tragedy; her death; her martyrdom; instead of which she had married, quite unexpectedly, a bald man with a large buttonhole who owned, it was said, cotton mills at Manchester. And she had five boys!

She and Peter had settled down together. They were talking: it seemed so familiar—that they should be talking. They would discuss the past. With the two of them (more even than with Richard) she shared her past; the garden; the trees; old Joseph Breitkopf singing Brahms without any voice; the drawing-room wallpaper; the smell of the mats. A part of this Sally must always be; Peter must always be. But she must leave them. There were the Bradshaws, whom she disliked. She must go up to Lady Bradshaw (in grey and silver, balancing like a sea-lion at the edge of its tank, barking for invitations, Duchesses, the typical successful man's wife), she must go up to Lady Bradshaw and say...

But Lady Bradshaw anticipated her.

"We are shockingly late, dear Mrs. Dalloway, we hardly dared to come in," she said.

And Sir William, who looked very distinguished, with his grey hair and blue eyes, said yes; they had not been able to resist the temptation. He was talking to Richard about that Bill probably, which they wanted to get through the Commons. Why did the sight of him, talking to Richard, curl her up? He looked what he was, a great doctor. A man absolutely at the head of his profession, very powerful, rather worn. For think what cases came before him—people in the uttermost depths of misery; people on the verge of insanity; husbands and wives. He had to decide questions of appalling difficulty. Yet—what she felt was, one wouldn't like Sir William to see one unhappy. No; not that man.

"How is your son at Eton?" she asked Lady Bradshaw.

He had just missed his eleven, said Lady Bradshaw, because of the mumps. His father minded even more than he did, she thought "being," she said, "nothing but a great boy himself."

Clarissa looked at Sir William, talking to Richard. He did not look like a boy—not in the least like a boy. She had once gone with some one to ask his advice. He had been perfectly right; extremely sensible. But Heavens—what a relief to get out to the street again! There was some poor wretch sobbing, she remembered, in the waiting-room. But she did not know what it was—about Sir William; what exactly she disliked. Only Richard agreed with her, "didn't like his taste, didn't like his smell." But he was extraordinarily able. They were talking about this Bill. Some case, Sir William was mentioning, lowering his voice. It had its bearing upon what he was saying about the deferred effects of shell shock. There must be some provision in the Bill.

Sinking her voice, drawing Mrs. Dalloway into the shelter of a common femininity, a common pride in the illustrious qualities of husbands and their sad tendency to overwork, Lady Bradshaw (poor goose—one didn't dislike her) murmured how, "just as we were starting, my husband was called up on the telephone, a very sad case. A young man (that is what Sir William is telling Mr. Dalloway) had killed himself. He had been in the army." Oh! thought Clarissa, in the middle of my party, here's death, she thought.

She went on, into the little room where the Prime Minister had gone with Lady Bruton. Perhaps there was somebody there. But there was nobody. The chairs still kept the impress of the Prime Minister and Lady Bruton, she turned deferentially, he sitting four-square, authoritatively. They had been talking about India. There was nobody. The party's splendour fell to the floor, so strange it was to come in alone in her finery.

What business had the Bradshaws to talk of death at her party? A young man had killed himself. And they talked of it at her party—the Bradshaws, talked of death. He had killed himself—but how? Always her body went through it first, when she was told, suddenly, of an accident; her dress flamed, her body burnt. He had thrown himself from a window. Up had flashed the ground; through him, blundering, bruising, went the rusty spikes. There he lay with a thud, thud, thud in his brain, and then a suffocation of blackness. So she saw it. But why had he done it? And the Bradshaws talked of it at her party!

She had once thrown a shilling into the Serpentine, never anything more. But he had flung it away. They went on living (she would have to go back; the rooms were still crowded; people kept on coming). They (all day she had been thinking of Bourton, of Peter, of Sally), they would grow old. A thing there was that mattered; a thing, wreathed about with chatter, defaced, obscured in her own life, let drop every day in corruption, lies, chatter. This he had preserved. Death was defiance. Death was an attempt to communicate; people feeling the impossibility of reaching the centre which, mystically, evaded them; closeness drew apart; rapture faded, one was alone. There was an embrace in death.

But this young man who had killed himself—had he plunged holding his treasure? "If it were now to die, 'twere now to be most happy," she had said to herself once, coming down in white.

Or there were the poets and thinkers. Suppose he had had that passion, and had gone to Sir William Bradshaw, a great doctor yet to her obscurely evil, without sex or lust, extremely polite to women, but capable of some indescribable outrage—forcing your soul, that was it—if this young man had gone to him, and Sir William had impressed him, like that, with his power, might he not then have said (indeed she felt it now), Life is made intolerable; they make life intolerable, men like that?

Then (she had felt it only this morning) there was the terror; the overwhelming incapacity, one's parents giving it into one's hands, this life, to be lived to the end, to be walked with serenely; there was in the depths of her heart an awful fear. Even now, quite often if Richard had not been there reading the *Times,* so that she could crouch like a bird and gradually revive, send roaring up that immeasurable delight, rubbing stick to stick, one thing with another, she must have perished. But that young man had killed himself.

Somehow it was her disaster—her disgrace. It was her punishment to see sink and disappear here a man, there a woman, in this profound darkness, and she forced to stand here in her evening dress. She had schemed; she had pilfered. She was never wholly admirable. She had wanted success. Lady Bexborough and the rest of it. And once she had walked on the terrace at Bourton.

It was due to Richard; she had never been so happy. Nothing could be slow enough; nothing last too long. No pleasure could equal, she thought, straightening the chairs, pushing in one book on the shelf, this having done with the triumphs of youth, lost herself in the process of living, to find it, with a shock of delight, as the sun rose, as the day sank. Many a time had she gone, at Bourton when they were all talking, to look at the sky; or seen it between people's shoulders at dinner; seen it in London when she could not sleep. She walked to the window.

It held, foolish as the idea was, something of her own in it, this country sky, this sky above Westminster. She parted the curtains; she looked. Oh, but how surprising!—in the room opposite the old lady stared straight at her! She was going to bed. And the sky. It will be a solemn sky, she had thought, it will be a dusky sky, turning away its cheek in beauty. But there it was—ashen pale, raced over quickly by tapering vast clouds. It was new to her. The wind must have risen. She was going to bed, in the room opposite. It was fascinating to watch her, moving about, that old lady, crossing the room, coming to the window. Could she see her? It was fascinating, with people still laughing and shouting in the drawing-room, to watch that old woman, quite quietly, going to bed. She pulled the blind now. The clock began striking. The young man had killed himself; but she did not pity him; with the clock striking the hour, one, two, three, she did not pity him, with all this going on. There! the old lady had put out her light! the whole house was dark now with this going on, she repeated, and the words came to her, Fear no more the heat of the sun. She must go back to them. But what an extraordinary night! She felt somehow very like him—the young man who had killed himself. She felt glad that he had done it; thrown it away. The clock was striking. The leaden circles dissolved in the air. He made her feel the beauty; made her feel the fun. But she must go back. She must assemble. She must find Sally and Peter. And she came in from the little room.

"But where is Clarissa?" said Peter. He was sitting on the sofa with Sally. (After all these years he really could not call her "Lady Rosseter.") "Where's the woman gone to?" he asked. "Where's Clarissa?"

Sally supposed, and so did Peter for the matter of that, that there were people of importance, politicians, whom neither of them knew unless by sight in the picture papers, whom Clarissa had to be nice to, had to talk to. She was with them. Yet there

was Richard Dalloway not in the Cabinet. He hadn't been a success, Sally supposed? For herself, she scarcely ever read the papers. She sometimes saw his name mentioned. But then—well,
she lived a very solitary life, in the wilds, Clarissa would say,
among great merchants, great manufacturers, men, after all,
who did things. She had done things too!

"I have five sons!" she told him.

Lord, Lord, what a change had come over her! the softness
of motherhood; its egotism too. Last time they met, Peter remembered, had been among the cauliflowers in the moonlight,
the leaves "like rough bronze" she had said, with her literary
turn; and she had picked a rose. She had marched him up and
down that awful night, after the scene by the fountain; he was to
catch the midnight train. Heavens, he had wept!

That was his old trick, opening a pocket-knife, thought
Sally, always opening and shutting a knife when he got excited.
They had been very, very intimate, she and Peter Walsh, when
he was in love with Clarissa, and there was that dreadful, ridiculous scene over Richard Dalloway at lunch. She had called
Richard "Wickham." Why not call Richard "Wickham"? Clarissa
had flared up! and indeed they had never seen each other since,
she and Clarissa, not more than half a dozen times perhaps in
the last ten years. And Peter Walsh had gone off to India, and
she had heard vaguely that he had made an unhappy marriage,
and she didn't know whether he had any children, and she
couldn't ask him, for he had changed. He was rather shrivelled-
looking, but kinder, she felt, and she had a real affection for
him, for he was connected with her youth, and she still had a
little Emily Brontë he had given her, and he was to write, surely?
In those days he was to write.

"Have you written?" she asked him, spreading her hand, her
firm and shapely hand, on her knee in a way he recalled.

"Not a word!" said Peter Walsh, and she laughed.

She was still attractive, still a personage, Sally Seton. But
who was this Rosseter? He wore two camelias on his wedding

day—that was all Peter knew of him. "They have myriads of servants, miles of conservatories," Clarissa wrote; something like that. Sally owned it with a shout of laughter.

"Yes, I have ten thousand a year"—whether before the tax was paid or after, she couldn't remember, for her husband, "whom you must meet," she said, "whom you would like," she said, did all that for her.

And Sally used to be in rags and tatters. She had pawned her grandmother's ring which Marie Antoinette had given her great-grandfather to come to Bourton.

Oh yes, Sally remembered; she had it still, a ruby ring which Marie Antoinette had given her great-grandfather. She never had a penny to her name in those days, and going to Bourton always meant some frightful pinch. But going to Bourton had meant so much to her—had kept her sane, she believed, so unhappy had she been at home. But that was all a thing of the past—all over now, she said. And Mr. Parry was dead; and Miss Parry was still alive. Never had he had such a shock in his life! said Peter. He had been quite certain she was dead. And the marriage had been, Sally supposed, a success? And that very handsome, very self-possessed young woman was Elizabeth, over there, by the curtains, in red.

(She was like a poplar, she was like a river, she was like a hyacinth, Willie Titcomb was thinking. Oh how much nicer to be in the country and do what she liked! She could hear her poor dog howling, Elizabeth was certain.) She was not a bit like Clarissa, Peter Walsh said.

"Oh, Clarissa!" said Sally.

What Sally felt was simply this. She had owed Clarissa an enormous amount. They had been friends, not acquaintances, friends, and she still saw Clarissa all in white going about the house with her hands full of flowers—to this day tobacco plants made her think of Bourton. But—did Peter understand?—she lacked something. Lacked what was it? She had charm; she had extraordinary charm. But to be frank (and she felt that Peter was an old friend, a real friend—did absence matter? did distance matter? She had often wanted to write to him, but torn it up, yet felt he understood, for people understand without things being said, as one realises growing old, and old she was, had been that afternoon to see her sons at Eton, where they had the mumps), to be quite frank then, how could Clarissa have done it?—married Richard Dalloway? a sportsman, a man who cared only for dogs. Literally, when he came into the room he smelt of the stables. And then all this? She waved her hand.

Hugh Whitbread it was, strolling past in his white waistcoat, dim, fat, blind, past everything he looked, except self-esteem and comfort.

"He's not going to recognise *us*," said Sally, and really she hadn't the courage—so that was Hugh! the admirable Hugh!

"And what does he do?" she asked Peter.

He blacked the King's boots or counted bottles at Windsor, Peter told her. Peter kept his sharp tongue still! But Sally must be frank, Peter said. That kiss now, Hugh's.

On the lips, she assured him, in the smoking-room one evening. She went straight to Clarissa in a rage. Hugh didn't do such things! Clarissa said, the admirable Hugh! Hugh's socks were without exception the most beautiful she had ever seen—and now his evening dress. Perfect! And had he children?

"Everybody in the room has six sons at Eton," Peter told her, except himself. He, thank God, had none. No sons, no daughters, no wife. Well, he didn't seem to mind, said Sally. He looked younger, she thought, than any of them.

But it had been a silly thing to do, in many ways, Peter said, to marry like that; "a perfect goose she was," he said, but, he said, "we had a splendid time of it," but how could that be? Sally wondered; what did he mean? and how odd it was to know him and yet not know a single thing that had happened to him. And did he say it out of pride? Very likely, for after all it must be galling for him (though he was an oddity, a sort of sprite, not at all an ordinary man), it must be lonely at his age to have no home, nowhere to go to. But he must stay with them for weeks and weeks. Of course he would; he would love to stay with them, and that was how it came out. All these years the Dalloways had never been once. Time after time they had asked them. Clarissa (for it was Clarissa of course) would not come. For, said Sally, Clarissa was at heart a snob—one had to admit it, a snob. And it was that that was between them, she was convinced. Clarissa thought she had married beneath her, her husband being—she was proud of it—a miner's son. Every penny they had he had earned. As a little boy (her voice trembled) he had carried great sacks.

(And so she would go on, Peter felt, hour after hour; the miner's son; people thought she had married beneath her; her five sons; and what was the other thing—plants, hydrangeas, syringas, very, very rare hibiscus lilies that never grow north of the Suez Canal, but she, with one gardener in a suburb near Manchester, had beds of them, positively beds! Now all that Clarissa had escaped, unmaternal as she was.)

A snob was she? Yes, in many ways. Where was she, all this time? It was getting late.

"Yet," said Sally, "when I heard Clarissa was giving a party, I felt I couldn't *not* come—must see her again (and I'm staying in Victoria Street, practically next door). So I just came without an invitation. But," she whispered, "tell me, do. Who is this?"

It was Mrs. Hilbery, looking for the door. For how late it was getting! And, she murmured, as the night grew later, as people went, one found old friends; quiet nooks and corners; and the loveliest views. Did they know, she asked, that they were surrounded by an enchanted garden? Lights and trees and wonderful gleaming lakes and the sky. Just a few fairy lamps, Clarissa Dalloway had said, in the back garden! But she was a magician! It was a park.... And she didn't know their names, but friends she knew they were, friends without names, songs without words, always the best. But there were so many doors, such unexpected places, she could not find her way.

"Old Mrs. Hilbery," said Peter; but who was that? that lady standing by the curtain all the evening, without speaking? He knew her face; connected her with Bourton. Surely she used to cut up underclothes at the large table in the window? Davidson, was that her name?

"Oh, that is Ellie Henderson," said Sally. Clarissa was really very hard on her. She was a cousin, very poor. Clarissa *was* hard on people.

She was rather, said Peter. Yet, said Sally, in her emotional way, with a rush of that enthusiasm which Peter used to love her for, yet dreaded a little now, so effusive she might become—how generous to her friends Clarissa was! and what a rare quality one found it, and how sometimes at night or on Christmas Day, when she counted up her blessings, she put that friendship first. They were young; that was it. Clarissa was pure-hearted; that was it. Peter would think her sentimental. So she was. For she had come to feel that it was the only thing worth saying—what one felt. Cleverness was silly. One must say simply what one felt.

"But I do not know," said Peter Walsh, "what I feel."

Poor Peter, thought Sally. Why did not Clarissa come and talk to them? That was what he was longing for. She knew it. All the time he was thinking only of Clarissa, and was fidgeting with his knife.

He had not found life simple, Peter said. His relations with Clarissa had not been simple. It had spoilt his life, he said. (They had been so intimate—he and Sally Seton, it was absurd not to say it.) One could not be in love twice, he said. And what could she say? Still, it is better to have loved (but he would think her sentimental—he used to be so sharp). He must come and stay with them in Manchester. That is all very true, he said. All very true. He would love to come and stay with them, directly he had done what he had to do in London.

And Clarissa had cared for him more than she had ever cared for Richard. Sally was positive of that.

"No, no, no!" said Peter (Sally should not have said that—she went too far). That good fellow—there he was at the end of the room, holding forth, the same as ever, dear old Richard. Who was he talking to? Sally asked, that very distinguished-looking man? Living in the wilds as she did, she had an insatiable curiosity to know who people were. But Peter did not know. He did not like his looks, he said, probably a Cabinet Minister. Of them all, Richard seemed to him the best, he said—the most disinterested.

"But what has he done?" Sally asked. Public work, she supposed. And were they happy together? Sally asked (she herself was extremely happy); for, she admitted, she knew nothing about them, only jumped to conclusions, as one does, for what can one know even of the people one lives with every day? she asked. Are we not all prisoners? She had read a wonderful play about a man who scratched on the wall of his cell, and she had felt that was true of life—one scratched on the wall. Despairing of human relationships (people were so difficult), she often went into her garden and got from her flowers a peace which men and women never gave her. But no; he did not like cabbages; he preferred human beings, Peter said. Indeed, the young are beautiful, Sally said, watching Elizabeth cross the room. How unlike Clarissa at her age! Could he make anything of her? She would not open her lips. Not much, not yet, Peter admitted. She was like a lily, Sally said, a lily by the side of a pool. But Peter did not agree that we know nothing. We know everything, he said; at least he did.

But these two, Sally whispered, these two coming now (and really she must go, if Clarissa did not come soon), this distinguished-looking man and his rather common-looking wife who had been talking to Richard—what could one know about people like that?

"That they're damnable humbugs," said Peter, looking at them casually. He made Sally laugh.

But Sir William Bradshaw stopped at the door to look at a picture. He looked in the corner for the engraver's name. His wife looked too. Sir William Bradshaw was so interested in art.

When one was young, said Peter, one was too much excited to know people. Now that one was old, fifty-two to be precise (Sally was fifty-five, in body, she said, but her heart was like a girl's of twenty); now that one was mature then, said Peter, one could watch, one could understand, and one did not lose the power of feeling, he said. No, that is true, said Sally. She felt more deeply, more passionately, every year. It increased, he said, alas, perhaps, but one should be glad of it—it went on increasing in his experience. There was some one in India. He would like to tell Sally about her. He would like Sally to know her. She was married, he said. She had two small children. They must all come to Manchester, said Sally—he must promise before they left.

There's Elizabeth, he said, she feels not half what we feel, not yet. But, said Sally, watching Elizabeth go to her father, one can see they are devoted to each other. She could feel it by the way Elizabeth went to her father.

For her father had been looking at her, as he stood talking to the Bradshaws, and he had thought to himself, Who is that lovely girl? And suddenly he realised that it was his Elizabeth, and he had not recognised her, she looked so lovely in her pink frock! Elizabeth had felt him looking at her as she talked to Willie Titcomb. So she went to him and they stood together, now that the party was almost over, looking at the people going, and the rooms getting emptier and emptier, with things scattered on the floor. Even Ellie Henderson was going, nearly last of all, though no one had spoken to her, but she had wanted to see everything, to tell Edith. And Richard and Elizabeth were rather glad it was over, but Richard was proud of his daughter.

And he had not meant to tell her, but he could not help telling her. He had looked at her, he said, and he had wondered, Who is that lovely girl? and it was his daughter! That did make her happy. But her poor dog was howling.

"Richard has improved. You are right," said Sally. "I shall go and talk to him. I shall say good-night. What does the brain matter," said Lady Rosseter, getting up, "compared with the heart?"

"I will come," said Peter, but he sat on for a moment. What is this terror? what is this ecstasy? he thought to himself. What is it that fills me with extraordinary excitement?

It is Clarissa, he said.

For there she was.

Contributors

FRANCINE PROSE is the author of ten highly acclaimed works of fiction, including *Bigfoot Dreams, Household Saints, Hunters and Gatherers, Primitive People,* and *Guided Tours of Hell.* Her work has appeared in the *New Yorker,* the *Atlantic Monthly, GQ,* and the *Paris Review;* she is a contributing editor at *Harper's,* and she writes regularly on art for the *Wall Street Journal.* The recipient of numerous grants and awards, including a Guggenheim and a Fulbright, Francine Prose is a director's fellow at the Center for Scholars and Writers at the New York Public Library. She has taught at the Iowa Writers' Workshop, the Sewanee Writers' Conference, and Johns Hopkins University. She lives in New York City.

VIRGINIA WOOLF (1882–1941) is one of the major literary figures of the twentieth century who transformed the art of the novel. The author of numerous novels, collections of letters, journals, and short stories, she was an admired literary critic and a master of the essay form.

KATHERINE MANSFIELD was born in Wellington, New Zealand, in 1888 and died in Fountainebleau in 1923. Her first book, *In a German Pension,* was published in 1911, and the following year she began to write for a literary magazine edited by John Middleton Murray, her future husband. Her relationship with Virginia Woolf was often a turbulent one; although they were friends and greatly respected one another's talent, they also deeply distrusted each other and regarded each other as singular rivals. Mansfield was an experimenter, in life as well as writing; and she influenced and affected Woolf in complex ways. The story reprinted here, "The Garden-Party," was published in 1922 and provides a good example of their important intellectual relationship—it is a story set during one day, a day spent planning a party. In her journal, Woolf described spending time with Katherine Mansfield:

"We talked about solitude, & I found her expressing my feelings as I had never heard them expressed... [I have] a queer sense of being 'like'—not only about literature; to no-one else can I talk in the same disembodied way about writing." Likewise, Mansfield once wrote to Woolf, "You are the only woman with whom I long to talk work." It is no coincidence that after Mansfield's death in 1923 Woolf described her vivid dreams of her friend and rival, and lamented the loss of their highly charged relationship for the remainder of her own life.

MARGO JEFFERSON is a cultural critic for the *New York Times*. Her incisive writing on theater, books, and the arts in general garnered her the Pulitzer Prize for criticism in 1995. A contributor to the *Nation, Harper's, Vogue,* and *Grand Street,* among others, she has also served as a consultant and commentator for several documentaries, including Ric Burns's *New York* and Ken Burns's *Jazz.* She was also a senior fellow at Columbia University's National Arts Journalism Program.

JAMES WOOD is the author of *The Broken Estate: Essays on Literature and Belief* and *The Book Against God,* a novel.

MARY GORDON is the author of *The Company of Women, The Rest of Life,* and *The Other Side,* and the memoir, *The Shadow Man.* Winner of the Lila Acheson Wallace Reader's Digest Award, a Guggenheim Fellowship, and the 1996 O. Henry Prize for best short story, she teaches at Barnard College and lives in New York City.

ELAINE SHOWALTER is the author of *The Female Malady: Women, Madness, and English Culture, 1830–1980, Teaching Literature, Hystories, A Literature of Their Own,* and *Daughters of Decadence: Women Writers of the Fin De Siecle.*

MICHAEL CUNNINGHAM is the author of three novels: *A Home at the End of the World, Flesh and Blood,* and *The Hours. The Hours* won the 1999 PEN Faulkner and Pulitzer prizes. His fiction has also appeared in the *New Yorker,* the *Atlantic Monthly,* and the *Paris Review.*

E. M. FORSTER was born in 1879 in London and attended King's College, Cambridge, where he later became an honorary fellow. After leaving Cambridge, Forster lived in Greece and Italy as well as in Egypt and India. He is the author of six novels, *Where Angels Fear to Tread, A Room with a View, Howards End, Maurice, A Passage to India,* and *The Longest Journey,* as well as numerous essays and short story collections. Forster and Woolf enjoyed a literary friendship for over two decades, and she wrote extensively in her journals and letters about his influence on her work. He died in 1970 in Coventry, England.

DANIEL MENDELSOHN is the book critic for *New York Magazine* and contributes to many other publications. He divides his time between Manhattan and New Jersey, where he teaches the classics at Princeton University. *The Elusive Embrace: Desire and the Riddle of Identity,* a memoir comprised of five essays, explores Mendelsohn's family history, his evolving sexual identity as a boy in Long Island, and his life as a gay man.

SIGRID NUNEZ is the author of the novels *A Feather on the Breath of God* and *For Rouenna.* She is also the author of *Mitz: The Marmoset of Bloomsbury,* a biography of Leonard and Virginia Woolf's pet monkey. She has been the recipient of a Whiting Writer's Award and of the Rome Prize in Literature and has just been elected to membership in the American Academy of Arts and Sciences.

DEBORAH EISENBERG's first two short story collections are available as *The Stories (So Far) of Deborah Eisenberg.* Her third collection is *All Around Atlantis.* She is the recipient of a Whiting Writers' Award, a Guggenheim Fellowship, the Rea Award for the Short Story, and four O. Henry Awards. She teaches part time at the University of Virginia.

ELISSA SCHAPPELL is the author of *Use Me,* which was a finalist for the PEN/Hemingway award. She currently writes the "Hot Type" column for *Vanity Fair* and is a founding editor of the new literary magazine *Tin House.* She has been a senior editor at the *Paris Review* and has contributed to numerous magazines including *Vogue,* the *New York Times Book Review, GQ,* and *Spin.* She teaches in the low-residency M.F.A. program at Queens in North Carolina and lives in Brooklyn.

Permissions and Acknowledgments

Katherine Mansfield's "The Garden-Party" is from *The Short Stories of Katherine Mansfield* by Katherine Mansfield, copyright 1923 by Alfred A. Knopf, a division of Random House, Inc., and renewed 1951 by John Middleton Murry. Used by permission of Alfred A. Knopf, a division of Random House, Inc.

Margo Jefferson's "Unreal Loyalties" is copyright 2003 *The New York Times*.

James Wood's essay "Virginia Woolf's Forgetful Selves" first appeared in *PEN America: A Journal for Writers and Readers,* published by PEN American Center, and is reprinted by permission of James Wood.

Mary Gordon's essay "Bodies of Knowledge" first appeared in *PEN America: A Journal for Writers and Readers,* published by PEN American Center. It is reprinted by permission of Sterling Lord Literistic, Inc., and is copyright by Mary Gordon.

Elaine Showalter's essay "Invigorating Life" first appeared in *PEN America: A Journal for Writers and Readers,* published by PEN American Center, and is reprinted by permission of Elaine Showalter.

Michael Cunningham's essay "First Love," copyright © 2001 by Michael Cunningham, first appeared in print in *PEN America: A Journal for Writers and Readers,* published by PEN American Center, and is reprinted with permission of Brandt & Hochman Literary Agents, Inc.

E. M. Forster's "The Early Novels of Virginia Woolf" is used by permission of the Provost and Scholars of King's College, Cambridge, and the Society of Authors as the Literary Representatives of the Estate of E. M. Forster.

Daniel Mendelsohn's "Not Afraid of Virginia Woolf" was originally published in the *New York Review of Books*.

British
Museum

BLOOMSBURY

Gower Street

Oxford Street

EVERSHOLT STREET

EUSTON ROAD

EUSTON

TOTTENHAM COURT ROAD

GOODGE STREET

GREAT PORTLAND STREET

ALBANY STREET

CIRCLE

Portland   Place

OUTER

Harley   Street

MARYLEBONE ROAD

MARYLEBONE HIGH

NEW CAVENDISH STREET

MORE

Regent's Park

INNER   CIRCLE

BAKER STREET

MARYLEBONE

GLOUCESTER

PLAC

ROAD

ALBERT

OUTER   CIRCLE

PARK ROAD

PRINCE

EDGWARE ROAD

*Mrs. Dalloway Prepares
for Her Party*

●●●●●●● Mrs. Dalloway's Walk